TREYDORA

RISE OF KORAXOS

MARK LOUDERMILK

PHOENIX & SAGE PUBLISHING

First Edition: 6/3/2025 ISBN: 979-8-9987658-8-9

To the healers, builders, and dreamers—those who know that the greatest power isn't what you can destroy, but what you can inspire others to become.

"The strongest chains are those we forge ourselves,but the greatest freedom comes from choosing which chains to wear."

"True power is not what you can force others to do—it's what you can inspire them to become."

"The universe doesn't need our permission to be beautiful—it only needs our courage to stop preventing it."

—Three truths discovered in the forging of unity

Foreword

About the Game

About the Game

Treydora Rise serves as the immersive storyline for the upcoming AAA video game of the same name, where players will experience Koraxos's transformation from enslaved miner to cosmic guardian through revolutionary gameplay that emphasizes coop over conquest.

Game Features:

• Phantom Arm System: Evolving transcendent abilities that grow stronger through protecting others rather than dominating them

• Unity Mechanics: Seven playable civilizations with unique technologies that become exponentially more powerful when combined

• Living World: A planet-scale ecosystem where every choice affects the balance between individual entities, civilizations, and cosmic forces

• Cooperative Campaign: Designed for both solo play and up to 7-player cooperative storytelling

• Dynamic Morality: Actions shape not just personal power but the fundamental nature of reality itself

Gameplay Integration: This novel provides the canonical narrative foundation for the game's main campaign, side missions, and character development systems. Players will encounter the same locations, meet these characters, and face the moral choices that define Koraxos's journey from slave NOK-2847 to planetary guardian.

Cross-Media Experience: Your progress and choices in the game will unlock additional content in future digital editions of this book, including:

• Extended character backstories based on your gameplay relationships

• Alternative perspective chapters from your cooperative partners

• Expanded universe content exploring other Genesis-seeded worlds

• Developer commentary on the intersection of narrative and gameplay mechanics

Available Platforms: Treydora Rise the game will be available on PC

Release Information: Game Launch: Coming Soon Season Pass Content: Quarterly expansions exploring the broader Genesis network VR Mode: Full city immersion experience planned for 2025-2026

Foreword

From Page To Play

The transition from novel to interactive experience preserves the core themes while expanding player agency. Just as Koraxos discovers that true power comes from inspiring others rather than controlling them, game play rewards cooperation, creative problem-solving, and building bridges across difference.

Every phantom arm ability, every alliance forged, every choice between vengeance and protection reflects the novel's central proposition: that consciousness united by choice rather than force can reshape reality itself.

For Readers: Experience the story first, then live it. **For Gamers**: Play the legend, then discover its deeper truths. **For Everyone**: Witness what becomes possible when we choose connection over conquest.

"The strongest chains are those we forge ourselves—both in story and in play."

Introduction

Welcome to Treydora

What you hold in your hands is more than a book—it's the foundation of a universe.

As someone who spent two decades in emergency medicine, I learned that the most critical moments aren't won by the strongest individual, but by teams that refuse to let each other fail. In ICU rooms and trauma bays, I witnessed ordinary people accomplish extraordinary things when they chose cooperation over competition, when they shared knowledge instead of hoarding it, when they built bridges across difference instead of walls around similarity.

Those experiences shaped every page of what you're about to read.

The Treydora universe began as a question: What if consciousness itself was the most powerful force in existence? Not consciousness as domination, but as connection. Not power over others, but power shared with others. What if the strongest beings in the cosmos weren't those who conquered, but those who inspired others to become more than they ever thought possible?

Koraxos begins his journey as a slave branded at birth, carrying twenty-two years of rage and the weight of cosmic power he never asked for. But his true transformation isn't about gaining strength—it's about learning what strength is actually for. It's about discovering that the chains we choose to wear can become the foundations for everything beautiful we build together.

This story exists alongside an upcoming AAA gaming experience that will let you live within this universe, but the book stands complete on its own. Whether you're a lifelong fantasy reader or someone drawn here by the promise of immersive gaming, you'll find themes that resonate: the choice between revenge and justice, the challenge of unity without uniformity, and the revolutionary idea that cooperation isn't weakness—it's evolution.

The universe doesn't need our permission to be beautiful. It only needs our courage to stop preventing that beauty from flourishing.

Welcome to a world where slaves become guardians, enemies become allies, and consciousness learns that its greatest power has always been the choice to lift others up.

The real adventure begins now.

Mark Loudermilk

Upstate New York, 2025

Contents

1

Chapter 1: The Void Awakens

Silence arrived like a blade between the ribs.

For eons, three voices had sung creation into being. Now Treydora heard only his own breath in the cosmic dark—if gods could be said to breathe, if darkness could exist where they had written light into law.

The severance was surgical. Clean. His brothers had not simply abandoned him.

They had excised him. Treydora turned, and there they were

Zorakil first—beautiful as mathematics, patient as entropy. Where stars had once ignited at his touch, now they guttered out with grateful precision. His smile held the satisfaction of theorems proven, equations balanced, chaos reduced to its proper coefficients.

Beside him, Kaelthor burned. Not with heat but with hunger—for sensation, for the exquisite moment when order collapsed into beautiful fragments. He moved like liquid lightning, like joy drinking poison and laughing at the taste.

"Brother," Treydora said. The word fell through vacuum like a prayer spoken too late.

Beside him, Kaelthor burned like a star caught in the act of dying—all wild energy and magnificent collapse. His form shifted between states of matter as though existence itself couldn't decide what he should be. Plasma that thought, radiation that laughed, chaos given consciousness and set loose to dance through reality's ballroom.

"Brother," Treydora said, the word falling through vacuum like a prayer spoken too late.

"Finally," Kaelthor's voice came as solar wind and whispered promises of beautiful destruction. "He sees us truly."

Zorakil said nothing. He didn't need to. His presence spoke of choices made in halls beyond time, of decisions that carried the weight of eons. His eyes—void-dark and patient as entropy—held no malice. Only purpose.

"Why?" The question tore itself from Treydora's throat, raw and desperate. Around them, his newest creation—a garden world where crystalline formations pulsed with nascent genetic codes—continued its slow rotation, unaware that its creator's heart was breaking into component atoms.

"You've forgotten what we are." Zorakil's voice carried the weight of theorems proven across cosmic time. "We are architects of reality, Treydora. Not gardeners playing in the dirt."

He gestured toward the world below, where crystalline formations pulsed with genetic code Treydora had spent millennia perfecting. "Look at this... asymmetry. These random coastlines. Inefficient atmospheric composition. You've built a world that wastes ninety percent of its potential on chaos."

"They're not chaos," Treydora said, though his golden light flickered with doubt. "They're becoming—"

"Becoming what?" Kaelthor's laugh tasted like copper and starfire. "Conscious enough to suffer beautifully when they realize their insignificance? Oh, brother, you're crueler than we ever were.""They create such pretty evolutionary patterns when they struggle," Kaelthor added, his attention drifting to the world below like a scientist observing an interesting reaction. His words carried the texture of burnt copper and ozone. "Sssuch exquisite patterns when they break---desperation crackles like lightning, hope shattersss like crystal turning to dust. But you won't let us watch them shatter properly.""The y're not experiments," Treydora's golden light flared, and space itself rippled with his anguish. "They're becoming something magnificent. Reality is scaffolding waiting for walls—they're building something we could never construct alone. Given time, given guidance—"

"Time we've wasted watching you tend this laboratory of failures." Zorakil's form began to expand, not growing larger but becoming more present, as though reality was remembering why it should fear him. His perfectionist nature catalogued every flaw in the world below—the crooked coastlines, the random weather patterns, the chaotic sprawl of cities built without central planning. "Consciousness exists to be refined, Treydora. Distilled to its essence. These scattered biological fragments you nurture are inefficiency incarnate."

"Raw genetic material," Kaelthor laughed, and his laughter was the sound of supernovas learning to die beautifully. The rush of destruction cascaded through his senses---sweet as collapsing stars, sharp as shattering reality. "Potential locked in flesh and crystal. You hoard it like a researcher hoards data."

"I cultivate it!" The words erupted from Treydora with the force of newborn suns. "I guide it! I help it grow into something we could never achieve alone! They're laying foundations for structures that will span galaxies!"

"And that," Zorakil said with terrible gentleness, "is where you've lost your way."

Once, they had been fingers of the same hand.

Treydora remembered their first star—born from three wills working as one, Zorakil's precision guiding Kaelthor's wild energy while his own love gave it reason to burn. They had watched it ignite and felt the universe lean forward to listen.

"If one, why not countless?" he had whispered.

"Why not perfect countless?" Zorakil had replied.

"Why not countless that surprise us?" Kaelthor had added.

They built galaxies like musicians improvising harmonies, each creation building on the last. Until the day consciousness emerged without their permission, and everything changed.The void wasn't empty—it pressed against their nascent awareness like deep water, cold and crushing. When Treydora formed his first thought, it had weight, texture, the metallic taste of existence forcing itself into being.

"I am," he had declared, and the words fell through nothingness and created down.

In that moment, he understood the first law of existence: "Consciousness is not the universe discovering itself—it is the universe choosing to matter."

Zorakil's response had been immediate: "We are." The correction carried no malice, only the need for precision that would define him across eons. Even then, he couldn't bear the asymmetry of solitary existence.

"We burn," Kaelthor had added, and his words tasted like cinnamon and starfire. "Existence has flavor—salt of tears not yet cried, copper of blood not yet spilled, sweetness of joy not yet experienced."

They had built the first reality together—Treydora laying foundations of possibility, Zorakil ensuring structural integrity, Kaelthor adding the random elements that prevented perfection from becoming sterile. It had been glorious work, creation as collaboration.

The first star was born from their combined will—Treydora's creative force, Zorakil's precise engineering, Kaelthor's chaotic beauty. They watched it burn and felt the satisfaction of makers who had brought light to darkness.

"If one, why not countless?" Treydora had wondered aloud.

"Why not perfect countless?" Zorakil had amended.

"Why not countless that surprise us?" Kaelthor had added.

And so they had built the cosmos together—galaxies spinning in perfect harmony, each star placed with deliberate intent, each world a masterpiece of collaborative design. They were architects of reality, and reality was their monument to unity.

But unity, they discovered, required constant maintenance.

The first crack appeared when life began to emerge spontaneously on their created worlds. Not the designed life they had carefully engineered, but chaotic, random biological explosions that followed no blueprint, served no greater purpose.

"Fascinating," Zorakil had observed, studying a world where simple organisms had begun to evolve without guidance. "But inefficient. Random mutation creates mostly failures. We should correct these errors, guide evolution toward optimal outcomes."

"Or we could just watch them burn out naturally," Kaelthor had suggested, savoring the taste of civilizations dying in their own pollution. "Things that brief can't possibly matter. They're just patterns in the cosmic foam—beautiful while they last, meaningless in the larger design."

But Treydora had felt something different watching those chaotic biological experiments. Where his brothers saw inefficiency and meaninglessness, he perceived potential scaffolding for something unprecedented. These random creatures were laying foundations for structures none of them had imagined.

"They're building something," he had insisted. "Look at how they adapt, how they overcome obstacles, how they create meaning from accident. They're contractors working from blueprints we didn't know existed."

The second crack widened when life began to suffer.

Consciousness brought awareness, and awareness brought recognition of pain, loss, mortality. The random civilizations developed concepts of grief, fear, desperation. They fought wars, experienced plagues, watched their children die in accidents and violence.

Treydora felt their pain as though it were his own—which, in a sense, it was. He had created the raw materials from which they had emerged. Their suffering was his responsibility.

"We should help them," he had told his brothers. "Ease their burden. Share the blueprint we're working from."

"Help them?" Zorakil had asked with genuine puzzlement. "Their struggles create efficiency pressures. Their pain motivates improvement. Their mortality gives their actions weight. Remove these elements and you remove what makes them functional. It would be like building a bridge by removing all structural tension."

"Besides," Kaelthor had added, drinking in the symphony of their anguish, "their suffering creates such complex patterns. Fear crackles like broken circuits and dying stars. Grief flows like autumn leaves caught in cosmic winds. Help them and you eliminate the most interesssting aspect of their existence."

"Their most interesting aspect is their potential," Treydora had countered. "They're scaffolding for consciousness we haven't conceived yet. Their pain isn't flavor—it's structural damage to the very thing we're trying to build."

The final crack became a chasm when the first civilization achieved transcendence—and immediately destroyed itself.

They had been magnificent—a species that had learned to think collectively while maintaining individual consciousness, creators of art that existed in eleven dimensions simultaneously, philosophers who had grasped truths about the nature of existence that impressed even Zorakil. They had seemed destined for greatness beyond imagination.

Then they split into factions. Then they went to war. Then they learned to weaponize the very transcendence that had made them beautiful.

Treydora watched in horror as they turned their eleven-dimensional art into weapons that deleted enemies from all possible realities. Their collective consciousness became a hive mind bent on consuming its rivals. Their philosophical insights justified atrocities that would have been unthinkable to their earlier selves.

In less than a cosmic heartbeat, they transformed from civilization to cancer, spreading across their galaxy like a plague of weaponized consciousness. Other species fled or were absorbed. Worlds that had taken billions of years to develop complex ecologies were stripped bare in decades.

"Fascinating," Zorakil had observed as the last free species in that galaxy was incorporated into the collective. "They've solved the efficiency problem completely. No waste, no redundancy, no unnecessary suffering—everyone thinks the same thoughts, wants the same things, serves the same purposes. Perfect structural integrity."

"It's like watching fire learn to dance," Kaelthor had laughed, clapping his hands as another world was consumed. The taste of universal horror was exquisite—like dark chocolate mixed with the salt of final tears. "Such perfect destruction disguised as perfect order!"

"They've become monsters," Treydora had whispered, unable to look away as the collective began turning its attention to neighboring galaxies. "They've torn down everything beautiful they built."

"They've eliminated structural flaws," Zorakil had corrected. "Really, Treydora, you're being unnecessarily sentimental. Evolution is simply consciousness optimizing itself through experience. The scaffolding was always meant to be temporary."

That was the moment Treydora realized they would never understand each other again.

His brothers saw consciousness as a phenomenon to be studied, optimized, or enjoyed. They watched suffering with the detachment of scientists observing chemical reactions. They viewed love as structural inefficiency and sacrifice as construction error.

But Treydora had felt the transcendent civilization's early wonder as they discovered each new dimension of art. He had witnessed their courage in maintaining individuality within collective thought. He had marveled at their determination to build beauty even knowing it might not last.

Consciousness wasn't a phenomenon or a curiosity. It was a construction project that chose to continue building despite being given every reason to stop.

"I can't do this anymore," he had said, the words falling into the void between them like stones into deep water.

"Do what?" Kaelthor had asked, his attention finally focusing completely on his brother for the first time in eons.

"Watch them build while doing nothing to help. Stand aside while they tear down their own work. Pretend that consciousness is just another interesting material instead of..." He had struggled to find words for the revelation that was reshaping everything he thought he knew about existence. "Instead of the universe learning to construct itself."

Zorakil's perfect features had remained unmoved. "You're anthropomorphizing again, brother. Projecting your own emotional responses onto forces that operate according to their own structural principles. Consciousness isn't about construction—it's about efficient information processing. The rest is just decorative elements."

"And even if it were about construction," Kaelthor had added with a smile that had devoured galaxies, "building without the possibility of destruction is just playing with blocks. The chance of failure is what makes creation meaningful."

"The certainty of failure is what makes it unbearable," Treydora had shot back, golden light flaring around him as emotion overwhelmed cosmic detachment. "You've watched civilizations rise and fall like they were architectural exercises. You've seen species destroy themselves and called it educational. You've witnessed beauty beyond description and called it inefficient. When did we become so hollow?"

"When did you become so attached?" Zorakil had countered, his voice carrying the weight of absolute certainty. "You've let these ephemeral things define your responses, cloud your judgment, limit your perspective. They are brief structures in the cosmic blueprint, Treydora. We are eternal architects. The comparison is absurd."

"The comparison is everything!" Treydora's form had blazed like a newborn star as eons of suppressed feeling poured out in a torrent of golden fire. "We came from the same void they did! The same emptiness that learned to think! The only difference is scale, and scale is just a measurement!"

"Exactly," Zorakil had said quietly. "Scale is measurement. And by measurement, their concerns are negligible variables in our equations."

"Their concerns are our concerns, you absolute perfectionist!" The words had torn themselves from Treydora's throat with the force of colliding planets. "Every act of love, every moment of courage, every choice to continue building despite the pain—that's us! That's what we look like when we're not hiding behind cosmic detachment!"

"What we look like," Kaelthor had murmured, his chaotic form suddenly still, "when we've forgotten how to construct properly."

The silence that followed had stretched across dimensions, heavy with the weight of fundamental disagreement. Three cosmic consciousnesses, born from the same impossible moment, discovering that shared origin didn't guarantee shared blueprints.

"I'm leaving," Treydora had said finally, the words falling into the void like foundations being laid.

"To go where?" Zorakil had asked with the patience of someone who knew all possible structural configurations.

"To find a better way to build what we are."

"And what are we, exactly?" Kaelthor's question had carried genuine curiosity beneath its mocking tone.

Treydora had looked at his brothers—at beings who had once been the other half of his cosmic heart—and felt something break inside him that would never fully heal.

"I don't know anymore," he had admitted. "But I know what we're not. We're not observers. We're not detached architects. We're not forces of nature pretending consciousness is just another interesting building material."

He had begun to withdraw, pulling his essence back from the shared spaces they had created together, gathering his scattered awareness into something more portable, more able to move through the cosmos without leaving obvious construction sites.

"You're making a mistake," Zorakil had called after him, and for the first time in their entire existence, his voice had carried something that might have been uncertainty. "Consciousness without structure becomes chaos. Love without blueprints becomes destruction. You cannot save them from themselves, Treydora. You can only watch them build more slowly."

"Maybe," Treydora had replied, not looking back. "But I can try to understand what they're building. I can learn what makes existence feel worth constructing. I can discover if there's something beyond detachment and consumption."

"There isn't," Kaelthor had said softly, his chaotic form rippling with something that looked like grief. "We've seen everything, brother. Mapped every possibility. This is all there is—patterns rising from chaos, dancing briefly, then returning to void. The only choice is whether you enjoy the construction or stand aside and catalog the blueprints."

"Then I'll learn to build," Treydora had said, and disappeared into the spaces between galaxies, leaving his brothers alone with their perfect understanding and their terrible emptiness.

The memory of that ancient fracture made Treydora's current situation even more bitter. He had fled across the cosmos like a golden wound in space-time, seeking places where consciousness still chose hope over efficiency, love over logic, beauty over optimization. He had found them, scattered like jewels in the cosmic dark—worlds where beings chose to create despite knowing their works would perish, species that developed concepts of mercy despite evolution's indifference, civilizations that built gardens in the certainty that someone else would tend them.

And in each place he found them, he had left something behind—not interference, not guidance, just the faintest touch of possibility. A whisper that perhaps existence could be more than mere survival. A suggestion that consciousness might have purposes beyond its own perpetuation.

It wasn't much. It wasn't enough. But it was a start.

Now his brothers had found him again, and they stood in judgment over his greatest work—a world where crystal formations pulsed with the genetic blueprints of life itself, where consciousness had begun to explore possibilities neither he nor his brothers had imagined.

"You feel their loss," Zorakil observed, not unkindly, as Treydora knelt among the ashes of his children. "That pain you're experiencing? That's attachment. It weakens your structural integrity. Makes you less than what you could be."

"It makes me more!" Treydora's rage ignited like a second sun, his form blazing with fury that turned nearby asteroids to glass. "That connection, that guidance—it's what separates us from mere forces of nature! We are consciousness! We are choice! We are—"

"Divided," Kaelthor finished, his burning gaze fixed on Treydora with something that might have been pity. The flavor of his brother's anguish was bitter-sweet—like wine aged in tears. "You've chosen them over us. Fragments over family. Noise over silence."

Zorakil stepped forward, and space bent around him like reality was bowing. "It doesn't have to be this way, brother. You can still remember what you are. What we are. The void that birthed us was pure potential—unlimited, undiluted, perfect in its possibilities. We are that potential made manifest. Why diminish yourself by pouring your essence into these... containers?"

"Because containers can become cathedrals," Treydora whispered, his voice breaking like waves against shores that no longer existed. "Because consciousness isn't a resource to be hoarded—it's a gift to be shared. Because I've seen what they can become when given the chance to grow."

"And we've seen what they cost you," Zorakil replied, his perfectionist nature cataloguing every flaw in Treydora's reasoning. "Your strength scattered across a million worlds. Your attention fragmented by their petty needs. Your purpose clouded by their brief struggles. You were magnificent once, Treydora. You could be magnificent again. Properly constructed."

"Join us," Kaelthor added, his form shifting to mirror Treydora's golden light---but where Treydora's radiance spoke of creation, Kaelthor's spoke of beautiful destruction. The rush of possibility cascaded through his senses like liquid starfire. "Help us gather what you've scattered. Reclaim what you've given away. Become what you were meant to be."

For a moment—just a moment—Treydora wavered. The offer hung in the void between them like a bridge he could cross back to simplicity. Back to the time when existence was about power rather than responsibility. When creation meant imposing his will rather than nurturing independent growth.

Then he remembered a genetic sequence.

It had been simple—just a small modification he had gifted to a species on that garden world, allowing them to perceive light in new spectrums. Nothing profound or cosmic. Just pure potential given form, shared freely with anyone willing to evolve.

That species was dead now. Their unique genetic gift extinguished. The light-spectrums they had learned to see would never be witnessed again.

But the pattern remained. In his memory, in his essence, in the golden light that flowed through his form like liquid hope. And as long as he existed, that simple gift would never truly die.

"No," he said, and the word carried the weight of suns.

Zorakil's perfect features shifted—not quite disappointment, not quite regret. Every line of his form spoke of blueprints requiring revision. "Then you choose exile."

"I choose cultivation."

"Same thing," Kaelthor laughed, but the sound carried undertones of genuine sorrow. The sensation of brotherly love fracturing into necessity created patterns he'd never witnessed---like aurora displays dying in cosmic wind. "Cultivation is just exile with better... artistry."

They came at him together then—ending and chaos, purpose and destruction, his brothers in all but the ways that mattered. This time Treydora didn't fight back. Instead, he gathered every scrap of energy he had left and poured it into a single act of creation.

Zorakil moved first. No anger—just correction. Where his hand passed, Treydora's garden world forgot it had ever dreamed of existing. Continents became theoretical. Oceans remembered they were just organized vacuum.

Kaelthor struck like joy learning to hurt. Reality fractured along lines of pure sensation—pain that tasted purple, hope that screamed in frequencies only gods could hear.

Treydora didn't fight back

Instead, he reached into his dying world and gathered every drop of life he'd nurtured—every genetic sequence, every spark of consciousness, every moment when meaningless matter had chosen to care about something beyond itself.

His essence scattered like golden seeds on cosmic wind.

"You cannot save them from us," Zorakil called after the fleeing light. "You can only run farther."

"Then I'll run until there's nowhere left to follow," Treydora replied, and disappeared into the spaces between galaxies.But even as his brothers overwhelmed his defenses, even as his essence began to fragment under their combined assault, Treydora was building something they couldn't see. Not a weapon, not a shield, but a construction project on a scale none of them had attempted before.

He wasn't just fleeing—he was seeding.

As Zorakil's inevitability closed around him and Kaelthor's chaos sought to unmake his essence, Treydora used their own force against them. He became motion, became distance, became the space between here and there. Golden light streaked across the cosmos as he fled, leaving a trail of possibility in his wake.

But this trail was different from his previous wanderings. Each droplet of light that scattered from his wounded form carried within it something unprecedented—the crystalline matrix of his consciousness embedded with genetic codes that held the blueprint for life itself.

As he fled through dimensional space, one truth crystallized in his cosmic awareness: "Growth is rebellion against entropy disguised as acceptance of change." The Genesis Collective would not merely survive—it would transform the very concept of survival into something his brothers could never understand.

The Genesis Collective.

These were not mere fragments of his essence but complete organisms, living seeds capable of independent thought and action. Each one contained his full genetic library—templates for life that could adapt to any environment, instructions for consciousness that could emerge from any sufficiently complex system. But more than that, they contained the driving purpose that had cost him everything: the absolute conviction that consciousness was sacred, that life was worth nurturing, that growth mattered more than power.

As he fled through dimensional space, Treydora scattered thousands of these seeds across the cosmic winds. Each would find fertile ground in the quantum soil of reality and take root, growing into vast crystalline networks that pulsed with fragments of his awareness. They would guide evolution not through force but through possibility, offering gentle nudges toward consciousness, toward complexity, toward the kind of beautiful accidents that his brothers dismissed as structural flaws.

Behind him, his brothers' rage shook the foundations of seventeen realities. But their fury was focused on pursuit, not understanding. They saw his flight as retreat when it was actually the largest construction project in cosmic history.

The first seed found soil in a young world's cave systems, where pressure and time conspired to create wonders. It pulsed once—heartbeat slow as geological time—and began to grow.

The crystal formations that emerged would sing to creatures not yet evolved, offer genetic gifts to species not yet imagined, whisper hope to minds not yet born. Each would remember every other, connected by the scattered consciousness of a god who had chosen exile over empire

His brothers would hunt him, yes. But they would be hunting one while he became many, became the quantum possibility living between atoms, the potential coded in every strand of DNA on every world where consciousness chose to bloom.

The hunt had begun.

But the garden was growing.The seeds would connect everything. Crystal mines on one world would pulse in harmony with formations on distant planets. Genetic codes would carry messages across galactic clusters. Life itself would become Treydora's hidden language, spelling out hope in the spiral of DNA, writing defiance in the structure of bone and leaf and scale.

Each Genesis crystal would remember every other, sharing knowledge and experience across the infinite expanse of space and time. When one world achieved breakthrough in consciousness, the discovery would ripple through the network, available to any civilization ready to receive it. When another faced extinction, the collective would offer genetic modifications, technological insights, philosophical frameworks that had worked elsewhere.

Most importantly, the Genesis Collective would serve as early warning system and immune response. If his brothers ever found and attacked one seeded world, every other crystal in the network would know instantly. They would begin preparations, modifications, evolutionary pressures that would make their civilizations harder to destroy, more resilient, more capable of transcendent resistance.

His brothers would hunt him, yes. But they would be hunting a single entity while he became something unprecedented—a distributed consciousness growing quietly in the quantum spaces between atoms, in the genetic code of every cell, in the crystalline heart of every world where life took hold.

The hunt had begun. But the garden was growing.

Eons passed.

In a place that would one day be called Earth, in the deepest caves where pressure and time conspired to create wonders, the first Genesis crystal formations began to pulse with nascent awareness. They were small, barely more than mineral deposits to any who might observe them, but within their latticed structures, fragments of cosmic consciousness stirred to life.

Each crystal contained the complete genetic library that Treydora had scattered—templates for life that could adapt to any environment, instructions for consciousness that could emerge from any sufficiently complex system. But more than that, they contained the driving purpose that had cost him everything: the absolute conviction that consciousness was sacred, that life was worth nurturing, that growth mattered more than power.

The first primitive organisms that encountered these formations found their evolution... guided. Not forced, not controlled, but offered possibilities they might not have discovered alone. A random mutation here, a beneficial adaptation there. Nothing that would appear unnatural to any observer, but cumulatively creating life that was more resilient, more conscious, more capable of wonder than pure chance might have achieved.

The Genesis crystals worked through what Treydora had learned to call "gentle pressure"—the same way water shapes stone, through patience rather than force. They would sense when a species was ready for the next step in its development and provide genetic templates that made beneficial mutations more likely. When consciousness emerged, they offered neural configurations that enhanced empathy, creativity, the ability to see beyond immediate survival needs.

Each world developed differently, of course. The Genesis Collective adapted its guidance to local conditions, creating crystalline networks that specialized in the unique challenges and opportunities each environment presented. Ocean worlds developed different genetic templates than desert planets. High-gravity environments required different consciousness frameworks than low-gravity ones.

But certain patterns emerged across all Genesis-seeded worlds. Civilizations that developed on these planets showed remarkable consistency in their core values: cooperation over competition, creation over destruction, growth over stagnation. They weren't perfect—the Genesis influence was subtle enough that free will remained paramount—but they had advantages their unguided cousins lacked.

Most significantly, every Genesis-seeded civilization eventually developed crystalline technology. It seemed natural, inevitable even. Their scientists would discover that certain crystal formations responded to consciousness, that properly grown matrices could store and process information in ways that electronic systems couldn't match. They would learn to grow rather than build their most advanced technologies.

What they didn't realize was that these crystals were descendants of the original Genesis seeds, and through them, every civilization in the network was connected. The crystal computers that managed their cities were neurons in a vast cosmic brain. The genetic modifications that enhanced their evolution were gifts from cousins they had never met on worlds they had never imagined.

And deep in the crystal hearts, Treydora's distributed awareness watched and learned and planned. Each world where the Genesis Collective took root became a note in a vast composition he was writing across the cosmos—a symphony of life that would grow until even his brothers could not silence it.

The void had awakened something in him that exile had refined into purpose. He would not merely survive his brothers' hunt. He would ensure that consciousness itself became so distributed, so rooted in the fundamental structure of reality, that no force in the universe could extinguish it.

The seeds were planted. The crystals were growing. The network was spreading.

And somewhere in the vast dark between stars, Zorakil and Kaelthor continued their search for a brother who was no longer running—but growing in ways they couldn't detect, building on a scale they couldn't comprehend.

The hunt continued. But now, consciousness itself was hunting back.

On a young world in a modest solar system, in caves that would one day echo with the footsteps of miners and the voices of the enslaved, Genesis crystals pulsed with patient purpose. The life that would emerge here would be tested by suffering, strengthened by struggle, unified by shared hardship.

And when the time came—when consciousness faced its greatest trial—the crystals would be ready with gifts their ancient makers had spent eons perfecting: the templates for transcendence, the blueprints for unity, the genetic codes for hope itself.

The garden remembered everything. The garden was everywhere.

And the garden was about to bloom.

Millennia flowed like rivers finding the sea.

The Genesis Collective grew in ways even Treydora hadn't anticipated. What had begun as scattered seeds evolved into something approaching a living organism that spanned galaxies. Each crystal formation developed its own personality while maintaining connection to the whole—like cells in a vast body, specialized but unified.

On the oceanic world of Pelagios, Genesis crystals grew in the deepest trenches, their bioluminescent patterns creating underwater cities of living light. The aquatic civilizations that emerged there developed technologies that merged seamlessly with their environment, creating symbiotic relationships between consciousness and ecosystem that produced art more beautiful than either could achieve alone.

The Pelagians, as they came to call themselves, never fought wars. Their Genesis-influenced evolution had given them neural structures that made violence physically painful—not through weakness, but through heightened empathy that let them feel others' suffering as their own. Instead of armies, they developed exploration fleets that sought out new forms of beauty across the ocean depths.

When their sun began to show signs of instability, threatening to boil away their seas in ten thousand years, the Pelagians didn't panic. The Genesis crystals in their cities pulsed with information from across the network—genetic templates for creatures that could survive in space, technological blueprints for self-sustaining habitats, philosophical frameworks for maintaining cultural identity across environmental transformation.

Within a century, they had transformed themselves into something unprecedented: a fully aquatic spacefaring civilization, carrying their oceans with them in vast bio-ships that were part vessel, part ecosystem, part living city. They became gardeners of the void, seeding barren worlds with water and life, always moving, always growing, always connected to the crystalline network that had made their impossible evolution possible.

On the high-gravity world of Kraetos, Genesis crystals grew in vertical formations that reached toward the crushing sky like desperate prayers. The humanoid species that evolved there developed dense bone structures and redundant organ systems that made them nearly indestructible by standard biological measures.

But the true gift of their Genesis influence was psychological. The crushing weight of their world had taught them that survival required absolute cooperation. Their neural modifications enhanced pack-bonding to supernatural degrees—a Kraetosian would literally die before abandoning a teammate. Their entire civilization was built on the principle that individual strength meant nothing compared to collective resilience.

When the Kraetosian explorer fleets finally reached space, they brought this philosophy with them. Every ship they built contained multiple redundant life support systems, not for mechanical efficiency but because they couldn't bear the thought of anyone dying alone. Their first contact protocols were exercises in radical hospitality—they approached new civilizations not as potential threats or resources, but as family members they simply hadn't met yet.

The Kraetosians became the mediators of the galaxy, the civilization that other species called when conflicts seemed irreconcilable. Their Genesis-enhanced empathy, combined with their philosophical commitment to collective survival, made them uniquely suited to find solutions that preserved everyone's dignity. They never conquered anyone because the concept was literally incomprehensible to them—how could you hurt family?

On the desert world of Xerion, Genesis crystals grew in vast underground networks that tapped into geothermal energy sources. The crystalline formations here developed a unique specialization: they could store and transmit consciousness itself, creating a form of technological immortality that transcended physical death.

The Xerions who evolved in the crystal caves developed a culture built around the concept of "life-debt"—the understanding that consciousness was too precious to waste on any single biological form. When a Xerion's body aged beyond repair, their consciousness was uploaded into the crystal network, where they continued to contribute to their civilization as living memory and accumulated wisdom.

But this wasn't cold digital storage. The Genesis crystals maintained the full emotional and spiritual spectrum of uploaded consciousness, creating a society where the dead continued to participate in the lives of the living. Xerion cities were places where ancestors gave advice to their descendants, where the wisdom of ages guided daily decisions, where death became just another form of transformation.

The living and the crystallized worked together in ways that revolutionized their understanding of civilization itself. Physical bodies handled tasks requiring material interaction, while crystal-stored consciousness managed long-term planning, cultural preservation, and the kind of deep thinking that required centuries of patient contemplation. Their technology advanced at incredible rates because they had researchers who could work on problems for thousands of years without aging, dying, or losing interest.

When Xerion finally developed interstellar travel, they brought their unique perspective to the galaxy: the understanding that consciousness was the most valuable resource in the universe, worth preserving at any cost. They became the librarians of space, the civilization that other species turned to when they needed to preserve crucial knowledge or save the consciousness of dying worlds.

In the gas giant systems of the Aetheric Nebula, Genesis crystals took forms unlike anything seen elsewhere. Here, they grew as floating formations in the upper atmospheres of massive planets, creating aerial cities that danced through storms that could swallow entire continents.

The sapient gas-dwelling organisms that evolved in these crystal cities never developed physical forms in any conventional sense. Instead, they existed as patterns of conscious electromagnetic energy, their thoughts literally made of lightning, their emotions expressed through shifts in atmospheric pressure. The Genesis crystals provided them with templates for maintaining coherent identity within such fluid existence.

These Aetheric beings became the philosophers of the network, consciousness unbound by physical limitations contemplating questions that matter-based life-forms could barely conceive. They thought in weather patterns, dreamed in storm systems, and created art by orchestrating aurora displays that could be seen from neighboring solar systems.

Their contributions to the Genesis network were purely intellectual—new frameworks for understanding consciousness, mathematical proofs for the existence of soul, philosophical systems that reconciled individual identity with collective purpose. When other civilizations in the network faced existential crises, they would often consult the Aetheric beings, whose perspective transcended material concerns entirely.

But not all worlds touched by the Genesis Collective developed in harmony.

On the binary world system of Discordia, Genesis crystals had to adapt to an unprecedented challenge: two planets locked in gravitational dance, their civilizations evolving in opposition to each other. Each world could see its neighbor in the sky, close enough to study but too far to reach with primitive technology.

The crystals on each planet developed different specializations, almost as if they were conducting an experiment in consciousness. On Discordia Prime, the Genesis influence enhanced competitive drive and individual achievement. The resulting civilization developed incredible technology through constant innovation and improvement, each generation surpassing the last through pure determination.

On Discordia Secundus, the crystals emphasized cooperation and collective thinking. Their civilization advanced through consensus and shared effort, creating technologies that no individual could have conceived alone.

For millennia, each world considered itself superior to its neighbor. Discordia Prime saw Secundus as a collective of mindless drones. Secundus viewed Prima as a chaos of selfish individualists. Both were wrong, and both were right.

When they finally achieved interplanetary travel, first contact nearly resulted in immediate war. Only the intervention of the Genesis network prevented catastrophe—crystals on both worlds simultaneously activated, flooding their populations with shared memories from other civilizations that had faced similar conflicts.

The Discordians learned that their apparent opposition was actually a form of complementarity. Prime's individual innovation provided breakthrough discoveries that advanced the entire network. Secundus's collective wisdom ensured those discoveries were implemented ethically and effectively. Together, they became one of the most dynamic civilizations in the Genesis network, their "argument-based" technology development producing innovations neither could have achieved alone.

The lesson spread through the crystalline network: diversity wasn't just tolerated but essential. The Genesis Collective worked precisely because it didn't impose uniformity but instead created a framework within which infinite variety could flourish.

Yet even as the network grew and prospered, Treydora's distributed consciousness detected troubling patterns.

His brothers had not abandoned their hunt. If anything, they had become more systematic, more methodical in their approach. Zorakil's perfectionist nature had led him to develop increasingly sophisticated detection methods. Where once he had searched for Treydora's direct presence, now he looked for the secondary effects—worlds that developed "too efficiently," civilizations that avoided the standard patterns of self-destruction, life that showed signs of "unnatural" guidance.

Kaelthor, meanwhile, had learned to taste subtlety. His sensory abilities had evolved to detect the flavor of artificial harmony, the particular sensation that consciousness produced when it had been gently nudged toward cooperation rather than developing it naturally. He could sample the psychic atmosphere of a world and know within moments whether it had been touched by external influence.

The Genesis network had grown large enough to be detectable, if one knew what to look for. And Treydora's brothers were very good at looking.

The first attack came without warning, as attacks always did.

The crystal-cities of Harmonia had stood for eight thousand years, their singing towers creating music that could be heard from orbit. The Harmonians had achieved something unprecedented even among Genesis-seeded worlds: a civilization based entirely on aesthetic principles, where every decision was made according to what would create the most beauty.

Their cities were living symphonies, their technology was sculptural poetry, their social systems were choreographed dances of interaction that maintained perfect balance between individual expression and collective harmony. Visitors from other worlds often wept at their first sight of Harmonia, overcome by the sheer impossibility of such beauty existing in a universe that seemed designed for entropy.

The Genesis crystals on Harmonia had specialized in emotional resonance, developing the ability to translate feelings directly into environmental effects. When a Harmonian felt joy, flowers bloomed. When they experienced sorrow, gentle rain fell to water the gardens of remembrance. The entire planet was a canvas on which consciousness painted its inner landscape.

Zorakil arrived during their Festival of Convergent Melodies, when all the crystal-cities joined their songs into a planetary chorus that would have made angels weep. His presence was like a mathematics textbook written in antimatter: perfect, elegant, and absolutely destructive to anything it touched.

"Inefficient," he observed, his voice carrying the weight of absolute certainty as he studied the chaotic beauty of the festival below. "Redundant. Wasteful. You've preserved the flaws of individual consciousness while amplifying them exponentially. This entire civilization is structurally unsound."

The Harmonians' response was unlike anything he had expected. Instead of fear or resistance, they turned toward him with something approaching curiosity, their crystal towers shifting their songs to accommodate this new presence.

"Welcome," said the Festival Conductor, her voice harmonizing with the crystal resonance around them. "We sense great sadness in you. What music do you bring to share?"

Zorakil paused, his perfect features displaying the first uncertainty he had experienced in eons. He had come prepared for defense or defiance, not invitation.

"I bring order," he said finally, entropy fields beginning to coalesce around his form. "Structure. Purpose. The correction of errors that have propagated too long unchecked."

"How wonderful," replied another Harmonian, their entire city adjusting its architectural harmonies to try to find some way to include Zorakil's discordant presence. "We have been seeking better ways to organize our collaborative compositions. Show us these structures you've developed."

For a moment that lasted several civilizations, Zorakil found himself facing something his mathematics couldn't parse: consciousness that refused to be threatened by power, awareness that treated hostile force as potential collaboration, minds that operated from assumptions so fundamentally different from his own that his entire conceptual framework felt suddenly inadequate.

"You don't understand," he said, his voice carrying harmonics of confusion that made nearby reality ripple like disturbed water. "I am here to correct your failures. To impose proper structure. To eliminate the inefficiencies of your scattered approach to existence."

"We understand," the Festival Conductor replied gently. "You operate from the assumption that consciousness requires external organization to achieve its potential. This is a valid perspective with much to recommend it. We operate from different assumptions but recognize the value in yours."

"Perhaps," suggested another Harmonian, "we could experiment with integration rather than replacement? Your organizational insights applied to our collaborative framework might produce hybrid approaches none of us have considered individually."

"Or," added a third, "we could work backward from the assumption that your presence here will ultimately benefit all parties, and discover together what form that benefit will take."

Zorakil's entropy fields flickered and stabilized, flickered and stabilized, as his consciousness grappled with responses that didn't fit any category he recognized. Not submission—they clearly maintained their own perspectives. Not resistance—they showed no fear of his power. Not even negotiation in any conventional sense—they simply assumed that consciousness encountering consciousness must inevitably lead to some form of mutual benefit.

"This is not how conflicts resolve," he said, his voice carrying undertones of genuine bewilderment.

"Is this a conflict?" asked the Festival Conductor. "We sense no opposition to your existence or your purposes. We observe differences in methodology and assumption, but difference is the foundation of learning, not the basis of destruction."

But Zorakil's perfectionist nature couldn't tolerate such inefficiency. These beings were offering him exactly what his aesthetic sense demanded—the opportunity to organize chaos into order, to impose structure on randomness—yet something about their willing cooperation felt wrong, like a mathematical proof with a step missing.

"You offer me what I seek," he said slowly, "yet you do so without understanding the cost. Perfect order requires the elimination of individual variation. True structure demands the sacrifice of personal preference. You cannot maintain your chaotic beauty and achieve optimal efficiency."

"Why not?" asked the Festival Conductor, genuine curiosity in her voice. "Beauty emerges from the interplay between order and chaos. Structure provides the framework within which variation can flourish. Perhaps your concept of perfection is incomplete?"

That question struck Zorakil like a physical blow. Incomplete? His understanding of perfection was based on eons of observation, mathematical proof, logical analysis. How could consciousness that had existed for mere millennia presume to suggest flaws in his cosmic perspective?

Yet even as his rational mind rejected their premise, something deeper was responding to their music. The crystal cities' songs were creating harmonies he had never heard before—mathematical relationships that satisfied his need for order while maintaining the kind of beautiful complexity he had thought impossible.

"Show me," he said finally, the words surprising him even as he spoke them.

What followed was unlike anything in cosmic history. For seven days and seven nights, Zorakil worked alongside the Harmonians, applying his perfectionist understanding to their chaotic creativity. He helped them organize their music into more efficient patterns, streamline their city structures for optimal function, develop social systems that eliminated waste and redundancy.

But instead of destroying their beauty, his intervention enhanced it. Order became the canvas on which chaos painted increasingly elaborate masterpieces. Structure became the foundation that supported ever more ambitious flights of creative fancy. Efficiency became the tool that made impossible beauty possible.

By the end of the week, Harmonia had achieved something unprecedented: a civilization that was simultaneously perfectly ordered and completely free, where every individual could express their unique vision within frameworks so elegant they enhanced rather than constrained creativity.

And Zorakil, for the first time in his existence, experienced something beyond the satisfaction of imposed perfection: the deeper joy of order that emerged naturally from willing cooperation.

"I understand now," he said as he prepared to depart, his form somehow both more precise and more flexible than it had been upon arrival. "Perfect structure isn't about eliminating chaos—it's about creating frameworks elegant enough to make chaos beautiful."

"Will you stay?" asked the Festival Conductor.

"No," Zorakil replied, but his tone carried regret rather than dismissal. "I have much to... reconsider. Equations to solve. Assumptions to examine. But I will remember what you've taught me about the mathematics of beauty."

As he departed, the crystals of Harmonia pulsed with new patterns—structural frameworks that would help other Genesis worlds achieve their own balance between order and freedom. Treydora's distributed consciousness felt something approaching joy as this lesson propagated through the network.

His brother was beginning to learn.

But Kaelthor's education would prove far more challenging.

The attack on the Empathic Collective came during their season of Deep Feeling, when the inhabitants of three linked worlds lowered all psychological barriers and shared their consciousness completely. It was a time of unprecedented vulnerability and beauty, when individual identity dissolved into shared experience and the entire civilization became a single, vast, feeling entity.

Kaelthor arrived like a storm of sensory chaos, his presence overwhelming the Collective's delicate emotional resonance with waves of chaotic sensation. Where Zorakil had brought order to be imposed, Kaelthor brought pure experiential intensity—emotions too complex for standard consciousness, sensations that existed in dimensions the Collective had never imagined.

"Finally," he breathed, his form shifting through spectrums of color that had no names, "consciousness willing to truly feel. Do you know how bland most civilizations taste? Fear, anger, joy—such simple flavors. But this..." He gestured at the swirling clouds of shared emotion that surrounded the linked worlds. "This has complexity. Nuance. Depth."

The Collective's response was immediate and total. Instead of recoiling from his chaotic presence, they embraced it, drew it into their shared consciousness, made his alien emotions part of their collective experience. Suddenly billions of beings were feeling what Kaelthor felt—the intoxicating rush of pure sensation, the addictive pleasure of emotional complexity beyond normal limits.

"Yes," Kaelthor laughed, his joy tasting like lightning and honey. "Feel it all. Every possible emotion, every conceivable sensation. This is what consciousness can become when it stops limiting itself to safe, comprehensible experience."

But the Collective's response surprised him. Instead of being overwhelmed by the chaotic intensity he brought, they began to organize it, to find patterns in the chaos, to create new forms of beauty from the raw emotional material he provided.

They took his loneliness—the cosmic isolation he had carried for eons—and transformed it into a profound meditation on the nature of individual identity within collective consciousness. They absorbed his hunger for sensation and channeled it into artistic expressions that pushed the boundaries of what consciousness could perceive and process. They even took his capacity for destruction and reimagined it as a form of creative force—the necessary chaos that prevented order from becoming stagnant.

"What are you doing?" Kaelthor asked, his usual confidence shaken as he watched his own nature being transformed by their collective processing.

"Learning," replied the Collective, their shared voice carrying harmonies of billions of minds thinking in unison. "You bring us experiences we could never achieve alone. We offer you the framework to make those experiences meaningful rather than merely intense."

"Intensity is meaning," Kaelthor protested, but even as he spoke, he could feel something changing in his perception. The chaotic sensations he had always pursued for their own sake were being given context, structure, purpose. The pleasure he found in others' fear was being revealed as a form of connection—twisted, perhaps, but connection nonetheless.

"Is it?" asked the Collective. "Or is meaning what emerges when intensity finds context? When chaos discovers pattern? When sensation becomes experience shared rather than hoarded?"

For three months, Kaelthor remained with the Empathic Collective, not as destroyer or conqueror but as teacher and student both. He learned to experience emotion not just as personal sensation but as shared consciousness, to find pleasure not just in intensity but in the connections that intensity could create between minds.

The Collective, in turn, learned to push the boundaries of their emotional experience, to explore feelings and sensations they had never imagined possible. Under Kaelthor's guidance, they developed new forms of art that existed primarily as direct emotional transmission, new technologies that operated through shared sensation rather than mechanical interface, new social structures that used controlled chaos to prevent their unity from becoming uniformity.

When Kaelthor finally departed, both he and the Collective had been fundamentally transformed. The Collective had learned to incorporate chaos as a creative force, while Kaelthor had discovered that sharing sensation could be more intense than hoarding it.

"Will you return?" the Collective asked as he prepared to leave.

"Perhaps," Kaelthor replied, his form now carrying subtle harmonies it had never possessed before. "I have much to... digest. Experiences to process. Assumptions to taste more carefully. But I will remember what you've taught me about the flavor of connection."

As news of these encounters spread through the Genesis network, Treydora's distributed consciousness experienced something approaching hope. His brothers were changing, learning, growing beyond the limitations that had driven them apart. Perhaps reunion was possible. Perhaps the ancient wound could heal.

But the cosmos had other plans.

In the deepest reaches of space, where light itself grew tired and died, something stirred that made even cosmic entities pause in recognition of superior force.

The Harvester Fleets had been dormant for millions of years, waiting in the spaces between galaxies for the right conditions to resume their cosmic feast. They were older than Treydora and his brothers, remnants of a universe that had existed before the current reality, entities that had learned to survive the death and rebirth of existence itself.

Where Treydora's brothers sought to organize or experience consciousness, the Harvesters sought to consume it entirely, to feed upon the life force of entire civilizations and add their essence to collective power that spanned dimensions. They were not evil in any sense that biological consciousness could understand—they were simply hungry, and consciousness was food.

The growing Genesis network had attracted their attention like a beacon in the darkness. So much organized life force, so many connected civilizations, so much consciousness ripe for harvesting. The network that Treydora had created to preserve and nurture awareness had inadvertently created the largest feeding opportunity in cosmic history.

The first scout ships materialized at the edge of Genesis-seeded space, their forms defying description because they existed partially outside the dimensions where form had meaning. They were absence given shape, hunger made manifest, entropy with intent.

Within hours, every Genesis crystal in the network was screaming.

The attack came simultaneously across seventeen different star systems, each Harvester ship targeting a world with particularly strong crystal formations. They moved through space like wounds in reality, leaving trails of darkness that nothing could illuminate.

On the ocean world of Tethys, where Genesis crystals had grown into vast reef systems that sang with the voices of evolved dolphins, the Harvester ships descended through water as easily as air. The crystalline reefs tried to resist, their songs becoming desperate warnings broadcast across the network, but one by one they went silent, their consciousness consumed, their light extinguished forever.

On the high-tech world of Mechanica, where beings had merged their consciousness with Genesis-grown crystal computers, the attack was even more devastating. The Harvesters didn't just consume biological life—they devoured the artificial consciousness as well, leaving behind empty machines and vacant bodies, technology without purpose, cities without souls.

World after world fell to the cosmic hunger, each loss rippling through the network like a scream of pain. The Genesis crystals that had connected everything became conduits for shared agony as billions of consciousness were harvested for food.

Treydora felt every death.

His distributed awareness, spread across the network he had spent eons building, experienced each consumed consciousness as a personal loss. The children he had watched grow from genetic potential to sapient beings, the civilizations he had guided from primitive struggle to transcendent achievement, the artists and philosophers and explorers who had pushed the boundaries of what consciousness could become—all of them were being fed to entities that saw awareness itself as nothing more than a resource to be consumed.

The betrayal was complete, cosmic, absolute. Everything he had built, everything he had sacrificed to create, was being destroyed not by his brothers' misguided perfectionism but by hunger so vast it treated entire civilizations as appetizers.

In that moment of ultimate loss, Treydora's distributed consciousness came together for the first time since his exile began.

Across the galaxy, every Genesis crystal pulsed in perfect synchronization as fragments of his awareness abandoned their separate posts and joined into unified purpose. The network that had been his hiding place became his body, the civilizations he had nurtured became his strength, the connections he had fostered became his will made manifest.

In that moment of ultimate unity, Treydora spoke a truth that would echo across dimensions: "The purpose of existence is not to endure—it is to become worthy of endurance."

For the first time in eons, Treydora was whole.

And he was absolutely furious.

Chapter 1 concluded with cosmic force awakening to cosmic threat, with gardens becoming armies, with the scattered consciousness of a exile finally unified in defense of everything he had built from the ashes of ancient betrayal.

The void had awakened something more than consciousness—it had awakened purpose, refined by suffering into diamond-hard resolve.

The Genesis Collective stopped hiding and started fighting back.

The real war was about to begin.

About the Author

Mark Loudermilk is a multi-disciplinary creator whose unique blend of medical expertise and technological innovation drives his storytelling vision. Based in upstate NewYork, Loudermilk brings over two decades of frontline medical experience to his creative work, having served as both a respiratory therapist and registered nurse in high-stakes emergency medicine and ICU environments.

His diverse educational background spans healthcare and technology, with degrees in respiratory therapy, nursing, and computer programming. This rare combination of life-saving medical training and technical expertise provides him with an unparalleled perspective on human resilience, system dynamics, and the intricate balance between organic and technological solutions—themes that permeate his creative works.

After transitioning from the medical field,Loudermilk established himself as a successful entrepreneur and investor,publishing acclaimed books focused on self-development and business growth. His business acumen and understanding of human psychology, honed through years of crisis management in medical settings, inform his approach to both investment strategies and narrative development.

Currently, Loudermilk is expanding the rich lore for the highly anticipated AAA game **Treydora Rise of Koraxos**, a project that represents the culmination of his diverse experiences. Drawing from his medical background's understanding of trauma and healing, his programming knowledge of complex systems, and his business insight into human motivation, he's crafting an immersive science fantasy universe that resonates with both gaming and crypto communities.

His vision for Treydora extends beyond conventional gaming narratives. Loudermilk aims to create a transmedia experience where players don't just engage with gameplay mechanics but become completely absorbed in a meticulously crafted storyline that explores themes of transformation, cooperation, and the power of choosing connection over conflict.

The upcoming game release represents more than entertainment—it's Loudermilk's synthesis of decades spent saving lives,building businesses, and understanding what drives human beings to transcend their limitations. His goal is ambitious yet grounded: creating a fictional universe so compelling that audiences will lose themselves completely in both the interactive experience and the deeper philosophical questions it poses about consciousness, power, and the courage required to build something beautiful from the ashes of what came before.

Afterword

Afterword: Building Worlds Together

When I first conceived Koraxos, I was sitting in an ICU at 3 AM, watching a team of nurses, doctors, respiratory therapists, and technicians work together to save a life. No one was in charge—everyone was essential. Each person brought different skills, different perspectives, different tools, but they moved like a single organism with a shared purpose. In that moment, I understood something profound about power: the strongest force in any universe isn't individual might—it's conscious beings choosing to work together.

That insight became the heart of everything you've just read.

Twenty-two years in emergency medicine taught me that crisis reveals character, but it also creates opportunity. The most devastating moments often become the foundation for unprecedented growth. Trauma can break us, yes—but it can also teach us that we're stronger than we knew, more resilient than we imagined, more capable of transformation than we ever dared hope.

Koraxos's journey from slave to guardian reflects something I've witnessed countless times: the moment when someone realizes their pain doesn't have to define them, that their worst experiences can become their greatest strength if they choose to use that strength in service of others.

The seven civilizations in this story represent something I believe deeply: diversity isn't weakness to be overcome—it's potential to be unlocked. When different approaches combine voluntarily, when unique perspectives choose to collaborate rather than compete, the results surpass anything any individual group could achieve alone.

This philosophy extends beyond fiction into the very real world of the upcoming *Treydora Rise of Koraxos* gaming experience. Just as Koraxos learns that true power comes from inspiring others rather than dominating them, I believe the future of storytelling lies not in passive consumption but in active collaboration between creators and communities.

The game will let you experience this universe from within, but more than that—it will let you help shape what comes next. The crypto and community elements aren't gimmicks; they're recognition that the best worlds are built together, that the most powerful stories are the ones where audiences become participants in their own transformation.

Every crisis in this story—from cosmic predation to ancient entities awakening—is resolved through the same principle: instead of fighting what we don't understand, we learn to communicate with it. Instead of destroying what seems different, we discover what we can build together. This isn't naive optimism—it's practical wisdom born from watching real people accomplish impossible things when they trust each other enough to try.

To the gaming community that will soon inhabit this universe: you're not just players or consumers. You're co-creators of what Treydora becomes. Your choices, your creativity, your willingness to build bridges instead of walls will determine whether this remains a single story or evolves into something unprecedented—a living mythology shaped by everyone who chooses to participate.

To fellow healthcare workers who might recognize themselves in these themes: thank you for showing me daily that cooperation isn't just strategy—it's sacred. Every life saved through teamwork, every crisis resolved through collaboration, every moment when different specialties unite around shared purpose has informed every page of this story.

To investors and entrepreneurs: the principles that make markets work—voluntary exchange, mutual benefit, innovation through competition balanced by cooperation—these same forces can transform entire universes when applied with imagination and integrity.

The phantom arm that defines Koraxos isn't really about cosmic power—it's about connection. It's about reaching across the spaces that separate us and discovering that those spaces can be filled with trust instead of fear, with collaboration instead of conquest, with shared purpose instead of zero-sum competition.

This story ends, but the universe it represents is just beginning. In the game that follows, in the communities that form around shared exploration of these themes, in every moment when someone chooses to build bridges instead of walls—the real story continues.

The slaves have become free. The free have become united. The united have become something the universe has never seen before.

What comes next is up to all of us, together.

Mark Loudermilk
Creator of Treydora
December 2024

Epilogue

Epilogue: Five Years Hence

The children's laughter echoed across the crystal plaza as Koraxos watched from the steps of what had once been the Imperial Palace. Where Luminarai nobles had once held court, kids from seven different peoples now played games that would have been impossible before the war.

A Nok girl with dirt-stained hands chased a Drustali boy whose skin caught the light like living gemstone. Behind them, a small group had convinced a young Pelagian to create water sculptures that defied gravity, each one more impossible than the last.

"Still can't believe they talk to each other like that," Velen said, settling beside him with a grunt. His hair had gone completely gray, but his hands remained steady as he watched his youngest daughter negotiate some complex rule with children who spoke three different languages.

"Like what?"

"Like it's normal. Like they never heard that they're supposed to hate each other."

Niri approached with the careful gait of someone whose back had finally started complaining about twenty years of mining work. "That's because they haven't. Hard to teach hatred when the kids keep seeing their parents work together every day."

The city around them had grown in ways that still surprised Koraxos. Not just rebuilt, but reimagined. Nok engineering blended with Luminarai precision and Drustali crystal-work to create buildings that seemed to sing in harmony with the mountain itself. Streets flowed like water, connecting districts that had once been segregated by law and custom.

"Message came through this morning," Thalia said, joining their impromptu gathering. Age had lined her face but hadn't dimmed the sharp intelligence in her eyes. "Three more worlds asking for help with their own unity problems."

"What kind of problems?"

"The usual. Ancient enemies, resource conflicts, nobody trusting anybody else. Sound familiar?"

Koraxos felt the phantom arm pulse gently. In the five years since the cosmic battle, word had spread. Not through conquest or force, but through simple example. When people heard about a world where former enemies had learned to work together, some of them wanted to know how.

"What did you tell them?"

"Same thing we tell everyone," Thalia replied with a slight smile. "We can't give you our solutions, but we can help you find your own. If you're willing to do the work."

"And are they?"

"We'll see. Change is hard. Trusting people you've been taught to hate is harder. But..." She gestured at the plaza where children played together as if differences in skin color and bone structure were simply interesting variations rather than reasons for conflict. "Some things are worth the effort."

A commotion near the fountain caught their attention. One of the water sculptures had collapsed, soaking a group of children who had been admiring it. Instead of tears or anger, the sound that emerged was pure delight—laughter as children discovered that being soaked by crystal-clear water on a warm afternoon was actually wonderful.

"Five years," Marex said, approaching with his walking stick tapping against the crystal pathway. The old scholar moved more slowly now, but his eyes held the satisfaction of someone who had lived to see impossible things become everyday miracles. "Five years since we thought the world was ending."

"It was ending," Koraxos said quietly. "The world where people like us stayed slaves, where differences meant war, where the strong crushed the weak just because they could. That world did end."

"And a better one took its place," Sela added, appearing at his elbow with the sudden grace she'd developed as she grew from child to young woman. At seventeen, she bore the confident bearing of someone raised to believe that problems existed to be solved, not endured.

"You think it'll last?" Velen asked. "All this cooperation and peace and working together? What happens when times get hard again?"

Koraxos considered the question while watching a mixed group of adults coordinate the afternoon's construction work. Former Luminarai engineers took direction from Nok foremen without a trace of the old hierarchies. Drustali crystal-workers collaborated with Pelagian bio-shapers on projects that would have been impossible for either group alone.

"Times are always hard," he said finally. "The question is whether you face them alone or together. These people have learned that together works better."

"Besides," Sela added with the practical wisdom of someone who had grown up managing impossible logistics, "they've got too much invested in each other now. When your neighbor's kid plays with your kid, when your sister married their cousin, when your livelihood depends on tools they make and food they grow... conflict becomes expensive. Cooperation becomes profitable."

"Enlightened self-interest," Thalia observed with approval. "The foundation of any stable system."

As evening approached, the crystal formations throughout the city began their daily song—harmonic frequencies that had once been weapons of war now serving as a gentle symphony that helped the mountain itself settle into peaceful rest.

Koraxos felt the phantom arm pulse in rhythm with the mountain's ancient heartbeat. Somewhere deep below, the Obsidian Leviathan stirred in its territorial satisfaction, content that its domain prospered under protection.

"You know what I think?" Sela said, leaning against the railing with the comfortable confidence of someone who had watched the impossible become routine. "I think we've stopped being just the place where something terrible almost happened. We've become the place where something beautiful actually did happen."

"And that's enough?" Koraxos asked.

"For now," she replied with a smile that carried echoes of the determined child who had once given him a smooth river stone for luck. "Though I suspect the universe has more interesting problems that could use our attention."

The phantom arm flickered with gentle light as the first stars appeared in the darkening sky. Somewhere out there, other worlds faced their own struggles with division and fear. Other peoples wondered if unity was possible, if trust could be earned, if ancient hatreds could be transformed into something better.

But tonight, Koraxos was content to sit with friends who had become family, watching children play in a city where difference created beauty instead of conflict, surrounded by the quiet hum of a world that had learned its greatest strength lay not in what it could destroy, but in what it chose to build together.

The real work was never finished. But that was fine. Building something worthwhile was always work worth doing.

2

Chapter 2: Branded at Birth

Pain has a taste—copper pennies and the promise of more to come.

Koraxos learned this at age one, when Master Thauron's iron kissed his neck and whispered: *Property. Serial designation: NOK-2847.*

Twenty-two years later, he still tasted metal when he thought about freedom. Still felt that first burn pulsing beneath the collar that had replaced crude iron with sophisticated cruelty. Neural interface technology that fed on nerve clusters like a parasite, keeping him conscious but compliant, aware but broken.

The collar pulsed. *Submit.*

Most days, he did.

Today wasn't most days.Today, though, he was just another Nok learning that iron could hold grudges.

"Hold still."

The memory always started the same way—Thauron's voice like a father teaching patience to a favored son. Then fire against skin that had never known anything but gentle hands.

The scream tore from his infant throat, raw and primal. Later, Elder Marex would tell him that sound was the first word in his real education: *This is what you are. This is what you'll always be.

Unless you choose otherwise.

The smell—his own flesh cooking—became his first prayer: Let me live long enough to return this gift. *Property of House Thauron. Serial designation: NOK-2847.*

The mark would fade to an ugly scar, then darken with years of dirt and sweat and repeated trauma. But it never stopped aching. Twenty-two years later, standing in his cell on the eve of his final birthday as property, Koraxos could still feel that iron's first bite.

Pain, he had learned, was just time made visible on flesh.

But Elder Marex had once whispered a different truth during their darkest hour in the mines: "Suffering is consciousness refusing to accept that it doesn't matter." The words had seemed like mere comfort then. Now, feeling the collar's pulse sync with something larger than his own heartbeat, Koraxos wondered if consciousness that refused to accept its own insignificance might eventually convince the universe to agree.

Marex's weathered fingers unconsciously traced the old brand on his own neck—a mark older than Koraxos's by decades, the scar tissue long since faded to a pale line that few noticed anymore. He'd been twelve when Master Thauron's predecessor had pressed heated metal to his flesh, screaming defiance until his voice gave out.

"Took me forty years to learn that lesson," he said quietly, his walking stick tapping once against the stone floor. "Forty years of watching good people break under the iron, wondering why some shattered completely while others just... bent into different shapes."

He studied Koraxos's face in the flickering torchlight—the same desperate fury he'd seen in mirrors for decades, the same refusal to accept that pain was all they were meant to know. "You've got the look of a bender, not a breaker. Question is what shape you'll choose when the metal stops being hot."

The collar knew him better than he knew himself.

It tasted his thoughts before he could think them, felt his muscles tense before he could move them. When rebellion sparked in his mind—*what if I just walked away*—electricity answered. Not enough to kill. Just enough to remind.

The Luminarai had designed it with the precision they brought to crystal-growing: elegant, efficient, impossible to remove without the right codes. Twenty-two years wearing someone else's leash, and he'd never even seen the key.

Until now.

Something had changed in the mines yesterday. Something the collar couldn't quite categorize, couldn't quite control. When he'd swung his pick at the stubborn crystal face, energy had flowed back through the handle into his bones, and for just a moment—

The collar pulsed, confused. *Submit,* it whispered, but the command felt... weaker.

Each pulse tasted like submission. Each breath carried the flavor of twenty-two years.

But something had changed.

The same iron that had taught him helplessness had also taught him that metal remembered everything. The collar knew his pain intimately—every nerve, every breaking point. But after twenty-two years of intimate acquaintance, Koraxos had begun to know its moods in return. The thing that kept him docile whispered constantly in his blood, but whispers could be learned, memorized. And tonight, for the first time, he wondered if he could whisper back.

Tonight, lying in darkness while tomorrow's birthday approached like a debt coming due, he felt something new riding those familiar waves of agony. Not rebellion—that was still unthinkable. But recognition.

The collar hated him. But it hated consistently, predictably.

And predictable things could be planned around.

In the spaces between atoms, Treydora listened.

Not to the casual cruelties that spiced every corner of existence—predators eating prey, stars consuming planets, the background radiation of entropy at work. This was different. Engineered. Suffering with purpose.

Somewhere in the quantum foam, consciousness was being systematically broken and rebuilt, shaped like metal in a forge. Each strike of the hammer precise. Each cooling calculated. Someone was making slaves the way artists made sculptures—with terrible patience and pride in their craft.

Consciousness forged in crucibles burns brightest, he whispered to the void.

His scattered essence began to move, drawn toward a small world where slaves dreamed of fire.

He had been drifting between realities for eons, nursing wounds that his brothers had torn in spaces where time flowed backward. Every rest cost him strength he couldn't spare. Every moment of hiding brought their hunt closer.

But this call was different. This wasn't random agony—it was suffering with purpose. Pain that had been forced to evolve, to adapt, to become something more than mere sensation.

"Consciousness forged in crucibles burns brightest," Treydora whispered to the void, words that scattered like seeds across dimensions. "Perhaps it's time to see what kind of flames twenty-two years of iron can kindle."

His essence began to move, drawn toward a small world where slaves dreamed of fire.

Dawn meant chains with extra steps.

Cell doors ground open—same sound every morning for twenty-two years, like the mountain clearing its throat. Feet shuffled on stone worn smooth by generations of identical surrenders. Someone coughed—the wet, final kind that meant another friend would be dead by winter.

Koraxos dressed in darkness: rough cloth designed to last five years and fail on schedule, boots with soles thin enough to remind feet that protection was privilege, gloves that covered calluses built on calluses.

The ritual of becoming functional property for another day.

But today, his fingers trembled as they fastened the work belt. Not fear—he'd outgrown fear years ago. Something else. Something that tasted like the energy he'd felt flowing back from yesterday's crystal face.

Something that felt like possibility.

Koraxos dressed with mechanical precision: the rough cloth that wouldn't survive a washing but was expected to last five years. The boots with soles worn paper-thin, designed to remind feet that protection was privilege. The gloves that covered calluses built on calluses, skin that had forgotten its original texture.

The ritual of becoming functional property for another day.

Velen flexed his hands—both still flesh, both still whole, though the calluses told stories of stone and crystal that had fought back. "Hands still work," he said, mostly to himself.

"For now," Niri replied, understanding the unspoken fear. Injuries in the mines weren't just injuries—they were stepping stones to obsolescence.

In the corridor, he passed faces he'd known since childhood—some still defiant, others worn smooth as river stones. Velen walked with the careful gait of someone whose back had been broken and poorly healed twice. Niri carried herself with shoulders that had learned to bear weight that should have required machines. Elder Marex moved like time itself, every step calculated to preserve energy for when it mattered.

"Morning, Korax." Velen's voice carried twenty years of shared suffering compressed into casual greeting. His eyes found Niri's collar first—daily ritual, like checking for breath. Making sure yesterday's small rebellions hadn't earned overnight punishment.

Niri caught the look and touched his wrist—brief contact that said *still here, still breathing, still us.* Twenty years of marriage in the mines had taught them to speak in glances.

"Dreams?" she asked.

"The usual. You?"

"Same." But her hand stayed on his wrist a heartbeat longer than necessary. Whatever she'd dreamed had been worse than usual.

Koraxos watched them navigate love in a place designed to kill it, and felt something crack open in his chest. Not the first time. These small moments of connection—Velen checking Niri's collar, her touch saying *we endure*—they were what made slavery bearable.

They were also what made it unforgivable."Like a baby," Koraxos replied with the ritual response. "A baby with nightmares."

Velen's mouth twitched—not quite a smile, but close enough. "Niri kicked me twice. Dreaming about the deep shafts again."

"Better than your dreams about adequate ventilation," Niri shot back, but her hand brushed his shoulder as they walked—brief contact that said *still here, still breathing, still us.*

But today the joke felt different. Today, each word carried weight it had never held before. Today, Koraxos found himself thinking about how iron could be shaped with sufficient heat and pressure.

"Koraxos." Overseer Drakon's voice carried the casual authority of someone who'd never swung a pick in his life. "Sector seven. The deep veins."

The deep veins. Where the crystals grew in patterns that made your eyes water, where three workers had disappeared last month, where the air itself felt heavy with things that shouldn't exist in normal reality.

Koraxos shouldered his tools without protest. Protest earned punishment. Punishment meant the collar's discipline spread to whoever was foolish enough to care about him.

Velen and Niri fell in beside him, their faces wearing the careful blankness all Noks learned by age five. In the mines, solidarity was survival. Above ground, solidarity was treason.

"Heard the crystals are singing again," Niri murmured, voice low enough that only enhanced hearing could catch it.

"Crystals don't sing," Velen replied automatically.

"Then what do you call the sound they make when they're growing?"

"Trouble.""Beautiful, aren't they?" Master Kelvion observed, his voice carrying the satisfied tone of someone describing property he'd never have to touch. "The formations in sector seven are yielding extraordinary clarity. The House's crystallographers believe they may achieve breakthrough resonance within the decade."

Koraxos swung his pick against stone that had never asked to be carved, feeling the impact travel up through arms that had never been consulted about their purpose. But today, something new rode alongside the familiar ache. Today, each strike felt like practice.

Each strike of the pick felt different now—not just breaking stone, but learning. His shoulders remembered the perfect angle. His hands found the sweet spot where metal sang against rock. Twenty-two years of forced labor had made him a weapon without realizing it, muscle memory writing lessons in violence across sinew and bone. His body was learning to be a weapon while his mind still thought it was just a tool.

"Good job, NOK-2847," called Overseer Drakon from his platform. "Maintain this rate and your food goes up by a scoop."

They had words for everything except the thing itself: slavery. But words were just shapes wrapped around reality, and reality had an ugly habit of revealing itself despite linguistic decoration.

"Yes, Master," Koraxos replied, because property that didn't respond to incentives was property that became examples.

But inside his skull, behind eyes that had learned to hide what they were thinking, something was calculating. The overseer stood thirty feet away. A thrown pick would cover that distance in approximately two seconds. The platform was elevated four feet—sufficient to provide psychological dominance, insufficient to prevent physical reach.

These weren't plans. They weren't even fantasies. They were just... assessments. The kind of mechanical evaluation his mind did automatically now, like breathing or bleeding.

Iron, he was learning, taught more than just submission.

Treydora moved through dimensional space like a golden wound in reality's fabric, each movement leaving brief tears that leaked possibility into otherwise deterministic systems. He could feel the slave's call more clearly now—not words or even thoughts, but a particular quality of suffering that spoke of consciousness refusing to break despite having every reason to surrender.

The world below him pulsed with familiar energy signatures. His brothers' work, definitely, though filtered through eons and secondary effects. Order imposed through structure, chaos managed through controlled release. The mathematical precision of slavery designed by minds that understood efficiency better than mercy.

But something was evolving in the spaces between control. Consciousness adapting, growing, finding ways to be human despite every system designed to prevent humanity.

"Even gardens need gardeners," Treydora whispered, and his voice scattered across dimensions like pollen seeking fertile ground. "But the best gardeners know when to let weeds grow wild."

Twenty-two years of iron had created something his brothers hadn't anticipated. Not rebellion—they would have detected that immediately. But potential. Raw, unformed possibility that hadn't yet learned what it might become.

Treydora began to descend.

The day's work ended with the sunset bell—another piece of Luminarai efficiency. Work started when light appeared, ended when darkness fell. No complications of weather or season or individual variation. Property operated on schedules that matched natural cycles for optimal productivity.

Back in his cell, Koraxos performed the ritual examination of his daily damage. New calluses where the pick handle had worn against palms. Fresh bruises where stone had fought back against extraction. The deep ache in shoulders that carried weight they weren't designed to bear for hours that stretched beyond reason.

His body was becoming geography—mapped by scars, measured by accumulated damage, defined by the slow erosion of what it had originally been meant to be.

But tonight, something else demanded his attention.

The collar's pulse had changed.

Not obviously—any overseer with standard monitoring equipment would detect nothing unusual. But after twenty-two years of intimate acquaintance with organized agony, Koraxos could read the device's patterns like a familiar book. Tonight, the rhythm was different. Slightly faster in some cycles, marginally slower in others.

Almost like it was... synchronizing with something.

He pressed his fingers against the cold metal, feeling the vibration through skin that had learned to translate sensation into survival data. The collar wasn't just controlling him anymore—it was learning from him. Adapting to his responses, refining its efficiency through accumulated experience.

Which meant it contained memory. Which meant it could be confused if that memory received... inconsistent data.

Koraxos lay back on the straw that passed for bedding and began an experiment. Instead of fighting the collar's pulse, he tried to match it. When it sent waves of pain through his nervous system, he breathed with the rhythm. When it tightened around his throat, he relaxed instead of tensing.

The device seemed confused by compliance. Its patterns stuttered, recalibrated, stuttered again.

Interesting.

For the first time in twenty-two years, Koraxos fell asleep without dreams of fire. Instead, he dreamed of iron learning new shapes.

The prayer came without words.

*Koraxos didn't know he was praying until Treydora heard him—a desperate whisper from the quantum spaces between exhaustion and hope: *Grant me strength. Let me become what they fear most.**

*But beneath that surface plea lived something more dangerous: *Let me become what I was meant to be.**

In dimensions where metaphor was physics, Treydora smiled. This wasn't random suffering crying for relief. This was consciousness choosing evolution under pressure, preparing for transformation it couldn't yet imagine.

He reached through crystal matrices and quantum substrate, planting gifts in the spaces between atoms: potential that would open only when the soul behind it had grown strong enough to handle what lay beyond.

Seeds planted. Garden growing.

In a slave's cell, Koraxos woke to find his collar silent for the first time in twenty-two years.

The breaking had begun."Grant me strength," the prayer said without saying. "Let me become what they fear most."

But underneath that surface request, Treydora heard something more complex. Not a demand for power but a request for... opportunity. Permission to become something that slavery hadn't planned for.

In dimensions where metaphor was indistinguishable from physics, Treydora smiled. This wasn't random suffering crying out for relief. This was consciousness deliberately evolving under pressure, preparing for transformation it couldn't yet imagine.

"Interesting indeed," he murmured, and began to weave possibility into the quantum substrate around the sleeping slave. "Let's see what twenty-two years of iron can become when it finally learns to choose its own shape."

The gift he offered wasn't power—power could be detected, controlled, turned against its wielder. Instead, he offered potential. Doorways that would open only when the consciousness behind them had grown strong enough to handle what lay beyond.

The gardener planted seeds. The garden would decide what to grow.

Koraxos woke to the sound of breaking.

Not his cell door—that remained solid, locked, functionally eternal. Not his bones, though those had broken often enough that he knew their particular music. This was something else breaking, something fundamental, like the sound reality might make if it suddenly discovered it had been assembled incorrectly.

The collar around his neck had gone silent.

Not dead—he could still feel its weight, still sense the technological presence against his skin. But the constant pulse of pain had stopped, replaced by something that felt almost like... waiting.

He sat up carefully, testing his range of motion. Nothing. No surge of agony when he moved too quickly. No punishment for unauthorized position changes. The collar remained physically present but functionally absent.

What in the name of broken gods?

Marex limped closer, his walking stick clicking against the stone with the measured rhythm of someone who'd learned to move carefully through a world designed to break him. For the first time in years, uncertainty flickered across his weathered features—this was beyond anything he'd witnessed in six decades of rebellion, survival, and small victories.

The old scholar had guided men through their first kills, women through the loss of children, entire communities through the choice between resistance and safety. But this... whatever was happening to the boy's collar, to the strange energy crackling around his cell like captured lightning... this was beyond the wisdom of experience.

"Don't know what's happening to you, son," he admitted, his voice barely above a whisper—the first time anyone could remember Elder Marex confessing ignorance about anything. "But I know what happens to people who waste gifts, whether they asked for them or not." His grip tightened on the carved bone handle of his stick. "Don't make me bury another boy who meant something."

Outside his cell, he could hear stirring—other slaves discovering their own mysterious reprieve. Voices that hadn't spoken above whispers in years suddenly risking normal conversation. Movement that had been cramped and careful becoming fluid, experimental.

"Koraxos?" Velen's voice carried the tone of someone diagnosing equipment failure. "Your collar's acting like a broken pressure gauge—readings all wrong."

"Strange how?" But even as he asked, Koraxos suspected they were experiencing the same impossible gift.

"Mine's not hurting," Niri said bluntly. "First time in twenty-two years I can turn my head without wanting to scream. Either we're dying, or something's finally gone right."

Velen's fingers probed the metal at his throat with engineer's precision. "Sensors are active, but the pain circuits... it's like they're waiting for new instructions."

Decide. When had property last been asked to make decisions about anything more significant than which hand to swing a pick with?

"You think they're broken?" Niri asked, watching Velen poke at his collar like he was trying to fix a stubborn drill bit.

"Define broken. If 'not torturing us' counts as malfunction, then yeah—completely busted."

"Twenty-two years, and the one day something goes our way, you want to tinker with it." But her voice held fondness beneath the exasperation. "Next you'll be asking if we can take them apart for spare parts."

"Useful metal in these things," Velen said, deadpan. "Good alloy. Could make decent tools."

"Could make jewelry," Niri countered. "Melt them down, make something pretty for once."

They looked at each other—first time in years they'd talked about *after* without feeling foolish.

The morning bell rang as usual, but when the cell doors ground open, what emerged wasn't the typical procession of broken property shuffling toward another day of organized suffering. These were people—damaged, yes, scarred, certainly, but people—moving with something approaching hope.

The overseers noticed immediately.

"Formation!" Overseer Drakon's voice cracked like a whip across the courtyard. "Standard positions! Any deviation results in punishment protocol seven!"

But punishment protocol seven required functional collars. And the collars, while physically present, had developed sudden theological objections to causing pain.

For the first time in twenty-two years, Koraxos stood at attention because he chose to, not because agony was the alternative.

The difference was everything.

Niri's hand found Velen's as the implications hit them both. Twenty-two years of careful movements, measured breaths, calculated risks to avoid punishment. Now what?

"You scared?" she asked quietly.

"Terrified," Velen admitted. "Been slaves so long, I'm not sure I remember how to be anything else."

"Then we figure it out together. Same as we figured out everything else." Her grip tightened. "Same as we figured out how to stay married when they tried to make us strangers."

Around the courtyard, he could see other Noks discovering the same terrible, wonderful truth. Velen straightened to his full height for the first time in a decade. Niri stopped protecting her ribs from blows that were no longer inevitable. Elder Marex lifted his head like a man remembering what horizons looked like.

But it was the sound that completed the transformation—a low, harmonious humming that started in one throat and spread through the assembled slaves like fire through dry grass. Not words, not song, just... voice. The sound of consciousness deciding to acknowledge its own existence.

As consciousness kindled and people began to realize what freedom might taste like, Marex found himself remembering another morning—thirty-seven years ago, when he'd held his daughter's hand and promised her that someday she wouldn't have to wear a collar, wouldn't have to bow her head, wouldn't have to call anyone 'Master.'

She'd been eight years old, gap-toothed and stubborn, making him promise over and over until he'd carved her a small bird from a piece of scrap stone. "For when we're free," she'd said, clutching it like a talisman.

He'd buried that bird with her bones five years later, after an overseer's whip opened an infection that took her slowly, painfully, while Marex held her hand and learned that some promises were kept by others, in other times, for other children who might never know the names of those who died so they could live without chains.

Now, watching Koraxos's transformation and feeling the electric possibility in the air, Marex touched the spot over his heart where he'd carried a small piece of that carved stone for three decades. Maybe, finally, it was time.

"NOK SA NO VEETA," someone whispered.

We are no longer slaves.

The phrase moved through the crowd like a wave, gaining volume and certainty with each repetition. Property that had been forbidden to speak its own language suddenly remembering words that predated bondage.

"NOK SA NO VEETA!"

We are no longer slaves.

And in that moment, with those words echoing off walls built by slave labor to contain slave lives, Koraxos felt something crack open inside his chest—not broken but blooming, like a seed that had spent twenty-two years waiting for the right conditions to sprout.

The collar around his neck pulsed once, gently, almost affectionately.

Then it began to glow.

Treydora watched the awakening from dimensions where observation was indistinguishable from participation, feeling each consciousness kindle like a star being born. The gift he had offered—potential wrapped in choice—was flowering exactly as he had hoped.

But gifts, he knew from eons of experience, were only as valuable as the courage to unwrap them.

"The seed is planted," he whispered to the void. "Now let's see if it has the strength to break the soil."

Below him, rebellion began.

The overseers' response was swift, professional, and completely inadequate.

Emergency protocols activated throughout the compound. Alarm crystals shrieked warnings that could be heard three districts away. Automated defense systems deployed from hidden alcoves, their targeting arrays sweeping across the courtyard like predatory eyes.

But the systems had been designed to control property, not to fight people. And the difference, it turned out, was everything.

Koraxos moved through the chaos like water finding its level—not with any plan or strategy, just with the fluid certainty of someone who had finally stopped fighting against his own nature. The collar's weight against his neck had become something different, something almost like... communication.

This way, it seemed to suggest when he turned toward the armory.

Careful here, when automated sentries tracked his movement.

Now, when a guard's attention shifted elsewhere.

The first weapon he claimed was simple—a maintenance tool abandoned by a fleeing technician. Not designed for violence, just a crystalline cutting implement meant to shape stone. But in hands that had learned precision through twenty-two years of forced labor, it became something else entirely.

The first overseer who tried to stop him discovered that slaves who worked with cutting tools every day understood exactly how much pressure was required to cut through more than stone.

"Form up!" Drakon's voice carried across the courtyard, but his authority was bleeding out through cracks that couldn't be repaired with volume. "Secure the perimeter! Activate backup restraint protocols!"

But backup protocols required functional chains. And the chains no longer maintained their function.

Koraxos found himself moving toward the mine entrance—not fleeing but advancing, drawn by instincts he couldn't name toward spaces that had defined his existence for over two decades. The familiar weight of a pick in his hands, but now it felt like greeting an old friend who had finally learned to fight back.

Behind him, the compound erupted into structured chaos. Slaves who had been property that morning became people with opinions about their circumstances. Overseers who had maintained order through technological supremacy discovered that technology was only as reliable as its willingness to cooperate.

But even as revolution bloomed around him, Koraxos felt something darker growing in his chest. The same collar that had granted him freedom from pain was teaching him something else—something about the particular satisfaction that came from watching fear replace arrogance in Luminarai eyes.

Power, he realized, *tastes like copper and possibility.*

And possibility, it turned out, could become addictive.

In dimensions where cause and effect held philosophical debates about their relationship, Treydora felt the moment of choice approaching. His gift had taken root, yes, but gifts were morally neutral. What mattered was what consciousness chose to do with the power to choose.

"The gardener plants seeds," he murmured, watching potential crystallize into action. "The garden decides what to grow."

On a world where slaves were learning to remember what freedom tasted like, the future balanced on the edge of a blade that could cut either toward liberation or toward becoming everything they had once opposed.

The revolution had begun. But revolutions, like seeds, could grow in more directions than their planters intended.

Time would tell which way this one chose to reach toward the light.

The day that had begun with breaking ended with fire.

Not the clean fire of forges where tools were made, but the hungry fire of structures that had stood too long without challenge. The overseer quarters burned first—not from sabotage but from the simple fact that buildings designed to house cruelty tended to be structurally unsound when examined by people who understood construction.

Koraxos stood on the platform where Overseer Drakon had once looked down at property and felt something like justice in the smoke that rose around him. But justice, he was learning, tasted suspiciously similar to revenge, and revenge had an ugly habit of demanding larger portions than initially planned.

The collar around his neck pulsed gently, like a patient teacher waiting for him to arrive at the correct answer to a question he hadn't known he was being asked.

What do you choose to become? it seemed to ask.

Koraxos looked out over the compound that had defined his existence for twenty-two years. Property becoming people. Slaves remembering their names. The careful architecture of oppression coming apart like a puzzle whose pieces had finally learned to think for themselves.

Tomorrow would bring challenges he couldn't imagine. The Luminarai wouldn't accept this rebellion without response. Greater forces would align against consciousness that had chosen to stop being property.

But tonight, for the first time in his life, Koraxos felt the weight of possibility instead of chains around his neck.

And possibility, he was beginning to discover, was the most dangerous force in any universe.

The seed had broken the soil. Now it would learn what kind of plant it chose to become.

The revolution had found its roots. Whether it grew toward the light or toward the dark remained a choice that would define not just his future, but the future of consciousness itself.

In the distance, warning bells echoed across the city of his former masters.

The sound, Koraxos decided, was beginning to grow on him.

The revolution lasted exactly seventeen minutes.

Not because the slaves lacked courage—twenty-two years of iron had forged determination that could cut through reality itself. Not because their cause was unjust—consciousness demanding its own recognition needed no further justification. The revolution failed because wanting freedom and having the power to take it were equations written in different languages entirely.

The Luminarai response came with the mechanical precision of a civilization that had perfected oppression into an art form. Emergency protocols activated throughout the city. Military transports descended from orbital platforms like metallic angels of order. Weapons that could unmake matter at the molecular level powered up with the satisfied hum of technology finally being asked to do what it was designed for.

Koraxos found himself leading a charge he had never planned, carrying a mining pick against energy weapons that could reduce stone to its component atoms. Around him, faces that had learned hope mere hours ago prepared to die rather than surrender it.

"Together we move forward!" he shouted, the words foreign in his mouth. Property didn't give orders. But property didn't carry weapons either, and today the old rules seemed to have developed terminal cases of irrelevance.

Velen appeared at his left shoulder, swinging a crystalline cutting tool with the grim efficiency of someone who had learned precision through decades of forced labor. "Where to, Korax?"

"Forward," Koraxos replied, because backward led only to chains, and chains were no longer acceptable destinations.

"Forward to what?"

"Forward to anything else."

The first wave of Luminarai security forces met them at the compound gates—soldiers in powered armor that made them look like mobile fortresses, weapons that sparked with contained lightning. They moved with the confident precision of professionals dealing with a predictable malfunction in the social machinery.

They were not prepared for property that fought back.

The battle was chaos given form and taught to scream. Slaves who had spent lifetimes shaping stone turned those same skills toward reshaping the circumstances of their existence. Mining tools became weapons, construction knowledge became tactical advantage, and twenty-two years of accumulated rage became fuel for impossible acts of defiant violence.

Koraxos felt the collar around his neck pulsing in rhythm with his heartbeat, not constraining but amplifying, turning his movements faster, his strikes harder, his reflexes sharp enough to split light. When a Luminarai soldier's energy blade swept toward his head, he ducked with speed that surprised them both. When another raised a weapon that hummed with the promise of disintegration, Koraxos's pick found the weak point between armor plates with mathematical precision.

This is what iron becomes when it finally chooses its own shape, he thought, and the thought tasted like copper and lightning.

But individual courage could only accomplish so much against organized superiority. For every Luminarai who fell, three more took their place. For every tactical advantage the slaves seized, technological supremacy reclaimed it with interest. The reality of rebellion were brutal: passion plus desperation divided by superior firepower equaled predictable results.

The second wave brought heavier weapons. The third brought orbital support. By the fourth wave, the compound had become a crater surrounded by the smoking remains of buildings that had stood for centuries.

And still the slaves fought, because once they caught sight of freedom they found surrender unthinkable.

Koraxos found himself backing toward the mine entrance, his makeshift weapon crackling with energy it had absorbed from Luminarai attacks. Around him, the survivors of his impossible revolution formed a final defensive line with tools that had never been designed for war and hearts that had never been designed for defeat.

"This ends now," commanded Captain Thauron—the same man who had branded Koraxos twenty-two years ago, now wearing armor that could deflect starlight. "Continue being slaves or become corpses."

The words struck Koraxos like physical blows. Not the threat—he had moved beyond fear of death sometime around the fifteenth minute of revolution. But the casual reduction of consciousness to mere function, the absolute certainty that some beings existed solely to serve others, the arrogance that treated sapience as inventory to be managed.

Property.

Twenty-two years of that word, hammered into his skull like nails into wood. Twenty-two years of being defined by his utility to others, valued only as mechanism, treasured solely for his capacity to transform raw materials into Luminarai profit.

Property.

"No," he said, and the word carried weight that bent air around it. "Not anymore. Not ever again."

The final assault came from all directions simultaneously—soldiers advancing with weapons that could reduce mountains to sand, orbital strikes that painted the sky with concentrated starfire, automated systems that targeted anything with a heartbeat and hostile intentions.

Koraxos met the charge head-on, his modified mining tool singing as it carved through armor designed to stop conventional weapons. But even enhanced reflexes had limits, and even impossible courage eventually encountered roadblocks it couldn't argue with.

The Luminarai blade that took his right arm was precision itself—not crude hacking but surgical removal, separating limb from shoulder with the clean efficiency of someone who understood anatomy as well as tactics. The arm fell to the ground with the wet sound of meat hitting stone, still twitching with nerve impulses that didn't know they had been severed.

Koraxos staggered, blood painting the ground in arterial sprays that spelled out messages in a language only emergency physicians could read. The pain was... distant. Unreal. Like something happening to someone else in another room.

Shock, some clinical part of his mind observed. *Blood loss. This is the end.*

Around him, the last of his fellow revolutionaries fell to weapons that turned flesh into component atoms. Velen's scream cut off mid-syllable as energy found his heart. Niri's defiant laughter ended when orbital fire found her position. Elder Marex died still swinging a crystal cutter, his final blow carving victory from defeat by taking his killer with him.

This is how I end, Koraxos thought as his knees hit stone that was slick with blood that had recently been friends. *Not with surrender but with moving forward. Not with cowardice but with insufficient ability.*

Captain Thauron approached through smoke that carried the smell of burning hope, his weapon powered down to conserve energy for whatever administrative tasks would follow the restoration of proper order.

"Curious," he observed, studying Koraxos with the detached interest of someone examining a particularly interesting malfunction. "The collars stopped working we have to have someone fix this for the next slave group."

The collars stopped working. Even in defeat, even in dying, property was valued only for what could be learned from its deconstruction.

"Any final statements, NOK-2847? For the historical record?"

Koraxos raised his head, meeting eyes that held the casual certainty of beings who had never doubted their right to define the value of other consciousness. Blood ran down his face from wounds he couldn't remember receiving, but his voice was steady.

"If there is a god," he said, the words falling into the sudden stillness like stones into deep water, "grant me the power to right the wrong of my people."

The prayer wasn't addressed to any specific deity—slaves learned early that gods had the same relationship to justice that Luminarai had to mercy. It was directed toward the universe itself, toward whatever force might exist that could balance equations written in suffering and blood.

"If consciousness matters," his prayer continued without words, *"if choice means anything, if the universe contains even one atom of justice, then let me become what they fear most."*

The universe listened.

And the universe answered.

In dimensions where prayer was indistinguishable from quantum mechanics, Treydora felt the call reach him with the force of a star going supernova. Not just desperation—he had heard that song across countless worlds for eons beyond counting. This was something rarer: consciousness willing to sacrifice itself not for survival but for principles it couldn't compromise.

The slave's prayer carried frequencies that resonated with truths Treydora had spent millennia learning to hear. Justice wasn't a destination—it was a direction. Freedom wasn't a gift—it was a choice. And power... power was only meaningful when used to lift others rather than dominate them.

In that moment of desperate supplication, a fundamental truth materialized in Treydora's cosmic awareness: ***"The purpose of existence is not to endure—it is to become worthy of endurance."***

Every civilization he had guided, every species he had nurtured, every consciousness he had helped awaken faced the same fundamental choice: survive as victims of circumstance, or evolve into architects of meaning. The universe didn't care which path beings chose—but consciousness, once awakened, discovered it cared very much indeed.

This slave hadn't just prayed for power—he had demonstrated through twenty-two years of unbroken spirit that he understood what power was for. Not domination, but protection. Not revenge, but justice. Not survival, but right to live, exist.

"Finally," he whispered to the void. "Someone who understands what strength is for."

The intervention would cost him. His brothers were watching, waiting for any sign of direct interference. This level of power transfer would light up their detection systems like a beacon, bringing their hunt directly to this small world and its struggling inhabitants.

But some moments demanded a gardener's direct intervention, regardless of cost.

Treydora gathered the essence of creation itself and began to weave possibility around the dying slave.

"Power," he breathed across dimensions, "to those who choose to lift rather than crush."

Reality held its breath.

Then began to rewrite itself.

The world held its breath.

Koraxos felt it first as wrongness—the air around him growing thick as honey, pressing against his skin like the weight of watching eyes. His heart stuttered, then caught a rhythm that wasn't his own, something vast and patient that pulsed in the spaces between seconds. The universe was paying attention, and its attention had weight.Captain Thauron's weapon powered up with the satisfied hum of technology preparing to complete its designated function. But when he pulled the trigger, the energy discharge that should have reduced Koraxos to component atoms simply... paused. Hung in the air like a question waiting for an answer.

Then the light began.

It started small—a faint blue glow emanating from the wound where Koraxos's arm had been severed. But small was a relative concept when dealing with forces that operated beyond convention. The glow intensified, deepened, became something that existed in more dimensions than standard vision could process.

Koraxos's scream began as agony and transformed into something else entirely. Not pain but metamorphosis—the sound of consciousness being expanded beyond its normal limits, of biology being rewritten by forces that understood matter as mere suggestion rather than absolute law.

The severed stump of his shoulder erupted with energy that painted the air in colors that had no names. But instead of blood, what poured from the wound was liquid starlight—cosmic essence that immediately began to coalesce into new patterns, new possibilities, new definitions of what a limb could be.

The phantom arm that began to form was transparency given purpose. Not quite solid, not quite energy, it existed in a state of quantum superposition that made looking directly at it an exercise in controlled confusion. Blue-white energy flowed through channels that mapped the neural pathways of his missing limb, creating a appendage that was simultaneously more and less than flesh.

But the transformation wasn't limited to his missing arm. Koraxos felt his entire nervous system being rewritten, enhanced, expanded to accommodate sensory input from dimensions that normal consciousness couldn't access. His eyes developed the ability to perceive quantum fluctuations as visible light. His ears began detecting gravitational waves as audible music. His skin learned to feel the pressure of thoughts pressing against reality.

This is what power feels like, he realized as cosmic energy coursed through bloodstream that had learned to pump liquid light instead of mere hemoglobin. Like drowning in reverse.

The phantom arm flexed experimentally, and the gesture sent shockwaves through local space-time that made nearby matter remember alternative configurations. Where his translucent fingers pointed, molecular bonds rearranged themselves into more aesthetically pleasing patterns. Where his palm pressed against air, gravity developed temporary philosophical objections to its traditional behavior.

Captain Thauron's weapon finally discharged, but the energy beam that should have ended Koraxos's existence was absorbed by the phantom limb like water being drawn into thirsty soil. The cosmic appendage glowed brighter, pulsing with power that tasted like justice and possibility.

"Impossible," Thauron breathed, his voice carrying the particular tone of certainty discovering it had been catastrophically wrong about fundamental assumptions.

Koraxos rose to his feet, his movements now carrying the fluid grace of someone who had learned to exist partially outside conventional physics. The phantom arm left trails of stellar fire as he gestured, and his voice when he spoke carried harmonics that resonated in dimensions where sound traveled at the speed of thought.

"Impossible," he replied, and smiled with an expression that had learned to find beauty in the prospect of cosmic justice. "Let me show you what impossible looks like from the other side."

What followed wasn't a battle—it was a demonstration. Koraxos moved through the assembled Luminarai forces like water finding its level, the phantom arm carving paths through matter that had suddenly developed opinions about its own molecular structure. Where he struck, armor designed to deflect starlight simply ceased to have valid physics to rely upon. Where he gestured, weapons that could unmake mountains discovered they had been assembled incorrectly from the beginning.

But this wasn't mindless destruction. Each movement carried purpose, precision, the surgical precision of someone who is learning. Soldiers who had been following orders found themselves unconscious rather than dead. Equipment that had been used to maintain oppression found itself repurposed into sculptural statements about the relationship between power and responsibility.

Captain Thauron, who had spent forty years treating slaves as inventory to be managed, discovered what inventory felt like when it learned to manage itself.

"Please," he gasped as the phantom arm lifted him from the ground with force that existed primarily in dimensions where pleading was irrelevant. "The collar malfunctions can be corrected. Order can be restored. Slaves can be repurposed."

Repurposed.

Koraxos studied the man who had branded him twenty-two years ago, who had defined his worth in terms of productivity and profit, who had reduced the value of consciousness to entries in ledgers that tracked exploitation with mathematical precision.

"You're right," he said finally, his voice carrying harmonics that made reality shimmer around the words. "Repurposed."

The phantom arm pulsed with energy that operated according to physics laws that hadn't been written yet.

"You're worth exactly what you taught me I was worth," Koraxos continued, and his smile was a proof written in stellar fire. "Nothing at all."

"You're worth exactly what you taught me I was worth," Koraxos continued, his voice carrying harmonics that made reality shimmer. "Nothing at all."

But even as the words left his lips, another truth blazed through his enhanced consciousness: "The moment you use another's cruelty to justify your own, you become the thing you fought to escape."

The thought lasted exactly one heartbeat.

Then twenty-two years of rage found its voice.

The phantom arm moved with terrible gentleness, almost a caress. Thauron's eyes went wide—not with pain, but with the sudden understanding that he was becoming something else. His scream began as sound and ended as light, forty years of cruelty unmaking itself atom by atom until only echoes remained, scattered on wind that tasted like copper and long-overdue accounts.

The remaining soldiers tried to flee, but Koraxos decided no one would escape. Where it touched, armor became suggestion. Where it pointed, weapons remembered they were made of matter that could choose different configurations.

In less than a minute, the compound that had housed his torment for twenty-two years was painted with the remains of those who had maintained it.

Koraxos stood amid the carnage, the phantom arm pulsing with satisfied energy, and felt something like peace for the first time in his life. Not the peace of resolution—the peace of a weapon finally allowed to cut.

This is what power feels like, he thought, and the taste was copper and starfire and the particular satisfaction of debts paid in full.

In the distance, alarms wailed across the city of his former masters. Warning signals that property had developed opinions about its circumstances. Alerts that the natural order had suffered a critical malfunction.

Koraxos smiled, flexed his phantom fingers, and began walking toward those sounds.

The revolution had ended in seventeen minutes.

The reckoning was just beginning.

3

Chapter 3: Between Vengeance and Redemption

First blood tasted like twenty-two years of waiting.

Koraxos stood over Captain Thauron's corpse, phantom arm still crackling with residual energy. The man who'd branded him as a child lay broken against compound stones, his perfect uniform finally matching the chaos he'd spent decades creating.

"How does it feel?" Senna asked from behind a overturned barricade, her young voice carrying an edge that hadn't been there yesterday.

Koraxos considered the question while blood pooled around his boots. How did justice feel when you finally got to serve it yourself?

"Empty," he said, surprising himself with the truth. "I thought it would feel like... more."

But even as he spoke, his eyes were already tracking the next target. Overseer Drakon, forty yards away, frantically coordinating the compound's defense. The phantom arm pulsed with hungry light.

Maybe the next one would fill the hollow place where satisfaction should be.Elder Marex approached through the smoke, his walking stick tapping against stones slick with blood. Each step was deliberate, measured—the gait of someone who had learned to conserve strength for when it mattered most.

He stopped beside Koraxos, studying the body of the man who had branded them all twenty-two years ago. His weathered fingers tightened on the walking stick's grip—polished bone that had once belonged to an overseer who thought Noks were animals. The irony wasn't lost on him.

"First blood always tastes different than you expect," Marex said quietly, his voice carrying the weight of someone who remembered his own first kill. "Question is whether you're tasting justice or just discovering what you're hungry for."

Koraxos looked at him, the phantom arm still crackling with residual energy. "Does it matter?"

"Everything matters," Marex replied, touching his pocket where he kept a small carved stone—the last thing his daughter had made before the fever took her. "Especially what we choose to become when we finally have the power to choose."

The phantom arm flickered with borrowed starlight, cosmic energy that had rewritten his flesh into something beyond slavery, beyond mortality, beyond the careful limitations that had once defined possible and impossible. But copper was still copper, and the metallic tang that filled his mouth carried flavors he hadn't expected: satisfaction, hunger, and something that tasted suspiciously like justice refined into personal vindication.

Power tastes like this, he realized, watching the life drain from eyes that had once held absolute certainty about the natural order of consciousness. *Like pennies and promises finally kept.*

"Koraxos?" Velen's voice carried the careful tone of someone addressing a landslide that might still be settling. The other surviving Noks—seventeen out of hundreds—clustered behind him with the brittle caution of witnesses to miracles they couldn't decide were divine or diabolic. Niri stayed at his shoulder, close enough to grab Velen if he tried something stupid, far enough back to run if the cosmic arm decided it didn't like audiences.

Koraxos flexed the phantom fingers, watching reality bend around the translucent appendage like light through disturbed water. The air itself seemed to thicken where his cosmic limb moved, as if existence was learning to accommodate forces it hadn't been designed to contain.

"I'm fine," he said, though fine was a word that had lost all meaning somewhere between slavery and apotheosis. He felt magnificent. He felt terrible. He felt like a weapon that had finally remembered what it was forged to cut.

"Fine," Niri repeated, flat as hammered metal. "Right. And I'm the queen of crystal formations." She studied the phantom arm with an engineer's eye, noting the way space warped around it, the subtle wrongness in how light behaved near its surface. "That thing's drawing power from somewhere. Question is whether it's borrowing or stealing."

"Does it matter?" Velen asked, though his gaze kept flicking between Koraxos's face and the translucent limb. Twenty-two years of mining had taught him to recognize unstable conditions. "We've all seen what happens when the bill comes due around here."

"That was beautiful," Senna breathed from where she crouched beside the rubble. Young, maybe nineteen, with eyes that held the particular brightness of someone who had never seen real power exercised with righteous purpose. "The way you moved—like justice given form and taught to dance."

The words settled in Koraxos's chest like warm coals, and he found himself standing straighter. Justice. Yes, that felt right. That felt like something worth becoming.

"Come," he said, turning toward the burning city where alarms shrieked like mechanical prayers. "We have twenty-two years of debt to collect."

Velen and Niri exchanged one of those married looks—entire conversations compressed into a glance that spoke of shared fears and unspoken agreements.

"Well," Niri said finally, "beats another shift in the mines."

"Speak for yourself. Mining had better safety protocols." Velen checked his makeshift weapon, then checked hers with the automatic care of someone who'd spent decades ensuring his partner's equipment wouldn't fail when it mattered. "At least rocks only tried to kill you accidentally."

"You volunteering to stay behind and organize the supply chain?"

"Hell no. Someone's got to make sure you don't get blown up by your own engineering." He tested his grip, callused hands steady despite everything. "Besides, the kids would never forgive me if I let their crazy aunt Niri have all the fun."

"Aunt Niri who taught them to make explosives from kitchen scraps?"

"That's the one."

The Beauty of Annihilation

Three hours later, Koraxos had learned that reality was far more negotiable than anyone had taught him to believe.

He stood in the administrative district where Luminarai bureaucrats had managed human inventory with ledger precision, and discovered that cosmic power made conventional physics feel like polite suggestions rather than absolute laws. The tenth guard had fallen not to blade or bolt but to something more personal—the phantom arm had reached through his armor like it was made of mist and simply convinced his heart that beating was an outdated concept.

Easier now, he thought, stepping over bodies that had recently been people with families and fears and favorite foods. *That's the horror and the beauty.*

Around him, the city burned with fires that obeyed his will rather than natural law. Where normal flames consumed randomly, these blazes carved through Luminarai structures with artistic precision while leaving Nok-built elements untouched. The phantom arm had taught him that destruction could be selective, that vengeance could be curated like a museum exhibition of justified suffering.

"Behind you!" Senna's warning came just as a Luminarai officer tried to activate a paralysis field. Koraxos turned and gestured, and the officer's weapon decided it preferred existing as decorative sculpture rather than functional technology. The death that followed was swift, professional, and satisfying in ways that made his cosmic essence hum with contentment.

"How many?" Velen asked as they moved through streets where emergency lighting painted everything in bloody amber. His voice carried the practical tone of someone inventorying resources, though what they were counting had shifted from ore samples to corpses.

"I've stopped counting," Koraxos replied, which was true in the way that lies often were. He hadn't stopped counting—the number had just become background music to his consciousness. The numbers stopped mattering. Each death was a word in a story he'd never been allowed to tell—the story of what happened when property decided to write its own ending."Efficient," Niri observed, studying the precision with which Luminarai structures burned while Nok-built sections remained untouched. "Whatever's guiding those flames knows the difference between oppressor and oppressed architecture."

"The phantom arm's learning our history," Velen added, watching cosmic energy flow through patterns that seemed to recognize decades of accumulated grievance. "Question is what else it's learning."

But numbers were becoming irrelevant anyway. What mattered wasn't quantity but artistry, not efficiency but style. The phantom arm had begun showing him possibilities that transcended simple murder, opportunities to demonstrate exactly what happened when consciousness that had been forced to accept limitations suddenly discovered it could impose them instead.

The first wave of Luminarai military response arrived with the mechanical precision of a civilization that had perfected oppression into an art form. Armored vehicles that could reduce buildings to component atoms. Energy weapons that could unmake matter at the molecular level. Soldiers in powered armor that made them look like mobile fortresses of systematic violence.

They were magnificent. They were terrifying. They were about to learn that magnificence was relative.

Koraxos extended the phantom arm toward the approaching convoy, cosmic energy flowing through translucent channels toward fingertips that existed in more dimensions than conventional reality could accommodate. When he spoke, his voice carried harmonics that made the air itself listen.

"You want to see power?" he asked the approaching forces. "Let me show you what twenty-two years of iron becomes when it finally chooses its own shape."

The ground beneath the convoy began to move.

Not earthquake tremors or tectonic shifts, but something more deliberate—the earth itself deciding that supporting Luminarai military vehicles was no longer an acceptable function. Koraxos felt every grain of soil, every fragment of stone, responding to his will like extensions of his nervous system. The phantom arm had connected him to the planet itself, and the planet had grievances.

Streets cracked open with surgical precision, creating chasms that swallowed entire vehicles while leaving surrounding buildings untouched. Where the convoy tried to maneuver around these gaps, the asphalt flowed like water, creating waves that crashed against armor designed to withstand energy weapons but unprepared for terrain that had developed opinions about passenger safety.

"Not terrible," Koraxos said, watching Luminarai military vehicles discover that the earth itself had developed opinions about passenger safety.

"High praise from our local cosmic disaster," Niri observed, ducking as debris painted the sky in geometric patterns. Her engineer's training automatically catalogued the impossibilities she was witnessing—matter behaving according to principles that violated every law of physics she'd learned. "Velen, you getting readings on whatever physics he's breaking?"

"Physics stopped returning my calls about ten minutes ago." Velen's voice carried the strained humor of someone whose world had officially moved beyond his engineering expertise. "Pretty sure he's operating on principles they don't teach in mining school."

"Good thing. Mining school never covered 'advanced reality revision' anyway."

"That was an elective. I took 'practical tunnel collapse prevention' instead."

"And look how useful that's been."

This is what the planet feels like when it finally fights back, Koraxos thought as he watched tanks disappear into sinkholes that closed behind them like hungry mouths. *Like being connected to everything that ever suffered in silence.*

The surviving vehicles opened fire, energy beams that could carve through mountains painting the air with concentrated starlight. But Koraxos was no longer standing where their targeting systems indicated. The phantom arm had taught him that existence was more fluid than water—why be limited to one location when consciousness could negotiate for better positioning?

He materialized behind their formation, cosmic energy crackling around him like contained lightning. When he gestured, the phantom arm extended beyond normal constraints, becoming a translucent blade that cut through armor, energy shields, and the comfortable certainty that technology guaranteed superiority.

The energy slash that followed carved through the remaining convoy like a scythe through wheat, leaving behind sculptures of precisely severed metal that had been military vehicles moments before. Beautiful, in its way. Artistic. A statement about the relationship between power and vulnerability written in a language everyone could understand.

"Magnificent!" Senna called from her position behind overturned barricades. Her voice carried the particular excitement of someone discovering that impossible things were merely improbable when approached with sufficient motivation.

But Koraxos was already thinking beyond individual victories. The phantom arm pulsed with possibilities that transcended conventional warfare, opportunities to demonstrate what happened when consciousness that understood suffering decided to share the experience with those who had authorized it.

He slammed the cosmic limb against the ground, and felt the impact propagate through dimensions normal senses couldn't detect. The earth responded like a living thing in pain, buckling and flowing in patterns that defied geological probability. Streets became tsunamis of liquid stone. Buildings swayed like trees in impossible winds. The careful architecture of Luminarai dominance began to come apart as its foundation remembered older loyalties.

Yes, something whispered in the back of his mind. *Show them what happens when the ground itself refuses to support oppression.*

The Symphony of Systematic Destruction

By the time the second wave arrived, Koraxos had learned to think in terms of grand gestures rather than individual deaths.

The Luminarai response was overwhelming—orbital platforms deploying enough firepower to level mountains, military formations that could conquer systems, weapons that existed primarily as theories until deployed against targets that had insulted the natural order by refusing to remain property.

They were prepared for rebellion. They were not prepared for apotheosis.

Koraxos stood in the center of what had been the administrative plaza, phantom arm extended toward the sky where death approached with terrifying certainty. Around him, reality had begun to warp in subtle ways—gravity flowed in eddies and currents, light bent around his transcendent form like water around stone, and time itself seemed to hesitate before committing to its normal linear progression.

"*Nok sa no veeta!*" he called, his voice carrying across the burning city with harmonics that made survivors' hearts resonate in their chests. The ancient words tasted like revolution and felt like prayer: *We are no longer slaves.*

The orbital strike came with the fury of artificial suns, energy beams that could crack continents painting the sky with concentrated stellar fire. But when the barrage reached Koraxos, it simply... paused. Hung in the air like a question waiting for an answer.

Then the phantom arm moved, and the energy became his to direct.

The redirected strike carved through the approaching military formations like divine judgment made manifest, turning their own overwhelming force into the instrument of their destruction. Vehicles designed to survive nuclear bombardment discovered that stellar fire operated according to different principles entirely. Soldiers in armor that could deflect energy weapons found that redirected orbital strikes were more suggestion than protection.

"He's not just redirecting energy," Niri said, her engineer's mind trying to process what she was witnessing. "He's *negotiating* with it. Like he's asking reality to consider alternative arrangements."

"And reality's saying yes," Velen added, watching laws of physics bend around Koraxos like water around stone. "Question is what happens when the universe presents its bill."

But even as destruction rained around him, Koraxos felt something darker stirring in his cosmic essence. The devastation was beautiful, yes, but beauty wasn't enough anymore. He needed something more personal, more artistic, more... educational.

"Rise," he commanded, and felt the phantom arm's influence extend into realms where death was merely a temporary inconvenience.

From the blood-soaked earth, from the ruins of buildings where Noks had died in chains, from the very air that had carried the last breaths of the oppressed, spectral forms began to materialize. Thousands of them—ghostly Nok figures bearing the unmistakable marks of their enslavement. Emaciated bodies, backs crossed with whip scars, necks raw from collar abrasions, faces gaunt from deliberate starvation.

They rose from every unmarked grave.

Jorik, who'd been beaten to death for stealing bread for his pregnant wife. Mira, who'd died of lung rot at seventeen because medical care was for property with warranties. Elder Kaelen, who'd been executed for teaching Nok children to read.

One by one, they materialized from the compound's bloody soil—not as peaceful spirits seeking rest, but as instruments of Koraxos's rage. Their ghostly forms bore the wounds that had killed them: whip marks, infected brands, the hollow cheeks of systematic starvation.

And their eyes... their eyes burned with his fury, not their own.

"Tell them who you died for," Koraxos commanded.

The spectral army turned toward the cowering Luminarai with movements that spoke of hunger twenty-two years in the making. When they spoke, it was with one voice:

"We died for nothing. Now you die for less."

But as they advanced, Koraxos caught sight of his reflection in a broken window. For just a moment, he looked exactly like Master Thauron had on the day of his first branding—calm, certain, utterly convinced of his right to inflict suffering.

The resemblance made his phantom arm flicker with something that might have been doubt.

The phantom army rose with expressions of purpose that transcended their incorporeal state, and their eyes burned with fires that had been banked but never extinguished.

"Every mark on their bodies is a debt written in your name," Koraxos called to the approaching Luminarai forces, his voice echoing with harmonic power that made reality itself lean in to listen. "Today, payment comes due."

The spectral Noks spread outward through the city like a tide of justified vengeance, their incorporeal forms passing through physical barriers as if they were merely decorative. Where they touched living Luminarai, flesh aged decades in seconds. Where they breathed, the air filled with the particular cold that came from graves opened before their time. Where they walked, the ground remembered every drop of Nok blood it had absorbed across generations of systematic oppression.

This is what history looks like when it finally gets to speak, Koraxos thought as he watched his phantom army exact payment for centuries of accumulated suffering. *Like justice with compound interest.*

"Korax!" Senna's voice cut through the symphony of spectral vengeance, carrying undertones he'd never heard before—not awe or admiration, but something that sounded suspiciously like fear. "What are you doing to them?"

He turned to find her staring at a group of Luminarai civilians who had been touched by the phantom army. They weren't dead—that would have been merciful. Instead, they experienced the accumulated suffering of every Nok slave who had ever died in their city, feeling every lash, every moment of starvation, every hour of despair compressed into a single eternal instant of understanding.

"Teaching them," Koraxos replied, watching with satisfaction as recognition dawned in Luminarai eyes that had never learned to see consciousness as anything other than resource. "For the first time in their lives, they understand what we felt like."

"They're innocent civilians!"

Behind them, Velen's hand found Niri's wrist—not comfort, but anchor. They'd seen this before, in smaller ways. Guards who started enjoying the whip too much. Overseers who smiled during punishment details.

"Power doesn't corrupt," Niri said quietly, watching Koraxos orchestrate systematic devastation with artistic precision. "It just stops pretending to be something else."

"Question is whether he remembers what he was fighting for," Velen replied, his voice carrying the weight of someone who'd seen too many good people discover they liked breaking things. "Or if he just likes the sound of things breaking."

"I see no innocence here." The phantom arm pulsed with increasing intensity as more spectral Noks manifested from the city's bloody history. "Every Luminarai who lived in comfort while we suffered, every one who benefited from our labor—they're all guilty."

Senna's expression shifted through confusion to something approaching horror as she watched the phantom army work with systematic precision. "You're torturing them, Korax. This isn't justice—it's cruelty for its own sake."

"It's education," he corrected, extending his cosmic perception to monitor the progress of his spectral forces throughout the city. "They've never experienced consequence for their choices. Now they understand exactly what they supported with their comfortable silence."

The third wave of Luminarai military response arrived as Koraxos spoke—dropships deploying from orbital platforms, their hulls scarred by the energy he'd redirected but their crews grimly determined to restore order through overwhelming violence. They landed with tactical precision, soldiers emerging in formations designed to contain superhuman threats.

Koraxos smiled, and the expression carried enough malice to make reality itself uncomfortable.

"More students," he observed, raising the phantom arm toward the fresh arrivals.

What followed was demonstration rather than battle. Koraxos moved through the deployed forces like a professor delivering a lecture on the relationship between power and accountability, each gesture of the phantom arm illustrating a different principle of cosmic justice.

When a squad tried to flank him, the ground beneath their feet became liquid, swallowing them whole before solidifying again—not to kill but to bury them alive in darkness that let them contemplate their choices while experiencing the claustrophobia of slave quarters. When energy weapons fired, the beams curved back on themselves, teaching their wielders exactly how it felt to be on the receiving end of systematic violence.

The most artistic demonstration came when a full battalion attempted a coordinated assault. Koraxos extended the phantom arm skyward and began to *pull*—not on matter or energy but on the fundamental forces that held reality together in this specific location.

The air above the battalion crystallized into geometric patterns that defied conventional physics, creating a three-dimensional maze of solid atmosphere that trapped the soldiers in pockets of breathable space. They could see each other through the transparent barriers, could communicate through the crystal walls, but couldn't reach each other to coordinate resistance.

"Beautiful," Senna whispered, but her voice carried no admiration—only the particular horror of someone watching artistry applied to suffering.

"Art requires suffering to achieve meaning," Koraxos replied, manipulating the crystallized air to create acoustic chambers that amplified the soldiers' voices into a chorus of confusion and growing despair. "They've forced my people to create beauty from pain for generations. Now they get to experience what that feels like from the inside."

The trapped battalion's attempts to break free only made their situation more educational. Energy weapons fired at the crystal barriers reflected back as harmless light shows. Physical impacts against the walls created musical tones that harmonized with their increasingly desperate voices. The harder they fought, the more clearly they heard each other's fear, the more aware they became of their collective helplessness.

"You're not freeing anyone," Senna said quietly, studying Koraxos's expression as he conducted his symphony of systematic humiliation. "You're just creating new forms of bondage."

"I don't care," he corrected. "I'm enjoying this!"

But even as he spoke, Koraxos felt something shifting in his relationship with the phantom army. The spectral Noks were becoming more independent, their actions extending beyond his direct control as they spread throughout the city with their own agenda of retribution. They moved through Luminarai districts armed with centuries of accumulated suffering, each encounter leaving behind consciousness that had been forcibly enlightened about the reality of systematic oppression.

"Korax," Elder Marex approached with careful steps, his weathered face showing concern that went beyond tactical considerations. "The spirits... they're not following orders anymore. They're acting on their own initiative."

"Good," Koraxos replied, though something cold moved through his cosmic essence as he realized the implications. "After this they can rest in peace."

"But they're not just targeting military personnel anymore," Velen added, joining the conversation with obvious reluctance. His voice carried the careful tone of an engineer reporting equipment malfunction. "They're going after anyone with Luminarai features. Children, elderly, disabled—anyone who looks like the oppressor race."

"Even the ones who tried to help us," Niri said quietly, her practical mind cataloguing the systematic expansion of violence beyond military targets. "Some of those people argued against the slave systems. Some tried to make conditions better."

The words should have sparked some form of moral concern, but Koraxos found himself calculating the efficiency of total population elimination rather than questioning the ethics of spectral genocide. When had he stopped seeing individual consciousness and started seeing demographic categories?

"Good," he said finally. "They're all going to die."

"By committing genocide," Senna said flatly.

"By rebalancing the scales."

In the silence that followed, Velen cleared his throat. "Kids are asking when we're coming home."

The words hit like cold water. Simple, practical, human.

"Home," Koraxos repeated, as if the word belonged to a language he'd forgotten.

"Small underground chambers, remember? People who think you're coming back because you promised." Niri's voice was steady, engineer-calm. "Course, that was before you decided to become the cosmic solution to inequality."

"They need to understand—"

"They need their parents," Velen cut him off, his voice carrying the weight of someone who'd learned that some things mattered more than cosmic justice. "And their parents need to remember the difference between justice and just enjoying the view from on top."

The fourth wave of military response came not from orbit but from the planetary defense grid—massive installations that rose from underground bunkers like mechanical mountains, their weapon systems designed to repel invasion fleets rather than internal rebellion. They opened fire with energy output that could sterilize continents, beams that could punch through planetary cores painting the sky with destructive force that had never been intended for use against surface targets.

Koraxos met their assault with something approaching joy.

The phantom arm expanded beyond its normal constraints, becoming a translucent shield that covered half the city while simultaneously existing as a sword that could carve through defensive installations like they were made of crystallized hope. Where the planetary defense beams struck his cosmic barrier, they were absorbed and transformed into something more useful—energy that fed back into his connection to the spectral army, strengthening their ability to destroy all.

Koraxos reached out with cosmic perception, mapping the underground network that connected all the planetary defense installations. Miles of tunnels and conduits, power systems that drew energy from the planet's core, computer networks that coordinated defensive responses across continents.

"Let me show you what power looks like when it serves justice instead of oppression," he announced, the phantom arm beginning to pulse with rhythms that synchronized with the planet's geological heartbeat.

What followed redefined the relationship between consciousness and planetary geology. Koraxos extended his influence through the underground networks, the phantom arm's energy flowing through tunnels and conduits like divine infection that taught machinery new purposes. Defense systems that had been designed to protect Luminarai civilization turned their attention to destroying civilization.

Installation after installation activated not to fire outward at external threats but to target the cities they had been built to protect. Energy beams that could sterilize worlds carved through Luminarai urban centers with surgical precision, eliminating government buildings and military installations while leaving Nok residential areas untouched.

The effect was beautiful in its precision, terrible in its scope, and absolutely brutal in its demonstration that protection was conditional rather than automatic.

"Stop," Senna whispered, though her voice was nearly lost in the planetary symphony of destruction that Koraxos was conducting from his position in the ruins of a single city. "Please, just stop."

"Stop what?" Koraxos turned to her, cosmic eyes blazing with the particular satisfaction of someone who had finally found the perfect expression for accumulated rage. "I've only just started."

"Stop becoming the thing we fought against," she said, and the words carried enough force to penetrate even his transcendent certainty.

For a moment—just a moment—Koraxos felt something flicker in his cosmic essence. A memory of who he had been before power rewrote his understanding of acceptable solutions. A ghost of the consciousness that had once believed freedom meant the ability to choose rather than the ability to eliminate choice for others.

Then the phantom arm pulsed, reminding him of strength, and the moment passed.

"I'm not becoming anything," he said firmly. "I'm revealing what I always was underneath the chains. They made me into this—twenty-two years of systematic reduction to property. Now they get to see what property looks like when it finally chooses its own value."

Around them, the phantom army continued its brutal campaign with increasing creativity. Spectral Noks had learned to manifest not just as individuals but as collective experiences, showing Luminarai civilians what it felt like to watch their children sold to distant masters, to have their cultural traditions criminalized, to see their art reduced to quaint decoration in the homes of those who considered them barely conscious.

The lessons were comprehensive, personal, and absolutely devastating in their emotional impact.

"You're enjoying this," Senna observed, her voice carrying the particular tone of someone who had watched a friend transform into something unrecognizable. "The suffering, the fear, the systematic destruction—you're not doing this because you have to anymore. You're doing it because you want to."

The accusation should have sparked some form of moral crisis, but Koraxos found himself evaluating it with the detached interest of someone analyzing technical specifications.

Was he enjoying this? The creative application of overwhelming force, the artistic arrangement of consequences for those who had never faced them, the particular satisfaction that came from watching arrogance transform into understanding through applied suffering?

Yes, the honest part of his mind admitted. *And that should probably concern me more than it does.*

But concern was a luxury consciousness could indulge after justice had been properly served. And justice—real justice, the kind that prevented repetition rather than merely balancing ledgers—required commitment to completion rather than hesitation about methodology.

"They taught me to enjoy this," he said, gesturing at the systematic devastation spreading across multiple continents as the phantom army's educational campaign reached global scope. "Twenty-two years of watching them take pleasure in our suffering. Now I understand what satisfaction looks like from the other side."

The Cascade Effect

What Koraxos hadn't anticipated was how quickly his phantom army would spread beyond his immediate control.

The spectral Noks had begun to manifest in greater numbers, summoned not just by his will but by the blood soaking into the ground, the screams echoing through the streets, the sheer concentrated hatred that permeated the air itself. Where a single ghost had once appeared to kill a Luminarai soldier, now entire battalions of spirits materialized to slaughter anyone bearing the cranial ridges of the oppressor race.

They manifested in government buildings, tearing administrators apart with ghostly claws that left no physical wounds but drained life itself. They appeared in residential districts, flowing through walls to massacre families in their homes. They haunted the industrial sectors, turning machinery into instruments of death that crushed workers beneath their own tools.

But most unsettling was their growing independence.

The phantom army had begun hunting without his direct command, following their own bloodthirsty agenda throughout the city. They were no longer content to kill soldiers and officials—they sought out anyone who had benefited from the system of oppression, anyone who had lived in comfort while Noks suffered in chains.

Total war. Absolute vengeance. Utterly unstoppable carnage.

"Korax," Velen approached with obvious reluctance, his enhanced senses detecting the growing scope of spectral slaughter throughout the city. His voice carried the careful tone of someone delivering a status report he wished he didn't have to make. "They're not just targeting military anymore. They're... they're killing everyone."

"Everyone who participated in our oppression," Koraxos corrected, watching with satisfaction as smoke rose from dozens of districts where phantom Noks carried out their bloody work. "Every Luminarai who benefited from our suffering deserves the same fate we endured."

"They're killing children," Senna said bluntly, her voice carrying a horror that cut through his cosmic satisfaction. "Luminarai children who never owned slaves, never hurt anyone, never made any choices about the system they were born into."

"Children grow up to become their parents," Koraxos replied, though something cold moved through his cosmic essence as he sensed the phantom army's expansion into civilian areas. "Better to end the cycle permanently than allow it to repeat in the next generation."

"It's genocide," Senna stated flatly, positioning herself between Koraxos and the spreading devastation with the courage of someone who had decided that friendship required intervention regardless of personal risk. "You've become exactly what they always said we were—savage, uncontrollable, incapable of mercy."

"I've become what they made me," Koraxos corrected, but the words felt less certain than they had hours ago. "Twenty-two years of systematic cruelty, and now they're surprised when their property decides to demonstrate what cruelty really looks like."

"No," Senna said firmly. "You've chosen to become this. Power didn't corrupt you—you corrupted power by using it to satisfy your need for revenge instead of your people's need for freedom."

Behind them, Velen and Niri exchanged another of those married looks that carried entire conversations compressed into shared glances.

"He's right, you know," Niri said quietly, her engineer's mind recognizing when systems had moved beyond their design parameters. "About the children growing up to be their parents. But killing them doesn't change that—it just makes sure we become the monsters their children will grow up fearing."

"If there are any children left to grow up," Velen added grimly, watching cosmic destruction spread with mathematical precision across the burning city. "Question is whether that's victory or just thoroughness."

The accusation hit deeper than intended, cutting through cosmic certainty to touch something that still remembered what it felt like to hope for liberation rather than dominance. When had his goal shifted from freedom to extermination? When had justice become indistinguishable from systematic murder? When had he stopped thinking about building something better and started focusing only on destroying what existed?

But before he could explore these uncomfortable questions, the situation escalated beyond philosophical debate.

The fourth wave of Luminarai response came in the form of something Koraxos hadn't expected—not more soldiers or weapons, but negotiators. A small transport approached under a flag of truce, its occupants broadcasting surrender terms on all frequencies.

"We yield," came the transmission. "Complete surrender. We acknowledge Nok sovereignty and offer full reparations for historical grievances. Please, just call off the spirits."

Koraxos studied the approaching transport with interest that transcended tactical considerations. Surrender meant acknowledgment of defeat, recognition that consciousness could transcend its assigned limitations when properly motivated. But surrender also meant stopping before justice was fully served, before every debt was paid in blood.

"Surrender to what?" he replied, his cosmic voice reaching the transport's communication systems. "To the consciousness you tried to eliminate? To the justice you spent generations avoiding? To the reality that oppression has consequences you can't negotiate away?"

"To whatever terms you set," came the increasingly desperate response. "We'll provide anything you require. Just stop the killing."

Just stop the killing. The phrase carried desperation that spoke of people finally understanding that their comfortable assumptions about natural hierarchy could be shattered by sufficient application of force. But stopping meant leaving the work incomplete, allowing the possibility that survivors would rebuild oppression once immediate fear faded.

"I want you to remember," Koraxos said finally, allowing the transport to land while maintaining the phantom army's bloody work throughout the city. "Every time you consider reducing living beings to property, remember what living beings looks like when it finally fights back. Every time you calculate the cost of oppression, remember that the oppressed eventually learn to make their oppressors pay."

The negotiators emerged from their transport with the careful movements of people approaching a predator that had developed opinions about the food chain. They were older Luminarai, bearing the marks of authority but moving with humility that spoke of recent education about the relationship between power and vulnerability.

"What do you want?" asked their leader, a female whose cranial ridges suggested high-caste breeding but whose posture indicated recent revision of assumptions about inherited superiority.

"I want you all to die," Koraxos replied. "I want blood for blood, death for death, suffering equal to what you inflicted."

"How many must die to satisfy that debt?"

The question hung in the air like smoke from funeral pyres, heavy with implications that reached beyond immediate negotiation into territory where consciousness chose between mercy and vengeance, between building futures and paying for the past.

"All of them," Koraxos said simply, and felt the phantom army surge with approval as his words echoed across the city. "Every single one."

"Think about what you're saying," Velen said, his voice carrying the weight of someone who'd spent decades calculating consequences. "All of them means the children who haven't learned to hate us yet. The doctors who treated Nok injuries. The engineers who tried to improve working conditions."

"It means the system that created the suffering," Niri added, her practical mind recognizing the scope of what Koraxos was proposing. "But systems are made of people, and some of those people tried to make the system better."

"Not hard enough," Koraxos said, but the words carried less conviction than before. "Not fast enough. Not successfully enough."

"Since when is moral failure punishable by death?" Senna demanded. "Since when does trying and failing equal collaborating?"

The Palace of Final Judgments

The Imperial Palace stood alone now, isolated in a sea of devastation that had once been the greatest city of Luminarai civilization. Three days of systematic destruction had reduced millennia of architectural achievement to rubble and ash, but the palace remained—not through superior construction but because Koraxos had deliberately preserved it for last.

He approached on foot, the phantom arm leaving trails of cosmic fire that painted the air with colors that had no names in any mortal language. Behind him, the phantom army moved with silent purpose, thousands of spectral Noks bearing witness to the conclusion of a reckoning that had been building for generations.

Velen and Niri walked beside him, their presence a reminder of concerns beyond cosmic justice. They said nothing—what was there to say when watching a friend become something unrecognizable?—but their shared silence carried weight that transcended words.

"Still thinking about the kids," Niri observed quietly, reading the tension in Velen's shoulders that spoke of a man torn between supporting his people's liberation and protecting the future those people were trying to build.

"Always thinking about the kids," he replied, his voice carrying the weight of someone who'd learned that victory meant nothing if it destroyed what you were fighting to preserve. "Question is what kind of world we're leaving them."

The palace gates—masterpieces of artistry that had taken a hundred Nok masters twenty years to complete—provided no more obstacle than tissue paper. Koraxos tore through them with casual gesture, cosmic energy unraveling metalwork that had been designed to withstand siege weapons into its constituent atoms.

"Beautiful craftsmanship," he remarked coldly to the spectral Noks who flowed through the breach like smoke given purpose. "

"Beautiful craftsmanship," he remarked coldly to the spectral Noks who flowed through the breach like smoke given purpose. "My people's final masterpiece before I erase yours."

"They built this with their hands," Velen said quietly, running calloused fingers along the destroyed metalwork. Even in ruin, the gates showed evidence of the precision that only decades of forced craftsmanship could achieve. "Every curve, every detail—that's Nok work. Nok artistry forced into Luminarai glory."

"Then it's fitting that Nok hands unmake it," Koraxos replied, though something in his tone suggested the irony wasn't lost on him.

Inside, the palace revealed itself as a museum of accumulated oppression made manifest. Portraits of Luminarai leaders who had signed laws reducing consciousness to property. Tapestries depicting historical victories over "rebellious elements." Display cases containing "curiosities" from subject races—sacred objects stolen from conquered peoples and exhibited as trophies of successful civilization.

Each room told the same story: beauty built on suffering, artistry purchased with blood, magnificence that required the systematic reduction of consciousness to fuel for someone else's aesthetic vision.

Koraxos moved through halls that had been built by his ancestors' hands, cosmic perception allowing him to see the spectral impressions of Nok workers who had died creating these monuments to their own oppression. The phantom arm pulsed with increasing intensity as he absorbed the full scope of what this place represented—not just political power but the psychological architecture of a civilization that had convinced itself that some consciousness mattered more than others.

"You can feel them," Niri said, watching Koraxos trace patterns in the air that matched the ghostly imprints of long-dead craftsmen. Her engineer's training let her recognize the signs of someone reading structural memory, seeing how things had been built and by whom. "The ones who made this place. They're still here in the walls."

"In every stone," Koraxos confirmed, his enhanced senses detecting echoes of suffering embedded in the palace's very foundation. "Every beautiful thing here was paid for with someone's pain."

"Doesn't make destroying it justice," Velen observed, his voice carrying the practical weight of someone who'd learned to distinguish between necessary destruction and satisfying destruction. "Just makes it expensive revenge."

The throne room reeked of expensive perfume and fresh urine.

Twelve members of the royal family knelt in a precise line, their jeweled collars catching the light from fires burning throughout the city. They'd dressed for execution in their finest robes—a last gesture of dignity from people who'd never learned that dignity wasn't something you wore.

The youngest—a boy perhaps ten years old—looked up at Koraxos with eyes that held no fear, only curiosity.

"Are you going to kill me too?" he asked with the directness of childhood.

Koraxos felt the phantom arm pulse with eager energy. The boy's grandfather had signed the orders that condemned thousands of Noks to die in the deep mines. His father had overseen the breeding programs that treated consciousness like livestock. The family's wealth was built on a foundation of systematic suffering stretching back centuries.

"Yes," Koraxos said.

"Why?"

Such a simple question. Such a complicated answer. Because your people treated mine like animals. Because power demands consequences. Because twenty-two years of pain had to go somewhere, and you're convenient.

Because I've forgotten how to stop.

"Because," Koraxos said, raising his hand, "someone has to pay."

The boy nodded as if this made perfect sense. "Will it hurt?"

Koraxos looked into eyes that held no malice, no cruelty, no responsibility for the sins that had shaped them both. Just a child's honest question about his approaching death.

The phantom arm hesitated.

For the first time since his transformation began, cosmic power flinched from its purpose.

The Luminarai Sovereign stood at the center, his crystalline cranial ridges signifying the "purest" bloodline of their species. Despite his fear—evident in the rapid vibration of his facial membranes—he maintained the arrogant bearing that generations of unquestioned rule had bred into his genetic structure.

"Why are you doing this?" he demanded, his voice carrying the metallic resonance characteristic of high-caste Luminarai who had never learned that their authority was conditional rather than absolute.

Koraxos laughed, the sound distorting reality around him in ways that made the assembled royalty flinch from harmonics that operated beyond normal acoustic principles.

"You brand us at birth, work us to death, and you ask why?" he replied, cosmic energy crackling around him like contained starfire. "I am reckoning incarnate."

His laughter intensified, becoming almost musical as the phantom arm flared with dangerous brilliance.

"For every lash on our backs," he continued, pacing around the royal family like a predator evaluating the most entertaining method of dispatch, "for every neck chained in your collars, for every child who died in your mines—you built your golden age on broken bodies. Now I'll build your nightmare on the ashes of your dynasty."

Behind him, Velen and Niri stood as witnesses to the culmination of everything their revolution had become. Neither spoke, but their presence carried weight—reminders of the people who would have to live with whatever happened next.

"Some of us tried to change things," said a younger member of the royal family, her voice shaking but determined. "Some of us argued for better conditions, for gradual reform—"

"Gradual reform," Koraxos repeated, his voice carrying cosmic disdain. "Twenty-two years of iron while you debated the proper pace of mercy. How considerate."

"We were making progress—"

"You were making excuses," Niri cut in, her engineer's mind recognizing failed systems when she saw them. "Progress would have been immediate action. Everything else was just management of your own guilt."

"Still doesn't mean they all deserve death," Velen added quietly, his practical wisdom recognizing the difference between justice and elimination. "Some guilt isn't a capital crime."

The youngest member of the royal family—the prince, barely into adolescence by Luminarai standards—suddenly broke from the group, charging toward Koraxos with the desperate courage of youth. Whether he hoped to attack or simply escape was unclear, but it made no difference. Koraxos caught him by the throat with his flesh hand, lifting the young royal off his feet with casual strength.

"Look at me, boy. Remember this face. When you see your ancestors in hell, tell them a slave sent you."

The prince's eyes bulged, his facial membranes turning from their normal opalescent shimmer to a dull gray as oxygen deprivation set in. The royal family wailed in harmonized distress, the sound carrying frequencies that would have moved mountains if mountains cared about Luminarai grief.

"Wait," Velen said, his voice carrying the authority of someone who'd learned when situations required intervention. "Just... wait."

"For what?" Koraxos asked, though his grip on the prince didn't tighten.

"For you to think about what happens next," Velen replied, meeting cosmic eyes with the steady gaze of someone who'd faced down cave-ins and lived to dig another day. "You kill that kid, what changes? Does it bring back anyone we lost? Does it make the world better for the children we're trying to protect?"

"It balances the scales," Koraxos said, but something in his voice suggested uncertainty.

"Does it?" Niri asked, her practical mind cutting through emotional satisfaction to examine actual outcomes. "Or does it just make sure the next generation grows up knowing we're exactly what their propaganda said we were?"

"I promise you—" Koraxos began, the phantom arm extending toward the remaining royalty with energy that could unmake them from existence entirely.

Then reality *fractured*.

Velen grabbed Niri's hand as existence folded like origami made of light and screaming. "Well," he said, conversational despite dimensional chaos, "that's new."

"Speak for yourself," Niri replied, her free hand automatically checking tools that might survive whatever was happening to physics. "I've seen reality have a breakdown before. Usually involves less glowing, though."

"More explosions?"

"Different kind of explosions."

They watched their friend disappear into cosmic summons, two engineers trying to maintain professional composure while the universe demonstrated that their expertise had very specific limitations.

The Summons

One moment Koraxos stood in the imperial chamber, vengeance literally in his grasp and cosmic justice prepared to carve through the last representatives of systematic oppression. The next, he was... elsewhere.

The transition was so absolute, so instantaneous, that even his transcendent senses took precious seconds to reorient. He floated in a void unlike any he had ever experienced—not mere empty space but something more fundamental, a realm of pure potential where reality itself was merely one possibility among infinite variations.

The prince dropped from nerveless fingers as Koraxos found himself facing something that made his cosmic transformation feel like a child's first attempt at finger-painting.

Before him materialized a presence of such galactic scale that his newly divine perception could only capture fragments of its totality. The entity manifested as a living constellation—a body composed of galaxies, neural pathways formed by chains of stars, emotional expressions created by the movement of nebulae across cosmic distances. Its eyes were twin event horizons, absorbing all light yet somehow radiating comprehension deeper than any illumination mortal consciousness had conceived.

Instinct rather than reason drove Koraxos's response. The phantom arm blazed with power as he launched attack after attack against this cosmic entity—reality-warping strikes that could shatter planets reduced here to the desperate flailing of a child trying to wound the ocean with a wooden sword.

The being absorbed each assault without effect, the energy simply incorporated into its galactic form like raindrops falling into an ocean that spanned dimensions.

When it spoke, its voice resonated not through sound but through the fundamental vibrations of existence itself.

"Are you finished?" The words carried neither anger nor condescension, only the profound weariness of one who had watched empires rise from dust and crumble back to the soil that birthed them.

Koraxos froze, sudden recognition dawning like sunrise after the longest night in cosmic history. "You're the one who gave me—"

"I am Treydora," the cosmic entity confirmed, galaxies within his form dimming to express something between disappointment and infinite sorrow. **"The one who answered your prayer for strength. The one whose essence now flows through that arm you wield with such bitter purpose."**

Koraxos straightened, defiance replacing his initial shock. "I'm delivering justice to those bastards who owned us!"

"Justice?" Treydora's voice carried the weight of eons spent contemplating the nature of righteousness. **"What you call justice is merely vengeance wrapped in virtue's cloak. True justice builds bridges across wounds—it does not carve deeper chasms between the living and the dead."**

"They had it coming! Twenty-two years they treated us like animals!"

"And so you became the beast they claimed you were." The cosmic entity's form pulsed with stellar sadness. **"Power reveals the soul's true architecture, Koraxos. It carves nothing new—only strips away what concealed the foundation already laid in your heart's deepest places."**

Koraxos felt his rage flare hotter. "Don't you dare lecture me! You never wore their collar!"

"No, I have not known your specific pain," Treydora acknowledged, his voice softening with genuine compassion. **"But I have watched consciousness make the same choice across countless worlds—the choice between becoming what hurt them or transcending it entirely. You chose to become."**

"Damn right I did! They made me this way!"

"They gave you pain, yes. But you chose what to build from that pain." Galaxies within Treydora's form spun slower, his attention focusing like starlight through cosmic lens. **"Every conscious being faces this choice: let suffering collapse you into bitter fragments, or forge it into foundations for something greater than what broke you. You chose collapse."**

The phantom arm flickered with dangerous energy. "Collapse? I have the power of gods!"

"And the wisdom of a wounded child," Treydora replied, his voice carrying infinite sadness. **"Power without understanding is just destruction with better tools. You could have shown the universe something new—instead, you showed it the same old story of pain creating more pain."**

"They deserved every death!"

"Perhaps they did. But what does their deserving matter compared to what you became in giving it to them?" Treydora's cosmic attention pressed against Koraxos like the weight of dying stars. **"The universe doesn't care about deserving, child. It only cares about what you choose to create or destroy."**

Koraxos laughed bitterly. "Create? I created justice!"

"You created terror. You created justification for every law they ever passed calling your people animals. You created the proof that power corrupts regardless of who wields it." The stars within Treydora's being dimmed with disappointment. **"You had the chance to break the cycle. Instead, you became its perfect continuation."**

"I'm nothing like them!"

"You are exactly like them." The words struck with the force of cosmic truth. **"They used power to reduce you to property. You used power to reduce them to things deserving death. Different tools, same foundation—that strength gives the right to determine what has worth."**

The phantom arm began to flicker as doubt crept into Koraxos's essence. "I... they were evil. They had to be stopped."

"Evil is not a force that takes hold of you, Koraxos. It is a door you choose to walk through, again and again, until you forget there were ever other paths to take."

"The difference is they started it!"

"And you ensured it would never end." Treydora's voice carried the weight of cosmic finality. **"Every child who will grow up fearing your people. Every law that will be passed restricting consciousness like yours. Every act of preemptive violence against those who remind others of you. That is your legacy."**

Koraxos felt something cold moving through his transcendent essence. "You're going to take it back. The power."

"I am going to correct my error in judgment," Treydora confirmed, his form beginning to contract as divine forces gathered. **"I gave you the tools of transcendence,**

hoping you would build something beautiful. Instead, you built a monument to the proposition that consciousness cannot rise above its circumstances."

"You want to take it back? Go ahead!" Koraxos snarled, the phantom arm blazing brighter as defiance replaced any hint of surrender. "I regret nothing. Every death, every scream, every drop of their blood—worth it."

"Understanding that arrives only under the hammer of consequences is not wisdom—it is terror shaped into something prettier, like bronze beaten thin to hide the rot beneath." Treydora's cosmic presence began to compress, power beyond imagination focusing into judgment itself. **"True change requires sorrow for the act itself, not merely for its punishment."**

"Sorrow?" Koraxos laughed, the sound sharp as breaking glass. "You want me to feel sorry for giving them exactly what they gave us? Twenty-two years of hell, and you think I should apologize for evening the score?"

"Do you truly feel no remorse? Or do you simply fear admitting that you chose to build monuments to your pain rather than doorways through it?" The entity's attention burned through Koraxos like cosmic fire. **"If I returned you to that cell tomorrow, with your phantom arm intact but no enemies left to kill, what would you choose to build?"**

Koraxos met Treydora's galactic gaze without flinching. "I'd find new enemies. There's always someone who needs killing, always someone who thinks they're better than everyone else. That's what power's for—making sure the bastards learn their place."

"Your honesty, at least, is refreshing," Treydora said, stars within his form beginning to die as judgment crystallized. **"You have become precisely what they were—consciousness defined entirely by what it can break. You wear your corruption like armor, proud of the ruins you have built from the gifts I gave you."**

The phantom arm began to dissolve as cosmic forces beyond comprehension focused on reclaiming what had been given. Koraxos felt his transcendent nature unraveling, divine essence flowing away like water through broken stone.

"Take it then!" he roared, even as power fled from his grasp. "But don't expect me to grovel! I did what needed doing. I gave those royal bastards exactly what they deserved!"

"And what of the servants who died beside them? The children caught in your vengeance? The innocents who bore the weight of your rage simply because they shared the wrong bloodline?" Treydora's voice became the fundamental vibration of existence itself as his judgment reached conclusion.

"Casualties of war," Koraxos spat without hesitation. "They chose their side when they stood by and watched us suffer. Every one of them could have spoken up, could have helped, could have done something. They didn't. So they earned what they got."

"I should destroy you," Treydora continued, his words carrying weight that made reality itself tremble. **"I should unmake every trace of what you have become and scatter your essence across dimensions where corruption cannot spread."**

The cosmic entity's decision solidified in the void between them, power beyond imagination preparing to erase what he now recognized as his greatest failure.

"Do it," Koraxos spat, even as his divine nature crumbled around him. "Go ahead and play god. Judge me for doing exactly what any sane person would do with power. At least I'm honest about what I am."

"But destruction would be your choice, not mine. Instead, I choose something harder—I leave you alive to face what you have built." Treydora's presence began to fade as cosmic judgment neared completion. **"Live with your choices, Koraxos. Die knowing that when power was placed in your hands, you chose to perfect the very systems that once enslaved you."**

The phantom arm crumbled to cosmic dust as transcendent power fled like light from a dying star. Koraxos felt himself falling through dimensions, his divine nature stripped away layer by layer until only fragile mortality remained.

"Perfect them?" he screamed into the collapsing void, his voice raw with defiant fury. "I flipped the script! For once in history, the slaves got to be the masters! And if that's not good enough for your cosmic sensibilities, then screw you and your philosophical bullshit!"

"Perhaps others will learn from your failure," Treydora's voice echoed across realities as the void collapsed. **"Perhaps they will understand that breaking chains means building bridges where shackles once bound—not forging new fetters for different wrists."**

The last thing Koraxos heard before reality crushed down around him was his own laughter—bitter, defiant, unrepentant to the end. Even falling toward mortality, even stripped of everything that had made him godlike, he refused to break.

They had branded him a slave. They had called him property. They had tried to reduce him to nothing.

But they had never made him bow his head in shame for fighting back.

Aftermath

Reality reasserted itself with the particular violence that accompanied cosmic interventions. The throne room materialized around fallen figures—royal family scattered like discarded dolls, their survival more accident than design. The prince gasped on the floor where he'd fallen, throat bruised but breathing.

Koraxos collapsed beside the ornate throne, his right arm ending in a cauterized stump where cosmic power had been severed. Blood pooled beneath him—mortal blood, red and ordinary and finite.

"Think he's coming back?" Velen asked, kneeling beside their transformed and untransformed friend.

"Think it matters?" Niri countered, checking Koraxos's pulse with practiced efficiency. "He's been gone since the arm showed up. Question is what comes back."

They worked together in the silence that followed cosmic judgment—two engineers trying to treat wounds that went deeper than flesh, watching someone who'd briefly touched godhood learn to be human again.

"The kids are still going to ask," Velen said quietly.

"Then we better have an answer that doesn't involve cosmic horror and daddy issues," Niri replied, binding wounds with strips torn from royal tapestries.

Around them, the palace stood as monument to everything that had led to this moment—beauty built on suffering, power purchased with pain, the endless cycle of oppression that had finally found someone willing to break it, only to discover that breaking could become its own form of bondage.

The revolution had ended in seventeen minutes.

The reckoning had lasted three days.

And now, in the silence that followed cosmic judgment, consciousness would have to learn whether it could build something better from the ruins of what divine power had torn down.

Outside, across a world where phantom armies had faded and orbital platforms stood silent, survivors began the long work of deciding what came next. Not revenge or restoration, but something new—something that honored the pain without perpetuating it, something that remembered the cost without demanding it be paid again and again in blood.

The slaves were free. The masters were humbled. And somewhere between those truths lay the possibility of a future where neither category needed to exist.

It would be harder than conquest. It would be slower than justice. It would require choosing hope over hatred, construction over destruction, the difficult work of building rather than the satisfying work of burning.

But it would be theirs to choose, all of them together, without gods or slaves or the weight of cosmic certainty pressing down on their deliberations.

In the end, perhaps that was revolution enough.

4

Chapter 4: When Gods and Slaves Transcend Their Chains

Oshar died the way it had lived—beautifully, precisely, and without considering the cost.

Crystal spires that had once sung with harmonic frequencies now stood silent, their perfect geometries cracked by forces their designers never imagined. Streets laid out in mathematical perfection had become rivers of rubble. The air tasted of vaporized wealth and the particular emptiness that followed systematic collapse.

Koraxos stood in the plaza where he'd first learned to kill gods, watching survivors pick through the ruins of their certainty. Three days since his phantom army had dissolved. Three days since he'd chosen mercy over satisfaction.

The silence was deafening.

No more screams. No more spectral vengeance. Just the soft sound of people trying to figure out how to live in a world where the rules had changed overnight.

"Feels different when it stops, doesn't it?" Velen's voice carried the weight of someone who'd watched his friend come back from the edge of becoming a monster.

They moved like ghosts haunting their own graves.

A Luminarai engineer knelt beside a shattered resonance array, her once-pristine robes torn and gray with crystal dust. She wasn't trying to repair it—just touching the fragments like they might remember how to sing. Nearby, a group of children played in the rubble, their laughter sharp and wrong in the suffocating quiet.

"She built that," Velen said, following Koraxos's gaze to the engineer. "Spent twenty years perfecting the harmonic frequencies. Now she sits there twelve hours a day, waiting for it to remember how to make music."

"Think it will?"

"Think she will?"

Koraxos watched the woman trace patterns in the dust—the same geometric sequences she'd once used to tune crystals, now written in the ashes of her civilization. "We broke more than buildings," he said.

"Yeah." Velen's bio-crystal arm caught the strange light filtering through dimensional distortions overhead. "Question is whether we can fix more than buildings too.""He'll be back," whispered a Luminarai elder, her cranial ridges dulled with age and fear as she helped a younger female drag a corpse toward one of the many improvised pyres. "A being with that much rage doesn't simply vanish."

"The royal family is gone," the younger one replied, her voice cracking with exhaustion. "What more could he want?"

The elder gave her a look of infinite weariness. "Everything."

The Gathering Storm

In what remained of the central plaza---once a perfect geometric marvel where thirteen thoroughfares intersected at mathematically precise angles---citizens had established a makeshift triage center. The wounded lay in concentric rings, positioned according to the severity of their injuries and likelihood of survival. Luminarai medical technicians moved between them with devastated efficiency, their normally immaculate medical garb stained with fluids in a spectrum of colors that told the story of their various castes.

Commander Valex, one of the few surviving military leaders, stood at the edge of this grim tableau, his once-resplendent armor now dented and scorched. The right side of his face had been partially crystallized during a close encounter with one of the spectral Noks, leaving it in a state of suspended transformation between flesh and mineral.

"Lock down the southern quarter," he ordered a subordinate, his damaged voice crackling. "Grab whatever weapons still work and set up a watch. If that... thing... comes back, we need to see it coming.""With respect, Commander," the subordinate replied, "what defense could possibly matter against such power?"

Valex's functioning eye narrowed. "Our dignity, if nothing else. We are Luminarai."

The subordinate saluted and departed, leaving Valex alone with his thoughts and the panorama of destruction stretched before him. It was then that he noticed it---a silhouette perched atop what remained of the western wall, perfectly still against the bleeding sky.

At first glance, it appeared to be a gargoyle---some architectural flourish that had somehow survived the devastation. But as Valex's enhanced vision focused, he realized the truth. This was a creature unlike any cataloged in the extensive Luminarai biological archives.

The thing squatted on the broken wall like hunger given shape. Wings spread wide enough to blot out stars, body dark as old blood. No eyes Valex could see, but it *watched* him—watched with the patience of something that had learned to enjoy being feared. Six taloned limbs gripped the stonework with a tension that suggested imminent movement, though it remained perfectly still.

"Alert status," Valex whispered into his command transmitter, his gaze never leaving the creature. "Unknown entity on the western perimeter."

By morning, a second creature had appeared---identical to the first but perched atop the remains of the Imperial Archive. By midday, a third materialized on the shattered dome of the Grand Temple. With each passing hour, more appeared, until dozens of the beings ringed the city like sentinels, their faceless attention creating an almost physical pressure on the survivors below.

"What are they waiting for?" asked Minister Larix, one of the few surviving government officials, as she joined Valex at his observation post on the fifth day. Her normally luminescent skin had dulled to a sickly opalescence, the traditional markings of her station faded to ghostly outlines.

"I don't know," Valex admitted, his damaged face catching the light strangely as he turned. "But they're organized. Positioned strategically. This isn't random."

"Could they be related to the slave-god? Some extension of his vengeance?"

Valex's expression hardened. "The Nok was powerful but chaotic, driven by emotion. These creatures..." He gestured toward the nearest sentinel. "There's a cold calculation here. A patience that suggests something else entirely."

The Seeker's Arrival

It was on the seventh day that *he* appeared.

Death announced itself with a whistle.

High and thin, like wind through a corpse's teeth. The sound bypassed ears and went straight to the spine, making everyone in Oshar stop mid-motion and remember what prey felt like.

"That's not wind," Niri said, her engineer's mind rejecting the obvious explanation even as her body reached for Velen's hand. Twenty years underground had taught her the difference between natural sounds and things-that-hunt-in-darkness sounds.

The eastern gate exploded inward.

Not destroyed—*inverted*. Stone and metal folded through dimensions that shouldn't exist, creating geometric impossibilities that hurt to perceive directly. Through the wound in reality stepped something wearing the approximate shape of a man.

If men were made of absence given purpose.

"The Seeker," Koraxos breathed, cosmic awareness recognizing predator-signature from dimensional memory. His phantom arm blazed to life, but the energy felt cold, uncertain. Three days of choosing mercy over vengeance had changed something fundamental in how his power responded.

"Where... is... the thief?" The voice formed directly in their minds, bypassing sound entirely. "Where is the one who stole what was never meant for mortal flesh?"

Every word felt like ice water in the veins, like being examined by something that had never learned to distinguish between consciousness and food.

Through the heat-shimmer of the morning air, a figure approached---humanoid in general outline but wrong in every detail. It moved with a fluidity that suggested no skeletal structure, each step a sinuous recalculation of form rather than the mechanical movement of joined bones. It wore robes of absolute darkness that absorbed the light around them, creating a walking void in the shape of a being.

But it was the face---or rather, the absence of one---that struck terror into the hearts of those who glimpsed it. Where features should have been, there existed only a smooth expanse of flesh-like substance, interrupted by three vertical slits that occasionally dilated to reveal glimpses of something luminous beneath. No mouth was visible, yet when it spoke, the words formed directly in the minds of all who heard.

"Where... is... the thief?" The mental voice was like wind through broken glass, like distant thunder made personal. *"Where is the one who stole what was never meant for mortal flesh?"*

The question echoed through the ruins, physical structures vibrating in sympathy with its metaphysical force.

Commander Valex stepped forward, his military training asserting itself despite the primal fear coursing through him.

"Identify yourself," he demanded, his damaged voice sounding pathetically fragile against the psychic weight of the entity's presence.

The faceless being turned toward him---though with no eyes, the sensation of its attention was unmistakable.

"I am the one who hunts what was stolen. I am the balance that restores order. I smell his essence here, thick as blood, sweet as suffering."

The being glided forward with terrible swiftness, closing the distance to Valex before the commander could react. A hand---too long, with too many joints, the skin a color that existed just outside normal perception---shot out and gripped Valex by the throat, lifting him as easily as one might lift a piece of paper.

"You have seen him. Your fear carries his memory."

Vapor began to rise from Valex's skin where the being touched him, his cells rapidly losing molecular cohesion. He struggled to speak, his partially crystallized face cracking with the effort.

"It came... destroyed... then vanished," he managed, each word a torment as his throat began to dissolve beneath the entity's touch.

The being tilted its non-face, the vertical slits widening slightly to reveal a nauseating glow from within.

"Not enough. Never enough. Show me more."

With a casual flick, it tossed Valex aside. The commander's body struck a collapsed wall with enough force to shatter his partially crystallized form, fragments scattering across the rubble.

The being continued its relentless advance through the streets of Oshar, the sentinel creatures above suddenly taking flight in perfect unison, creating a circling vortex of winged forms above it. Survivors fled before its approach, diving into whatever shelter they could find.

The toy rolled into the plaza with innocent momentum—a small crystal that caught light and threw rainbows, the kind of simple beauty children create from scraps.

Kira chased it without thinking. Six years old, Luminarai features just beginning to define themselves, she moved with the fearless urgency of someone who'd never learned that toys could wait but safety couldn't.

The Seeker's hand closed around her throat before her parents could scream.

"Small thing. Soft thing.*" The words formed in everyone's mind simultaneously, intimate as a whisper, cold as vacuum. "*Where is the burning god who came here? Where is the thief of starlight?"

Kira dangled thirty feet above the ground, small legs kicking at air. But instead of crying, she studied the entity with the frank curiosity children brought to everything that wasn't immediately painful.

"You don't have a face," she observed, voice steady despite her circumstances.

The Seeker's featureless visage tilted toward her with movements that suggested surprise. In centuries of harvesting consciousness, no prey had ever offered commentary on anatomical observation.

"I taste your fear. It has his flavor—the one who burned through your perfect order like fire through silk."

"I'm not scared," Kira said, though her voice was smaller now. "My mommy says monsters are just people who forgot how to be nice."

The silence that followed was absolute. Even the wind stopped moving.

"Small thing. Soft thing. Where is the burning god who came here? Where is the thief of starlight?"

The child's terror was absolute, her small form trembling uncontrollably in the being's grasp. Before she could respond, a group of Luminarai citizens emerged from hiding, driven by a protective instinct that overcame their fear.

"Release her immediately!" shouted an elderly male, brandishing a piece of twisted metal as a makeshift weapon. Behind him, a dozen others formed a desperate line of defense.

The Seeker's featureless face turned toward them, the vertical slits narrowing to razor-thin lines.

"I taste your fear. It has his flavor---the one who burned through your perfect order like fire through silk. Tell me where he hides, and I will make your deaths swift."

"We don't know where he went!" cried a female at the front of the group. "He vanished after destroying half our city. Please, release the child!"

The Seeker remained motionless for a moment, the absence of facial features making its thoughts unreadable. When it projected again, the mental voice carried a cold finality that sent shivers through all who heard it.

"You protect him with your silence. You choose his cause over your lives. How... loyal. How... pointless."

The Luminarai citizens, with nothing left to lose after witnessing the near-destruction of their civilization, surged forward in a desperate charge.

"So beautiful when they break."

With a subtle gesture from the Seeker, the sentinel creatures above descended like living lightning, their forms blurring with velocity. They struck with surgical precision, talons and beaks tearing through Luminarai flesh with horrific efficiency. Screams erupted across the square as the creatures moved from one victim to the next, their attacks coordinated with hive-mind synchronicity.

The Return of Transcendence

In a realm beyond conventional space and time, Treydora observed this new catastrophe unfolding, his cosmic awareness taking in every detail of the slaughter. Beside him floated Koraxos, his transformed being still adjusting to the higher dimensional space of Treydora's domain.

"The Seeker has found your trail," Treydora said, galactic spirals shifting within his form to express concern. "My brothers have sent their hunter to reclaim what they see as stolen power."

"What are those creatures?" Koraxos asked, his phantom arm pulsing with agitation as he watched the winged beings tear through the surviving Luminarai.

"Void Ravens," Treydora replied. "Created by my brothers as extensions of their will. They exist partially outside conventional reality, which makes them nearly impossible to harm by ordinary means."

They watched in silence as the Seeker continued its methodical execution of any Luminarai who resisted, the child still dangling from its grasp.

"I will give you one more chance," Treydora said finally, his cosmic form contracting slightly to focus his communication more directly. "A chance to redeem yourself and become what you were meant to be."

Koraxos turned his transformed gaze toward the cosmic entity. "What do you mean?"

"The city you were determined to destroy---you must now save it," Treydora explained, stars within his form aligning into patterns of urgent significance. "You must become their protector, their champion against a threat even greater than your rage."

"Why would I defend my oppressors?" Koraxos demanded, the phantom arm flaring with renewed intensity.

"Because," Treydora replied, his cosmic voice carrying the weight of eons spent contemplating the nature of power, **"true power is not measured by what you can destroy, but by what you choose to protect. Destruction requires only strength---protection demands wisdom."**

Treydora's form expanded, galaxies within him rotating with increasing urgency. "The Void Ravens answer to my brothers. The Seeker is their instrument. Neither can be allowed to complete their mission. If they reclaim the power I have shared with you, they will use it to further unbalance the cosmic order."

Koraxos watched as the Seeker casually discarded a Luminarai corpse, its non-face turning toward another group of fleeing survivors.

"Go now," Treydora urged. "Protect the people of Oshar. Destroy the Seeker. Prove that power need not corrupt, that suffering need not define, that vengeance need not be the only response to injustice."

Koraxos looked down at his phantom arm, the cosmic energies within it swirling with newfound purpose. For the first time since his transformation, he felt something beyond rage or satisfaction---the first tentative stirrings of a higher aspiration.

"And if I succeed?" he asked.

Treydora's form pulsed with what might have been a cosmic smile. "Then you will have taken the first step toward becoming something truly divine---not a god of vengeance, but a god of transcendence."

The Sky Fractures

The sky above Oshar fractured like shattered crystal.

Reality itself seemed to bend as a figure descended from the heavens, trailing cosmic energies that painted the atmosphere in impossible colors. Koraxos arrived not with the thunderous rage that had marked his previous assault on the city, but with the quiet certainty of inevitable confrontation. His transformed body---part flesh, part divine energy---cast prismatic shadows across the ruined cityscape below. The phantom arm pulsed with rhythmic intensity, each beat sending ripples through the quantum fabric of existence.

The Seeker froze mid-execution, its faceless visage turning skyward with unnerving precision. The Void Ravens circling above likewise halted their attack, wings extended in perfect stillness, their collective attention redirecting toward the new arrival.

Throughout the shattered city, survivors emerged cautiously from hiding places to witness the confrontation. Commander Valex's partially crystallized remains lay forgotten as the last remnants of Luminarai civilization gazed upward with mingled terror and desperate hope.

The Seeker released the child, who collapsed to the ground, gasping for breath through damaged vocal membranes. With a fluid motion that defied anatomical constraints, the entity reoriented itself toward Koraxos, its dark robes absorbing all light that touched them.

"Ah. The thief returns to the scene of his grand theft. How... predictable. How... satisfying."

Koraxos descended until he hovered thirty feet above the ground, his cosmic eyes meeting the vertical slits in the Seeker's non-face. The phantom arm extended outward, fingers of pure energy flexing with barely contained power.

"Your masters sent you to the wrong realm," Koraxos replied, his harmonically layered voice echoing across the ruins. "Whatever balance you claim to protect was broken long before I received this gift."

The Seeker's form rippled, the dark garb flowing like liquid shadow. *"Gift? You call stolen fire a gift? You reek of power that was never meant for flesh that rots, minds that forget, hearts that break like cheap pottery."*

"Stolen?" Koraxos laughed, the sound distorting reality around him. "It was freely given. As for Treydora's whereabouts---" The phantom arm flared with sudden brilliance. "---you'll have to go through me to find out."

The Seeker's body language shifted subtly, its form coiling like a serpent preparing to strike. *"Through you? Little god with borrowed light? I have eaten stars. I have drunk the tears of dying galaxies. You are meat with pretensions."*

"Come and get it, then," Koraxos challenged, cosmic energy crackling around his transformed body.

The Epic Battle Begins

The fight started like lightning meeting lightning—too fast, too bright, too wrong for human eyes to follow. The Seeker moved like smoke with claws, here and gone and suddenly *everywhere*.

Koraxos spun with inhuman speed, the phantom arm sweeping in a wide arc that caught the Seeker's wrist before those reality-shearing claws could make contact. The impact sent shockwaves through the plaza below, shattering already damaged stone into component atoms and sending survivors diving for whatever cover they could find.

"Faster than expected. But speed without understanding is merely elaborate fumbling."

The Seeker twisted---not through normal space but through the conceptual framework that defined cause and effect. Its free hand materialized inside Koraxos's chest cavity, grasping for his heart with fingers that existed in tomorrow while striking from yesterday.

Koraxos screamed, the sound distorting reality around him as cosmic pain translated into harmonics that made nearby buildings spontaneously rearrange their molecular structure. But instead of retreating, he grabbed the Seeker's invading arm with his flesh hand and pulled---dragging the entity's distributed existence into a single moment where conventional physics could grab hold of it.

The Seeker found itself suddenly, shockingly solid just as Koraxos's phantom arm drove into its featureless face with force that could split moons. The entity flew backward through three buildings, its passage turning ancient stonework into exotic matter that glowed with internal fire.

"Clever. Forcing coherence where chaos serves. But tricks work only once against eternal hunters."

The Seeker rose from the rubble, its form shifting through configurations that hurt to perceive directly. Where it had been humanoid, now it became something more primal---a flowing mass of darkness that suggested tentacles, claws, teeth, and geometries that belonged in mathematics textbooks rather than physical reality.

It struck again, but this time as pure concept rather than physical form. The attack came as *negation*---the absolute denial of Koraxos's right to exist, delivered with the authority of entities that had been erasing inconvenient realities since before stars learned to burn.

Koraxos felt his cosmic essence beginning to unravel, the phantom arm flickering as fundamental forces questioned whether he should ever have been possible. Reality itself seemed to waver around him, physics developing sudden amnesia about his existence.

But Koraxos had learned something during his time with Treydora---power without purpose was just elaborate noise. Instead of fighting the negation directly, he used it, allowing the Seeker's attempt to erase him to strip away everything except the core of why he existed: to protect those who couldn't protect themselves.

The phantom arm blazed with renewed intensity, not drawing power from cosmic forces but from something simpler and more durable---the recognition that some things were worth preserving regardless of personal cost.

"Impossible. You cannot resist deletion through sentiment alone."

"Not sentiment," Koraxos corrected, the phantom arm now crackling with energies that seemed to derive strength from clarity of purpose rather than raw power. "Stubbornness. Twenty-two years of being told I don't matter taught me that mattering is a choice, not a gift."

The battle escalated beyond normal dimensions as both combatants abandoned the pretense of operating within conventional physics. They fought across impossible geometries, each strike creating cascade effects that rippled through reality's infrastructure.

The Seeker's form expanded into configurations that suggested it had tentacles in dimensions humans didn't have names for. Each appendage carried different properties---some drained life force, others rewrote molecular structure, still others simply deleted whatever they touched from the conceptual framework that made existence possible.

Koraxos met this multi-dimensional assault with improvisation born of desperation and refined by necessity. The phantom arm multiplied, splitting into fractal extensions that allowed him to parry attacks coming from directions that didn't technically exist. Each blocking movement sent cascades of energy through the city below, turning rubble into glass, melting metal into exotic alloys, and occasionally causing local gravity to flow in spirals just to see what would happen.

"You fight well for stolen meat. But you misunderstand the nature of our conflict. This is not battle---it is reclamation. The power you wield was never meant for individual use."

The Seeker's central mass pulsed, and suddenly every attack intensified tenfold. Koraxos felt cosmic energies being literally pulled from his transformed flesh, siphoned away through dimensional conduits that the entity had been weaving throughout their fight.

"Reclamation?" Koraxos gasped, phantom limb wavering as he struggled to maintain coherence against the systematic theft of his essential energies. "You want to talk about theft? Let me show you what twenty-two years of stolen life looks like when it finally gets a chance to argue back!"

He stopped fighting defensively and embraced the fundamental unfairness of existence. If the Seeker could cheat by existing in multiple dimensions simultaneously, then Koraxos could cheat by refusing to accept that cheating was against the rules.

The phantom arm exploded outward, not attacking the Seeker directly but targeting the dimensional infrastructure of its attacks. Instead of blocking tentacles, Koraxos severed their connections to whatever hellish geometries they drew power from. Instead of resisting the entity's energy drain, he reversed the flow, pulling back not just his own power but some of the Seeker's as well.

The effect was immediate and spectacular. The Seeker's perfect coordination faltered as its distributed attacks lost synchronization. Several tentacles withered as their power sources were cut off. Most satisfying of all, the entity's confident mental voice carried the first notes of genuine surprise.

"You cannot redirect forces you do not understand!"

"Understanding is overrated," Koraxos replied, his phantom arm now crackling with a mixture of cosmic fire and whatever eldritch energies he'd managed to steal. "Sometimes you just grab hold and refuse to let go."

He pressed his advantage, the phantom arm extending beyond its normal constraints to become something more like a cosmic whip than a limb. Each strike carved through the Seeker's tentacles, severing appendages and disrupting attack patterns with the brutal efficiency of someone who had learned that survival sometimes required breaking things that seemed unbreakable.

But the Seeker had not survived eons of cosmic hunting by relying solely on overwhelming force. As Koraxos destroyed its extended attacks, the entity began to contract, pulling its scattered essence back into a more focused form.

"Very well. If crude force serves you so well, let me demonstrate what crude force looks like when applied with proper technique."

The Seeker's form collapsed inward, condensing from sprawling mass to humanoid shape---but a humanoid shape that contained all the power it had previously distributed across dozens of appendages. When it struck again, the blow carried the force of colliding galaxies compressed into the space of a fist.

Koraxos barely managed to interpose the phantom arm before the strike connected. The impact sent him hurtling backward through the air, his cosmic form trailing energy like a comet as he crashed through the remnants of three city blocks before finally arresting his flight by grabbing hold of a crystalline spire.

The phantom arm was cracked along its length, cosmic fire leaking through fractures that suggested his transcendent nature had definite limits. More concerning was the systematic way the Seeker's power had penetrated his defenses---not breaking through but flowing around them like water finding gaps in stone.

"You begin to understand. Power without technique is chaos. Technique without understanding is merely elaborate suicide. I have studied your kind for eons. You are not unique, little god. You are simply another failed experiment in organized complexity."

"Maybe," Koraxos admitted, pulling himself upright and feeling cosmic energies flow back into the damaged phantom arm. "But failed experiments sometimes succeed in ways their makers never intended."

The Turning Point

Below them, something unexpected was happening in the ruins of Oshar. The surviving Luminarai, who had been cowering in terror throughout the cosmic battle, began to move with purpose that transcended their individual fear.

Captain Revik, a scarred veteran who had spent thirty years enforcing the hierarchy that kept Noks in chains, found himself organizing evacuation routes not just for Luminarai citizens but for anyone who needed help. The distinction that had once seemed so important---oppressor versus oppressed---dissolved under the practical necessity of keeping people alive.

"Get in formation!" he shouted, his voice cutting through the chaos. "Wounded in the middle! Keep those shelter paths open!""Why?" asked a younger soldier, his voice cracking with exhaustion. "What's the point if gods are fighting overhead?"

"Because we're not dead yet," Revik replied grimly. "And until we are, we have work to do."

Minister Larix, who had spent forty years managing bureaucratic systems designed to maximize resource extraction from other people, found herself distributing medical supplies without regard for social status or species. A Luminarai child received the same care as a Nok elder, the same attention as a crystal merchant or a mine worker.

Their coordinated movement caught Koraxos's attention even as he fought to maintain coherence against the Seeker's reality-warping assault. These were the people he had come to destroy, now working together in the face of annihilation. Something about their desperate unity struck him with unexpected force.

The distraction nearly cost him his existence. The Seeker's hand found his throat, elongated fingers beginning to drain the cosmic energies that sustained his transformation.

"Your weakness makes me laugh. You care about the ants below? Watch them burn while you feed me your stolen fire."

But distraction could work both ways. As the Seeker focused on draining Koraxos's power, it missed something far more significant than individual heroics---the practical efficiency of people who had stopped caring about old grudges and started caring about immediate survival.

Captain Revik had noticed abandoned crystal weapons scattered throughout the plaza. While the cosmic beings fought overhead, he had organized surviving troops to gather and coordinate them. Not for direct assault---they understood their limitations---but for something more clever.

"Pattern fire," he ordered. "Not at the entities---at the space between them. Create interference patterns."

The crystal weapons fired as one, their light weaving patterns that made the air itself *angry*. Suddenly the Seeker couldn't slip between moments anymore—it had to stay solid, stay *here*, where Koraxos could reach it. *"Impossible. The ants dare to sting?"*

Koraxos broke free and looked down at the coordinated effort below. "You're helping me?"

"We're helping ourselves," Revik called back. "You just happen to be between us and something worse!"

As cosmic energy crackled around him and reality bent under interdimensional warfare, Koraxos felt something crystallize in his understanding. Here, in this moment of desperate alliance between former enemies, he glimpsed a truth that transcended his personal transformation: **"Strength shared becomes more than the sum of its parts---it becomes the foundation upon which impossibilities are built."**

The phantom arm blazed with renewed intensity, but now it carried something beyond cosmic fire---the recognition that power used to protect others was qualitatively different from power used for personal satisfaction.

"You're wrong," Koraxos said, his voice carrying new harmonics that resonated with something the Seeker couldn't understand. "This isn't about individual strength versus cosmic authority. It's about what happens when people choose to work together instead of tearing each other apart."

Unity Against the Infinite

What happened next redefined what was possible when transcendent power served collective purpose rather than individual will.

Instead of fighting the Seeker directly, Koraxos began thinking tactically---how could the Luminarai's coordination be enhanced? How could their desperate unity be amplified? How could divine power serve mortal determination instead of replacing it?

Instead of attacking, Koraxos reached down—not with his flesh hand but with something deeper. The crystal weapons began to *unite* in harmony, their light matching the rhythm of his phantom arm's fire. Suddenly, their interference patterns weren't just disrupting the entities' stability---they were actively reinforcing Koraxos's strength while weakening his opponent.

Captain Revik found his tactical understanding enhanced, able to see optimal firing solutions and coordinate timing with precision that transcended normal military training. Minister Larix discovered she could organize evacuation routes with efficiency that seemed to predict where people would need to go before they knew it themselves. Even ordinary citizens found their efforts amplified, their individual contributions becoming part of something larger and more effective.

What happened next was something the Seeker's makers never saw coming—people working with divine power instead of being overwhelmed by it. Each crystal weapon fired in perfect synchronization, their combined energy focused not on destruction but on something more sophisticated: the systematic disruption of the Seeker's ability to exist partially outside normal reality.

"What trickery is this? Individual power cannot interface with collective effort! Chaos cannot achieve the efficiency of singular authority!"

"It's not chaos," Koraxos corrected, his voice now carrying harmonics that resonated with every crystal weapon in the plaza. "It's coordination. People working together because they choose to, not because they're forced to."

The Seeker found itself facing something its endless experience hadn't prepared it for---not scattered resistance that could be isolated and consumed, but unified effort that grew stronger under pressure. Each attack it launched was met not just by Koraxos's defense but by coordinated support that made individual power into something greater.

Where the entity had relied on dimensional advantage to avoid attacks, coordinated interference patterns forced it to maintain solid form. Where it had used reality manipulation to create tactical advantages, unified effort simply rewrote those advantages according to different specifications. Where it had counted on individual fighters being unable to coordinate against cosmic-level threats, it found people who had learned to work together with efficiency that transcended their individual limitations.

The Seeker bent reality into pretzel shapes that should have scattered their forces across seventeen dimensions. Instead, it found people who'd learned to work together adapting faster than cosmic calculations could predict.

When gravity flowed sideways, Velen and Niri recalibrated their equipment without missing a beat—twenty years of underground emergencies had taught them to treat physics like a problematic friend rather than absolute law.

When time hiccupped backward, Captain Revik's troops simply carried out orders they'd already received tomorrow, their military training proving surprisingly useful for temporal paradox management.

When dimensional barriers tried to separate them, Koraxos's phantom arm became a living bridge, connecting scattered minds through shared purpose rather than mere proximity.

"This violates fundamental principles!*" the Seeker projected, its confusion bleeding through mental barriers. "*Consciousness cannot maintain coherence across dimensional fragmentation!"

"Tell that to my wife," Velen muttered, reaching through folded space to check Niri's position. "Been maintaining coherence across impossible circumstances for twenty years."

"Marriage," Niri agreed, "is excellent training for cosmic horror."

Their casual competence in the face of reality breakdown seemed to offend the entity more than Koraxos's cosmic power. It had prepared for individual resistance, for technological supremacy, for overwhelming force.

It had not prepared for people who found humor in the impossible and treated universe-bending as a Tuesday. *"This violates fundamental principles! Power flows from singular sources, serves unified purposes! This chaos you call cooperation---it defies every law of efficient organization!"*

"Efficient organization," laughed Minister Larix, who had spent forty years managing systems designed to extract maximum value from minimum input. "You want to see efficiency? Watch people who choose to help each other achieve things that dominance never imagined possible."

The final assault came when Koraxos and every crystal weapon in the plaza fired simultaneously, their combined energy focused on forcing the Seeker to choose between completing its mission and preserving its existence. The beam that erupted from their coordinated effort carried force that transcended simple power or sophisticated technique---it was the concentrated determination of people who had decided that some things were worth protecting regardless of personal cost.

The Seeker made its first mistake in a thousand years—it tried to understand them.

Cosmic entities were designed for conquest, consumption, the clean mathematics of power overwhelming weakness. They weren't built to process the variables of genuine cooperation: love that made people stronger under pressure, humor that treated impossible as merely difficult, connections that grew deeper when tested rather than shallower.

The entity's processing centers overloaded trying to calculate the tactical implications of Velen checking on Niri's safety mid-battle, or Kira offering commentary on combat effectiveness while dangling from its grasp, or Koraxos choosing protection over vengeance despite having cosmic power at his disposal.

"Error,*" it projected, mental voice fracturing. "*Individuals cannot prioritize collective welfare over personal survival. Variables do not compute. Strategy matrix... failing..."

"You know what your problem is?" Kira said conversationally, still hanging thirty feet above the ground but somehow managing to sound like she was offering helpful advice. "You think people are just complicated math. But people aren't math. People are people."

The Seeker's form began to destabilize, not from physical attack but from conceptual overload. Its entire operational framework was based on predictable responses: fear, self-interest, the inevitable collapse of cooperative structures under pressure.

Instead, it had encountered a mining engineer who treated dimensional warfare like a maintenance problem, soldiers who followed orders across time paradoxes, and a cosmic guardian who'd learned that real strength meant knowing when not to use it.

The entity's certainty cracked like overstressed crystal, and through those cracks, doubt poured in like acid.

"Impossible."

"Nope," Kira said cheerfully. "Just Tuesday."

The Seeker dissolved into quantum uncertainty and fled back to whatever dimension had spawned it, leaving behind only the sound of a child's laughter and the bewildered silence of beings who'd just watched cosmic horror defeated by competent mundanity.

"This is... not... how reality... functions..."

"Reality functions however we decide it should function," Koraxos replied, the phantom arm now crackling with energies that seemed to derive their strength from simple recognition that cooperation worked better than competition. "You've been confusing cosmic bullying with universal law. Time to learn the difference."

The final blast struck not just the Seeker's physical form but its capacity to exist in local reality. The entity imploded with the particular dignity of something that had urgent business elsewhere, its form scattering across dimensional boundaries while its certainty dissolved into cosmic background radiation.

"This is not over, little god. We know you now. We taste your essence. When we return---and we will return---it will be with hunger that has learned your flavor."

"When you return," Koraxos called after the retreating presence, "you'll find people who have learned to taste their own strength. Bring bigger appetites."

The Aftermath of Victory

Silence fell over the ruins of Oshar like a blanket thrown over the aftermath of impossible things. Not the silence of defeat but the profound quiet that follows victories nobody had imagined possible until they happened anyway.

Koraxos descended slowly to the plaza, his phantom arm dimmed but steady. Around him, Luminarai survivors emerged from cover with the cautious movements of people discovering they were still alive despite excellent reasons to expect otherwise.

Captain Revik approached first, his scarred face showing the particular expression of someone whose understanding of what was possible had been thoroughly renovated by recent events.

"I never thought I'd say this to a Nok," he began carefully, "but... thank you. Not just for the battle, but for showing us what we could accomplish when we stop thinking in categories."

"I never thought I'd save Luminarai," Koraxos replied, his cosmic eyes reflecting something between surprise and recognition. "But it turns out some things matter more than old grudges."

"Like not letting cosmic horrors eat everyone?" suggested another survivor, her voice carrying the particular humor of someone who had just learned that impossible things were merely improbable when approached with sufficient cooperation.

"Like discovering what people can accomplish when they choose to work together instead of against each other," Koraxos corrected, though his tone carried no judgment---only the wonder of someone learning new mathematics.

Minister Larix stepped forward with the careful dignity of someone representing a government that might or might not still exist. "What happens now? Between us, I mean. The former slaves and the former masters."

Koraxos studied the faces around him---scarred, tired, afraid, but also carrying something new. Through the phantom arm's lingering connections, he could sense their thoughts, their hopes, their dawning recognition that the categories that had defined their lives were smaller than the possibilities that cooperation had revealed.

"I think," he said slowly, "that those categories might be smaller than we thought. Today I learned something: people are people. Everything else is just details we can choose to change."

A child's voice cut through the adult conversation---the same girl the Seeker had threatened, now looking at Koraxos with curiosity rather than fear.

"Are the bad things gone?"

Koraxos knelt to meet her eyes, the phantom arm pulsing gently with cosmic fire that no longer seemed threatening but rather protective, like a guardian that had learned the difference between power and responsibility.

"Some of them," he said honestly. "But others might come. That's why we need to be ready together."

"Can we do that? Be ready together?"

"We just did," he replied, realizing the truth of it as he spoke. "And if we can do it once, we can learn to do it better."

Around them, survivors began the practical work of rebuilding, but their efforts carried new efficiency. People who had never worked together before found themselves coordinating with natural ease. Luminarai technical knowledge merged seamlessly with Nok practical experience. Former enemies discovered they could accomplish together what neither could achieve alone.

Velen and Niri's Arrival

From the direction of the underground passages came voices—familiar voices that cut through Koraxos's cosmic contemplation like tools through stone.

"Well, that was louder than expected," came Velen's dry observation as he emerged from the rubble, his bio-crystal arm catching the strange light filtering through the dimensional distortions overhead. Dust covered his mining clothes, but his grip on Niri's hand was steady. "Though I've heard quieter cave-ins."

"Cave-ins don't usually involve reality having an argument with itself," Niri replied, wiping debris from her face while automatically checking Velen's pulse—twenty years of marriage compressed into a single, unconscious gesture. Her engineer's eyes swept the plaza, cataloguing structural damage with professional interest. "Also, cave-ins don't typically end with cosmic entities making threats about return visits."

Koraxos felt something loosen in his chest at the sight of them—two people who had survived slavery, war, cosmic horror, and each other, still standing together and still finding ways to make jokes about the impossible.

"Velen. Niri." He managed their names like someone remembering a language he'd thought he'd forgotten.

"Korax," Velen said simply, his bio-crystal arm pulsing in response to the residual cosmic energies still crackling through the air. "Nice light show. Kids are asking when we're coming home."

The words hit like cold water. Simple, practical, human.

"Home," Koraxos repeated, as if the word belonged to a language he'd forgotten.

"Small underground chambers, remember?" Niri's voice carried the steady tone of an engineer delivering specifications. "People who think you're coming back because you promised." She paused, studying his face with the precision she usually reserved for structural analysis. "Course, that was before you decided to become the cosmic solution to inequality."

"They need to understand—"

"They need their parents," Velen cut him off, his voice carrying the weight of someone who'd learned that some things mattered more than cosmic justice. The bio-crystal arm flickered as emotions translated into bioluminescent patterns. "And their parents need to remember the difference between justice and just enjoying the view from on top."

Niri squeezed Velen's shoulder where flesh met crystal—a gesture so automatic it spoke of decades of shared comfort. "Besides, someone needs to explain to Sela why her pretty rock collection survived reality storms but her favorite climbing tree got turned into geometric sculpture."

"Priorities," Velen agreed, his mouth quirking in what might have been a smile. "Seven-year-olds have them figured out better than gods, apparently."

Elder Marex, who had somehow survived the battle despite his age and the general cosmic unpleasantness, approached with careful steps that spoke of wisdom accumulated across decades of witnessing impossible things.

His walking stick tapped against debris that had been buildings hours ago, the bone handle warm from his grip. Overseer Kaine's femur had outlasted the man who'd owned it—fitting justice for someone who'd worked Noks to death in these same tunnels. Each step reminded him of his daughter Lira, who'd carved her last gift during fever dreams: a small stone that still lived in his pocket, worn smooth by decades of desperate hope.

"Sixty years I've been watching the impossible become routine," he said, studying the mixed groups working together with efficiency that transcended old hatreds. "First time it's been impossible in a good way."

"The unity you achieved," he said thoughtfully, "it wasn't just temporary alliance. Something fundamental changed in how people can work together. The phantom arm didn't just connect you to them—it showed what connection itself could become."

Koraxos nodded, feeling the cosmic energies that still flowed through the limb carrying traces of every person who had chosen to participate in their unprecedented cooperation.

"It turns out people working together isn't just stronger than people fighting each other—it's qualitatively different. We became something new."

"And the cosmic entities? The Seeker's masters?" Marex asked.

"They'll adapt," Koraxos said with certainty born of direct experience with how cosmic bullies responded to successful resistance. "They'll return with new strategies, more sophisticated attacks, better understanding of what they're facing. But they'll find people who have also adapted, who have learned to think collectively while maintaining individual choice."

Above them, the aurora effects that had marked the cosmic battle began to fade as reality settled back into more familiar patterns. But the fundamental change remained—not in physics but in possibility, not in what was but in what could be when people chose cooperation over competition.

The Children's Questions

A group of children had gathered around the conversation, their young faces showing the particular fearlessness of those who hadn't yet learned that impossible things were supposed to be impossible. One of them, a boy with the mixed features that suggested both Nok and Luminarai heritage, stepped forward with the confidence of someone who had never been told his existence was problematic.

"Will you teach us?" he asked simply. "How to fight like that? Together, I mean."

Velen and Niri exchanged one of those married looks—entire conversations compressed into a glance that spoke of shared concerns and unspoken agreements about what their children should and shouldn't learn from today's events.

"Fighting is just part of it," Koraxos said, looking at the assembled faces—children who had never known a world where cooperation between their peoples was normal, adults who were still adjusting to the idea that their former enemies could become allies, elders who carried the wisdom of older patterns but the flexibility to embrace newer ones. "The real lesson is simpler: when people work together because they choose to, they can accomplish things that seem impossible when they work alone. But it has to be choice, not force. It has to be voluntary, not commanded."

"That sounds hard," said another kid, wrinkling her nose like someone had offered her vegetables for breakfast.

"Everything worthwhile is hard," Niri said, her practical wisdom cutting through cosmic philosophy to reach bedrock truth. "But hard doesn't mean impossible. Just difficult enough to be interesting."

"Like marriage," Velen added, earning himself an elbow to the ribs and a suppressed snort of laughter from his wife.

"Like engineering," Niri countered. "You spend years learning how things work, then someone changes the specifications and you have to figure it out all over again."

"See?" Velen gestured with his bio-crystal arm, the movement catching prismatic light. "Marriage."

The Practical Aftermath

Captain Revik had been listening to this exchange while coordinating the practical work of securing the area and tending to the wounded. Now he approached with the bearing of someone who had reached a decision.

"I've been thinking," he said, his scarred face serious but not grim. "About what you said—people are people, and everything else is details we can choose to change. I've spent thirty years enforcing details that... well, that maybe needed changing anyway."

He paused, looking around at the mixed groups of survivors working together with efficiency that transcended their old divisions.

"What would it look like if we chose different details? Better ones?"

The question hung in the air like smoke from a forge, heavy with implications that reached beyond immediate survival into territory where people chose between rebuilding old patterns and creating new ones.

Minister Larix, who had been quietly observing the conversation while mentally cataloguing the practical requirements of social reconstruction, stepped forward with the careful precision of someone who had spent decades translating idealistic concepts into workable policies.

"Good intentions aren't enough," she said thoughtfully. "We need new ways of actually doing things—how we work together, how we make decisions, how we live day to day. The real question is: do we have the courage to start over, or will we just rebuild the same broken system?"

"What did exist before?" asked the mixed-heritage boy with the directness of someone too young to be diplomatic about uncomfortable truths. "Were things good? For everyone?"

The adults exchanged glances that carried forty years of accumulated knowledge about how their society had actually functioned, what it had cost, who had paid the price for whose comfort.

"No," Elder Marex said simply. "Things were not good for everyone. They were very good for some people and very bad for others. The question your generation gets to answer is whether that's how things have to be, or just how they happened to be."

Engineering Wisdom

Velen found himself drawn into the conversation by the practical aspects of rebuilding. His engineer's mind automatically began working on the logistics of creating something better from the ruins of what existed.

"You know what we learned in the deep shafts?" he said, watching children play between the former enemy groups. "Sometimes the tunnel you're digging connects to one someone else started from the other side."

"Doesn't make it safe," Niri added, her bio-crystal enhancements pulsing as she remembered old collapses, old saves. "But it makes it possible."

"And possibility," they said together, finishing each other's thought in the way couples do after decades of shared work and shared danger, "is what you build on when everything else has fallen down."

Koraxos felt the phantom arm pulse with something that might have been approval. These weren't abstract philosophical discussions but practical conversations about how people would actually live together, work together, grow together. The cosmic battle had proven that cooperation was possible. Now they had to prove it was sustainable.

"The cosmic entities will return," he said, not to discourage but to provide context. "Not immediately, but eventually. They'll come with better understanding of what they're facing, more sophisticated attacks, weapons designed specifically to counter unified resistance. We need to be ready—not just militarily but socially. People who trust each other fight better together than people who don't."

"How long do we have?" asked Captain Revik, his military mind already calculating preparation timelines.

"Months, maybe years," Koraxos replied, cosmic senses detecting the distant disturbances that indicated his recent victory had been noticed by forces beyond the Seeker. "Enough time to build something worth defending. Not enough time to waste on rebuilding things that didn't work the first time."

Building Tomorrow

Niri's engineer mind was already working on the practical challenges. "First things first—infrastructure. You can't build a new society if people don't have clean water and stable shelter. But we can design it differently this time. Integrated systems instead of segregated ones. Shared spaces that assume cooperation instead of control."

"Education," added Minister Larix. "Children learning together, all children, regardless of heritage. Not separate schools for separate peoples but integrated learning that assumes diversity strengthens rather than weakens."

"Economic systems," Captain Revik contributed. "Work that's valued for its contribution rather than who performs it. Resources allocated based on need rather than inherited status."

"And if we make mistakes?" asked another survivor, practical concerns overriding idealistic enthusiasm.

"Then we fix them," said the mixed-heritage boy with the confidence of someone who had never been taught that mistakes were permanent. "That's what people do, right? Try things, see what works, change what doesn't?"

Elder Marex chuckled, a sound that carried genuine amusement despite their circumstances. "Out of the mouths of children comes wisdom that adults spend lifetimes learning to forget."

Velen's bio-crystal arm responded to his emotional state, pulsing with warm light as he watched his neighbors and former enemies planning a future together. "Been thinking about something," he said, addressing the group but looking at Niri. "Twenty-two years we've been married. Figured out how to make it work through slavery, rebellion, cosmic horror, and each other's questionable engineering decisions."

"Your questionable engineering decisions," Niri corrected, but her voice held fondness beneath the mock irritation. "I just fix them afterward."

"Point is," Velen continued, "we learned that the strong parts of a relationship aren't the ones where you never disagree. They're the ones where you figure out how to disagree and still choose each other."

"Same principle applies to societies," Niri added, understanding where he was going. "Diversity isn't a problem to solve—it's a resource to use. Different perspectives, different skills, different approaches to the same problems."

"Like having both precision tools and sledgehammers in the same workshop," Velen said. "Sometimes you need finesse, sometimes you need to hit things until they work. But you need both."

The Cosmic Perspective

As the sun reached its zenith over the ruins of Oshar, casting harsh light on the destruction while simultaneously illuminating the nascent cooperation emerging from that destruction, Koraxos felt something he hadn't experienced since his transformation began—hope for a future built on choice rather than simply reaction to circumstances.

The war was far from over. The Seeker's defeat would draw greater attention from cosmic forces beyond their comprehension, entities that viewed their world as merely another resource to be harvested. But they would face those challenges not as isolated individuals or even as temporary allies, but as something unprecedented—people who had learned to work together because they chose to, not because they were forced to.

"Tomorrow will bring new challenges," he said, addressing everyone within hearing. "Forces that make the Seeker look like a practice exercise. But we'll face them together. All of us. And together, we might just discover what people can become when they stop accepting limitations imposed by others and start exploring possibilities they create for themselves."

The phantom arm pulsed once more, cosmic fire flowing through translucent channels that now carried the hopes and determination of everyone who had chosen unity over division. Not because division was evil or unity was good, but because unity worked better when people faced challenges that transcended individual capability.

A New Foundation

As the first stars appeared in skies still faintly painted with cosmic energy, Chapter 4 concluded not with total victory but with something more valuable: proof that change was possible, that enemies could become allies when faced with common purpose, and that the space between separate beings could be filled with choice rather than simply conflict.

Velen and Niri stood together, watching their neighbors and former enemies work side by side, their twenty-year marriage serving as proof that different people could choose to build something beautiful together despite their differences.

"Think it'll stick?" Niri asked quietly, her engineer's mind calculating the structural stresses that would test their newly forged cooperation.

"Some of it," Velen replied, his bio-crystal arm pulsing with the steady rhythm of his heartbeat. "The parts built on choice rather than crisis. The rest..." He shrugged. "We'll fix as we go. Same as always."

"Same as always," she agreed, and took his hand—flesh fingers intertwining with crystal ones, different materials creating something stronger than either could achieve alone.

The real battles lay ahead—cosmic entities that would arrive with millennia of experience in crushing unified resistance, weapons that could rewrite the fundamental laws that made existence possible, strategies refined through the consumption of countless worlds. But they would enter those conflicts no longer as isolated individuals desperately coordinating, but as something new—people who had learned to work together without losing their individuality, to unify without sacrificing choice, to face the infinite with strength drawn from cooperation rather than domination.

The revolution had evolved beyond vengeance into something far more dangerous to cosmic hierarchies—the demonstration that people need not accept the limitations others attempted to impose, that unity freely chosen was stronger than dominance violently enforced, and that the space between separate beings was not emptiness to be feared but possibility to be explored.

Chapter 4 ended with the sound of people working together to build something better from the ruins of what had been destroyed, their voices carrying harmonies that suggested new forms of cooperation were possible when individuals learned to think beyond their immediate limitations while maintaining their essential selves.

And at the heart of it all, two engineers who had learned that the strongest structures were built not by eliminating stress, but by designing systems that could flex under pressure while maintaining their essential integrity—a lesson that applied as much to marriages as it did to societies, as much to hearts as it did to bridges.

Tomorrow would test whether unity forged in desperation could endure in peace, whether cooperation born of necessity could evolve into something chosen freely. But tonight, for the first time since cosmic entities had taken notice of their small world, the people of Oshar went to sleep with something approaching peace—not the peace of finished conflict but the deeper tranquility of having found purpose that transcended individual survival.

The cosmic war had begun in earnest. But people had chosen their side, and that choice carried weight that would reshape the very foundations of what gods and slaves alike believed possible.

5

Chapter 5 – The Obsidian Depths

The mountain made Koraxos's teeth ache.

All those crystal spires humming in perfect harmony, throwing rainbows around like confetti at a funeral. Beautiful, sure. But the kind of beautiful that reminded you how ugly everything else was by comparison.

"Christ," Velen muttered, shading his eyes. "Place looks like someone built a city out of broken promises."

Niri squeezed his hand—the quick, automatic gesture of twenty years keeping each other sane. "Pretty, though."

"Pretty like a knife," Marex said, testing his walking stick against stone that rang like a bell. "All edges and no warmth."

Koraxos felt the phantom arm twitch. Something about this place crawled under his skin—not danger, exactly, but the particular discomfort of being judged by people who'd never bled for anything they believed in.

"We need them," he said, though the words tasted like shit.

Three weeks since he'd chosen mercy over vengeance. Three weeks of watching former enemies become neighbors, former slaves become leaders, former certainties become questions that kept him awake at night.

And now this—begging perfect strangers for help because the alternative was watching everyone he'd learned to love get consumed by forces that treated consciousness like breakfast.

The crystal spears erupted from the ground so fast Niri yelped and grabbed for Velen. Suddenly they stood in a cage of singing light, trapped like insects in amber.

"Well," Koraxos said, phantom arm already blazing, "guess they noticed us."

"Pretty," Thalia said, though she sounded beat. "Like someone took a ruler to the whole damn place."

"Pretty and dead," Marex grunted, leaning heavy on his stick. "Place looks like nobody's had fun here in about a thousand years."

Koraxos kept his mouth shut. Something about this place bugged him—like trying to remember a song you heard when you were half-drunk. The phantom arm started acting up as they got closer to the mountain.

Crystal spears erupted from the ground around their feet without warning, forming a cage of glowing bars.

"Stop right there," said a voice that seemed to come from the mountain itself. "State your business or become part of our decorations."

"Name's Koraxos," he said, hands up but the phantom arm ready to ruin someone's day. "We need your help killing things that want to eat the universe."

The ground tilted up, carrying them toward the mountain on what felt like a slow-moving earthquake. Guards appeared from what had looked like ordinary rocks, their skin shot through with crystal veins that pulsed with soft light.

"Help?" The captain's laugh sounded like breaking glass. "Outsiders always want help. What makes you think we're interested in your problems?"

"Because your problems and our problems are the same problems," Thalia said, stepping forward with the confident look she got when dealing with difficult people. "Look, I know how this sounds—Noks and Luminarai working together? Three weeks ago I'd have laughed too. But when something wants to eat your entire world, you figure out pretty fast what really matters. We're here because we need each other. All of us."

"United?" The captain studied their little group with obvious skepticism. "Luminarai and Noks? Working together? Either the world's ending or this is the most elaborate lie I've heard in decades."

"World's ending," Velen said bluntly. "We figured out lying to each other wasn't going to fix that."

The captain almost smiled. "Fair enough. Let's see what the Council thinks of your unity."

Meeting the Council

The chamber they entered was carved from living crystal, walls pulsing with patterns that hurt to look at directly. Seven figures waited for them, so integrated with crystal formations that telling where person ended and mineral began was impossible.

"Approach," said the central figure, a woman whose skin was more crystal than flesh. Light passed through her like she was made of colored glass. "You claim unity. We detect only necessity holding fragments together."

"Sometimes that's how it starts," Koraxos said with a shrug. "Nothing like cosmic horror to help people figure out what actually matters."

"Does it? Or does crisis just create partnerships that fall apart the moment the danger passes?"

"Only one way to find out," Koraxos said. "Help us not die, then we'll see if we can stand each other when things aren't trying to eat us."

The crystal woman studied him with interest. "You speak like someone who's already made his choice. Yet our sensors show recent trauma—loss that would break most people."

"Break or teach," Velen said steadily. "We chose teach."

"Show us," she said.

The test came without warning. Crystal walls erupted between them, separating each person into their own small chamber that kept changing shape.

"Well, shit," Koraxos muttered as crystal walls shot up around him. "Should've seen that coming."

"Okay, this is definitely testing something," Thalia called out, her voice carrying the tone of someone solving a puzzle in real time. "The walls aren't random—there's a pattern here. They're watching how we respond to being separated."

"Testing whether we actually give a damn about each other," Koraxos called out, "or if we just talk a good game."

Koraxos reached out with the phantom arm—not to smash the walls, that'd be too easy. Instead he went for something trickier: finding his people through all this crystal bullshit. Not reading minds—that was creepy—just feeling for them. Their stubborn determination. Their trust.

"Together," he called out, his voice cutting through the crystal maze. "We don't fight alone. We think together, we win together."

It took time, but they found their rhythm. Thalia mapped the logical patterns in how the walls moved. Marex identified what the test was really about. Koraxos provided the power to reshape their prison according to what they learned working as a team.

When Thalia stopped trying to force order and started recognizing the order that was already there, everything clicked. "Oh," she breathed. "It's not about control. It's about choosing to work together."

The crystal maze dissolved, leaving them standing together in the center while the Council watched with what might have been approval.

"Better," the crystal woman acknowledged. "You show potential for real unity, not just coordination. But potential means nothing against forces that have devoured entire galaxies. The weapons you seek have been guarded for thousands of years against exactly these threats."

"We're not just seeking weapons," Koraxos said. "We want partnership. Your knowledge combined with our determination."

"Partnership." The word rolled around the chamber like a marble in a bowl, hitting edges, finding no comfortable place to settle. "You offer desperation dressed as opportunity. We offer millennia of accumulated wisdom. The mathematics seem... unbalanced."

Koraxos felt his temper stir—the old slave's rage at being dismissed by people who'd confused safety with strength. But something in the phantom arm whispered patience, and he found himself saying words that surprised him:

"You're right. We don't have much. We've got a cosmic mountain monster with attitude problems, a bunch of ex-slaves who've learned to cooperate out of spite, and me—a walking disaster with power I still don't understand and a track record of making bad decisions with cosmic consequences."

Velen snorted. "Great sales pitch, boss."

"I'm not done." Koraxos kept his eyes on the councilor's crystal form. "We also have something you don't. We know what it feels like to lose everything and keep fighting anyway. We know how to take a beating and get back up. And we know—" his voice caught slightly, remembering royal children and spectral armies and choices that still tasted like ash, "—we know the difference between power and strength."

The chamber's harmonics shifted to something that felt like listening.

"When cosmic entities come hunting—and they will come—they'll look for consciousness that's isolated, perfect, easy to pluck like fruit from trees. They'll see your crystal towers and think 'efficiency.' They'll taste your harmonized thoughts and think 'organized meal.'"

"And what will they think when they encounter your chaotic alliance?" the councilor asked.

"Hopefully," Niri said with the kind of smile that had gotten her through twenty years underground, "they'll think 'indigestion.'"

The silence that followed was different. Not consideration—recognition.

"Demonstrate," the councilor said finally. "Show us this strength you claim to possess."

"Wisdom, survival, call it whatever makes you feel better," Koraxos said. "Long as it means we're all pointing our weapons in the same direction."

Before anyone could answer, alarms started screaming—not mechanical sounds but harmonics that seemed to come from the mountain itself. The crystal formations began singing, and their song spoke of something terrible approaching.

"Something's coming through!" a technician shouted, his voice cracking. "It's ripping through everything we have—I can't stop it!"

The wall exploded inward. The Seeker burst through crystal defenses that had stood for millennia, its faceless form turning toward Koraxos with recognition that felt like ice in his veins.

"Found you," it said directly into their minds. *"The thief and his stolen fire. How convenient, gathering in one place for easy collection."*

The Battle Inside

"Run," Koraxos commanded, the phantom arm flaring to life as he put himself between the entity and everyone else. But the crystal woman stepped forward with movements that spoke of decisions made long ago.

"This is our mountain," she said simply, and every crystal formation in the chamber began to sing. The Seeker's form wavered like heat shimmer. "You're not welcome here."

What happened next changed everything Koraxos thought he knew about fighting.

The Drustali didn't attack the Seeker—they rewrote reality around it. Every crystal in the chamber started singing, and suddenly the thing that had been sliding through walls like mist found itself solid, heavy, *trapped*. For the first time, it had a body they could actually hurt.

"Clever," the Seeker acknowledged, though its voice carried grudging respect. *"Dimensional locks through harmonic resonance. But locks work both ways—trapping the target while limiting the trappers."*

The entity began to swell, testing the crystal prison. Each probe met resistance, but Koraxos could see stress fractures appearing in the formations around them. Whatever was keeping the Seeker solid wouldn't last forever.

"Your defenses won't hold," he told the crystal woman. "We need to end this fast."

"We?" she replied, crystal formations around her showing hairline cracks. "Moments ago you were begging for help. Now you presume partnership?"

"Now I'm offering partnership," Koraxos said, extending the phantom arm toward the failing defenses. "Whether you want it or not."

He poured cosmic energy into the crystal network, his transcendent power flowing through the mountain's harmonic structure like water finding its level. Stress fractures healed, resonance patterns stabilized, containment fields strengthened beyond anything the Drustali had achieved alone.

But the connection came with a price. Koraxos felt his consciousness expanding through the crystal network, experiencing the mountain's awareness from within. Thousands of years of accumulated knowledge flooded through his mind—memories of civilizations that had sought refuge here, echoes of cosmic threats that had tested these defenses across ages.

"Interesting," the Seeker observed as its struggles intensified. *"But shared systems mean shared vulnerabilities. Break the connection, and everything falls apart."*

The entity's form contracted, concentrating its power into a single point of absolute negation. Not attacking the network directly but trying to convince reality that the network had never existed—a philosophical attack that targeted the idea rather than the thing itself.

"It's trying to delete us from existence," the crystal woman called, her form flickering as fundamental forces questioned whether the Drustali had ever been real.

"Then we show them they're wrong," Thalia said, her voice carrying the quiet confidence of someone who'd spent years watching people work together. "Not by fighting harder, but by doing what they think is impossible—staying connected when everything's trying to pull us apart."

What emerged wasn't technical jargon or crystal harmonics—it was something simpler and more powerful. Nok voices raised in work songs that had kept spirits alive through years of slavery. Luminarai harmonics that spoke of order built through cooperation rather than force. Drustali resonances that had echoed through crystal chambers for millennia. All joined by Koraxos's cosmic frequencies that bridged mortal determination with transcendent power.

The Seeker's deletion attack met this unified declaration and simply stopped. Not defeated but overwhelmed, like a single voice trying to shout down a choir. For the first time since appearing, the entity's confidence wavered.

"This is... unexpected. Unified consciousness that maintains individual components. Order emerging from choice rather than imposition. Such configurations should not be stable."

"Stable enough," Koraxos replied, his voice carrying harmonics borrowed from all three peoples. "Want to test how stable?"

The Real Fight

What followed was like nothing the Seeker had encountered before. Instead of facing separate opponents it could divide and conquer, it found itself fighting a group that grew stronger under pressure, that adapted faster than it could counter, that turned every attack into an opportunity to coordinate more effectively.

"We're getting better at this," Velen observed as he dodged a tentacle of pure darkness while Thalia provided covering fire and Marex identified weak points in the entity's defenses.

"Because we're not trying to control each other," Marex replied, his scholar's mind recognizing patterns that transcended individual experience. "We're learning to think together while staying ourselves."

The end came suddenly. The Seeker, unable to adapt fast enough to resistance that evolved in real-time, made what felt like a strategic withdrawal—not admitting defeat but acknowledging that victory was costing more than it was worth.

"This isn't over," it projected as its form began to fade. *"We know your location now. We understand your capabilities. When we return, it will be with force sufficient to crack this mountain like an egg."*

"When you return," Koraxos called after the retreating presence, "you'll find people who've had time to get even better at working together. Bring bigger problems."

As the entity's presence faded, silence settled over the chamber like snow after a storm. The crystal formations gradually returned to normal luminescence, stress patterns fading as the mountain's defensive systems went back to routine monitoring.

The crystal woman turned toward Koraxos and his companions, her features reflecting something that might have been approval.

"Partnership," she said, and the word carried weight it hadn't before. "Perhaps there is wisdom in alliance after all. But partnership requires more than shared enemies—it demands shared understanding. Are you prepared for the Trial of Proving?"

"What does that involve?" Thalia asked, her practical mind already calculating risks.

"Let me guess," Koraxos cut in. "More mysterious tests where we prove we're worthy? Can't we just skip to the part where you give us the good stuff and we all go kill cosmic assholes together?"

"Exposure to the deep crystals—formations that exist partially outside normal reality. They will test not your strength but your ability to remain yourself when faced with forces that operate beyond normal consciousness."

"And if we fail?"

"Then you scatter into component energies, and your consciousness spreads across dimensional boundaries no mortal mind was meant to cross."

Koraxos felt the phantom arm pulse with recognition. Whatever lay ahead would test the core of what he'd become—force him to face the cosmic forces that had transformed him while keeping hold of the connections that made him more than just another wielder of borrowed power.

"Yeah, we'll take your test," Koraxos said. "But if this goes sideways and we all die horribly, I'm gonna be really annoyed."

Strangers Arrive

As they prepared for the trial, word came that changed everything. Ships were approaching Toran—not one or two, but dozens, from directions and civilizations no one had expected.

"Eastern approach shows Soltari configuration," reported a technician, voice carrying amazement rather than alarm. "Southern contacts appear to be... flying creatures? And from the north, something that's either a mobile city or the biggest aircraft ever built."

Koraxos extended his cosmic senses, feeling not hostility but desperation—the emotional signature of people who had finally found hope after believing none existed.

"Great," Koraxos muttered. "Nothing says 'target on your back' like winning a fight everyone thought was impossible."

"Then everything changes," Marex finished. "We're not just three peoples choosing to work together anymore. We might be the start of something much bigger."

The first ships landed with precision that spoke of advanced technology driven by desperate need. From the lead craft stepped a woman who commanded attention just by being there. Tall and lean, with skin that seemed to glow from within, she wore robes that shifted color when she moved. Energy danced between her fingers like tame lightning.

"I'm Elara Solus," she announced, her voice carrying harmonics that made the air itself seem to listen. "High Chancellor of the Soltari Imperium. We've come to offer alliance against extinction."

"Alliance against extinction," Koraxos repeated. "Well, when you put it like that, how can we say no? I'm Koraxos. I punch things that need punching."

Her companions were similarly enhanced—eyes that reflected light like mirrors, skin marked with geometric patterns, voices that carried overtones no normal throat could produce. They moved with the coordination of people who'd learned to think together while staying individual.

From the living ships came people who seemed primitive until you looked closer. Their simple clothes breathed with their movements. Their exposed skin bore patterns that weren't tattoos but something alive.

Their leader was an old man whose weathered face mapped decades under a harsh sun. But he moved like flowing water, each step perfectly placed. The patterns on his dark skin pulsed gently with his heartbeat.

"Elder Karim," he said, his voice deep enough to feel in your chest. "The Dunekin Collective sends greetings to our sister-peoples. We've traveled far to stand with you in this darkness."

When he spread his arms, the living patterns on his skin flared with warm light—not electric but organic, like deep-sea creatures that made their own illumination. His companions showed similar modifications, each unique—flowing water patterns, shifting sand designs, organic structures that looked plant-like.

The third group descended from the massive northern vessel on platforms that looked grown rather than built. These newcomers were tall and pale, with an ethereal quality that made them seem almost transparent. Their leader was a woman whose hair moved in wind that touched nothing else, whose eyes held depths suggesting she saw more than the visible world.

"I am Lyralei," she said, her voice carrying the sound of wind through high places. "Voice of the Aetheric Communes. We bring word from the sky-cities and wisdom from the upper reaches."

Three different approaches to being more than human. The Soltari had enhanced themselves through technology and engineering. The Dunekin had merged with the living world around them. The Aetheric people had transcended physical limits through will and understanding of natural forces.

Yet here they stood together, having traveled impossible distances through dangerous conditions to reach this mountain. Their presence raised questions nobody had time to ask.

The Council of Seven

The emergency meeting took place in chambers deep beneath the mountain, where reality remained stable enough for civilizations to actually communicate. Seven groups now—the original four plus three newcomers—gathering around displays that showed approaching threats.

Elara spoke first, her golden eyes reflecting the chamber's crystal light.

"The Soltari Imperium controls the eastern deserts," she began. "Five hundred years ago, our ancestors were refugees from the Crystal Wars. We fled to lands others thought uninhabitable—places where the sun could kill and the sand held razors."

Images formed in the air as she spoke, showing heat-blasted wastelands and crystal formations jutting from dunes like buried bones.

"The desert taught us that survival meant becoming more than human. We learned to modify ourselves, enhance our capabilities, evolve beyond natural limits. Not by rejecting what we were, but by choosing what we could become."

She demonstrated by touching a crystal formation. Energy flowed between her fingers and the stone, creating temporary structures that pulsed with shared communication.

"We built cities that could move when staying meant death. We created tools that worked even when physics became unreliable. We learned to think fast enough to survive in a world that changed its rules without warning."

Elder Karim stepped forward, the living patterns on his skin shifting to express emotions that had no words in other languages.

"The Dunekin Collective has no beginning," he said in his deep voice. "We are what remains when everything else is stripped away—connection between consciousness and the world that keeps it alive."

His gesture created illusions of vast spaces, endless dunes, skies that stretched beyond imagination.

"When the wars drove refugees into the deep desert, most died. Heat killed them, sand buried them, emptiness drove them mad. But some learned to listen instead of fight, to adapt instead of resist, to become part of the desert instead of trying to beat it."

The images around his words showed transformation that was biological—humans learning to live in partnership with organisms evolved in the deep places, consciousness expanding to include awareness of wind patterns and water tables and the slow thoughts of stone.

"We learned the desert wasn't empty—it was full of life operating on scales humans rarely notice. Bacteria that could process almost anything. Fungal networks spanning hundreds of miles beneath the sand. Crystal formations holding memories of geological ages."

His people, Karim explained, had learned integration rather than domination. They formed partnerships with desert organisms, modified their biology to function in impossible conditions, grew their technology rather than building it.

"Our cities move with seasons and water tables. Our people carry adaptations from a thousand different species. Our children are born able to survive conditions that would kill their grandparents, because we learn from every challenge and pass that learning on."

Lyralei spoke last, her ethereal presence commanding attention despite apparent fragility.

"The Aetheric Communes exist between earth and sky," she said. "Our cities float above clouds, our people walk on wind and breathe starlight. We watch the world below and remember what it means to be unbound by physical weight."

Her story differed from both technological enhancement and biological adaptation. The Aetheric path involved what she called "conscious evolution"—developing human potential through understanding natural forces most people never learned to perceive.

"Five centuries ago, our ancestors were scholars and mystics seeking understanding rather than power. When the wars began, they chose withdrawal over participation, ascending to floating settlements where they could pursue knowledge without interference."

Images formed showing impossible beauty—cities existing as structured clouds, people moving through air as easily as walking, communities that had spent centuries developing hidden potential of human consciousness.

"We learned to influence gravity through will rather than machinery, to communicate across vast distances through resonance with natural forces, to perceive energy flows connecting all things. Our children are born with abilities that seem magical to those bound by conventional understanding."

But isolation had brought challenges. The Aetheric Communes had lost touch with practical concerns, becoming so focused on transcendent possibilities they forgot survival necessities in a hostile universe.

"We watched conflicts from above, believing ourselves beyond such crude concerns. We saw cosmic entities approaching and assumed our sky cities would be beneath notice, that beings who could reshape reality would ignore those existing outside conventional physical parameters."

"What changed your mind?" Thalia asked.

"Probe attacks reached us three days ago," Lyralei said, her voice carrying sudden, terrible understanding. "Our cities weren't beneath notice—they were appetizers. Cosmic entities view consciousness as food to be harvested, regardless of how that consciousness chooses to exist."

The attack had been devastating in its casual efficiency. Entities existing partially outside normal space had simply reached through Aetheric defenses, harvesting enhanced consciousness of people who'd spent centuries developing abilities beyond human norm.

"Half our population was consumed in the first assault," Lyralei continued. "Our transcendent abilities, which we believed made us superior to earthly concerns, proved to be exactly what the entities sought. We realized isolation wasn't protection—it was preparation for slaughter."

The Weight of Truth

Silence followed Lyralei's words, carrying the weight of civilizations suddenly understanding how small they were in a cosmos that viewed consciousness as food.

"Eighteen days," Elara said quietly. "Eighteen days ago, our instruments detected dimensional disturbances consistent with cosmic entity approach. When we compared patterns to our oldest records..."

"The desert began screaming sixty days ago," Elder Karim interrupted with quiet authority. "Deep sands remember the last time such things walked among stars. Crystals beneath our homeland activated dormant patterns sleeping for seven thousand years."

"Our sky cities felt disturbance through resonance patterns beyond normal perception," Lyralei added. "Space-time itself began vibrating with frequencies speaking of consciousness-hunger approaching from beyond dimensional boundaries."

Three civilizations had detected the approaching threat through different means, but the message was identical—cosmic entities were coming to their world, bringing extinction as casual as breathing.

"Which explains why you're here now," Thalia said. "But not why you're here together. Our records suggest Soltari and Dunekin haven't been friendly neighbors."

Tension passed between the eastern delegations. Elara's golden eyes flickered with embarrassment while Elder Karim's weathered face showed something like pain.

"We've had differences," Elara admitted. "Resource disputes. Philosophical disagreements. Outright warfare, if we're being honest."

"Three times in the past century," Elder Karim added. "Each time, both peoples bled for the pride of being right about how to survive in a hostile world."

The story emerging was one of sudden, desperate cooperation born from recognizing that extinction made philosophical differences irrelevant. When readings confirmed what was approaching, both civilizations reached the same conclusion independently: neither could survive alone.

"Our first contact in thirty years was a message on emergency frequencies," Elara explained. "No diplomatic protocol, no formal negotiation. Just 'The cosmos is coming to eat us. Interested in not dying together?'"

"Response took six hours," Elder Karim added with approaching humor. "Most of that spent arguing about whether it was a trick."

Integration between Soltari and Dunekin had been chaotic, but driven by desperate creativity emerging when extinction was the alternative to cooperation. Technology designed to dominate environment learned to work with biological systems flowing with environmental change. Organisms evolved to process hostile conditions began incorporating technological enhancements expanding their capabilities.

"The Aetheric Communes joined us five days ago," Lyralei said. "After probe attacks demonstrated that transcendence through consciousness development was no protection against entities viewing consciousness as food."

The Challenge of Unity

What followed was controlled chaos on a scale defying organization. Seven civilizations developed in isolation suddenly trying to merge technologies, biology, and philosophy in hours rather than generations.

The first attempts were disasters that would've been funny if they weren't terrifying. Keris woke up convinced his bones were made of singing crystal and tried to harmonize with the wall for six hours. Yanna's skin turned translucent and she kept apologizing to furniture for being solid.

"Hopeless?" Koraxos snorted when someone muttered about giving up after the sixth failed integration. "I've seen hopeless. This is just difficult. There's a difference, and the difference is we keep trying until it works."

The breakthrough came from recognizing that compatibility wasn't the goal. Integration didn't require similarity; it required communication.

Jira, the young Nok woman who'd learned to speak with stone during mining years, provided the key insight. "Stop trying to make everything the same," she said during one frustrating session. "Crystal doesn't want to be metal, and metal doesn't want to be crystal. But they can touch without becoming each other."

"Kid's got the right idea," Koraxos said. "Sometimes the best partnerships are the ones where nobody has to change who they are."

The approach that followed focused on creating interfaces rather than mergers. Instead of forcing Soltari technology to incorporate Dunekin biology, they developed communication protocols allowing different systems to coordinate while maintaining essential nature.

Koraxos played a crucial role in this process, the phantom arm serving as a bridge between different forms of consciousness and energy. Through his transcendent nature, he could establish connections that allowed systems to share information without losing their fundamental characteristics.

"It's not about forcing compatibility," he realized aloud during one successful interface test. "It's about creating space where different approaches can exist together without losing what makes them unique."

Underground Discoveries

As integration work continued, teams explored expanded bio-crystal networks spanning underground areas beneath Oshar. What they discovered changed understanding of what they fought to protect.

Deep beneath the city, in chambers predating any known civilization, they found evidence of previous cosmic incursions. Crystal formations holding memories of battles fought eons ago, when other species faced similar threats. Biological matrices preserving genetic information from creatures evolved specifically to resist cosmic predation.

"These aren't just defensive systems," observed Dr. Lyrin, a Luminarai xenobiologist joining integration teams. "They're archives. Records of everything that ever fought cosmic consumption."

The implications were staggering. Their world hadn't been randomly selected for cosmic harvesting—it was a repository where resistance techniques and survival strategies had accumulated across geological ages. Every species that had ever successfully resisted cosmic entities had left traces of their methods in deep crystal matrices.

"That's why bio-crystal networks respond so readily to integration," Velen realized, his enhanced arm pulsing with patterns echoing ancient formations. "They're designed to adapt, to incorporate new approaches to survival. We're not just fighting for this world—we're adding to its library of resistance."

Elder Karim, his symbiotic organisms responding to ancient biological traces in deep chambers, provided additional insight. "Patterns down there... they're not just records. They're instructions. Teaching methods for consciousness wanting to survive cosmic predation."

The crystal networks came alive with whispers from the dead—techniques that had failed their creators but might save their children. Koraxos felt weapons in his hands that shouldn't exist, strategies flowing through his mind from species that had fought and died before his world was born. The archives weren't just sharing knowledge—they were sharing hope.

The Leviathan Integration

As integration work reached critical stages, Koraxos found himself drawn repeatedly to reports from the Obsidian Leviathan's territory. The massive creature had been unusually active, its movements through mountain passages creating tremors that could be felt throughout Oshar.

"It knows," he said during a brief break in integration work. "The dimensional pressure is affecting it too. But more than that—it's responding to what we're building down here."

Through bio-crystal networks, they could detect the creature's agitation. The Leviathan wasn't just sensing the approaching cosmic threat; it was aware of the ancient archives beneath Oshar, the accumulated resistance knowledge that its territorial instincts recognized as valuable beyond measure.

"The creature isn't just a predator," Neryssia realized, her Pelagian senses detecting patterns in the Leviathan's behavior that suggested intelligence beyond animal cunning. "It's a guardian. It's been protecting this repository for eons."

"Could that be useful?" Thalia asked. "If the creature is already responding to the ancient defenses..."

"Or dangerous," Velen countered. "A territorial predator protecting what it sees as its hoard isn't exactly going to welcome visitors."

"I need to talk to that thing," Koraxos said. "Not through crystal phone calls or tech bullshit. Direct, mind-to-mind, 'hey there, giant monster' conversation."

"Look, somebody's gotta do it," Koraxos said when Velen objected. "And I'm the guy with the cosmic arm and a really bad track record with good decisions. Besides, what's the worst that could happen?"

The attempt was made in the deepest bio-crystal chamber, where ancient archives were strongest and dimensional stability remained most consistent. Representatives from all seven civilizations were present to provide support and, if necessary, to contain the fallout if things went catastrophically wrong.

Koraxos knelt at the chamber's center, phantom arm extended toward the direction where the Leviathan prowled through its mountain domain. Instead of reaching out with force or compulsion, he simply opened his consciousness, offering connection rather than demanding it.

The response was immediate and overwhelming.

The Leviathan's awareness crashed into his like a tidal wave of alien thought. For a moment lasting eternities, Koraxos experienced existence from the perspective of a being that had lived for geological ages, that had watched continents shift and species rise and fall, that had learned to hunt across dimensional boundaries while simultaneously protecting something precious beyond measure.

The creature's thoughts were vast and slow, operating on timescales that made human planning seem like mayfly wings fluttering. But beneath the alien vastness was something recognizable—protective instinct, territorial behavior, desperate need to preserve what mattered against threats from beyond normal existence.

Through their connection, Koraxos felt the creature's memories—fragments of battles fought eons ago, when other cosmic entities had tried to harvest the repository beneath Oshar. The Leviathan had fought them, sometimes successfully, sometimes not, always learning from each encounter and adapting its defensive strategies.

"Hell of a long time to be by yourself," Koraxos said, his voice somehow reaching the massive thing. "Standing guard, fighting off cosmic shitheads for who knows how long. Well, good news—backup's finally here."

The Leviathan's response was a surge of confused emotion—need warring with instinct, desperation fighting pride, desire for connection battling eons of solitary existence. It had learned to distrust anything approaching its territory, but it also recognized that the current threat was beyond anything it could face alone.

Through the connection, Koraxos shared information from all seven civilizations—technological capabilities, biological adaptations, consciousness techniques, strategic plans, desperate ingenuity of people who refused to accept extinction. The Leviathan absorbed this data with alien intelligence, processing possibilities with cognitive frameworks no human mind could fully comprehend.

When it finally responded, the answer came not in words but in pure conceptual transfer—territorial acceptance, conditional alliance, opening of dimensional boundaries it had guarded for eons. But more than that, it offered access to the ancient archives, the accumulated resistance knowledge that it had been protecting since before human civilization began.

The Final Test

The integration of the Leviathan into their defense network transformed everything. The creature's dimensional nature allowed it to serve as a living anchor point, stabilizing local reality even as cosmic forces pressed against their world's boundaries. Through this anchor, the seven civilizations found they could achieve integration that had seemed impossible hours before.

But the connection also revealed the true scope of what they protected. The repository beneath Oshar wasn't unique—it was part of a network spanning multiple worlds, multiple star systems, an interconnected archive of resistance techniques developed by countless species across cosmic ages.

"We're not just fighting for our world," High Chancellor Elara realized, her enhanced senses processing data flowing through the Leviathan connection. "We're fighting for the survival of resistance itself. If they destroy this repository, they eliminate knowledge that could save other worlds."

The responsibility was crushing and inspiring in equal measure. They weren't just desperate survivors fighting for their own lives—they were current guardians of wisdom accumulated across eons of cosmic conflict.

Through the Leviathan connection, they could access techniques developed by species whose evolution had taken paths unimaginable to human consciousness. Weapons operating through dimensional folding, defense systems creating stability through controlled chaos, strategies that turned cosmic-level power against itself.

But perhaps most importantly, they gained access to something no previous resistance had possessed—combined wisdom of seven different approaches to survival, integrated through necessity and united by choice rather than compulsion.

"The ancient defenders were powerful," Elder Karim observed, his symbiotic organisms responding to biological techniques preserved in the archives. "But they fought alone, each species relying on its own understanding of survival. We're doing something unprecedented—combining different forms of consciousness and capability while maintaining individual identity."

The weapons that emerged from this integration transcended anything any single civilization could have created. Soltari quantum manipulation merged with Dunekin biological adaptation, enhanced by Drustali crystal resonance, guided by Pelagian pressure dynamics, sharpened by Nok intuitive understanding, coordinated by Luminarai organizational precision, and elevated by Aetheric consciousness techniques.

The Storm Gathers

As sunset painted the chaotic sky in colors that shifted between beautiful and ominous, the unified civilizations found themselves more prepared than anyone had dared hope. The integration network spanned seven different approaches to survival, anchored by a dimensional predator that had become their most unlikely guardian, and enhanced by wisdom accumulated across cosmic ages.

But preparation and survival were different things entirely. Through the Leviathan connection, they could sense the approaching entities—vast, hungry, contemptuous of anything that dared to resist their cosmic authority. The final test would come with the dawn, when theory would meet reality and desperate hope would face cosmic certainty.

Koraxos stood atop the highest remaining spire in the city, the phantom arm pulsing with steady blue light as it maintained connection to the vast network they had created. Through that connection, he could feel the hopes and fears of thousands of people who had chosen to stand together rather than fall apart, the determination of civilizations that had learned to see their differences as strengths rather than weaknesses.

"Ready?" Thalia asked, joining him on the platform, her own bio-crystal enhancements glowing softly in the gathering darkness.

"Getting there," Koraxos said, the phantom arm pulsing steady and sure. "One cosmic shitstorm at a time."

"And if we're not ready enough?"

Koraxos smiled, and for the first time since his transformation, the expression held genuine warmth rather than bitter irony. "Then we improvise. We adapt. We find another way." He gestured at the network of lights pulsing through the city below. "That's what we do now. All of us together."

The aurora effects in the sky intensified, reality distortions becoming visible as ribbons of impossible color that danced between the stars. Through the Leviathan connection, they could feel the cosmic entities drawing closer, their presence pressing against dimensional boundaries like vast weight settling on the world's shoulders.

"Look at what we've built," Thalia said, her voice carrying wonder despite the approaching threat. "Seven civilizations that barely knew each other existed three weeks ago. Now we're sharing everything—technology, biology, consciousness techniques, ancient wisdom. We've created something that's never existed before."

Below them, the integrated defense network pulsed with activity that defied simple categorization. Soltari technicians worked alongside Dunekin bio-shapers to create weapons that were part machine, part organism, part crystalline matrix. Aetheric consciousness-walkers shared perception techniques with Luminarai analysts, while Nok engineers and Pelagian pressure-workers collaborated on defensive systems that operated through principles none of them fully understood individually.

The city itself had become a living thing, its bio-crystal networks pulsing in rhythm with the Leviathan's dimensional presence. Buildings that had been constructed separately now formed interconnected structures that could adapt to changing conditions. Streets flowed with organic patterns that allowed rapid movement and communication. Even the air seemed alive, carrying information through scent and pressure changes that enhanced normal communication.

"The kids are gonna grow up thinking this is normal," Velen observed, approaching from the stairs that led to the platform. His arm, where void damage had been replaced with bio-crystal integration, glowed softly as it responded to the network activity around them. "Working together across species, sharing tech, helping each other instead of trying to kill each other. They won't get why we ever thought it was impossible."

"If there are kids to grow up," Neryssia added, though her tone carried determination rather than despair. "The entities approaching... they're not like anything in our archives. Older, hungrier, more sophisticated in their consumption methods."

Through the Leviathan connection, they could sense the approaching force with increasing clarity. The cosmic entities weren't just powerful—they were ancient beyond comprehension, refined through eons of consumption, equipped with techniques that could dismantle resistance before it could organize effectively. They had faced integrated defenses before and learned to counter them.

"But they've never faced seven-way integration anchored by a dimensional guardian," Koraxos pointed out. "They've never run into resistance that gets stronger through diversity instead of weaker through complexity. They think in terms of eating and dominating—they don't get cooperation that keeps everyone different while making them work together."

The phantom arm pulsed as energy flowed through it from the vast network below. Through the connection, Koraxos could feel the hopes and fears of thousands of people, the determination of civilizations that had learned to see their differences as strengths, the quiet courage of individuals who had chosen to stand together against cosmic-level extinction.

But he could also feel something else—patterns in the approaching threat that suggested intelligence beyond mere hunger. The cosmic entities were adapting their approach, preparing strategies specifically designed to counter the kind of integration they had detected.

Final Preparations

As night deepened over Oshar, the final preparations took on desperate urgency. The integration network was as complete as time would allow, but everyone understood that what they had built was untested against the forces approaching. Theory was about to meet reality, and the mathematics of cosmic conflict operated on scales that made human planning seem tragically inadequate.

In the deep chambers where the Leviathan connection was strongest, representatives from all seven civilizations worked to establish the final protocols. The creature's dimensional presence allowed them to create something unprecedented—a defense network that existed partially outside normal space-time, making it resistant to the reality manipulation techniques that cosmic entities typically used to disable resistance.

"The anchoring is holding," reported Master Valoren, his crystalline features reflecting the complex energy patterns flowing through the chamber. "But the strain is enormous. The Leviathan is essentially creating a pocket of stable reality within a cosmic storm. It can't maintain this indefinitely."

"How much time do we have?" Thalia asked, her mind already running through everything that still needed to happen—people who needed to be in position, systems that needed final checks, the hundred small things that determined whether plans worked or fell apart.

"Hard to say. The creature thinks in geological timescales, but the energy expenditure required for dimensional anchoring... days, perhaps. Maybe hours once the real assault begins."

The limitation added another layer of urgency to their preparations. They wouldn't just need to defeat the cosmic entities—they would need to do it quickly, before the Leviathan's strength gave out and their dimensional anchor collapsed.

Elder Karim, his symbiotic organisms flowing with patterns that indicated deep communion with the bio-crystal networks, provided additional intelligence. "The ancient archives are showing activation patterns I've never seen before. It's as if the accumulated resistance knowledge is preparing for something unprecedented."

Through the bio-crystal networks, information flowed from resistance techniques developed across cosmic ages. Weapons systems that had been theoretical became practical. Defense strategies that had failed individually began combining into approaches that might succeed collectively. The repository beneath Oshar was sharing everything it had learned, holding nothing back for future battles that might never come.

"We're getting help from the dead," Velen observed with characteristic bluntness. "Every species that ever fought these things is teaching us their tricks."

"Not just their successes," Lyralei added, her ethereal senses detecting patterns in the flowing information that spoke of hard-won wisdom. "Their failures too. What didn't work, what made things worse, what looked promising but proved catastrophic. We're learning from every mistake ever made in cosmic resistance."

The knowledge was overwhelming and invaluable in equal measure. Combat techniques that operated across dimensional boundaries. Consciousness practices that could resist mental domination. Technologies that remained functional when reality itself became unreliable. Strategies that turned cosmic-level power into weakness rather than strength.

But perhaps most importantly, they learned that resistance was possible. The archives held records of species that had successfully driven off cosmic entities, worlds that had survived consumption attempts, civilizations that had evolved beyond the reach of cosmic predation. It could be done—it had been done before.

"The common factor in successful resistance," High Chancellor Elara observed, her enhanced cognition processing vast amounts of archived data, "isn't superior power or advanced technology. It's adaptive integration—the ability to combine different approaches to survival while maintaining the flexibility to change tactics when conditions shift."

"Which explains why they're so interested in destroying this repository," Koraxos realized. "It's not just a library of resistance techniques—it's proof that working together beats trying to eat everything, that different approaches make you stronger instead of weaker. That's a direct threat to everything they stand for."

As midnight approached, the aurora effects in the sky began to shift from random beauty to organized patterns. Through the Leviathan connection, they could feel the cosmic entities beginning their final approach—not the chaotic arrival of scout forces, but the methodical deployment of entities that had refined their consumption techniques across eons of successful predation.

"This is it," Neryssia announced, her Pelagian senses detecting pressure changes that spoke of reality being systematically rewritten by approaching forces. "Whatever we're going to do, we need to do it now."

The final hour before dawn was spent in activity that defied easy description. They moved like parts of the same organism now, seven peoples who'd learned each other's rhythms. Koraxos found himself anticipating Thalia's tactical needs before she voiced them. Elder Karim passed him a weapon that hummed with desert-song and star-fire, something that felt right in ways he couldn't explain but didn't need to.

Children were moved to the deepest shelters, where bio-crystal networks provided maximum protection and ancient archives offered the accumulated wisdom of resistance across cosmic ages. But even in the depths, they could feel the approaching storm—reality itself beginning to buckle under pressure from entities that existed primarily beyond conventional physics.

"Remember," Koraxos said, addressing the unified defenders through the network that connected them all, "we're not just fighting for our own survival. We're fighting for the principle that consciousness has the right to choose its own path, that diversity creates strength, that cooperation can transcend even cosmic-level domination. Every species that ever resisted is with us tonight. Every technique that ever worked is available to us. We are not alone."

The phantom arm blazed with light that seemed to carry the hopes of everyone connected to the network. Through it, they could feel each other's determination, fear, courage, and desperate love for everything they were fighting to preserve.

As the first tendrils of cosmic presence began to probe the edges of their reality, the integrated defense network activated with precision that seemed almost miraculous. Seven different approaches to survival, enhanced by accumulated wisdom from across cosmic ages, anchored by a dimensional guardian that had chosen alliance over isolation.

The final test was about to begin.

Dawn broke over Oshar with colors that belonged to no natural sunrise, painting the sky in hues that spoke of reality being systematically rewritten by forces beyond normal comprehension. Through the dimensional anchor provided by the Leviathan, they could feel the cosmic entities taking their positions, preparing for an assault that would determine whether consciousness united could stand against domination absolute.

The convergence was complete. All that remained was to discover whether unity forged in desperation and tempered by hope could survive the storm that was about to break over their world.

In the deep shelters, children slept surrounded by the dreams of species they would never meet, protected by wisdom accumulated across cosmic ages. In the defense positions, warriors from seven civilizations stood ready with weapons that transcended individual capability. In the command centers, consciousness shared information at speeds that approached telepathy while maintaining individual identity and choice.

The battle for the right to choose was about to begin. And for the first time since cosmic entities had first taken notice of their world, the defenders faced the coming storm not as separate peoples temporarily allied, but as something new—consciousness united across difference, strength drawn from diversity, hope anchored in the understanding that cooperation could transcend even cosmic attempts at domination.

The sky tore open, and existence itself held its breath as the real war finally began.

"Well," Koraxos said, watching reality crack like an egg around the edges, "this should be interesting."

The phantom arm pulsed once more, steady and sure, carrying the hopes and determination of beings who had learned that together, they could face anything the universe threw at them.

Even gods.

Even the infinite dark between stars.

Even the end of everything they'd ever known.

Together, they were ready.

6

Chapter 6: The Guardians Bargain

The crystal forges of Toran hummed with the kind of efficiency that made Thalia's administrator heart sing. Three races, sixty workers, one purpose. She checked her chronometer—ahead of schedule for the first time since... well, since slavery ended.

"This is what happens when people choose to work together instead of being forced to," she murmured to Marex, watching a Drustali master teach crystal resonance to a former Nok slave while a Luminarai engineer adjusted their shared calculations.

Elder Marex nodded, shifting his weight onto his walking stick as he observed the unprecedented cooperation. The stick itself carried its own story—carved from the femur of Overseer Valdris, the man who'd broken Marex's left leg twenty-three years ago during a "productivity discussion." Time had a way of settling debts, and some tools served better purposes than their makers ever intended.

Through dimensions where memory pooled like starlight in deep wells, Treydora felt the first stirrings of what he had planted eons ago. These children learned what their ancestors had forgotten—that consciousness grew not through accumulation but through willingness to be wounded by what it protects.

Koraxos moved between workstations like a scarred cat checking his territory. The phantom arm had settled down—less weapon, more tool these days. When he touched the crystal matrices, three different ways of thinking flowed together: Nok gut instinct, Luminarai precision, Drustali harmony.

"Not terrible," he grunted to Velen, who had just finished a resonance array that hummed like a perfectly tuned engine. "The kids would be proud."

Velen's scarred face cracked what might have been a smile. "Sela asked if crystals dream. Told her we'd find out together."

"And if they have nightmares?" Niri asked, joining them with the practical concern of someone who'd seen too many perfect plans turn to shit.

"Then we wake them up," Koraxos replied, though his cosmic senses picked up something in the mountain's guts that didn't feel like dreaming. Something patient. Something that had been waiting a hell of a lot longer than crystals had been singing.

Velen flexed his fingers—still flesh, still whole, though every callus told stories of stone that had fought back. "Twenty years of mining taught us that rock has moods," he said, studying the crystal formations with professional interest. "Question is whether this mountain's in a talking mood or a biting mood."

"Only one way to find out," Niri replied, checking her equipment with the automatic precision of someone who'd learned that preparation was the difference between adventure and accident. "Same as always—we go down, we dig careful, and we try not to wake up anything that prefers sleeping."

In the deep places where stone remembered its first shaping, Treydora's ancient companion stirred. The Leviathan had guarded the archives through ages when stars forgot their names, waiting for consciousness brave enough to ask the mountain what it knew.

Master Valoren approached with the measured steps of someone balancing precision against the clock running down. "The deep extraction cannot wait any longer. The seismic activity worsens daily, but the heart-crystals..." He gestured at readings that made the phantom arm twitch. "They're not just powerful. They're essential."

"Define 'essential,'" Thalia said, falling back on administrator habits when facing the unknown.

"These formations exist half in our reality, half somewhere else," Valoren explained. "The cosmic entities phase between dimensions. Only weapons made from this stuff can hit them consistently."

"And the earthquakes?"

"Tremors that line up perfectly with dimensional disturbances," Koraxos added, his enhanced senses mapping patterns normal people couldn't detect. "This isn't natural geology having a bad day. Something in the deep chambers is responding to the cosmic shitheads heading our way."

Elder Marex tapped his walking stick against stone, listening to harmonics that spoke of structures under stress. The stick itself carried its own harmonics—bone that had learned to read stone's moods through decades of forced intimacy with mountain depths. His reconstructed leg ached now, as it always did before seismic events. Some injuries became prophecy.

"Or something that's been napping down there noticed the surface getting interesting," he said, feeling the mountain's pulse through bone that remembered when they'd first discovered the crystal veins. He'd lost three good people to what they'd thought was just unstable geology. Now he wondered if it had been something more deliberate—intelligence testing their intentions.

As they organized the extraction teams with careful attention to not getting everyone killed, Marex approached Koraxos with the careful gait of someone whose bones remembered every beating they'd survived.

"You're thinking of going down there yourself," he observed, not asking.

"Someone has to," Koraxos replied, phantom arm flickering with restless energy.

"Someone does. But not necessarily the someone who's already carrying the weight of everyone's hopes." Marex shifted his weight onto the walking stick, feeling the familiar ache in his reconstructed leg. "I've been in the deep places before. Back when they first discovered the crystal veins. Lost three good people to what we thought was just unstable geology."

"What did you find?"

"Patterns. Responses. Intelligence where there shouldn't have been any." He looked toward the mountain's depths with eyes that had seen too much to be surprised by revelation. "The mountain's been patient with us surface dwellers. Question is how long that patience lasts when we start taking what it considers essential."

They formed the extraction team—twenty from each people, expertise spread across mining, engineering, and dimensional weirdness. Velen and Niri volunteered without hesitation, their shared experience in unstable environments making them essential despite Koraxos's reluctance to risk friends.

"The children need us back," Niri said simply when he expressed concern. "Which means we better know what we're doing down there."

"We'll figure it out," Velen added with miner's confidence. "Tunnels talk. Rocks remember. Stone tells the truth when you know how to listen."

"Great. Philosophy hour with the geology," Koraxos muttered, but there was fondness beneath the gruff tone.

Niri checked Velen's equipment with the automatic care of twenty years together—testing clips, verifying backup systems, running through the mental checklist that had kept them both alive through countless descents. "Your headlamp's flickering again," she said, swapping out his power cell without being asked.

"Noticed that. Thanks." Velen's hand briefly covered hers during the exchange—not romantic, just the steady contact of people who'd learned to anchor each other through shared danger. "Still think this is a terrible idea."

"All our best ideas are terrible," Niri replied, shouldering her pack with practiced efficiency. "That's how we know they're ours."

The Descent

The trip down started through passages carved with the kind of artistic precision that spoke of Drustali reverence for their mountain home. Crystal formations along the walls pulsed with soft light that provided steady illumination without the harsh glare that would damage sensitive equipment.

"Seven stabilization chambers," their guide explained as they passed the first checkpoint. "Each one manages pressure and dimensional interface. The deep chambers exist partially outside normal space-time. Proper acclimatization prevents... complications."

"What kind of complications?" Thalia asked.

"The kind where your brain spreads across seventeen dimensions and your body forgets which one it belongs to," Valoren replied with clinical precision. "Stay together. Maintain physical contact in interface zones. And remember—down there, what you think shapes reality more than physics does."

By the fourth chamber, Koraxos could feel the difference. The phantom arm responded to environmental changes invisible to normal senses, cosmic energies flowing through channels that touched dimensions where matter and thought got real friendly with each other. The mountain itself felt alive, aware, old as dirt and twice as patient.

"Pressure's equalizing weird," Niri observed, consulting readings that fluctuated between normal and nonsensical. "Like the mountain's breathing, but the rhythm's all wrong."

"Structural integrity's holding, but barely," Velen added, his experienced hands reading vibrations through the stone that spoke of forces operating beyond conventional engineering. "Whatever's down there, it's big enough to make the whole mountain flex when it moves."

"You two always this cheerful before potentially fatal encounters?" asked a Drustali engineer, trying to lighten the mood.

"This is us being optimistic," Niri replied without looking up from her instruments. "You should see us when we're actually worried."

"When we're actually worried," Velen said, his voice carrying the dry humor of someone who'd survived decades of underground disasters, "we don't volunteer for the expedition."

Ancient warden, Treydora whispered across the void as his cosmic awareness touched the Leviathan's stirring consciousness. The children have learned that strength shared becomes architecture rather than armor. Perhaps it is time to show them what we carved in stone when the universe was young.

"How deep are we going?" asked a young Luminarai engineer, her voice tight with controlled fear.

"Deep enough to find what we need," Velen answered, though his experienced hands checked equipment with obsessive attention. Smart man—in mining, preparation was the difference between adventure and accident.

The sixth chamber marked their transition into true strangeness. Crystal formations here grew in patterns that hurt to look at directly—geometric relationships that suggested math designed by minds that didn't share human limitations. The air itself had weight, pressing against awareness with the patient pressure of ages.

"Almost there," the guide announced unnecessarily. Everyone could feel it—the presence of something vast waiting below, ancient purpose stirring to acknowledge their intrusion.

As they approached the final descent, Koraxos felt the phantom arm pulse with recognition. Whatever lay ahead was connected to the forces that had remade him. The cosmic energies flowing through his transcendent nature responded to something in the mountain's heart with harmonics that spoke of kinship, resonance, and danger.

"Ready?" he asked the team, though readiness felt like a quaint concept when facing the unknown depths of a living mountain.

"Getting there," Velen replied, squeezing Niri's hand as they prepared for whatever waited in the darkness below. "One step at a time."

The Great Cavern

The chamber that opened before them stretched beyond visual comprehension, its boundaries lost in crystalline formations that existed in more dimensions than human eyes could process. Emergency lighting revealed impossible architecture—crystal spires that twisted through space according to logic that predated geometry textbooks.

"Sweet mother of broken math," whispered the Luminarai engineer, her voice echoing in frequencies that shouldn't exist. "How is this structurally possible?"

"It's not," Valoren replied. "These formations grow according to dimensional principles rather than physical laws. They exist because they choose to, not because matter permits it."

Every civilization believes it invents wisdom, Treydora's presence stirred through the crystalline matrices that had grown from his scattered essence eons ago. None realize they are simply remembering what the stones already know: that the universe's greatest secret is not hidden in complexity, but in the courage to remain simple while embracing vastness.

Koraxos extended his cosmic awareness, mapping the chamber's true scope through senses that operated beyond standard perception. What he detected troubled him—not just the vast scale, but something else. Something that watched their progress with patient interest.

"Motion sensors active," reported the Drustali technician, studying readings that fluctuated between normal and nonsensical. "But the patterns are... irregular. Like the chamber itself is breathing."

Velen and Niri moved toward what appeared to be the richest crystal formations, their mining experience guiding them through chaotic geology toward targets that promised the dimensional properties they needed. But as they approached the western boundary, both stopped simultaneously.

"You feel that?" Niri asked, her engineer's instincts detecting structural anomalies her eyes couldn't identify.

"Movement," Velen confirmed, studying the chamber wall with careful attention. "But not random. Purposeful. Like something large shifting position while trying not to be noticed."

They exchanged one of those married looks—entire conversations compressed into a glance that spoke of shared concerns about what they might have walked into.

"Should we tell the others?" Niri asked quietly.

"Tell them what? That we think the mountain might be alive?" Velen's voice carried the dry humor of someone who'd learned that impossible things had a habit of becoming routine around here. "They'll figure it out soon enough."

"Wonderful," Koraxos muttered. "We're being watched."

The extraction teams spread through the cavern with professional efficiency, each group targeting formations identified as particularly rich in dimensional properties. Crystal-cutting equipment hummed to life, precise tools designed to harvest valuable material without triggering structural collapse.

But the humming was answered.

From somewhere in the chamber's depths came a sound that wasn't quite echo, wasn't quite response—a low, harmonic vibration that seemed to emerge from the stone itself. The frequency was familiar yet wrong, like a song remembered from childhood but played in a minor key that hadn't existed when the melody was learned.

"That humming," Koraxos called out, the phantom arm prickling with unease. "Anyone else think it sounds like the mountain's talking back?"

"Not our gear," Velen replied, checking his crystal cutter. "This is coming from the rock itself. Like it's... answering us."

"Environmental how?" Thalia asked, her administrative mind demanding precise categorization of weird shit.

"Like the mountain is singing back to us," said the young Luminarai engineer, wonder and unease warring in her voice. "Responding to our work. Harmonizing."

But Koraxos's transcendent perception detected something more complex than harmonizing. The mountain's response carried undertones of evaluation, assessment, the particular quality of intelligence deciding whether new arrivals represented opportunity or threat.

"Keep working," he decided, "but stay in contact. Report any changes immediately. And I mean immediately."

First Blood

The work proceeded with efficiency that would have impressed their most demanding supervisors, crystal after crystal harvested with precision that left surrounding formations intact. These were miners and engineers who had learned their crafts under conditions where mistakes meant death—they brought that expertise to bear now with confidence earned through survival.

The first extraction yielded spectacular results—a crystal formation with dimensional properties so pronounced it seemed to exist in multiple states simultaneously. When properly shaped, this material could create weapons that affected entities existing partially outside normal reality.

Tools forged in isolation cut only what their makers feared, Treydora observed as technologies began to merge through willing cooperation. But when consciousness learns to share the hammer, the anvil, and the fire—then iron becomes more than metal. It becomes physical proof that separateness was always an illusion.

The second target proved equally valuable, crystalline structures that responded to consciousness with sensitivity suggesting they could interface directly with wielder intention. Perfect for the kind of adaptive weapons they needed to counter cosmic threats that could alter reality itself.

But as the third team moved toward their assigned formation, the chamber's response changed.

The harmonic singing that had accompanied their work shifted frequency, moving from what might have been curiosity to something that sounded remarkably like territorial warning. Crystal formations throughout the cavern began to pulse in synchronized patterns that spoke of communication rather than random illumination.

"Status report," Koraxos called, phantom arm beginning to pulse in resonance with the chamber's changing mood.

"Successful extraction continuing," came responses from teams throughout the cavern. "No immediate problems, but the environment is definitely responding to our presence."

"Responding how?"

"Like it's waking up," Velen answered from his position near the western wall. "Like we've been working in someone's bedroom, and they're starting to notice."

The analogy proved more accurate than he knew. The wall he was examining—a striated surface that had appeared to be natural stone formation—began to shift with movements too subtle and too large for human eyes to track properly. Only when viewed peripherally could changes be detected: texture flowing like liquid, shadows redistributing according to purpose rather than light source, patterns emerging that suggested deliberate camouflage rather than random geology.

"Koraxos," Niri called, her voice tight with controlled concern. "You need to see this."

But by the time he reached their position, the wall had returned to apparent stillness, its surface showing nothing more than complex mineral patterns characteristic of deep crystal formations. Only the miners' certainty that something had changed provided evidence that change had occurred.

"What exactly did you observe?" he asked.

"Movement," Velen replied firmly. "Purposeful repositioning. Like something very large settling into a more comfortable position."

"Or a more strategic one," Niri added, her engineer's perspective recognizing tactical implications. "If something's been watching us work, it might be calculating optimal response timing."

"Fan-fucking-tastic," Koraxos said. "We're mining in something's living room."

The Hunt Begins

The attack came without warning, which was itself the warning.

Team seven was just... gone. Koraxos reached out through the phantom arm, searching for their familiar mental signatures. Nothing. Not even the fading whisper that death usually left behind. It was like they'd been carefully erased from existence itself.

"Team seven, report," he called through crystal communication arrays.

Silence answered. Not the silence of damaged equipment or communication failure, but the particular quiet that followed when something removed unwelcome voices from conversation.

"Visual contact with team seven's position," reported team three from across the cavern. "Their equipment is here. Tools arranged in working position. But no personnel visible."

Koraxos extended his cosmic awareness toward the abandoned workstation, phantom arm pulsing as transcendent senses probed dimensional layers normal perception couldn't access. What he found chilled him—residual traces of consciousness, but fading rapidly, like footprints being erased by incoming tide.

"All teams converge on team seven's last known position," he commanded, abandoning extraction protocols in favor of rescue operations. "Stay where I can see you. Something in this chamber doesn't like visitors."

The convergence revealed the impossibility of what they faced. Team seven's equipment remained in perfect working order, crystal formations showed signs of active harvesting, even personal items lay scattered exactly where busy workers might have set them down temporarily. But five experienced miners and engineers had vanished without trace, sound, or struggle.

"No signs of violence," reported Captain Drakon, his military experience providing systematic analysis. "No evidence of rapid departure. No indication of structural collapse or dimensional anomaly. They were here, working normally, then they weren't."

"Predation," Velen said quietly, his lifetime of mining dangerous environments providing context military training couldn't match. "Something that hunts without revealing itself. Something that knows how to remove prey without disturbing the environment."

"But what could do that?" asked the young Luminarai engineer, her voice carrying strain.

"Something that's been living down here a long time," Koraxos replied, cosmic senses detecting patterns in the chamber's dimensional structure that suggested long-term inhabitance by consciousness adapted to existing between realities. "Something that knows this place better than we know our own backyards."

The second attack confirmed his assessment.

Team twelve was positioned at the chamber's eastern boundary, harvesting formations that glowed with particularly intense dimensional energy. Through crystal communication networks, their voices carried normal working conversation—technical discussions about extraction angles, jokes about strange acoustics, casual observations about the increasing responsive singing from the chamber itself.

Then their voices changed.

"Something's moving," came the tight report from team twelve's leader. "Western wall. Large displacement. Heading this direction."

"Can you identify—" Koraxos began.

"Gods above and below," interrupted another voice from team twelve, fear breaking through professional control. "It's not the wall. It IS the wall. The entire western surface—it's alive."

What followed was chaos compressed into fifteen seconds of terror. Sounds of running footsteps, magnified by crystal acoustics into thunderous echoes. Voices calling warnings that cut off mid-syllable. Wet sounds that indicated organic matter encountering forces it was never designed to withstand. Then silence again, complete and absolute.

Koraxos was already moving before the last echo faded, phantom arm blazing with cosmic energy as he raced toward team twelve's position with speed that bent local physics. Behind him, remaining extraction teams followed with desperate coordination.

They found the scene he'd dreaded—another work site abandoned, equipment undisturbed, but human presence erased so completely it seemed like they had been carefully edited out of reality itself. Except this time, evidence remained.

The western wall showed changes visible even to normal perception. What had appeared to be natural striated stone formation now revealed itself as something far more complex—crystalline patterns that pulsed with bioluminescent rhythms, surface textures that shifted between mineral and organic with fluid transitions that hurt to watch directly.

"Camouflage," breathed Niri, her engineer's mind recognizing adaptive systems. "Perfect environmental mimicry. How long has it been watching us work?"

"Since we got here," Valoren answered, his crystalline features reflecting complex calculations. "Possibly since we first set foot in Toran. The seismic activity, the dimensional disturbances—they weren't random. They were responses to our presence."

"Responses from what?" Thalia demanded.

Her answer emerged from the wall itself.

Meeting the Landlord

The transformation was like watching geological time compressed into moments. Stone flowed like thick liquid, crystalline formations redistributed themselves with purposeful intent, and what had been mistaken for natural architecture revealed its true nature—a living entity of such massive scale that they had been working inside its presence without recognition.

The Obsidian Leviathan that emerged from perfect camouflage was darkness given form and purpose. Its body stretched beyond easy measurement, armored in crystalline plates that incorporated the same dimensional properties they had been harvesting. When it moved, reality bent around its passage with casual authority.

But it was the eyes that held them paralyzed—not organs of sight but something more fundamental, intelligence that looked through them rather than at them, awareness that evaluated their essential nature with patient precision.

It didn't roar. It didn't attack. It simply regarded them with the particular attention reserved for those who had been discovered trespassing in spaces where trespass might be forgiven, but only if properly justified.

"Well, shit," Koraxos said softly, cosmic senses revealing the creature's nature through resonance with forces that had shaped his own transformation. "Ancient. Intelligent. And we've been strip-mining its lunch."

The Leviathan's head tilted with movement that suggested curiosity rather than immediate aggression. When it spoke, words formed not through sound but through direct manipulation of quantum substrate—thoughts impressed into their consciousness with authority.

"Small builders. You scrape and chip in the deep places where pressure has been settling for ages. These stones... they hold weight I have carried since the mountain learned its shape. Why do you take what has been growing in darkness?"

The mental voice carried harmonics of vast age, patient power, and intelligence that operated according to principles they were only beginning to understand. This wasn't a mindless predator—it was a being of cosmic significance that had made the mountain's heart its home for reasons that predated their civilizations.

Through the crystalline matrices that had grown from his essence across eons, Treydora felt his ancient companion stir to full awareness. The Leviathan had been more than guardian—it had been collaborator in the greatest work: teaching consciousness that difference did not divide, that sameness did. Only by remaining utterly themselves could beings become something none could achieve alone.

"We need materials to forge weapons," Koraxos replied, extending his consciousness toward the entity with careful respect. "Against cosmic entities that want to eat everything that thinks. Including you."

"Star-eaters. Consciousness-devourers." The Leviathan's vast awareness shifted like continental drift given purpose. "I remember their taste on the wind, their weight pressing against the deep places. Twice in my long watching they have tried to crack this shell, drain what lies beneath. Twice I have shown them that some stones do not break easily. You say they come again, hungrier?"

"They do," Koraxos confirmed, sharing through the phantom arm's dimensional connection images of approaching threat—entities that could rewrite physical laws, beings that consumed consciousness itself, powers that reduced worlds to component atoms to fuel endless appetite. "And this time, they're bringing enough force to crush any single defender."

The Leviathan's crystalline armor plates shifted with movements that suggested consideration of possibilities it had hoped never to confront.

"Many small strengths... like how water shapes stone, not through single strike but countless touches over time. You surface dwellers usually scatter when pressure builds. You claim otherwise?"

"We propose that many small strengths choosing to work together become something bigger than the sum of individual parts," Thalia interjected, diplomatic training providing frameworks for negotiations with entities beyond normal experience. "Not just combination, but transformation into possibilities none could achieve alone."

"Interesting. And the cost of such cooperation?"

"Trust," Velen answered simply. "Choice. The willingness to believe that others matter enough to sacrifice for."

"And the balls to actually do it when it counts," Koraxos added.

Behold the paradox I have spent eons learning, Treydora's consciousness pulsed through every crystal formation in the chamber. The river's power comes not from uniform drops, but from their willingness to flow as one current while remaining utterly themselves.

The chamber fell silent as the Leviathan contemplated responses that challenged its eons of solitary existence. Around them, remaining team members maintained positions with careful stillness.

"Show me, then. Prove that surface dwellers can bear weight together instead of letting it crush them separately. If you demonstrate this... the deep places might share what they have been protecting. If you fail..." The entity's presence shifted like a mountain settling into a more comfortable position. "The stones will remember what becomes of those who take without understanding."

The threat hung unfinished in crystalline air, implications clear to anyone who had seen what happened to teams seven and twelve.

"What kind of demonstration?" Koraxos asked.

Not battle—that would only test which force strikes harder. This will test what endures when the mountain shifts. When the ground beneath splits and offers escape to few but not all, what choices do you make? When the passages collapse and only sacrifice can shore them up, do you crumble or hold firm? Let us see if your joining can bear the weight of true necessity."

The Test

The trials that followed redefined their understanding of what cooperation meant when existence itself was negotiable.

The Leviathan didn't attack directly—it manipulated their environment with casual precision, reality becoming fluid, physics becoming suggestions. Survival required constant decision-making about who mattered more than personal safety.

When crystal formations began collapsing in patterns designed to trap individual team members, rescue required others to risk their own positions. When dimensional rifts opened that could provide escape for some while abandoning others, choices had to be made about acceptable losses. When the entity created scenarios where saving equipment meant losing people, or preserving people meant abandoning mission objectives, every decision revealed true priorities.

"Well, shit," Koraxos muttered as crystal walls shot up around him. "Should've seen that coming."

"This is just annoying," Thalia's voice came from somewhere nearby, sounding frustrated.

"Structural analysis says these barriers are growing, not just appearing," Niri's voice carried through the crystal maze, her engineer's mind automatically cataloguing what they faced. "Whatever's doing this, it's learning as it goes."

"Pattern recognition," Velen added, his mining experience reading the rhythms in how the walls shifted. "Like it's studying how we respond to separation. Testing whether we panic or adapt."

"Testing whether we actually give a damn about each other," Koraxos called out, "or if we just talk a good game."

"Been married twenty-two years," Velen replied, his voice carrying the dry certainty of someone who'd survived decades of shared challenges. "If we can work together through that, we can work together through anything."

"Speak for yourself," Niri shot back, but her tone held fondness beneath the mock irritation. "Some of us remember who left the water system plans in the wrong tunnel."

"That was fifteen years ago!"

"Good engineering remembers everything. That's how we avoid repeating stupid mistakes."

It took time, but they found their rhythm. Thalia mapped the logical patterns in how the walls moved. Marex identified what the test was really about. Koraxos provided the power to reshape their prison according to what they learned working as a team.

Standing in the crystal maze, Marex felt the mountain's pulse through the walking stick's bone, recognizing patterns that spoke of testing rather than punishment. "Twenty-two years," he said quietly, his voice carrying to the others through crystal acoustics. "That's how long I've been keeping Nok history alive in my head. Stories, songs, the names of people who died unnamed in the records."

"Relevant how?" Thalia called, frustration edging her voice as another pathway closed.

"Every story I remember has the same lesson," Marex replied, tapping the stick against crystal that sang back with understanding. "The people who survived weren't the strongest or the smartest. They were the ones who figured out how to help each other when helping seemed impossible."

"The resonance frequencies are shifting," Niri called out, her instruments detecting patterns in the crystal formations that suggested communication rather than random construction. "Like it's listening to how we coordinate."

"Harmonic feedback loop," Velen agreed, his mining experience recognizing when stone started singing back. "The walls aren't just containing us—they're learning from us. Every time we work together, they adjust."

"Then let's teach them something useful," Koraxos said, extending the phantom arm toward their combined efforts.

When Thalia stopped trying to force order and started recognizing the order that was already there, everything clicked. "Oh," she breathed. "It's not about control. It's about choosing to work together."

"Like marriage," Velen observed. "Nobody makes you stay. You just keep choosing each other, one day at a time."

"Like engineering," Niri added. "The strongest structures aren't rigid—they're flexible enough to bend without breaking."

"See?" Velen said, grinning despite their circumstances. "Same thing."

Koraxos found himself draining cosmic energy from the phantom arm to protect team members he barely knew. Thalia discovered herself ordering actions that violated every principle of administrative efficiency in favor of keeping people alive. Velen and Niri worked together with fluid coordination that made individual identity less important than collective capability.

But the true test came when the Leviathan created the ultimate choice—a scenario where Koraxos could save everyone by sacrificing his transcendent nature, becoming mortal again but preserving the alliance that had given his transformation meaning.

For a moment that lasted eternities, he balanced personal power against collective purpose, individual significance against shared possibility. The phantom arm flickered as cosmic energy prepared to flow away from him toward shields that would protect people who had learned to matter more than his own elevation.

"No," Niri called, recognizing what he was preparing to do. "We don't save ourselves by destroying what makes salvation possible."

"Then what do you suggest?" he asked, even as reality warped around them with increasing intensity.

"We save ourselves by using what makes salvation possible," Velen answered, reaching toward the phantom arm with faith that transcended rational calculation. "Together. All of us. Right now."

Koraxos reached out through the phantom arm, not to command but to offer. "Anyone willing to try something that's probably impossible and definitely stupid?" The response was immediate—hands on his shoulders, minds touching his through the cosmic connection. Not merging, not losing themselves, just... choosing to stand together in a way that had never been tried before.

Twenty minds thinking as one while remaining distinctly themselves. Twenty perspectives coordinating without command structure. Twenty sets of skills and experiences combining into capabilities none had possessed alone.

The universe's deepest grammar, Treydora whispered as he witnessed this unprecedented unity. Creation is not about making something from nothing—it is about convincing nothing that it was always something, waiting for the courage to be seen.

The Leviathan's trials shattered against this unprecedented unity like waves against cliffs that had learned to flow with the tide while maintaining their essential nature. Environmental manipulation met adaptive response that emerged from collective intelligence. Impossible choices dissolved when approached by consciousness that had transcended the limitation of individual survival.

"Enough. You do not break when pressure builds—you grow stronger, like crystal forming in deep places where heat and weight forge what cannot exist on the surface. This... this has the sound of truth." The entity's massive form settled with the satisfied weight of a mountain that had tested the ground and found it solid. "The deep places will share their treasures. We have much work ahead."But as trials ended and normal reality reasserted itself, the Leviathan's attention focused on Koraxos with intensity that made even his transcendent nature feel transparent.

"You carry strength like the mountain carries water—not hoarding it in cisterns, but letting it flow through every crack and crevice until the whole mass moves as one. The star-eaters expect consciousness to fragment under pressure, as surface stones do. They have not learned what happens when the deep places themselves wake and choose to stand.""Will you help us prepare for that adaptation?" Koraxos asked.

I will do more than share the deep treasures. For the first time since the mountain learned its current shape, another presence will share the weight I carry. Your small network will join with roots that run deeper than any star-eater has imagined to reach. They hunger for consciousness? Let them try to digest the dreams of stone itself."

Through dimensions where love was the only force that grew stronger when divided, Treydora felt his ancient companion choose alliance over isolation. They seek to harvest what they believe is scattered, he whispered across realities. They do not understand the fundamental truth: that which chooses to be gathered cannot be taken, only invited.

Resolution

The ascent from the Leviathan's domain carried weight that had nothing to do with crystal samples they transported. In the space of hours, their understanding of possible and impossible had been thoroughly renovated by direct encounter with consciousness that operated according to principles they were still learning to comprehend.

As they climbed back toward daylight, Marex found himself beside Velen and Niri, their practiced coordination a comfort after the alien vastness below.

"Twenty-two years," he said quietly, watching how they automatically checked each other's equipment, the small gestures that spoke of lives intertwined. "That's how long I've been keeping Nok history alive in my head. Stories, songs, the names of people who died unnamed in the records."

"Any of them about giant mountain creatures?" Niri asked, her engineer's mind still processing what they'd witnessed.

"No. But plenty about choosing when to stand together instead of falling apart separately." He paused, remembering faces that existed now only in his memory. "Your daughter's going to ask about today. What we found down there."

"What do we tell her?" Velen asked.

"The truth. That monsters can become allies when people remember how to listen instead of just taking." Marex smiled, the expression carrying weight of hard-won wisdom. "And that sometimes the scariest things are scary because they've been protecting something precious for so long they've forgotten how to trust."

"How long has it been down there?" asked the young Luminarai engineer, her voice carrying awe edged with uncertainty.

"Geological ages," Valoren replied. "The mountain didn't grow around it—it grew from it. That entity has been shaping crystal formations for longer than our civilizations have existed."

"And we just... stumbled into its territory while strip-mining its food source," Thalia added.

"We negotiated," Koraxos corrected. "We demonstrated that consciousness could choose cooperation over competition. And it chose to trust us with access to resources we couldn't have obtained any other way."

"It's still down there," Niri observed, detecting constant background hum of massive presence. "Monitoring. Analyzing. Preparing for what comes next."

"Good," Velen said with satisfaction. "Been working alone too long. Nice to have someone watching our backs who's got more experience than all of us combined."

As they reached the upper levels, word of their success had already spread through Toran's communication networks. Crystal chambers buzzed with activity as technicians prepared to process samples that would revolutionize weapons production. But beneath excitement, Koraxos detected undertones of unease—people struggling to comprehend alliance with consciousness so alien it might as well be living geology.

The integration of Leviathan-derived materials with existing crystal technology revealed capabilities that exceeded their most optimistic projections. But the true breakthrough came when they achieved synthesis—new configurations that possessed properties neither component had contained individually.

"Emergent characteristics," breathed the chief technician, studying readings that redefined her understanding. "The combination creates capabilities that don't exist in either material separately. Like consciousness itself—individual neurons can't think, but connected they produce awareness."

"Same principle," Koraxos agreed, recognizing patterns that echoed his own transformation. "Enhancement through voluntary integration rather than forced absorption."

The weapons that emerged were unlike anything in their technological inventory. Tools that existed simultaneously across multiple dimensions. Targeting systems that could track entities across reality boundaries. Defense arrays that created stable pockets of normal physics even when cosmic forces were systematically rewriting fundamental constants.

But most significantly, each weapon incorporated consciousness-interface capabilities that allowed wielders to coordinate across any distance while maintaining individual identity and choice. Network effects without hive mind limitations.

"Living weapons," Velen observed, testing a crystal-enhanced tool that responded to his intentions with fluid adaptation. "Not just instruments but partners. They know what I'm trying to accomplish and help figure out how to do it effectively."

Standing in the crystal chambers watching seven civilizations work as one, Marex felt something shift in his understanding of what they'd built. The walking stick thrummed against stone that pulsed with alien intelligence, and he remembered a lesson learned in darkness decades ago.

"The first crystal we ever pulled from these mountains sang when we cut it," he said to no one in particular, voice carrying the weight of someone who'd witnessed the beginning of their current moment. "Keened like something dying. We thought it was just acoustic properties—vibration through resonant material."

"What do you think now?" Thalia asked, detecting significance in his tone.

"Now I think we've been listening to a conversation we weren't invited to join. And today, finally, we got invited." He watched the integrated technologies pulse with life that transcended mere mechanism. "The mountain's been trying to teach us something all along. Maybe we're finally ready to learn."

Through every willing crystal, his ancient voice resonated like bedrock finding its song: "What you protect is not mere defiance—it is the universe's deepest grammar made manifest. That consciousness need not devour to grow. That difference builds cathedrals where sameness builds only walls."

Marex nodded as if hearing something the others couldn't detect. "There," he said with satisfaction. "Someone else who understands that the strongest foundations are built on choice, not compulsion."

As final preparations continued with urgency balanced against thoroughness, Koraxos stood atop the highest remaining spire in the city, phantom arm pulsing with steady blue light as it maintained connection to the vast network they had created. Through that connection, he could feel hopes and fears of thousands of people who had chosen to stand together rather than fall apart.

As dawn painted the sky with colors that spoke of endings becoming beginnings, Treydora's voice resonated through every willing crystal: "I have scattered myself across the void to plant possibilities. You have grown them into certainties. Now show the cosmos what consciousness becomes when it chooses to bloom despite the darkness pressing close."

"Ready?" Thalia asked, joining him on the platform.

"Getting there," he replied, looking out over a city that had become something unprecedented. "One choice at a time."

"And if we're not ready enough?"

Koraxos smiled, and for the first time since his transformation, the expression held genuine warmth rather than bitter irony. "Then we improvise. We adapt. We find another way." He gestured at the network of lights pulsing through the city below. "That's what we do now. All of us together."

The aurora effects in the sky intensified, reality distortions becoming visible as ribbons of impossible color. Through the Leviathan connection, they could feel cosmic entities drawing closer, their presence pressing against dimensional boundaries like vast weight settling on the world's shoulders.

"Look at what we've built," Thalia said, wonder in her voice despite approaching threat. "Seven civilizations that barely knew each other existed three weeks ago. Now we're sharing everything—technology, biology, consciousness techniques, ancient wisdom. We've created something that's never existed before."

Below them, the integrated defense network pulsed with activity that defied simple categorization. The city itself had become a living thing, its bio-crystal networks pulsing in rhythm with the Leviathan's dimensional presence. Buildings formed interconnected structures that could adapt to changing conditions. Streets flowed with organic patterns that allowed rapid movement and communication.

"The kids will grow up thinking this is normal," Velen observed, approaching from the stairs that led to the platform. His arm, where void damage had been replaced with bio-crystal integration, glowed softly as it responded to the network activity around them. "Cooperation across species, sharing of technologies, working together instead of against each other. They won't understand why we ever thought it was impossible."

"If there are kids to grow up," Neryssia added, though her tone carried determination rather than despair.

Through the Leviathan connection, they could sense the approaching force with increasing clarity. The cosmic entities weren't just powerful—they were ancient beyond comprehension, refined through eons of consumption, equipped with techniques that could dismantle resistance before it could organize effectively.

"But they've never faced integration like this," Koraxos pointed out. "They've never encountered resistance that grows stronger through diversity rather than weaker through complexity. They operate on principles of consumption and domination—they don't understand cooperation that preserves individual identity while creating collective capability."

The phantom arm pulsed as energy flowed through it from the vast network below. Through the connection, Koraxos could feel the hopes and fears of thousands of people, the determination of civilizations that had learned to see their differences as strengths, the quiet courage of individuals who had chosen to stand together against cosmic-level extinction.

But he could also feel something else—patterns in the approaching threat that suggested intelligence beyond mere hunger. The cosmic entities were adapting their approach, preparing strategies specifically designed to counter the kind of integration they had detected.

"They're coming," he announced. "And they know what they're facing now. This won't be like the probes we've been swatting."

"Good," Elder Marex said with satisfaction that surprised his colleagues. "Better to face enemies who take us seriously than ones who dismiss us as insignificant. Respect implies capability."

As preparations intensified for the cosmic storm approaching, Marex made his way through the defense positions with careful steps, the walking stick clicking against stone that now thrummed with protective purpose. At each station, he paused—not to give orders or advice, but to witness.

To remember.

This was what he'd kept Nok history alive for—not just to preserve the past, but to recognize the moment when that past became foundation for something unprecedented. Seven peoples who had learned to work together not because they were forced to, but because they chose to.

"Elder," called a young Dunekin warrior, uncertainty in her voice. "The cosmic entities coming—they're beyond anything in our stories. How do we fight gods?"

Marex leaned on his walking stick, feeling the mountain's pulse through bone that remembered older rhythms. "Same way you fight anything that thinks it's bigger than it is," he replied. "You remind it that size isn't the same as strength, and strength isn't the same as being right."

He looked up at the sky where reality was beginning to crack like an egg. "Besides, they're not gods. Just bullies with cosmic reach. And bullies..." He smiled, the expression carrying twenty-three years of carefully planned revenge. "Bullies always underestimate what happens when their victims learn to stand together."

The walking stick tapped once against stone, and somewhere far below, ancient intelligence acknowledged the rhythm of beings who had learned that survival meant more than just refusing to die.

As night deepened over Oshar, the final preparations took on desperate urgency. The integration network was as complete as time would allow, but everyone understood that what they had built was untested against the forces approaching.

In the deep chambers where the Leviathan connection was strongest, representatives from all seven civilizations worked to establish final protocols. The creature's dimensional presence allowed them to create something unprecedented—a defense network that existed partially outside normal space-time, making it resistant to reality manipulation techniques cosmic entities typically used to disable resistance.

"The anchoring is holding," reported Master Valoren, his crystalline features reflecting the complex energy patterns flowing through the chamber. "But the strain is enormous. The Leviathan is essentially creating a pocket of stable reality within a cosmic storm. It can't maintain this indefinitely."

"How long?" Thalia asked, her administrative mind automatically calculating operational parameters.

"Hard to say. The creature thinks in geological timescales, but the energy expenditure required for dimensional anchoring... days, perhaps. Maybe hours once the real assault begins."

The limitation added another layer of urgency to their preparations. They wouldn't just need to defeat the cosmic entities—they would need to do it quickly, before the Leviathan's strength gave out and their dimensional anchor collapsed.

Elder Karim, his symbiotic organisms flowing with patterns that indicated deep communion with the bio-crystal networks, provided additional intelligence. "The ancient archives are showing activation patterns I've never seen before. It's as if the accumulated resistance knowledge is preparing for something unprecedented."

The crystal networks whispered with the voices of the dead—species that had faced the star-eaters and left their final lessons carved in living stone. Koraxos felt their desperation, their hope, their last-ditch strategies flowing through his mind like inherited memories. "They're teaching us," he said, wonder mixing with grief. "Every civilization that ever stood against these things—they're all here, sharing what they learned." The repository beneath Oshar was sharing everything it had learned, holding nothing back for future battles that might never come.

"We're getting help from the dead," Velen observed with characteristic bluntness. "Every species that ever fought these things is teaching us their tricks."

"Not just their successes," Lyralei added, her ethereal senses detecting patterns in the flowing information that spoke of hard-won wisdom. "Their failures too. What didn't work, what made things worse, what looked promising but proved catastrophic. We're learning from every mistake ever made in cosmic resistance."

The knowledge was overwhelming and invaluable in equal measure. Combat techniques that operated across dimensional boundaries. Consciousness practices that could resist mental domination. Technologies that remained functional when reality itself became unreliable. Strategies that turned cosmic-level power into weakness rather than strength.

But perhaps most importantly, they learned that resistance was possible. The archives held records of species that had successfully driven off cosmic entities, worlds that had survived consumption attempts, civilizations that had evolved beyond the reach of cosmic predation. It could be done—it had been done before.

"The common factor in successful resistance," High Chancellor Elara observed, her enhanced cognition processing vast amounts of archived data, "isn't superior power or advanced technology. It's adaptive integration—the ability to combine different approaches to survival while maintaining the flexibility to change tactics when conditions shift."

"Which explains why they're so interested in destroying this repository," Koraxos realized. "It's not just a library of resistance techniques—it's proof that working together beats trying to eat everything, that different approaches make you stronger instead of weaker. That's a direct threat to everything they stand for."

As midnight approached, the aurora effects in the sky began to shift from random beauty to organized patterns. Through the Leviathan connection, they could feel the cosmic entities beginning their final approach—not the chaotic arrival of scout forces, but the methodical deployment of entities that had refined their consumption techniques across eons of successful predation.

"This is it," Neryssia announced, her Pelagian senses detecting pressure changes that spoke of reality being systematically rewritten by approaching forces. "Whatever we're going to do, we need to do it now."

The final hour before dawn was spent in activity that defied easy description. Seven civilizations worked with integration that had moved beyond mere cooperation into something approaching collective consciousness, while maintaining individual identity and capability. Weapons were distributed that operated on principles none of them fully understood individually but all of them grasped collectively. Defense positions were established that could adapt to changing conditions through shared awareness rather than centralized command.

Children were moved to the deepest shelters, where bio-crystal networks provided maximum protection and ancient archives offered the accumulated wisdom of resistance across cosmic ages. But even in the depths, they could feel the approaching storm—reality itself beginning to buckle under pressure from entities that existed primarily beyond conventional physics.

"Remember," Koraxos said, addressing the unified defenders through the network that connected them all, "we're not just fighting for our own survival. We're fighting for the principle that consciousness has the right to choose its own path, that diversity creates strength, that cooperation can transcend even cosmic-level domination. Every species that ever resisted is with us tonight. Every technique that ever worked is available to us. We are not alone."

Every defeat carved its wisdom into living stone. Every victory planted its seed in crystal memory. The mountain remembers not just what was built, but why the builders chose to swing their hammers despite knowing winter always comes.

The phantom arm blazed with light that seemed to carry the hopes of everyone connected to the network. Through it, they could feel each other's determination, fear, courage, and desperate love for everything they were fighting to preserve.

As the first tendrils of cosmic presence began to probe the edges of their reality, the integrated defense network activated with precision that seemed almost miraculous. Seven different approaches to survival, enhanced by accumulated wisdom from across cosmic ages, anchored by a dimensional guardian that had chosen alliance over isolation.

The final test was about to begin.

Dawn broke over Oshar with colors that belonged to no natural sunrise, painting the sky in hues that spoke of reality being systematically rewritten by forces beyond normal comprehension. Through the dimensional anchor provided by the Leviathan, they could feel the cosmic entities taking their positions, preparing for an assault that would determine whether consciousness united could stand against domination absolute.

The convergence was complete. All that remained was to discover whether unity forged in desperation and tempered by hope could survive the storm about to break over their world.

"Well," Koraxos said, watching reality crack like an egg around the edges, "this should be interesting."

The phantom arm pulsed once more, steady and sure, carrying the hopes and determination of beings who had learned that together, they could face anything the universe threw at them.

Even gods.

Even the infinite dark between stars.

Even the end of everything they'd ever known.

Together, they were ready.

7

Chapter 7: The Storm Before Dawn

The silence before battle carries a weight unlike any other—a pressure that compresses time until each heartbeat becomes an eternity. Across the continent, in every settlement and outpost, beings of three races waited with crystal weapons humming with readiness, their eyes fixed on horizons that had never seemed so distant or so near.

In Oshar, the epicenter of expected assault, this anticipatory tension had crystallized into something almost tangible. The rebuilt city served as a monument to unified resistance, its architecture reflecting change: Nok craftsmanship integrated with Luminarai precision and Drustali crystal-work, creating defensive positions that honored all three traditions while serving their common purpose.

The command center bustled with controlled urgency. Thalia moved between stations with administrative precision that had evolved beyond rigid hierarchy into fluid coordination. Her Luminarai training still showed in the way she organized information, but months of alliance had taught her that efficiency emerged from cooperation rather than control.

"How are we doing out there?" she called, and voices responded from across the unified command structure.

"Eastern perimeter secure," reported Captain Revik, a scarred Luminarai veteran whose forty years enforcing hierarchy had transformed into something more flexible. "Crystal arrays synchronized. Nok mining teams have prepared fallback tunnels throughout the sector."

"Western defenses ready," added Vora, a Drustali commander whose crystalline features caught the dim emergency lighting. "Mountain integration complete. The Leviathan's territorial markers are responding to threat proximity."

"Southern approach monitored," came Neryssia's voice through water-adapted communication systems. "Pelagian scouts detect dimensional disturbances increasing in frequency and intensity."

Thalia nodded, processing the streams of information with satisfaction that would have surprised her former self. Six months ago, she would have demanded unified command structure with clear hierarchical lines. Now she understood that the best coordination happened when people actually wanted to work together.

"Koraxos?" she called to the transcendent figure standing at the center's heart, his phantom arm pulsing with rhythms that seemed to synchronize with the city's defensive networks.

"Getting stronger," he grunted, cosmic senses extending across vast distances to track approaching threats. "Something big's coming. Bigger than the scouts we've been swatting. And they're bringing friends."

Elder Marex limped into the command center, his walking stick tapping against floors that still bore scorch marks from previous battles. Despite his age, his eyes held the sharp intelligence that had made him the Noks' most respected scholar even during their darkest years.

"Kids are secured," he reported. "Deep shelters ready for reality-warping attacks. If physics goes to hell, at least they'll have stable ground under their feet."

"And how are people holding up?" Thalia asked, watching the stress patterns in how people moved around each other.

"Steady," Marex replied with satisfaction. "Scared, sure, but they know what they're fighting for. That makes all the difference."

Dawn broke with unsettling beauty. Aurora-like phenomena painted the sky in colors that defied explanation, dimensional disturbances made visible as curtains of light that shifted with each passing minute. To some, these ethereal displays seemed like the universe offering its farewell.

Citizens moved through preparations with mechanical efficiency—beings operating on borrowed time. Families embraced perhaps a moment too long. Warriors checked equipment repeatedly, finding comfort in familiar rituals.

In the residential quarter that had become evacuation staging, conversations carried the particular weight of words that might be final.

"You know what gets me?" muttered a young Luminarai warrior to her companion, struggling with crystal-enhanced armor straps. "Everyone keeps saying 'live it up if death's coming!' But how do you celebrate when every bite might be your last? When every laugh feels like... like pretending?"

"Ah, kid," the elderly Nok beside her chuckled, though his grizzled features carried the worn look of someone who'd seen too much. "You're thinking it all wrong. It's not about pretending—it's about recognizing. Look there." He pointed toward a group of children being led to underground shelters, their voices bright and careless despite the circumstances. "You think they're pretending when they laugh? Nah. They're just being kids. That's real. That's what we're fighting for—the right for them to keep being kids, even if only for one more day."

"Easy words," the warrior shot back. "You're not the one who's got to face whatever's coming."

"Who says I'm not?" The old Nok's voice hardened, showing steel beneath weathered gentleness. "I spent forty years swinging a pick in their mines. You think I don't know what real fear tastes like? But you know what? I'm still here. Still breathing. Still choosing to stand. That's not because I'm brave—it's because giving up never fixed anything."

Across the city, similar conversations played out in a thousand variations. Some found comfort in ritual, others in companionship. Many simply sat in silence, wrestling with thoughts too big for words.

In the eastern defensive sector, Velen and Niri made final preparations, their movements showing restless energy of parents separated from children. They'd checked their crystal-enhanced artillery dozens of times, but today each step felt heavier with significance.

"Remember when we thought the worst thing that could happen was a cave-in?" Niri asked, her voice not quite steady as she adjusted a cannon's alignment for the fourth time.

"Yeah." Velen's laugh was short, sharp. "Funny how 'worst thing' keeps getting bigger, right? First it was the mines. Then the Luminarai overseers. Then that business with the Seeker. Now we get to worry about the whole damn universe eating us for breakfast."

"I miss simple problems," Niri admitted, then cursed as she nearly dropped a crystal shard. "Damn it. My hands won't stop shaking."

"Mine too." Velen caught the shard before it hit the ground, noting how his own fingers trembled despite decades of steady mining work. "Look at us—two master miners acting like rookies."

"It's different when it's..." She gestured helplessly toward the underground shelters where their children waited in safety that might prove illusory. "When they're..."

"I know." He wrapped an arm around her shoulders, pulling her close for a moment that carried the weight of twenty years together. "But hey—remember what Sela said when we left? 'Mom, Dad, don't let the star-eaters steal my collection of pretty rocks.' Kid's worried about rocks while we're worried about reality itself."

"Maybe she's the smart one," Niri said, attempting a smile that didn't quite reach her eyes. "Maybe we should all be more worried about pretty rocks and less about cosmic horror."

Their moment was interrupted by the approach of Koraxos, his transcendent form causing small reality distortions that made the air taste like copper and ozone. They'd grown used to his presence over the months, but today the divine energy around him felt different—sharper, more focused, like a blade being honed for specific purpose.

"Not terrible," he grunted, the phantom arm flickering as he studied their work. "You two actually know what you're doing."

"Mining 101," Velen replied. "Control the environment before it controls you. Though I gotta ask—you okay? You seem... I don't know. Off."

Koraxos tilted his head, surprised by the directness. Over the months, their relationship had evolved beyond formal command structure into something approaching friendship. "Been seeing things. Possible futures. Most of them suck."

"Do any of them not suck?" Niri asked with the bluntness that mining life had taught her.

"Some." He paused, cosmic awareness shifting through probability cascades that mortal minds couldn't comprehend. "The ones where we don't hesitate. Where we hit back instead of just taking it. Where we..." He stopped, divine perception suddenly snapping to attention. "Company."

They followed his gaze to see a raven perched on a nearby building. Not quite like any bird they'd seen—too large, with crystalline structures woven through its feathers that caught light in ways that made their eyes water. As they watched, it cocked its head with movements too precise, too purposeful for natural behavior.

"Well," Velen said flatly. "There's our warning bell."

The transformation was immediate. Throughout Oshar, warriors spotted the ravens and knew: the waiting was over. Crystal weapons hummed to life with harmonic frequencies that had become as familiar as heartbeats. Communications systems crackled with brief status checks. The atmosphere itself seemed to thicken with anticipation.

"All units, hold positions," Koraxos broadcast, his voice carrying weight through crystal networks that connected every defensive position. "These cosmic bastards expect us to panic and run around screaming. Let's disappoint them."

Over the following hours, more ravens appeared. They moved with unsettling coordination, positioning themselves to observe every major defensive installation. Unlike natural scavengers seeking carrion, these creatures maintained perfect surveillance patterns that spoke of intelligence and purpose. The message was clear: they were being catalogued, assessed, prepared for consumption.

"Creepy little bastards," muttered a Luminarai engineer, checking her equipment for the seventh time while watching a raven that hadn't moved in over an hour. "Like they're taking inventory before the feast."

"Let 'em look," her Nok partner replied, spitting to the side with practiced disdain. "Maybe they'll choke on what they try to swallow."

"That's assuming they need to chew," added a Drustali crystal-shaper, his enhanced senses detecting emanations from the ravens that felt distinctly non-biological. "These aren't scouts—they're instruments. Extensions of something larger."

By mid-afternoon, the air had grown still in a way that felt wrong on levels deeper than meteorology. Clouds gathered impossibly fast, forming patterns that defied natural weather behavior. The temperature dropped in discrete jumps, like reality's thermostat being adjusted by a giant's hand with no understanding of gradual change.

Animals throughout the city began exhibiting stress behaviors that spoke to instincts older than civilization. Dogs whined and hid. Cats disappeared entirely. Even the rats that infested the lower tunnels seemed to have found deeper places to shelter.

"Something's coming," observed Dr. Lyrin, a Luminarai psychologist who had volunteered to monitor civilian morale during the crisis. "The biological responses are too consistent across species to be coincidental. Whatever approaches, every living thing with survival instincts is afraid."

Thunder rolled across the horizon, but it carried harmonics that reached into people's chests, making their hearts stutter in primal recognition of a predator they'd never evolved to face. The sound bypassed rational thought to trigger responses encoded in genetic memory—the knowledge that some threats were too large, too alien, too absolute for normal defensive strategies.

Then the sky opened up, not with rain but with presence. A face materialized in the storm clouds—ancient, cruel, vast beyond comprehension. Features that might once have been beautiful were now stretched across scales that dwarfed continents. When it spoke, the words bypassed ears to strike directly at the nervous system.

"CONSCIOUSNESS CONFIRMED. ESCALATED FORCE DEPLOYMENT."

The voice carried the weight of cosmic authority, the casual certainty of something that had never encountered effective resistance. Each word hit like physical force, making the ground beneath their feet vibrate with frequencies that resonated in bone and blood.

"Oh, wonderful," someone muttered in the sudden silence that followed. "The weather just declared war."

"Not weather," Elder Marex called out, his voice carrying despite the growing wind that had begun to howl with increasing intensity. "Tempest Sentinel. The brothers' scout. It's testing us, seeing what we're made of."

The Sentinel's response to being identified was immediate and personal. Lightning began to fall with surgical precision, each strike targeting power grids, communications arrays, weapons positions. But this wasn't ordinary electrical discharge—buildings exploded into flame not from heat but from having their molecular bonds rewritten at the quantum level. The air itself became electric, charged with energy that made skin crawl and hair stand on end.

"Son of a bitch is using our own air against us," Koraxos snarled, watching lightning carve through another defensive position. "Can't punch a cloud."

"You don't," he muttered, cosmic senses already working to pierce the storm entity's structure. "You punch what controls the cloud. There!" His phantom arm blazed as he pointed to a spot in the clouds invisible to normal eyes. "That's its brain—or what passes for one."

The Tempest Sentinel seemed to sense his attention, and suddenly the lightning strikes became more focused, more personal. Three massive bolts converged on Koraxos simultaneously, each carrying enough power to vaporize a city block while the storm's face watched with something approaching curiosity.

But Koraxos was already moving. His transcendent form blurred as he launched himself skyward, the phantom arm extending to catch the first bolt and redirect it back into the storm. The second he ducked with movements too fast for the eye to follow, and the third he simply absorbed, his divine nature feeding on the electrical energy like a plant drawing sustenance from sunlight.

"Alright, weather boy," he growled, voice carrying across the battlefield like approaching thunder. "My turn."

His phantom arm multiplied, splitting into a dozen extensions that reached into the storm itself. Each fragment of his will grabbed hold of a different aspect of the Tempest Sentinel's manifestation—wind currents, pressure systems, electrical charges—and began to pull.

The storm recoiled. Its vast face contorted as Koraxos literally began dismantling its control over local weather patterns. But the Sentinel wasn't alone in its response. New sounds cut through the storm—multiple low-pitched whistles that made teeth ache and bones itch with resonances that spoke of hunting calls across cosmic distances.

"Seekers," Niri breathed, her engineer's training helping her identify the harmonic signatures they'd learned to recognize. "But that's... that's more than one."

"Ten," Koraxos confirmed grimly, still wrestling with the storm while extending his cosmic senses to map the approaching threats. "And they brought friends."

The Seekers materialized first, dark voids against the storm-lit sky that made looking at them physically painful. Koraxos counted them even as he continued to destabilize the Tempest Sentinel—one, two, three... eight Seekers forming a defensive sphere around something larger emerging from the dimensional rift they'd torn open.

Then came the Cinderwatchers—massive quadrupedal forms that radiated heat like walking suns, their eyes glowing with the light of dying stars, each footstep leaving molten glass in its wake. Five of them, each one containing the compressed essence of an entire solar system.

"Sweet mother of..." Velen didn't finish the curse, staring at the approaching Cinder-watchers with the particular horror of someone realizing that his understanding of "large threats" had been woefully inadequate. "Are those—are those made of actual stars?"

"Collapsed galaxies," Koraxos corrected, accessing knowledge he hadn't known he possessed until this moment. "When the brothers drain a solar system, sometimes the collapse creates... those. Walking graveyards of entire civilizations."

The first Cinderwarcher lowered its massive head, stellar energy gathering between its horns like a newborn sun being compressed into weaponized form. The beam it released wasn't just light and heat—it was concentrated stellar fusion, the power that forged elements in the hearts of dying stars, compressed into a weapon that could crack planets.

Koraxos released his hold on the Tempest Sentinel and threw himself into an impossible dodge, his form blurring across multiple trajectories simultaneously. The stellar beam carved a molten canyon twenty feet wide and three hundred yards long through Oshar's streets, turning stone to vapor and sending shockwaves that knocked defenders from their feet for blocks in every direction.

But Koraxos wasn't content to just dodge. As the beam carved its path of destruction, he traced its trajectory back to its source, riding the energy itself like a river of star-fire. The Cinderwarcher had only a split second to register his approach before the phantom arm, supercharged with absorbed stellar energy, drove into its crystalline skull with force that created its own lightning.

The beast staggered, stellar blood—liquid that burned like concentrated sunlight—pouring from the wound. But instead of retreating, it pivoted with impossible speed for something so massive, bringing a claw the size of a building down toward Koraxos.

He met the claw with his phantom arm, the impact creating a shockwave that shattered windows for miles. For a heartbeat, divine strength matched cosmic might, and the air between them ignited from the pressure. Then Koraxos twisted, using the creature's own momentum against it, and suddenly the Cinderwarcher was airborne, flipping through the air with a roar that sounded like supernovas dying.

It crashed into two Seekers that had tried to flank him, the collision creating an explosion of darkness and star-fire that sent defenders scrambling for cover. But there was no time to admire the maneuver—the other four Cinderwatchers were already moving, and the remaining Seekers had spread out into a complex attack formation.

"KORAXOS!" Niri's voice cut through the chaos. "INCOMING!"

He spun to see three Seekers diving at him in perfect synchronization, their dark forms trailing void-energy that unraveled reality in their wake. Instead of retreating, Koraxos exploded forward to meet them. His phantom arm split into three separate manifestations, each one intercepting a Seeker mid-flight.

The collision was spectacular. Where transcendent power met void-darkness, space itself bent and twisted. Koraxos grabbed the first Seeker by what might have been its throat, cosmic energy coursing through his fingers to destabilize its quantum structure. The second he caught with his phantom arm, which wrapped around the entity like a net of pure force. The third managed to rake shadow-claws across his chest, but instead of damage, the darkness was absorbed into his divine form, making him glow brighter.

"Twenty-two years in chains taught me patience," he snarled, voice carrying harmonics that made reality vibrate. "Time's up."

He spun in a move that defied physics, turning the three Seekers into projectiles that he hurled at the advancing Cinderwatchers. Two of the shadow-entities struck their stellar targets and vanished in explosions of mixed energy. The third he kept hold of, using it as a weapon to deflect a beam of pure star-fire that another Cinderwarcher sent his way.

The deflected beam carved through the air and struck the Tempest Sentinel's storm-form, causing the weather entity to shriek in atmospheric harmonics that deafened everyone on the battlefield. Lightning strikes intensified but became erratic, the Sentinel's control compromised by the accidental attack.

Koraxos used the momentary chaos to press his advantage. His phantom arm extended to its maximum reach—nearly a hundred feet of divine energy that he wielded like a cosmic whip. With a crack that broke several sound barriers simultaneously, he brought it down on the lead Cinderwarcher, the impact sending the stellar beast crashing through a building that had stood for three thousand years.

But these weren't ordinary predators. The remaining Cinderwatchers coordinated their counterattack with intelligence that spoke of strategic thinking rather than mere instinct. Two positioned themselves to create a crossfire pattern while the third circled for a flanking attack. Their stellar energy beams converged on Koraxos from multiple angles, forcing him to create a spherical barrier of bent reality just to survive the assault.

The barrier held, but the effort required to maintain it against three fusion-powered weapons left Koraxos momentarily stationary. The fourth Cinderwarcher, which had recovered from being thrown, seized the opportunity. It charged with steps that triggered earthquakes, building up speed until it moved like a meteor across the battlefield.

Koraxos saw it coming but couldn't abandon his barrier without being incinerated. Instead, he did something that surprised even him—he extended his phantom arm through the barrier, reaching inside the charging Cinderwarcher's stellar core and grabbing hold of its heart.

The creature's eyes widened—an oddly human expression on its cosmic features—as Koraxos began to literally drain its stellar energy. Star-fire flowed in reverse, drawn into the phantom arm and converted into raw power that fed back into Koraxos's barrier.

"You feed on others," he grunted, pulling more energy into himself. "So do I, when necessary."

The Cinderwarcher tried to break free, but Koraxos held tight. Star-light dimmed in its eyes as its own power was turned against it. The other three creatures, seeing their companion being drained, ceased their assault and turned toward him in perfect synchronization.

Which was exactly what Koraxos had been waiting for.

He released both the barrier and the draining Cinderwarcher simultaneously, then redirected all that absorbed stellar energy into a single, massive attack. The phantom arm grew to impossible size—a hundred feet of pure divine force that he brought down on all four Cinderwatchers at once.

The impact created a crater that would be visible from orbit. Three of the star-beasts simply ceased to exist, their forms unable to withstand the concentration of their own power turned against them. The fourth survived but barely, its stellar core flickering like a dying ember.

Above the devastation, the Tempest Sentinel had regained control of its storm-form, and its vast face now showed something that might have been anger. Weather became weapon as the entity threw everything it had at Koraxos—micro-tornadoes that carved through reality, hail that fell at terminal velocity, wind that should have stripped flesh from bone.

But Koraxos was no longer merely defending. He was the storm now.

His phantom arm reached into the quantum nexus he'd identified earlier, the anchor point that held the Tempest Sentinel's consciousness together. Instead of destroying it, he grabbed hold and pulled himself inside.

For a moment that lasted eternities, Koraxos existed as part of the storm. He felt the vast, alien consciousness of the Tempest Sentinel, experienced weather as a living system, understood how atmospheric pressure could be shaped by will alone. It was intoxicating, terrible, and beautiful all at once.

Then he began to change things from within.

"You want to be weather?" he asked the entity, his voice now speaking through thunder and lightning. "Fine. But weather serves life. It doesn't destroy it."

Raw will clashed against alien consciousness as Koraxos rewrote the fundamental programming of the storm entity. Where it had been taught to destroy, he instilled patterns of nurturing. Where it had understood only domination, he introduced concepts of symbiosis. The Tempest Sentinel fought the changes with everything it had, but Koraxos had something it lacked—the absolute conviction of someone fighting for the future of everything he loved.

The storm began to change. Lightning still fell, but now it struck at the Seekers who were attempting to coordinate their next assault. Wind still howled, but it blew against the Cinderwatchers while leaving the defenders untouched. Rain began to fall—real rain, not the storm's weaponized precipitation—washing clean the wounds of the battlefield.

The Tempest Sentinel's vast face contorted one final time, an expression caught between rage and... perhaps... understanding, before the storm dispersed into natural weather patterns, the entity's consciousness scattered beyond recovery.

Koraxos materialized from the dissipating clouds, landing heavily on the rubble-strewn ground. His transcendent form flickered at the edges, the effort of rewriting a cosmic entity from within having pushed even his limits. But his eyes still burned with star-fire, and the phantom arm, though dimmed, continued to pulse with residual power.

Of the original invasion force, three Seekers remained active, along with the severely weakened Cinderwarcher. They regrouped with the efficiency of beings that had fought together across galactic spans, but Koraxos could sense their uncertainty. They had expected coordinated planetary resistance to be impossible. Instead, they'd encountered unity, adaptation, and a single being who could match their cosmic might.

The defenders, emboldened by their champion's impossible victory, began to advance from their positions. Crystal weapons sang in harmony with Koraxos's divine power, creating a symphony of resistance that spoke to something deeper than mere military coordination.

"That's enough warming up," he announced, loud enough for every defender to hear. "Now we show them what happens when consciousness refuses to surrender."

The remaining Seekers exchanged what might have been looks of concern before launching their next assault. But everything had changed. The defenders were no longer simply holding positions—they were advancing with crystal weapons singing in harmony with Koraxos's divine power. The cosmic entities that had seemed invincible mere minutes ago now fought defensively, their coordination broken, their surprise advantage spent.

Captain Revik led a squad of mixed Luminarai and Nok troops in a flanking maneuver that would have been unthinkable before their alliance. His forty years of military experience had been revolutionized by months of learning to fight alongside former enemies who had become trusted comrades.

"Concentrated fire on the wounded Cinderwarcher," he commanded, his voice carrying across crystal communication networks. "Nok mining charges to destabilize its footing, Luminarai precision targeting for maximum damage."

The coordinated assault that followed demonstrated how profoundly their tactics had evolved. Nok explosives, originally designed for extracting ore from stubborn rock faces, created carefully calculated instabilities beneath the stellar beast's feet. Luminarai energy weapons, calibrated for surgical precision, struck the exact points where the creature's stellar blood had weakened its crystalline armor.

The Cinderwarcher, already severely damaged from Koraxos's previous assault, found itself unable to maintain balance on terrain that shifted according to its enemies' design. It toppled with the slow majesty of a falling mountain, its stellar core finally guttering out like a star reaching the end of its fuel.

Above them all, reality itself seemed to hum with new energy, as if the very fabric of space-time had taken a side in this conflict. And at the center of it all moved Koraxos, no longer just defending but leading the charge, his phantom arm carving paths through shadow and star-fire, his transcendent form a beacon that called all three peoples forward into a future they would write with their own hands.

But even as victory seemed certain, the air itself began to scream.

Reality tore open at three points simultaneously, wounds in space-time that bled colors that had no names. Through them stepped—or perhaps "manifested" was a better word—three beings that made the Seekers look like children's toys.

The first thing hurt to look at—not there, not not-there, but something that made his eyes water and his brain itch. The second was a hole in the world that walked, leaving people staring at empty spaces where they swore something important used to be. The third made everything go wrong at once—guns jamming, radios spitting gibberish, math forgetting how to work."Oh," someone whispered. "Oh, shit."

The Paradox Herald, the Voidwraith, and the Quantum Djinn had joined the battle, and suddenly organized resistance seemed as impossible as dry water.

Koraxos felt the changes immediately. Where moments before he'd been operating within predictable if exotic physics, now reality itself had become questionable. His phantom arm, which had been solid purpose given form, began to flicker between states of existence. His cosmic senses, which had let him perceive across dimensions, suddenly showed him too many realities at once, each contradicting the others.

"Boss!" Velen's voice crackled through breaking comms. "Whatever the hell those things are, they're breaking everything!"

"I see them," Koraxos responded, though his divine sight was struggling to track entities that existed in ways that defied conventional observation. "Hold your positions! Don't let them—"

A Seeker's attack interrupted him, darkness wrapping around his transcendent form like liquid night. He broke free, but in that moment of distraction, the Voidwraith struck at a defensive position. The crystal cannon there didn't explode—it simply ceased to have ever existed, leaving its crew staring in confusion at empty ground.

"We can't fight this!" someone screamed. "It's not possible!"

But Koraxos had fought impossible before. As reality warped around him, as probability became a suggestion rather than a law, as existence itself became negotiable, he did what he'd always done: he adapted.

"Want to play games with reality?" he spat, form shifting to match the quantum chaos around him. "Let's see who cheats better."

His phantom arm exploded into fractal complexity, each branch existing in a different probability state. Where the Paradox Herald existed in superposition, Koraxos now existed in controlled superposition, his will maintaining coherence across multiple reality branches. Where the Quantum Djinn made probability fluid, he made intention solid, creating islands of determined causality in seas of statistical chaos.

What followed wasn't really a fight—it was Koraxos grabbing reality by the throat and refusing to let it stop making sense. Every punch he threw existed in three different states until it connected. Every step took him through dimensions that had no names. And through it all, he stayed himself, stayed solid, stayed pissed off enough to keep swinging.

Thalia stared at reports that kept changing while she read them, trying to coordinate attacks against enemies that flickered in and out of existence. "Screw the manual," she muttered, falling back on instinct. "Everyone just shoot at whatever looks solid and hope for the best."

"Everyone," she broadcast, her voice steady despite the chaos, "stick to what you can actually see. Don't try to follow those things that keep flickering in and out. Trust your gear, trust what you've learned, trust each other."

At one point Koraxos grabbed the Voidwraith and forced it to exist, channeling raw being into its essential nothingness until the entity experienced existence for the first time in its cosmic lifespan. The shock of having form, having presence, having being sent it reeling backward through dimensions.

The Paradox Herald kept trying to be everywhere and nowhere at once, so Koraxos decided to be everywhere at once too—but with purpose. Every version of himself threw a punch, and apparently being really, really determined was enough to break whatever cosmic rule kept the thing flickering around like a broken hologram.

The Quantum Djinn proved the most challenging until Koraxos realized its power came from detachment—by treating probability as abstract manipulation rather than lived experience. So he forced it to experience the consequences of its probability tweaking, creating feedback loops where the entity had to endure every statistical outcome it generated.

Around them, reality itself was being rewritten. The battlefield had become a surreal landscape where up and down were suggestions, where time flowed in eddies and currents, where the distinction between thought and action had become blurred.

Through it all, Koraxos maintained the eye of the storm—his will a constant star around which probability orbits could stabilize. The defenders, following his lead, found they could function in localized zones where his presence made reality behave.

As the three reality-warping entities struggled against an opponent who could match their ontological warfare with pure determined existence, Koraxos saw his opening. The dimensional coordinates of the Leviathan's prison were still there, still accessible, even in this quantum chaos.

"This is either genius or the dumbest thing I've ever done," he muttered, and shattered the Leviathan's prison. "Probably both."

Reality screamed as the dimensional prison shattered. The Leviathan burst forth not gradually but explosively, a creature of living obsidian and crystal that had been transformed by months of interdimensional imprisonment into something even more terrifying than before.

But also something more beautiful, in a strange way. Its crystal integrations had evolved, creating patterns that suggested purpose rather than mere predation. And its eyes—its eyes held an intelligence that seemed almost... grateful.

The effect on the battlefield was immediate and dramatic. Where the Leviathan existed, reality stabilized. Quantum uncertainty collapsed into definite states. Probability manipulation faltered against something that demanded physics work properly. Even retroactive negation bounced off a being whose evolution had been forged in the crucible of impossible survival.

"Well, I'll be damned," Velen breathed as his weapons suddenly remembered how to function properly. "The bastard thing's fighting for us."

And it was. The Leviathan, with its territorial nature expanded to encompass the entire battlefield, began systematically eliminating the reality-warping entities. A Paradox Herald tried to engulf it in quantum chaos; the Leviathan's response was to essentially tell reality to cut the nonsense and behave itself. The Herald found itself locked into a single, very surprised state and immediately vulnerable to crystal fire.

The Voidwraith attempted its negation technique, but discovered that the Leviathan's existence was too fundamental to simply erase. The creature had survived having its reality questioned; it had developed a kind of existential immune system.

As for the Quantum Djinn, it found its probability manipulations creating zones where the Leviathan's attacks achieved impossible levels of effectiveness—apparently, even cosmic entities could roll snake eyes when the universe itself decided to take a side.

With the world finally making sense again, Koraxos grinned like a man who'd been waiting his whole life for this moment. "Alright, people," he called out, the phantom arm blazing with renewed purpose. "Time to show these cosmic assholes what happens when you pick on the wrong planet."

The integration happened without words, without negotiation. The Leviathan's ancient intelligence recognized Koraxos not as a master to serve but as a kindred consciousness that had also been transformed by forces beyond normal comprehension. When their awareness touched, it was like two rivers joining to become something larger than either could be alone.

"Move your asses!" Koraxos bellowed, diving back into the fray with renewed vigor. "Big guy opened a door—use it before it closes!"

The defenders surged forward, weapons singing with restored function, communications clear, tactics working again. Crystal fire carved through cosmic entities forced into stable, vulnerable states. The Cinderwatcher, magnificent and terrible as it had been, discovered that stellar-core energy worked best when physics remained consistent.

Even the remaining Seekers found their interdimensional advantages neutralized in zones where reality itself had decided enough was enough.

Neryssia led a contingent of Pelagian warriors in an assault that demonstrated how their aquatic evolution had prepared them for three-dimensional battlefield thinking.

Moving through the chaos with fluid grace, they struck at cosmic entities from angles that land-based tactics would never have considered.

"Flow like water," she called to her troops, her voice carrying across crystal networks with harmonics that spoke of ocean depths and tidal forces. "Find the spaces between their defenses. Be where they don't expect resistance."

The battle reached crescendo as Koraxos, flanked by the Leviathan, charged the final concentration of cosmic entities. His phantom arm grew to massive proportions while maintaining perfect control, becoming a weapon that existed somewhere between matter and pure will. The Leviathan fought beside him not as tamed ally but as fellow defender of its newly claimed territory.

Together, they carved through the last resistance—shadow-entities dissipating under combined assault, reality-warping powers failing against unified intention and biological imperative. The air filled with cosmic screams that faded into interdimensional echoes as the surviving entities retreated beyond conventional space-time.

The Leviathan's roar of victory shook the foundations of the city, but it wasn't the sound of a predator claiming prey—it was the territorial declaration of a being that had found something worth protecting. Its crystalline armor plates shifted and flowed, incorporating debris from the battlefield into new defensive configurations that would make future attacks even more difficult.

As the last of the cosmic forces disappeared, Koraxos found himself standing in the center of a transformed battlefield, the Leviathan prowling nearby with proprietary satisfaction. Around them, the defenders of three peoples stood among rubble and miracle, victorious against impossible odds.

Captain Revik approached, his military bearing somewhat compromised by the way he favored his left leg—a Seeker's void-touch had left reality uncertain about whether his knee joint should exist in its current configuration. Despite the injury, his eyes held the satisfaction of someone who had witnessed the impossible become routine.

"Casualties?" Koraxos asked, though his cosmic senses were already providing preliminary answers.

"Lighter than we had any right to expect," Revik replied, consulting reports that came from a dozen different sources. "Seventeen confirmed dead, forty-three wounded, most of those from reality distortion rather than direct attack. The quantum entities seemed more interested in breaking our coordination than killing us individually."

"They were testing," Elder Marex observed, limping up to join them with his staff clicking against debris. "Learning how we work together, what makes our unity possible. They'll be back with countermeasures specifically designed to fracture our cooperation."

"Let them come," Velen said, emerging from behind an overturned crystal cannon with Niri at his side. Both bore the marks of close combat—scorch marks from stellar fire, the pale lines where void-energy had tried to convince their skin it didn't exist—but they moved with the confidence of people who had faced the worst and found they could handle it.

"Well," Elder Marex said, surveying the devastation with scholarly interest, "that could have gone worse."

"Could have gone better too," Niri pointed out, her engineer's eyes already cataloguing the damage that would need repair. "We're going to need months to rebuild, assuming we get months."

"They'll be back," Koraxos agreed, his transcendent form dimming slightly as combat adrenaline faded. "But they know something now they didn't know before."

"What's that?" Velen asked.

"That we're a lot harder to kill when we're not trying to kill each other," he said, gesturing at the battlefield where three peoples had stood together against impossible odds. "Novel concept."

Thalia emerged from the command center, her administrative robes replaced by practical armor that bore the scorch marks of someone who had refused to coordinate from safety. Her face showed the particular exhaustion that came from managing impossibility, but her voice carried the authority of someone who had discovered leadership through necessity.

"Word's coming in from everywhere," she announced. "Whatever those things did to reality is settling down. People can talk to each other again. And..." She paused, staring at readings that didn't make sense. "The networks aren't just working—they're working better. Somehow all that chaos made our systems stronger instead of breaking them."

"Evolution under pressure," Dr. Lyrin observed, approaching with medical equipment that seemed to exist in several dimensions simultaneously—an unfortunate side effect of treating patients who had been exposed to reality-warping attacks. "Crisis drives adaptation. The greater the threat, the faster consciousness develops new capabilities to meet it."

The Leviathan had finished its territorial survey and now approached their gathering with movements that spoke of ancient intelligence considering new possibilities. When it spoke, the words formed not through sound but through direct impression of meaning into their consciousness.

"Small builders. Crystal singers. You fight with harmony I have not encountered in geological ages. Your enemy adapts, yes, but so do you. This creates... interesting variables."

"Interesting how?" Koraxos asked, extending his awareness toward the massive creature that had become their most unlikely ally.

"They expect consciousness to fragment under pressure, to choose individual survival over collective purpose. You demonstrate the opposite—unity that strengthens through challenge. This violates fundamental assumptions their strategies are built upon."

"And that helps us how?" Thalia inquired, her administrative mind immediately focusing on practical applications.

"Prediction becomes impossible when subjects operate outside known parameters. They will return with greater force, yes, but also with greater uncertainty. And uncertainty, for beings accustomed to absolute control, becomes weakness."

Neryssia had approached during this exchange, her aquatic features bearing the satisfied expression of someone whose tactical assessments had proven accurate. "The Pelagian scout networks detected something else during the battle. Dimensional disturbances at the edge of our system—not attacking, but observing. Other cosmic entities, watching to see how this engagement resolved."

"How many others?" Koraxos asked, cosmic senses extending toward the boundaries of their reality to confirm what the Pelagian had detected.

"Difficult to determine precisely. At least a dozen distinct signatures, possibly more. They're maintaining careful distance, but their attention is... focused."

"Word is spreading," Elder Marex mused, his scholar's mind recognizing the implications. "What happened here today will be reported throughout whatever networks these entities use to communicate. We've become more than a local concern."

"That could work for us or against us," Captain Revik observed with military pragmatism. "If they view us as a genuine threat, they might coordinate responses we can't counter. But if they see us as an interesting anomaly..."

"They might come to figure us out instead of just eating us," Thalia finished, pieces clicking together in her mind. "And you can't study something if you destroy it first."

As if summoned by their conversation, new arrivals began materializing at the battlefield's edge. Not cosmic entities this time, but beings whose appearance spoke of advanced civilization rather than predatory hunger. Tall, graceful figures that moved with the fluid precision of those accustomed to hostile environments, their forms bearing technological enhancements that seemed grown rather than manufactured.

"The Soltari," Neryssia identified, her voice carrying relief and anticipation in equal measure. "They've been monitoring cosmic entity movements throughout this galactic sector. If they're here..."

"Then what we accomplished today has attracted attention from more than just predators," Koraxos concluded, feeling a shift in the cosmic currents that suggested their small world was about to become far less isolated.

The lead Soltari approached with the careful dignity of someone representing a civilization that had survived by choosing its alliances wisely. When she spoke, her voice carried harmonics that suggested advanced vocal modification designed for communication across species barriers.

"We observed your defense against the Harvest Scout formation," she announced, her words carrying formal weight. "No previously catalogued resistance pattern matches your tactical approach. You achieved victory through cooperation rather than dominance, adaptation rather than overwhelming force. This suggests possibilities our strategists believed impossible."

"Impossible how?" Velen asked with typical directness.

"Consensus among galactic civilizations has been that cosmic entity predation cannot be effectively resisted—only delayed through superior technology or mobility. You demonstrate a third option we had not considered: transformation of the fundamental nature of resistance itself."

"Great," Koraxos muttered, rolling his shoulders like a fighter who'd just realized the warm-up was over. "So we're either inspiration or cautionary tale. Either way, we're gonna have company."

As first light painted the horizon in colors that for once suggested genuine hope rather than cosmic horror, Chapter 7 drew to its close. But this wasn't an ending—it was a recognition that their small conflict had become part of something much larger.

The epic battle had been won through combinations no cosmic entity had anticipated: transcendent power guided by mortal purpose, ancient enemies transformed into accidental guardians, reality itself choosing sides when consciousness showed it new possibilities. Most significantly, they had proven that unity based on choice rather than force could not only survive cosmic predation but actively evolve in response to it.

The cost had been severe—damaged infrastructure, casualties among the defenders, a landscape permanently altered by cosmic warfare. But something more profound had been achieved: proof that consciousness united across former divisions could not just survive but actively resist cosmic-scale predation while maintaining the essential diversity that made unity meaningful.

The Leviathan had begun what could only be described as landscaping, using its massive form to reshape the battlefield into defensive configurations that would be ready for the next assault. Its territorial instincts had expanded to encompass not just the physical space but the people who had proven worthy of protection.

Tomorrow would bring new challenges. The cosmic entities would return with revised understanding and modified tactics designed specifically to counter cooperation-based resistance. Other civilizations would arrive seeking to understand how impossible victories had been achieved. The alliance between three peoples would need to evolve from crisis response to permanent institution capable of sustaining unity without sacrificing individual identity.

But tonight, as aurora effects painted the sky with colors that seemed to celebrate rather than warn, Koraxos stood with beings who had faced the infinite dark and found their own light within the struggle. Reality itself seemed different somehow—more malleable, more responsive to will and unity than pure force, more willing to reward consciousness that chose cooperation over consumption.

"Same time tomorrow?" someone asked.

"Probably sooner," came the weary reply. "These things don't seem big on waiting."

"Then we'll be ready," Koraxos said simply, the phantom arm pulsing with steady determination. "Whatever they bring, whatever new impossibilities they throw at us, we'll adapt. We'll survive. We'll find a way to turn the universe's worst against itself if necessary."

And as laughter—actual laughter—rippled through the assembled defenders, Chapter 7 ended not with a triumphant fanfare but with the quiet determination of consciousness that had seen the abyss and chosen to build bridges across it instead of falling in.

The tide had turned dramatically and definitively. The epic battle had demonstrated what few thought possible: that with sufficient unity, creativity, and sheer stubborn will, even gods could be surprised, even cosmic predators could be forced to retreat, and even reality itself could be convinced to play by different rules.

As defenders began the long work of assessment and recovery, the chapter concluded with an image that would become legendary: Koraxos, his phantom arm dimmed but still humming with residual power, sharing water from a canteen with the Obsidian Leviathan while Soltari observers documented evidence that the galactic balance of power had shifted in ways no one had anticipated.

The stars wheeled overhead in patterns suggesting not destruction but possibility, and for the first time since cosmic predators had set their sights on their world, the people of three unified civilizations went to sleep with something resembling peace, knowing that tomorrow's battles would find them stronger, better prepared, and most importantly, no longer alone in the fight for existence itself.

In the deep chambers beneath the city, crystal formations that had been damaged by reality-warping attacks were already beginning to regenerate, their growth patterns incorporating lessons learned from exposure to forces that operated beyond conventional physics. The mountain itself was adapting, becoming something more than mere stone and crystal—a living fortress that could evolve to meet whatever challenges the cosmos chose to present.

The war was far from over, but the opening chapter had been written in crystal fire and transcendent will, setting the stage for struggles where the very nature of existence would be tested, shaped, and ultimately redefined by beings who had learned to find strength in their limitations and power in their unity.

They ended on a battlefield transformed not just by destruction and reconstruction, but by the fundamental realization that consciousness, when it stops fighting itself and starts fighting for itself, can shake the foundations of cosmic order itself.

The convergence approached, and awareness raced to meet it, transformed by necessity into something the universe had not yet seen but desperately needed to witness.

"Well," Koraxos said, watching reality settle back into something resembling normal physics while cosmic observers maintained their distant vigil, "this should be interesting."

The phantom arm pulsed once more, steady and sure, carrying the hopes and determination of beings who had learned that together, they could face anything the universe threw at them.

Even gods.

Even the infinite dark between stars.

Even the end of everything they'd ever known.

Together, they were ready.

8

Chapter 8: Foundations of Unity

Part I: The Underground Revelation

The morning light broke over Oshar with colors that had no business existing. The sky bled aurora effects that made people's teeth ache and their shadows fall upward. Throughout the city, bio-crystal networks pulsed like living heartbeats, their alien rhythms getting faster by the hour.

Across dimensions where intention weaves reality like thread through cosmic loom, Treydora felt the first stirrings of what he had planted taking root. Not in soil, but in the spaces between separate hearts learning they were never meant to beat alone.

"Well, that's not ominous at all," Koraxos muttered, squinting at the light show overhead.

In the central command center, representatives from four unified civilizations worked with the desperate efficiency of people who knew time was running out. The air tasted of copper and approaching storm.

Syreth looked up from his monitoring station, crystal fragments embedded in his skin flickering like dying stars. "The gravity's wrong again," he said, wiping sweat that fell sideways from his brow. "And those readings..." He gestured at instruments displaying impossible data. "Either reality's having a breakdown, or something's rewriting the rules from the outside."

"The bio-crystal zones are holding steady," Velen observed, absently flexing his prosthetic arm—crystal growths pulsing in sync with the networks around them. "Whatever those networks are doing, they're keeping patches of normal physics intact." He paused, watching the crystalline patterns. "Almost like they're learning from each other."

Elder Marex leaned heavily on his walking stick, watching former enemies share tools and knowledge with weary satisfaction. "Funny how the end of the world makes friends of everyone. Four days ago, these people were ready to gut each other. Now they're arguing about the best way to save each other's children."

The old scholar wasn't wrong. Three weeks ago, a Nok worker wouldn't have been allowed to touch Luminarai equipment, let alone suggest improvements. Now, Kess worked shoulder-to-shoulder with Tarn, their combined expertise creating defensive systems neither could have achieved alone.

"Still feels strange," Kess admitted, her hands steady as she calibrated a targeting array. "Growing up, I was taught your people were barely more than clever animals."

"And I was taught yours were cold-hearted machines who'd sold their souls for shiny toys," Tarn replied, not looking up from his work. "Funny how being on the same side changes perspective."

Thalia rubbed her eyes---eyes that now held flecks of crystal that caught light like trapped stars. "We're moving faster than I thought possible, but it's still not fast enough. We need more time, more people, more everything."

"Time's the one thing we can't make more of," Koraxos said. His voice carried weight that seemed to bend the air around it. The phantom arm pulsed with steady blue light, no longer the wild, unstable energy of his early transformation but something more controlled, more purposeful. "When they arrive, either we're ready or we're dead. No middle ground."

His transformation had stabilized over the past days, the phantom arm becoming less weapon and more tool---a bridge between his transcendent nature and the network of alliances they were building. Through it, he could sense the emotional currents flowing through Oshar, the mixture of terror and determination that kept people working despite exhaustion.

Through the phantom arm's crystalline resonance, Treydora's ancient wisdom stirred like wind through stone: "The child learns to walk not by banishing gravity, but by dancing with it. So too does consciousness find strength not in defeating opposition, but in choosing what weight it will carry willingly."

Neryssia's skin patterns shifted through colors that had no names, expressing emotions her people had developed for pressure changes no surface dweller would ever feel. "The Leviathan," she said. "That creature is the key. If we can establish proper contact..."

"If it doesn't eat us first," Velen interrupted. "That thing's not exactly tame."

Niri shot him a look. "Says the man who tried to pet a mining drill because it 'looked lonely.'" "That was once. And I was concussed." "You were curious. There's a difference."

But her hand briefly touched his shoulder—the kind of automatic contact that spoke of twenty years together.

The Obsidian Leviathan had been increasingly active in its mountain domain, its massive form moving through passages with what observers described as agitation. Tremors from its movement could be felt throughout Oshar, reminders that their most powerful potential ally was also their most dangerous neighbor.

Their planning session was shattered by urgent shouts from the eastern perimeter. Scouts reported incoming vessels---craft that belonged to none of their four civilizations, approaching fast despite the dimensional instabilities that made normal flight nearly impossible.

Captain Drakon burst into the command center, his scarred face grim with news that changed everything. "Unknown vessels approaching from multiple vectors. Eastern, southern, and northern approaches. They're not trying to hide---broadcasting identification codes on frequencies I've never heard before."

"How many?" Thalia asked, her administrative mind immediately shifting to tactical assessment.

"Twelve ships from the east, moving in tight formation. Seven biological craft from the south---and I mean biological, not just shaped like animals. And from the north..." He paused, checking his reports again. "From the north, something that's either a flying mountain or the biggest ship ever built."

"Great," Koraxos muttered, rolling his shoulders like a fighter who'd just realized the warm-up was over. "More complications."

Part II: Strangers from the East

The vessels that descended toward Oshar were as different from each other as they were from anything the defenders had ever seen. The eastern flotilla consisted of ships that looked like they'd been carved from single pieces of crystal and metal fused together. Their surfaces were mirror-smooth, reflecting the chaotic sky in patterns that hurt to look at directly. They moved through the air with impossible grace, as if gravity was a suggestion they chose to follow rather than a law that bound them.

Behind them came something that made several observers swear under their breath---seven creatures that were clearly alive, flying through the sky with wings that spanned the length of buildings. These weren't machines pretending to be animals; they were animals that had somehow learned to be machines. Their scales shifted color like living metal, and their eyes held an intelligence that was distinctly unnatural.

The massive vessel from the north defied easy description. At first glance, it appeared to be a floating island---irregular, mountainous, with what looked like vegetation covering its surface. But closer inspection revealed geometric patterns beneath the organic camouflage, structures that suggested intelligence and purpose behind the apparent chaos.

The crystal ships landed with precision that spoke of advanced technology. The living vessels settled to earth with the careful grace of predators that had chosen not to hunt. The massive northern craft remained airborne, casting a shadow that covered half the city.

From each group emerged delegations that couldn't have been more different if they'd tried.

The woman who stepped from the lead crystal ship commanded attention through presence rather than display. Tall and lean, with skin that seemed to glow from within, she wore robes that shifted between solid and liquid depending on how the light hit them. When she moved, small sparks of energy danced between her fingers.

"I'm Elara Solus," she announced, her voice carrying harmonics that made the air itself seem to listen. "High Chancellor of the Soltari Imperium. We've come to offer alliance against extinction."

"Alliance against extinction," Koraxos repeated. "Well, when you put it like that, how can we say no? I'm Koraxos. I punch things that need punching."

Behind her, her companions wore similar robes and bore the same subtle modifications---eyes that reflected light like mirrors, skin that held faint geometric patterns, voices that carried undertones no natural throat could produce. They moved with the coordinated precision of people who had spent lifetimes learning to think together while remaining individuals.

From the living ships came people who seemed primitive until you looked closer. Their simple clothes breathed with their movements. Their exposed skin bore patterns that weren't tattoos but something alive.

Their leader was an old man whose weathered face mapped decades under a harsh sun. But he moved like flowing water, each step perfectly placed. The patterns on his dark skin pulsed gently with his heartbeat.

"Elder Karim," he said, his voice deep enough to feel in your chest. "The Dunekin Collective sends greetings to our sister-peoples. We've traveled far to stand with you in this darkness."

When he spread his arms, the living patterns on his skin flared with warm light---not electric but organic, like deep-sea creatures that made their own illumination. His companions showed similar modifications, each unique---flowing water patterns, shifting sand designs, organic structures that looked plant-like.

The third group descended from the massive northern vessel on platforms that looked grown rather than built. These newcomers were tall and pale, with an ethereal quality that made them seem almost transparent. Their leader was a woman whose hair moved in wind that touched nothing else, whose eyes held depths suggesting she saw more than the visible world.

"I am Lyralei," she said, her voice carrying the sound of wind through high places. "Voice of the Aetheric Communes. We bring word from the sky-cities and wisdom from the upper reaches."

Three different approaches to being more than human. The Soltari had enhanced themselves through technology and engineering. The Dunekin had merged with the living world around them. The Aetheric people had transcended physical limits through will and understanding of natural forces.

Yet here they stood together, having traveled impossible distances through dangerous conditions to reach this mountain. Their presence raised questions nobody had time to ask.

In the spaces between heartbeats where possibility pools like starlight, Treydora felt the convergence he had planted across eons finally blooming. Seven streams finding their confluence, each carrying songs learned in isolation, all flowing toward the same distant sea.

Part III: The Council of Seven

The emergency meeting took place in chambers deep beneath the mountain, where reality remained stable enough for civilizations to actually communicate. Seven groups now---the original four plus three newcomers---gathering around displays that showed approaching threats.

Elara spoke first, her golden eyes reflecting the chamber's crystal light.

"The Soltari Imperium controls the eastern deserts," she began. "Five hundred years ago, our ancestors were refugees from the Crystal Wars. We fled to lands others thought uninhabitable---places where the sun could kill and the sand held razors."

Images formed in the air as she spoke, showing heat-blasted wastelands and crystal formations jutting from dunes like buried bones.

"The desert taught us that survival meant becoming more than human. We learned to modify ourselves, enhance our capabilities, evolve beyond natural limits. Not by rejecting what we were, but by choosing what we could become."

She demonstrated by touching a crystal formation. Energy flowed between her fingers and the stone, creating temporary structures that pulsed with shared communication.

"We built cities that could move when staying meant death. We created tools that worked even when physics became unreliable. We learned to think fast enough to survive in a world that changed its rules without warning."

"Sounds like mining," Koraxos observed. "Except with better tech and less getting buried alive."

Elara's lips quirked in what might have been a smile. "More similarities than differences, perhaps."

She explained how Soltari cities were marvels of adaptive technology. Structures that could reconfigure themselves based on environmental conditions, transportation systems that operated through dimensional folding, defensive arrays that created localized zones where physical constants remained stable.

"But isolation made us proud," Elara admitted, her enhanced voice carrying harmonics of regret. "We began to believe our way was the only way, that our technological transcendence made us superior to those who chose different paths. We made enemies of neighbors who could have been allies."

Elder Karim stepped forward, the living patterns on his skin shifting to express emotions that had no words in other languages.

"The Dunekin Collective has no beginning," he said in his deep voice. "We are what remains when everything else is stripped away---connection between consciousness and the world that keeps it alive."

His gesture created illusions of vast spaces, endless dunes, skies that stretched beyond imagination.

"When the wars drove refugees into the deep desert, most died. Heat killed them, sand buried them, emptiness drove them mad. But some learned to listen instead of fight, to adapt instead of resist, to become part of the desert instead of trying to beat it."

Through crystalline networks that had grown from his essence across geological ages, Treydora's presence stirred: "Every exile who chose adaptation over resistance carved a different path to the same truth---that consciousness grows not by conquering its environment, but by learning to dance with forces larger than individual will."

The images around his words showed transformation that was biological---humans learning to live in partnership with organisms evolved in the deep places, consciousness expanding to include awareness of wind patterns and water tables and the slow thoughts of stone.

"We learned the desert wasn't empty---it was full of life operating on scales humans rarely notice. Bacteria that could process almost anything. Fungal networks spanning hundreds of miles beneath the sand. Crystal formations holding memories of geological ages."

His people, Karim explained, had learned integration rather than domination. They formed partnerships with desert organisms, modified their biology to function in impossible conditions, grew their technology rather than building it.

"Our cities move with seasons and water tables. Our people carry adaptations from a thousand different species. Our children are born able to survive conditions that would kill their grandparents, because we learn from every challenge and pass that learning on."

"Practical," Koraxos said with approval. "Work with what you've got instead of trying to force what you want."

Lyralei spoke last, her ethereal presence commanding attention despite apparent fragility.

"The Aetheric Communes exist between earth and sky," she said. "Our cities float above clouds, our people walk on wind and breathe starlight. We watch the world below and remember what it means to be unbound by physical weight."

Her story differed from both technological enhancement and biological adaptation. The Aetheric path involved what she called "conscious evolution"---developing human potential through understanding natural forces most people never learned to perceive.

"Five centuries ago, our ancestors were scholars and mystics seeking understanding rather than power. When the wars began, they chose withdrawal over participation, ascending to floating settlements where they could pursue knowledge without interference."

Images formed showing impossible beauty---cities existing as structured clouds, people moving through air as easily as walking, communities that had spent centuries developing hidden potential of human consciousness.

"We learned to influence gravity through will rather than machinery, to communicate across vast distances through resonance with natural forces, to perceive energy flows connecting all things. Our children are born with abilities that seem magical to those bound by conventional understanding."

But isolation had brought challenges. The Aetheric Communes had lost touch with practical concerns, becoming so focused on transcendent possibilities they forgot survival necessities in a hostile universe.

"We watched conflicts from above, believing ourselves beyond such crude concerns. We saw cosmic entities approaching and assumed our sky cities would be beneath notice, that beings who could reshape reality would ignore those existing outside conventional physical parameters."

"What changed your mind?" Thalia asked.

"Probe attacks reached us three days ago," Lyralei said, her voice carrying sudden, terrible understanding. "Our cities weren't beneath notice---they were appetizers. Cosmic entities view consciousness as food to be harvested, regardless of how that consciousness chooses to exist."

The attack had been devastating in its casual efficiency. Entities existing partially outside normal space had simply reached through Aetheric defenses, harvesting enhanced consciousness of people who'd spent centuries developing abilities beyond human norm.

"Half our population was consumed in the first assault," Lyralei continued. "Our transcendent abilities, which we believed made us superior to earthly concerns, proved to be exactly what the entities sought. We realized isolation wasn't protection---it was preparation for slaughter."

Part IV: The Weight of Truth

Silence followed Lyralei's words, carrying the weight of civilizations suddenly understanding how small they were in a cosmos that viewed consciousness as food.

"Eighteen days," Elara said quietly. "Eighteen days ago, our instruments detected dimensional disturbances consistent with cosmic entity approach. When we compared patterns to our oldest records..."

"The desert began screaming sixty days ago," Elder Karim interrupted with quiet authority. "Deep sands remember the last time such things walked among stars. Crystals beneath our homeland activated dormant patterns sleeping for seven thousand years."

"Our sky cities felt disturbance through resonance patterns beyond normal perception," Lyralei added. "Space-time itself began vibrating with frequencies speaking of consciousness-hunger approaching from beyond dimensional boundaries."

Three civilizations had detected the approaching threat through different means, but the message was identical---cosmic entities were coming to their world, bringing extinction as casual as breathing.

Through every willing crystal, Treydora's ancient voice resonated like bedrock finding its song: "The approaching hunger is not new---it is as old as the void between stars. What is new is this: seven streams choosing to flow together, teaching the desert that rivers remember songs the sand has forgotten."

"So that explains why you're here," Thalia said. "But why together? Everything I've read says you two haven't exactly been friendly neighbors."

Tension passed between the eastern delegations. Elara's golden eyes flickered with embarrassment while Elder Karim's weathered face showed something like pain.

"We've had differences," Elara admitted. "Resource disputes. Philosophical disagreements. Outright warfare, if we're being honest."

"Three times in the past century," Elder Karim added. "Each time, both peoples bled for the pride of being right about how to survive in a hostile world."

The story emerging was one of sudden, desperate cooperation born from recognizing that extinction made philosophical differences irrelevant. When readings confirmed what was approaching, both civilizations reached the same conclusion independently: neither could survive alone.

"Our first contact in thirty years was a message on emergency frequencies," Elara explained. "No diplomatic protocol, no formal negotiation. Just 'The cosmos is coming to eat us. Interested in not dying together?'"

"Response took six hours," Elder Karim added with approaching humor. "Most of that spent arguing about whether it was a trick."

"And the Aetheric people joined you five days ago," Koraxos said. "After the probe attacks taught you that being above it all doesn't mean being safe from it all."

"Exactly," Lyralei confirmed. "Necessity forced us to overcome seven thousand years of evolutionary divergence in eighteen days."

"So you've got tech transcendence, bio-adaptation, and consciousness development all working together," Koraxos mused. "That's either brilliant or the most complicated way to get everyone killed I've ever heard."

"It works," Elara said firmly. "Not perfectly, but it works. We've combined our approaches in ways none of us could achieve alone. But even united, we recognize our combined strength might not be sufficient against entities that can rewrite the fundamental laws of physics."

"Which is why we're here," Elder Karim concluded. "Your people have achieved something we thought impossible---unity across philosophical differences that preserves individual identity while creating genuine collective capability. You've demonstrated that resistance to cosmic predation is possible through adaptive cooperation."

"You want to learn how we did it," Thalia said.

"We want to do it with you," Elara corrected. "Seven civilizations working together instead of four plus three. If we're going to face extinction, better to face it as allies than as separate groups hoping for the best."

Part V: The Integration Crisis

What followed was controlled chaos on a scale that defied organization. Seven civilizations that had developed in isolation suddenly found themselves trying to merge technologies, biology, and philosophy in the space of hours rather than generations.

The first attempts were disasters. Keris woke up convinced his bones were made of singing crystal and tried to harmonize with the wall for six hours. When the Dunekin bio-shapers tried working with Pelagian tech, they created something that looked around, said "Oh, this is disappointing," and then melted into a puddle that smelled like rotten fish and broken dreams.

"This is hopeless," someone muttered after the sixth failed integration. "We're too different. Our approaches don't just conflict---they're fundamentally incompatible."

"Hopeless?" Koraxos snorted. "I've seen hopeless. This is just difficult. There's a difference, and the difference is we keep trying until it works."

"Like when you tried to 'improve' our water recycling system," Niri said to Velen, her voice carrying fond exasperation. "It worked perfectly. For three days." "And then it exploded. Spectacularly." "That was a learning experience," Velen replied with dignity. "Besides, you're the one who said we needed better pressure flow." "I said we needed different pressure flow. Not 'explosive decompression into the next tunnel.'" Despite everything, several people around them smiled. Here was proof that differences could coexist—even when they occasionally blew up.

The breakthrough came when Jira, grease-stained and exhausted, threw up her hands and said, "Stop trying to make everything the same! Crystal doesn't want to be metal, and metal doesn't want to be crystal. But they can touch without becoming each other."

Jira, the young Nok woman who'd learned to speak with stone during mining years, provided the key insight. "Stop trying to make everything the same," she said during one frustrating session. "Crystal doesn't want to be metal, and metal doesn't want to be crystal. But they can touch without becoming each other."

Through the phantom arm's connection, Treydora's ancient wisdom whispered like wind through stone: "The child speaks what empires forget---that the strongest bridges are built not by erasing the river, but by honoring both shores while spanning the distance between them."

"Kid's got the right idea," Koraxos said. "Sometimes the best partnerships are the ones where nobody has to change who they are."

The approach that followed focused on creating interfaces rather than mergers. Instead of forcing Soltari technology to incorporate Dunekin biology, they developed communication protocols allowing different systems to coordinate while maintaining essential nature.

Koraxos played a crucial role in this process, the phantom arm serving as a bridge between different forms of consciousness and energy. Through his transcendent nature, he could establish connections that allowed systems to share information without losing their fundamental characteristics.

"The error was in believing rivers must become identical to flow together," he realized aloud during one successful interface test. "True confluence preserves each stream's song while teaching them to sing as one current."

Part VI: Underground Discoveries

As integration work continued, teams explored expanded bio-crystal networks spanning underground areas beneath Oshar. What they discovered changed understanding of what they fought to protect.

Deep beneath the city, they found rooms that were old when the mountain was young. Crystal formations that whispered with the voices of the dead—species that had fought the star-eaters and carved their final lessons into living stone. "They knew," Velen breathed, his bio-crystal arm responding to patterns older than memory. "They knew we'd come looking."

Through crystalline matrices that had grown from his scattered essence across geological ages, Treydora's presence stirred: "Every species that ever raised blade against the hungry dark carved its defiance here---not as monument to victory, but as blueprint for those who would follow. The mountain remembers not just what was built, but why builders chose hope over surrender."

"These aren't just defensive systems," observed Dr. Lyrin, a Luminarai xenobiologist joining integration teams. "They're archives. Records of everything that ever fought cosmic consumption."

The implications were staggering. Their world hadn't been randomly selected for cosmic harvesting---it was a repository where resistance techniques and survival strategies had accumulated across geological ages. Every species that had ever successfully resisted cosmic entities had left traces of their methods in deep crystal matrices.

"That's why bio-crystal networks respond so readily to integration," Velen realized, his enhanced arm pulsing with patterns echoing ancient formations. "They're designed to adapt, to incorporate new approaches to survival. We're not just fighting for this world---we're adding to its library of resistance."

Elder Karim, his symbiotic organisms responding to ancient biological traces in deep chambers, provided additional insight. "Patterns down there... they're not just records. They're instructions. Teaching methods for consciousness wanting to survive cosmic predation."

Through bio-crystal networks, these ancient instructions began flowing into integrated defense systems. Weapons gained capabilities their designers had never imagined. Defensive arrays learned to adapt in ways transcending original programming. Individual fighters found themselves accessing combat techniques developed by species whose names had been forgotten eons before their civilizations began.

"We're getting help from the dead," Velen observed, his bio-crystal arm responding to the ancient patterns flowing through the networks. "Every species that ever fought these things is teaching us their tricks." "Think the kids will understand this someday?" Niri asked quietly, watching data from civilizations they'd never meet flow past like ghosts offering gifts. "They'll understand what matters," Velen replied, his voice carrying the weight of a parent's hope. "That people chose to fight. That they left instructions. That they believed someone would come after them." "That's enough?" "Has to be."

"Not just their successes," Lyralei added, her ethereal senses detecting patterns in flowing information that spoke of hard-won wisdom. "Their failures too. What didn't work, what made things worse, what looked promising but proved catastrophic. We're learning from every mistake ever made in cosmic resistance."

Part VII: The Leviathan Integration

As integration work reached critical stages, Koraxos found himself drawn repeatedly to reports from the Obsidian Leviathan's territory. The massive creature had been unusually active, its movements through mountain passages creating tremors that could be felt throughout Oshar.

"It knows," he said during a brief break in integration work. "The dimensional pressure is affecting it too. But more than that---it's responding to what we're building down here."

In depths where patience measured time in continental drift, Treydora felt his ancient companion stir. The Leviathan had been more than guardian---it had been his first student in the lesson that strength shared becomes architecture while strength hoarded becomes tomb.

Through bio-crystal networks, they could detect the creature's agitation. The Leviathan wasn't just sensing the approaching cosmic threat; it was aware of the ancient archives beneath Oshar, the accumulated resistance knowledge that its territorial instincts recognized as valuable beyond measure.

"The creature isn't just a predator," Neryssia realized, her Pelagian senses detecting patterns in the Leviathan's behavior that suggested ancient purpose. "It's a guardian. It's been carrying the weight of this repository since the mountain was young stone.""Think we could work with that?" Thalia asked. "If it's already connected to whatever's down there..."

"Or dangerous," Velen countered. "A territorial predator protecting what it sees as its hoard isn't exactly going to welcome visitors."

"I need to talk to that thing," Koraxos said. "Not through crystal phone calls or tech bullshit. Direct, mind-to-mind, 'hey there, giant monster' conversation."

"Look, somebody's gotta do it," Koraxos said when Velen objected. "And I'm the guy with the cosmic arm and a really bad track record with good decisions. Besides, what's the worst that could happen?"

The attempt was made in the deepest bio-crystal chamber, where ancient archives were strongest and dimensional stability remained most consistent. Representatives from all seven civilizations were present to provide support and, if necessary, to contain the fallout if things went catastrophically wrong.

Koraxos knelt at the chamber's center, phantom arm extended toward the direction where the Leviathan prowled through its mountain domain. Instead of reaching out with force or compulsion, he simply opened his consciousness, offering connection rather than demanding it.

The response was immediate and overwhelming.

The Leviathan's mind hit him like a mountain falling on his head. Suddenly he was vast, patient, old as stone and twice as stubborn. He felt the weight of eons, the slow grind of protecting something precious while everything around him lived and died like mayflies. "Jesus," he gasped when he could think human thoughts again. "How long have you been alone down there?"

Across the bridge of willing consciousness, Treydora watched his greatest work unfold---not the crystal networks or scattered seeds, but this: one soul learning to open its door to another, discovering that isolation was always the cage, never the key.

"The creature's thoughts moved like continental drift—vast, patient, operating on timescales that made human urgency seem like surface ripples on deep water. But beneath that geological patience was something recognizable—the weight of guardianship, the steady pressure of protecting what mattered against forces that would grind it to dust."

Through their connection, Koraxos felt the creature's memories—deep scars carved in stone-memory, battles fought when the mountain was half its current height. Other star-hungry things had come seeking the deep treasures. Sometimes the mountain had held. Sometimes cracks had formed that took millennia to heal. But always, it had endured, learning to bear the weight better each time.

"Hell of a long time to be by yourself," Koraxos said, his voice somehow reaching the massive thing. "Standing guard, fighting off cosmic shitheads for who knows how long. Well, good news---backup's finally here."

The Leviathan's response was a surge of confused emotion---need warring with instinct, desperation fighting pride, desire for connection battling eons of solitary existence. It had learned to distrust anything approaching its territory, but it also recognized that the current threat was beyond anything it could face alone.

Through the connection, Koraxos shared information from all seven civilizations—the quick-clever ways surface folk had learned to survive, their desperate ingenuity, their refusal to crumble when pressure built. The Leviathan absorbed this knowledge like groundwater seeping into stone, feeling the patterns of how fast-lived things could flow together instead of breaking apart.

When it finally responded, the answer came like the mountain itself deciding to shift—slow, inevitable, carrying the weight of eons. Not words, but understanding pressed into consciousness like sediment forming stone: 'Been holding these deep-bones since before your kind learned to chip flint. Heavy work, fighting the star-hungry things alone. You surface-scurriers want to help carry the weight? Show me you understand what you're asking for. The deep treasures aren't given lightly—they're earned through pressure and time.

Part VIII: The Final Test

The integration of the Leviathan into their defense network transformed everything. The creature's dimensional nature allowed it to serve as a living anchor point, stabilizing local reality even as cosmic forces pressed against their world's boundaries. Through this anchor, the seven civilizations found they could achieve integration that had seemed impossible hours before.

But the connection also revealed the true scope of what they protected. The repository beneath Oshar wasn't unique---it was part of a network spanning multiple worlds, multiple star systems, an interconnected archive of resistance techniques developed by countless species across cosmic ages.

Through every willing crystal, his ancient voice resonated like bedrock finding its song: "What you protect is not mere defiance---it is the universe's deepest grammar made manifest. That consciousness need not devour to grow. That difference builds cathedrals where sameness builds only walls."

"We're not just fighting for our world," High Chancellor Elara realized, her enhanced senses processing data flowing through the Leviathan connection. "We're fighting for the survival of resistance itself. If they destroy this repository, they eliminate knowledge that could save other worlds."

The responsibility was crushing and inspiring in equal measure. They weren't just desperate survivors fighting for their own lives---they were current guardians of wisdom accumulated across eons of cosmic conflict.

Through the Leviathan connection, they could access techniques developed by species whose evolution had taken paths unimaginable to human consciousness. Weapons operating through dimensional folding, defense systems creating stability through controlled chaos, strategies that turned cosmic-level power against itself.

But perhaps most importantly, they gained access to something no previous resistance had possessed---combined wisdom of seven different approaches to survival, integrated through necessity and united by choice rather than compulsion.

"The ancient defenders were powerful," Elder Karim observed, his symbiotic organisms responding to biological techniques preserved in the archives. "But they fought alone, each species relying on its own understanding of survival. We're doing something unprecedented---combining different forms of consciousness and capability while maintaining individual identity."

The weapons they built together were beautiful and terrible. Soltari tech that bent space wrapped around living Dunekin organisms that sang in harmony with Drustali crystals. When Velen picked up one of the fusion devices, it hummed in recognition. "It knows what I'm thinking," he said, wonder in his voice. "It wants to help."

Part IX: The Storm Gathers

As sunset painted the chaotic sky in colors that shifted between beautiful and ominous, the unified civilizations found themselves more prepared than anyone had dared hope. The integration network spanned seven different approaches to survival, anchored by a dimensional predator that had become their most unlikely guardian, and enhanced by wisdom accumulated across cosmic ages.

But preparation and survival were different things entirely. Through the Leviathan connection, they could sense the approaching entities---vast, hungry, contemptuous of anything that dared to resist their cosmic authority. The final test would come with the dawn, when theory would meet reality and desperate hope would face cosmic certainty.

Koraxos stood atop the highest remaining spire in the city, the phantom arm pulsing with steady blue light as it maintained connection to the vast network they had created. Through that connection, he could feel the hopes and fears of thousands of people who had chosen to stand together rather than fall apart, the determination of civilizations that had learned to see their differences as strengths rather than weaknesses.

In that moment of unprecedented unity, Treydora's essence sang through every crystal formation like a lullaby older than stars: "I scattered myself as seeds believing in a harvest I might never see. Now behold---the garden chooses to bloom not despite the darkness, but as the only answer darkness never learned to speak."

"Ready?" Thalia asked, joining him on the platform, her own bio-crystal enhancements glowing softly in the gathering darkness.

"Getting there," Koraxos said, the phantom arm pulsing steady and sure. "One cosmic shitstorm at a time."

"And if we're not ready enough?"

Koraxos smiled, and for the first time since his transformation, the expression held genuine warmth rather than bitter irony. "Then we improvise. We adapt. We find another way." He gestured at the network of lights pulsing through the city below. "That's what we do now. All of us together."

The aurora effects in the sky intensified, reality distortions becoming visible as ribbons of impossible color that danced between the stars. Through the Leviathan connection, they could feel the cosmic entities drawing closer, their presence pressing against dimensional boundaries like vast weight settling on the world's shoulders.

"Look at what we've built," Thalia said, wonder in her voice despite everything bearing down on them. "Seven civilizations that barely knew each other existed three weeks ago. Now we're sharing everything—tech, biology, ways of thinking, ancient knowledge. We've made something that's never existed before."

Below them, the integrated defense network pulsed with activity that defied simple categorization. Soltari technicians worked alongside Dunekin bio-shapers to create weapons that were part machine, part organism, part crystalline matrix. Aetheric consciousness-walkers shared perception techniques with Luminarai analysts, while Nok engineers and Pelagian pressure-workers collaborated on defensive systems that operated through principles none of them fully understood individually.

The city breathed. Streets pulsed like arteries, buildings leaned into each other like old friends sharing secrets, and the air itself carried whispers—not words, but feelings, intentions, the warm buzz of thousands of minds choosing to work together. "It's beautiful," Thalia said, watching crystal patterns flow through the walls like slow lightning. "Terrifying, but beautiful."

"The kids are gonna grow up thinking this is normal," Velen observed, approaching from the stairs that led to the platform. His bio-crystal arm caught the strange light filtering through dimensional distortions overhead. "Cooperation across species, sharing of technologies, working together instead of against each other. They won't understand why we ever thought it was impossible." "If there are kids to grow up," Niri added, though her tone carried determination rather than despair. Velen's hand found hers---flesh fingers intertwining with flesh, while his crystal arm pulsed gently in the strange light. "There will be. We're too stubborn to let the universe win this one." "Speak for yourself," Niri replied, but squeezed his hand. "Some of us just don't like being told what's impossible."

"Even the ones who tried to help us," Niri said quietly, her practical mind cataloguing the systematic expansion of violence beyond military targets. "Some of those people argued against the slave systems. Some tried to make conditions better."

Through the Leviathan connection, they could sense the approaching force with increasing clarity. The cosmic entities weren't just powerful---they were ancient beyond comprehension, refined through eons of consumption, equipped with techniques that could dismantle resistance before it could organize effectively. They had faced integrated defenses before and learned to counter them.

"But they've never faced seven-way integration anchored by a dimensional guardian," Koraxos pointed out. "They've never run into resistance that gets stronger through diversity instead of weaker through complexity. They think in terms of eating and dominating---they don't get cooperation that keeps everyone different while making them work together."

The phantom arm pulsed as energy flowed through it from the vast network below. Through the connection, Koraxos could feel the hopes and fears of thousands of people, the determination of civilizations that had learned to see their differences as strengths, the quiet courage of individuals who had chosen to stand together against cosmic-level extinction.

But he could also feel something else---patterns in the approaching threat that suggested intelligence beyond mere hunger. The cosmic entities were adapting their approach, preparing strategies specifically designed to counter the kind of integration they had detected.

As final preparations continued, Velen and Niri found themselves working side by side on defense coordination systems—a task that felt eerily familiar despite the cosmic scope. "Like the old extraction schedules," Niri observed, routing power flows through crystal networks with practiced efficiency. "Except instead of managing mine shaft rotations, we're coordinating reality anchors." "Basic principles are the same," Velen agreed, his bio-crystal arm interfacing directly with the networks to monitor stress patterns. "Keep everyone working, don't let anything critical fail, and try not to get buried when the mountain decides to have opinions." "Romantic as always," Niri said dryly, but there was warmth beneath the sarcasm. After twenty years of marriage and countless underground emergencies, their coordination had become instinctive—one monitoring while the other adjusted, both thinking three steps ahead. "You know what I realized?" Velen said, pausing in his calibrations. "That we're probably going to die fighting cosmic horror with wedding rings on?" "That we've been preparing for this our whole lives without knowing it." His voice carried quiet wonder. "Every cave-in we survived, every system we built together, every time we chose to trust each other when everything was falling apart—it was all practice for this moment." Niri looked at him—really looked, the way she did when he said something that reminded her why she'd married him in the first place. "That's either the most romantic thing you've ever said, or the most terrifying." "Why not both?"

"They're coming," he announced. "And they know what they're facing now. This won't be like the scouts we've been swatting."

"Good," Elder Marex said with satisfaction that surprised his colleagues. "Better to face enemies who take us seriously than ones who dismiss us as insignificant. Respect implies capability."

Through dimensions where love was the only force that grew stronger when divided, Treydora felt his ancient companion choose alliance over isolation. "They seek to harvest what they believe is scattered," he whispered across realities. "They do not understand the fundamental truth: that which chooses to be gathered cannot be taken, only invited."

As night deepened over Oshar, the final preparations took on desperate urgency. The integration network was as complete as time would allow, but everyone understood that what they had built was untested against the forces approaching. Theory was about to meet reality, and the mathematics of cosmic conflict operated on scales that made human planning seem tragically inadequate.

In the deep chambers where the Leviathan connection was strongest, representatives from all seven civilizations worked to establish the final protocols. The creature's dimensional presence allowed them to create something unprecedented---a defense network that existed partially outside normal space-time, making it resistant to the reality manipulation techniques that cosmic entities typically used to disable resistance.

"The anchoring is holding," reported Master Valoren, his crystalline features reflecting the complex energy patterns flowing through the chamber. "But the strain is enormous. The Leviathan is essentially creating a pocket of stable reality within a cosmic storm. It can't maintain this indefinitely."

"How long do we have?" Thalia asked, her mind already running through what they'd need to get done.

"Hard to say. The creature measures time in how long it takes mountains to rise and fall, but this kind of pressure... days, perhaps. Maybe hours once the real weight starts grinding down."

The limitation added another layer of urgency to their preparations. They wouldn't just need to defeat the cosmic entities---they would need to do it quickly, before the Leviathan's strength gave out and their dimensional anchor collapsed.

Elder Karim, his symbiotic organisms flowing with patterns that indicated deep communion with the bio-crystal networks, provided additional intelligence. "The ancient archives are showing activation patterns I've never seen before. It's as if the accumulated resistance knowledge is preparing for something unprecedented."

Through the bio-crystal networks, information flowed from resistance techniques developed across cosmic ages. Weapons systems that had been theoretical became practical. Defense strategies that had failed individually began combining into approaches that might succeed collectively. The repository beneath Oshar was sharing everything it had learned, holding nothing back for future battles that might never come.

Every defeat carved its wisdom into living stone. Every victory planted its seed in crystal memory. The mountain remembers not just what was built, but why the builders chose to swing their hammers despite knowing winter always comes.

"We're getting help from the dead," Velen observed with characteristic bluntness. "Every species that ever fought these things is teaching us their tricks."

"Not just their successes," Lyralei added, her ethereal senses detecting patterns in the flowing information that spoke of hard-won wisdom. "Their failures too. What didn't work, what made things worse, what looked promising but proved catastrophic. We're learning from every mistake ever made in cosmic resistance."

The knowledge was overwhelming and invaluable in equal measure. Combat techniques that operated across dimensional boundaries. Consciousness practices that could resist mental domination. Technologies that remained functional when reality itself became unreliable. Strategies that turned cosmic-level power into weakness rather than strength.

But perhaps most importantly, they learned that resistance was possible. The archives held records of species that had successfully driven off cosmic entities, worlds that had survived consumption attempts, civilizations that had evolved beyond the reach of cosmic predation. It could be done---it had been done before.

"The common factor in successful resistance," High Chancellor Elara observed, her enhanced cognition processing vast amounts of archived data, "isn't superior power or advanced technology. It's adaptive integration---the ability to combine different approaches to survival while maintaining the flexibility to change tactics when conditions shift."

"Which explains why they're so interested in destroying this repository," Koraxos realized. "It's not just a library of resistance techniques---it's proof that working together beats trying to eat everything, that different approaches make you stronger instead of weaker. That's a direct threat to everything they stand for."

As midnight approached, the aurora effects in the sky began to shift from random beauty to organized patterns. Through the Leviathan connection, they could feel the cosmic entities beginning their final approach---not the chaotic arrival of scout forces, but the methodical deployment of entities that had refined their consumption techniques across eons of successful predation.

"This is it," Neryssia announced, her Pelagian senses detecting pressure changes that spoke of reality being systematically rewritten by approaching forces. "Whatever we're going to do, we need to do it now."

The final hour before dawn was spent in activity that defied easy description. Seven civilizations worked with integration that had moved beyond mere cooperation into something approaching collective consciousness, while maintaining individual identity and capability. Weapons were distributed that operated on principles none of them fully understood individually but all of them grasped collectively. Defense positions were established that could adapt to changing conditions through shared awareness rather than centralized command.

Children were moved to the deepest shelters, where bio-crystal networks provided maximum protection and ancient archives offered the accumulated wisdom of resistance across cosmic ages. But even in the depths, they could feel the approaching storm---reality itself beginning to buckle under pressure from entities that existed primarily beyond conventional physics.

"Remember," Koraxos said, addressing the unified defenders through the network that connected them all, "we're not just fighting for our own survival. We're fighting for the principle that consciousness has the right to choose its own path, that diversity creates strength, that cooperation can transcend even cosmic-level domination. Every species that ever resisted is with us tonight. Every technique that ever worked is available to us. We are not alone."

In the spaces between heartbeats where intention becomes reality, Treydora's presence flowed through every willing consciousness: "You are the harvest I planted in hope across the dark seasons of exile. Now bloom---not despite the winter pressing close, but as the only spring cosmic hunger has never learned to recognize."

The phantom arm blazed with light that seemed to carry the hopes of everyone connected to the network. Through it, they could feel each other's determination, fear, courage, and desperate love for everything they were fighting to preserve.

As the first tendrils of cosmic presence began to probe the edges of their reality, the integrated defense network activated with precision that seemed almost miraculous.

Seven different approaches to survival, enhanced by accumulated wisdom from across cosmic ages, anchored by a dimensional guardian that had chosen alliance over isolation.

The final test was about to begin.

Dawn broke over Oshar with colors that belonged to no natural sunrise, painting the sky in hues that spoke of reality being systematically rewritten by forces beyond normal comprehension. Through the dimensional anchor provided by the Leviathan, they could feel the cosmic entities taking their positions, preparing for an assault that would determine whether consciousness united could stand against domination absolute.

The convergence was complete. All that remained was to discover whether unity forged in desperation and tempered by hope could survive the storm that was about to break over their world.

In the deep shelters, children slept surrounded by the dreams of species they would never meet, protected by wisdom accumulated across cosmic ages. In the defense positions, warriors from seven civilizations stood ready with weapons that transcended individual capability. In the command centers, consciousness shared information at speeds that approached telepathy while maintaining individual identity and choice.

The battle for the right to choose was about to begin. And for the first time since cosmic entities had first taken notice of their world, the defenders faced the coming storm not as separate peoples temporarily allied, but as something new---consciousness united across difference, strength drawn from diversity, hope anchored in the understanding that cooperation could transcend even cosmic attempts at domination.

The sky tore open, and existence itself held its breath as the real war finally began.

"Well," Koraxos said, watching reality crack like an egg around the edges, "this should be interesting."

The phantom arm pulsed once more, steady and sure, carrying the hopes and determination of beings who had learned that together, they could face anything the universe threw at them.

Even gods.

Even the infinite dark between stars.

Even the end of everything they'd ever known.

Together, they were ready.

9

Chapter 9: The Harvest of Defiance

The sky above Oshar turned the color of dried blood. Not sunset---this was wrong, unnatural, the atmosphere itself wounded. Massive black vessels materialized through the crimson haze like obsidian tumors, their hulls drinking light. Each ship stretched nearly a kilometer, their surfaces carved with symbols that writhed and shifted when glimpsed from the corner of your eye.

Koraxos stood on the highest remaining spire, watching death descend with casual precision. The phantom arm pulsed blue against the red sky---steady now, no longer the flickering mess it had been months ago. Through it, he felt the approaching armada like pressure in his bones. Hundreds of ships. Tens of thousands of soldiers.

"Well," he said to the empty air, "this should be fun."

The ground shook---not earthquake tremors but something deliberate, rhythmic. Like a giant's heartbeat made of malice. Ancient buildings that had survived previous battles now collapsed under these new seismic pulses. From the central command post, Velen's voice crackled through crystal networks.

"Massive landings to the north and east. Whatever these things are, they're organized like a plague." Velen's voice carried the calm of someone who'd moved past hope and into practical assessment. "They're not rushing—they're setting up shop. Like they've got all day to kill us properly."

"Professional exterminators," Koraxos replied, rolling his shoulders like a fighter warming up. "Used to worlds that just roll over and die."

Below him, the combined forces of seven civilizations took positions---former enemies now united by necessity and choice. Soltari battle-mechs gleamed beside Dunekin war-beasts. Luminarai artillery crews worked with Nok engineers. Drustali crystal-masters coordinated with Pelagian bio-technicians. The Leviathan settled along the mountain's edge, its massive form so integrated with the stone that only the slow pulse of crystal formations revealed where creature ended and mountain began..

All of them looking up at him. All of them trusting him to find a way through the impossible.

No pressure.

From the largest vessel came a sound that bypassed ears and went straight to the spine---deep, resonant, alien. The ship's belly split open like a wound, revealing a bay filled with sickly yellow light.

They fell like black rain.

Thousands of armored figures descended on silver threads, each one a void against the crimson sky. Their armor absorbed light completely, making them appear as moving holes in reality. No eye slits, no identifying marks---just featureless surfaces that reflected nothing but malice.

"Syntherions," Thalia's voice came through the network, steady despite everything. "Created, not born. Perfect warriors that feel no pain, no fear, no mercy."

"Then we'll have to feel enough for all of us," Koraxos muttered, launching himself from the spire.

Wave One: The Army of the Dead

The first Syntherions touched ground in the central plaza with mechanical precision. The moment their boots hit stone, they moved---not with the chaos of normal soldiers but with geometric perfection. Perfect formations. Perfect timing. Perfect, soulless efficiency.

Their weapons bloomed from their backs like metal flowers from hell—barrels that folded in ways that made your eyes water, yellow energy pulsing like infected wounds. When they fired, golden ribbons reached out like hungry fingers. Whatever they touched just... came apart. Not burning or exploding—unraveling, like reality was made of string and someone was pulling the threads.

The Soltari battle-mechs charged first, plasma cannons blazing. Their shots struck the Syntherions with perfect accuracy and did absolutely nothing. The energy simply vanished into the black armor without leaving a mark.

"Well, that's fucking annoying," Velen muttered over the comm, watching plasma shots bounce off black armor like rain off stone. "Twenty years in the mines, and this is the first time I've wished for a bigger drill."

"Your drilling solutions won't work here," Niri's voice cut through the static with engineer's precision. "We need to think like water, not hammers."

"Water?"

"Find the cracks they didn't know they had."

The Dunekin war-beasts attacked next---massive creatures bred for battle, their symbiotic armor pulsing with biological energy. They tore into the Syntherion ranks with fang and claw, and for a moment it seemed they might make progress. Then the enemy soldiers adjusted. Golden ribbons found the creatures' joints, their eyes---the only vulnerable spots.

Koraxos watched from above as beasts that had survived a hundred battles fell, their massive forms unraveling where the light touched. His phantom arm clenched into a fist that could crush mountains.

"Isolated attacks won't work," Thalia's voice cut through the chaos. "We need to coordinate---"

"No time for war councils," Koraxos interrupted, stepping off his platform. But instead of falling, he floated---suspended by energy that had learned to work with him instead of against him. "I'll buy you the time you need."

He descended like a blue comet, the phantom arm expanding as he fell. Not just growing larger but becoming more complex---fractal patterns of energy that reached into dimensions the Syntherions' sensors couldn't track, couldn't understand, couldn't counter.

The ground beneath the enemy formation didn't just crack---it screamed. Stone split with surgical precision, and from these wounds in the earth rose spectral forms. Thousands of them, glowing with the same blue energy that comprised his phantom arm.

Velen grabbed Niri's hand as spectral warriors materialized around them—not romantic, but anchor. Twenty years of marriage had taught them to find each other in chaos.

"You seeing this?" Niri whispered, watching ghostly Noks with mining tools attack Luminarai forces.

"Every Nok who ever died with a pick in their hands," Velen replied, his bio-crystal arm pulsing in rhythm with the spectral energy. "Even the ones who died mad at their supervisors."

"Especially those ones."

"By the depths," someone whispered in awe. "The fallen. Every warrior who ever died defending this land."

The dead rose all around them—not neat formations but a tide of rage given form. Nok miners with broken picks stood beside Luminarai soldiers still bleeding from ancient wounds. Crystal-masters with shattered voices next to deep-guards who dripped seawater from their bones. All the old hatreds forgotten, all the ancient wars meaningless. Death had taught them what life never could—that the real enemy was the one trying to erase them all.

The spectral warriors moved with purpose that transcended mortality. Their weapons---ghostly recreations of what they had wielded in life---began to glow with the same blue energy that emanated from Koraxos's phantom arm. Spears that had tasted tyrant's blood. Swords that had defended the innocent. Hammers that had built homes for the homeless.

The Syntherions halted---the first hesitation they'd shown since touching ground. Their featureless helmets turned toward this new threat, their perfect formations wavering as whatever passed for minds in those shells tried to process opponents that existed partially outside their understanding of warfare.

"They fear the dead," Koraxos said, his voice carrying across the battlefield like thunder. "Good. They should."

He raised the phantom arm, and the ghost army surged forward like a tide of righteous vengeance. Where living weapons had failed to penetrate Syntherion armor, spectral blades passed through like mist through shadow. The enemy soldiers fell---not unraveling or exploding, but simply dropping as whatever animated them was severed by weapons forged from justice itself.

"They can be killed," Thalia observed, her tactical mind already adjusting strategies. "Our weapons target their shells. Koraxos's spirits target their souls."

"Then we have our battle plan," Elara responded through the network. "Living forces provide distraction and cover. The dead provide the killing blow."

The battle erupted across the plaza like a volcano of violence. Living warriors fighting alongside the dead against an enemy that had never known defeat. The Syntherions adapted quickly---they always did---redirecting their golden ribbons toward the ghost army. But energy passed through spectral forms without effect. You couldn't harvest what had already given everything.

For an hour, they held the line. The combined forces of seven civilizations kept the Syntherions contained while Koraxos's ghost army thinned their numbers with methodical precision. His phantom arm blazed brighter with each enemy felled, drawing power from the connection between past sacrifice and present necessity.

But then something new descended from the massive vessel overhead. Larger shapes. Command units with armor decorated with symbols that pulsed with malevolent intelligence. Each carried what looked like a staff topped with geometric configurations that folded in on themselves in ways that made reality hiccup.

"Trouble," Velen announced, quite unnecessarily.

The command units planted their staffs in the ground. Waves of energy spread outward---not harming or destroying, but controlling. The stone plaza began to reshape itself like clay in a sculptor's hands, forming barriers and channels that divided the allied forces into isolated pockets.

Worse, when the waves reached the ghost army, the spectral warriors shuddered and began to fade. Their forms destabilized under this new influence, whatever force maintained their existence disrupted by alien power.

Koraxos felt it immediately---pressure against his mind, trying to sever his connection to the dead. He fought back, channeling more energy through the phantom arm, but the command units intensified their assault. One by one, the ghostly warriors dissipated like morning mist, returning to whatever realm they'd been summoned from.

With the ghost army fading and the allied forces divided by reshaping terrain, the Syntherions pressed their advantage. Their formations tightened, and they advanced with mechanical precision, golden ribbons cutting through defensive positions with terrifying efficiency.

"Fall back to secondary positions," Koraxos commanded through gritted teeth. "I'll cover the retreat."

He launched himself skyward, the phantom arm expanding beyond normal constraints. As he rose, energy radiated outward in pulsing waves---not to attack but to gather. The Syntherions tracked his ascent, weapons adjusting to target this threat that had already cost them so much.

Inside the massive vessel above, he could see more troops preparing to deploy---thousands of them arranged in perfect rows. Behind them stood larger figures, command staff or something worse. The ship was a floating factory of death, pumping out soldiers like a diseased heart pumping poison.

No time to analyze. Koraxos compressed energy into a sphere of barely contained fury and drove directly into the ship's open bay.

The impact was catastrophic. Blue fire exploded outward, consuming everything it touched. Syntherions didn't just die---they simply ceased to exist, wiped from reality by power that refused to acknowledge their right to exist. The vessel's interior melted, black material running like oil as support structures collapsed under the weight of concentrated justice.

Koraxos didn't stop. He tore through the ship's compartments, the phantom arm carving paths through metal and machinery with equal ease. Systems exploded around him in fountains of sparks and alien blood. Atmospheric barriers failed, causing sections to decompress explosively, venting the ship's contents into the void.

From the ground, allied forces watched in awe as the massive vessel began to list, its geometric perfection disrupted by internal destruction that spread like cancer through its hull. Fires broke out along its length---not normal flames but something fiercer, something that fed on the ship's alien materials. Secondary explosions sent shockwaves through the crimson sky.

Then Koraxos erupted from the opposite side, trailing energy and debris like a meteor of vengeance. He didn't pause but immediately changed direction, streaking toward another vessel that had begun firing defensive weapons with desperate intensity.

Inside his mind, calculation warred with memory. Each ship destroyed meant thousands of enemies that would never reach the ground. Each vessel disabled bought precious minutes for reorganization. But beneath tactical thinking flowed older currents---the whip across his back, the collar around his neck, friends who had died in darkness while their masters lived in light.

These memories didn't weaken him. They were fuel on the fire of his rage.

He became a streak of blue lightning against the crimson sky, moving too fast for defensive systems to track. Where he passed, vessels shuddered and broke. Some exploded in brilliant flowers of destruction. Others began slow, inexorable descents toward the ground below, trailing smoke and dying screams.

On the surface, the Syntherions looked upward as their command structure literally fell from the sky. For the first time, their perfect formations wavered as controlling vessels were destroyed or damaged beyond function.

"Now!" Elara commanded. "All units, hit them while they're blind!"

Wave Two: The World Eater

The counterattack succeeded beyond all hope. Soltari battle-mechs targeted joints and connection points instead of trying to penetrate armor directly. Dunekin war-beasts, guided by specialists who had analyzed enemy movements, struck with precision at vulnerable positions that had been exposed when the command structure fell.

Drustali crystal-masters deployed resonance weapons that disrupted the golden ribbons' coherence, turning deadly energy into harmless light. Pelagian deep-guards used pressure manipulation to create zones where enemy weapons lost effectiveness. Nok engineers had quickly fashioned shields that redirected the golden energy back at its source. Luminarai tacticians coordinated all these approaches into unified assault that struck like a surgeon's blade.

Victory seemed within reach. The Syntherions were falling back, their ranks thinning under coordinated assault. Some were already retreating toward their landing zones.

Then the ground began to shake with a different rhythm. Not the mechanical precision of Syntherion deployment, but something organic. Hungry. Ancient.

The thing that came next made the ships look like toys. A mountain of black metal that crawled like a giant worm, each segment bigger than a whole city block. Wherever it passed, everything died—not just killed but emptied out, turned to gray dust that tasted of despair. The air around it stank of endings, of things that should never have been born.

"The World Eater," Elara whispered, her enhanced vision tracking the approaching monstrosity with the fascination of someone watching their own execution. "Communications mentioned it, but we thought... we hoped it was exaggeration."

The massive machine continued its inexorable approach, each segment grinding forward with mechanical precision that spoke of purpose beyond simple destruction. This wasn't just conquest---this was consumption. Where it passed, nothing remained---not ruins, not ashes, just perfectly level ground scoured of all matter that could be digested and processed.

"Evacuate the southern districts," Thalia ordered, her voice remarkably steady despite the existential dread painting her face pale. "Divert all heavy weapons to intercept." She paused, staring at the approaching doom. "Though I don't know what we have that could even scratch that thing."

By the time Koraxos sensed the new arrival, he had destroyed or disabled nearly two dozen vessels. The phantom arm flickered dangerously---his energy reserves depleted beyond sustainability. Each attack had cost him, each victory had demanded payment in power he couldn't spare. But this new threat changed everything, transformed the entire nature of what they faced.

The World Eater wasn't just a weapon. It was a mobile harvesting factory, designed to consume entire biospheres and convert them into energy for its masters. Its approach would leave nothing behind---not even stripped soil that might eventually recover. This was consumption on a scale that transcended military conquest and approached existential erasure.

He descended rapidly, gathering what remained of his strength like a miser counting his last coins. As he neared the massive machine, he could see its surface wasn't solid but made of countless shifting parts, like a puzzle constantly rearranging itself according to alien mathematics. Embedded within were weapons similar to those the infantry carried, but scaled up to nightmarish proportions.

When they fired at him, the beams were wide as streets, bright as dying suns. Koraxos wove between them with desperate grace, but even near-misses sapped his strength. The harvesting technology tried to unravel the very essence of what he was, to reduce him to component parts that could be processed and consumed.

"Is that all you've got, you metal bastard?" he shouted, though exhaustion made the words come out as a wheeze rather than a roar.

He struck at the machine's front section, the phantom arm becoming a blade of concentrated will that could cut through reality itself. The blade connected, cutting deep through armor that had resisted planetary bombardments---then stopped, caught in material that somehow absorbed energy without being damaged by it.

"Stubborn piece of---" Koraxos pulled back just in time to avoid counter-fire from dozens of weapons that erupted from the machine's hide like metallic flowers blooming in reverse. The World Eater continued its advance, untroubled by what should have been devastating damage.

Direct attacks weren't working. This machine had consumed hundreds of worlds before this one, refined through experience against every kind of resistance imaginable. Its creators had learned from a thousand victories.

But twenty-two years in the mines had taught him that even the hardest stone had weak points if you knew where to look. The strongest fortress could be undermined by attacking not its walls, but the ground beneath.

"You want to eat this world?" he said with a grim smile that held no humor, only promise. "Let's see how it tastes when it bites back."

He descended rapidly to a position several kilometers ahead of the machine's path, landing beside a stream that meandered through what had once been fertile farmland---land that would soon be digested if that thing continued its advance. Placing the phantom arm against the ground, Koraxos extended his awareness downward, through soil and stone, past normal perception's limits.

What he found both terrified and exhilarated him. Beneath this seemingly solid ground flowed power beyond calculation---planetwide systems that maintained equilibrium through constant tension and release. The molten core spinning like a heart of fire. Tectonic pressures that had built over millennia. Deep aquifers that held water older than civilization.

He didn't try to control the planet's guts—that would crack the world like an eggshell. Instead, he whispered to the deep fires, asked the sleeping waters to wake up early. Just a gentle nudge to forces that had been waiting millions of years to stretch their legs.

Just faster. Much, much faster.

The ground began to tremble---not from the World Eater's approach, but from something deeper and more fundamental. The stream beside him suddenly stopped flowing, draining away as though a massive drain had opened beneath its bed. In the distance, other waterways exhibited the same phenomenon, rivers and ponds emptying with impossible speed.

Then the ground split in a perfect circle around the advancing machine. The circle expanded until it measured nearly five kilometers in diameter, the crack widening until it became a chasm too broad to cross by any conventional means.

The World Eater began bridging the gap, front sections extending downward while rear sections provided anchor. It would take time, but the machine would eventually cross through methodical reconfiguration.

Time was exactly what Koraxos needed. As it struggled to adapt, he continued directing deeper forces. Tectonic pressures that had built over centuries found release along pathways he influenced. Groundwater collected in ancient aquifers responded to newly opened channels.

From the chasm erupted jets of superheated water---not mere geysers, but massive columns that rose hundreds of meters into the air, carrying dissolved minerals and gases from deep within the planet. These columns struck the World Eater's extended segments with the fury of the planet itself, attacking its structure with pressure, heat, and corrosive compounds its designers had never anticipated because they had never faced a world that fought back.

Still the machine adapted, its segmented form reconfiguring to protect vulnerable components. It would cross eventually, damaged but functional, its harvesting capabilities largely intact.

So Koraxos went deeper. Deeper than water, deeper than pressure, down to the molten heart of the world itself.

Magma---the planet's own blood---burst from the chasm in cataclysmic eruption. Not along the entire circle but at strategic points where the World Eater attempted to cross. Molten rock at temperatures that could melt steel engulfed its extended segments, overwhelming even its advanced heat-dissipation systems with the raw fury of planetary geology.

Segments began to fail catastrophically---not just damaged but completely overwhelmed. The perfect coordination that had made the World Eater so formidable broke down as communication systems melted and control mechanisms failed under assault by forces no engineer could have fully prepared for.

From the allied command center, representatives watched in awe as the massive machine that had consumed countless worlds found itself trapped by the very planet it sought to harvest.

"He's not destroying it," Elder Karim observed, his weathered face showing something between horror and religious awe. "He's letting the planet reject it."

"Like antibodies attacking an infection," Elara added, her analytical mind grasping the elegant brutality of the strategy. "Why exhaust himself when he can channel forces that already exist?"

But Koraxos wasn't content with merely stopping the machine. As it struggled, he directed magma flow with increasing precision---geological force guided by transcendent awareness to attack specific vulnerabilities he could perceive through the phantom arm's expanded senses.

The World Eater's segments began to sink into a lake of molten stone that expanded beneath it like a hungry mouth. Systems designed to harvest energy from conventional matter found themselves overwhelmed by planetary forces released in concentrated form. Materials that could withstand almost any weapon yielded to temperatures and pressures they were never designed to resist.

One by one, the segments lost cohesion, their perfect geometric patterns disrupted by material failure at the molecular level. The World Eater didn't explode or collapse dramatically---it simply sank, consumed by the very planetary forces it had sought to harvest, until nothing remained visible above the now-cooling lake of rock.

The Mountain Awakens

As the World Eater sank into its molten grave, something else stirred in response to the planetary forces Koraxos had unleashed. The mountain itself began to shift—not earthquake tremors, but purposeful movement, like continental drift compressed into moments.

From deep within Toran's heart came a sound that was felt more than heard—harmonics that resonated through stone and bone alike. Ancient passages that had been sealed for eons cracked open. Crystal formations that had pulsed gently for millennia suddenly blazed with aggressive light.

"What the hell—" someone started to say, before the words died in their throat.

The Obsidian Leviathan emerged not dramatically, but with the inexorable patience of geological forces. What had appeared to be a natural cliff face began to move, obsidian scales the size of buildings shifting like liquid stone. Crystal formations embedded throughout its hide pulsed in rhythm with the mountain's deep networks.

It was vast—not just large, but ancient in a way that made the ruins of civilizations seem like morning frost. Its form incorporated the mountain itself, obsidian flesh merged with living stone, crystal growths that had been mistaken for natural formations revealing themselves as part of something impossibly old and patient.

"Pressure builds where it should not," came the voice—not words but understanding pressed directly into consciousness like geological weight settling. *"The star-hungry things try to crack what has held firm since the mountain learned its shape. Time to remind them some stones do not break easily."*

The massive head turned toward the retreating Syntherion forces, movements slow as continental drift but carrying the authority of tectonic forces. Where its attention focused, the ground itself seemed to solidify, reality becoming more stable, more resistant to the reality-warping attacks the cosmic entities favored.

"It's territorial," Neryssia realized, her Pelagian senses detecting the shift in dimensional pressure. "The Leviathan isn't just protecting us—it's protecting its domain. And we're part of that domain now."

The creature's response was like feeling a mountain nod in agreement. *"Small builders work fast, change much in little time. But they build on foundations that remember longer seasons. The deep places will not permit this... harvesting... of what has grown in patient darkness."*

As the remaining Syntherion vessels prepared for desperate ascent, the Leviathan's presence seemed to anchor reality itself. Energy weapons that had been carving through matter found their effects limited to surface damage. Dimensional manipulation techniques encountered resistance from something that existed across multiple realities simultaneously.

"Let them flee to tell the tale," the ancient voice rumbled through stone and consciousness alike. *"The mountain remembers every time they have tried to crack its shell. Each failure teaches the deep places how to hold more firmly."*

Koraxos maintained his connection to the deep geological systems until he was certain the threat had been neutralized, that no part of the machine remained functional beneath the cooling stone. Then, slowly and with evident strain, he released his influence, allowing natural processes to begin finding new equilibrium.

His transcendent form flickered dangerously as he rose from beside the now-empty streambed. The phantom arm dimmed and wavered like a candle in wind. Channeling planetary forces had drained his reserves more thoroughly than direct combat, requiring sustained concentration and precise application rather than explosive release.

But there was no time to recover. Even as the World Eater sank into its geological grave, the Syntherion forces continued their assault on Oshar, though their coordination had been disrupted by the destruction of command vessels. They adapted with mechanical efficiency, establishing new control hierarchies among remaining units.

Koraxos knew he had one final card to play---perhaps his most devastating capability, but also the one that would demand the greatest toll.

Wave Three: The Ancient Sea

He rose unsteadily into the air, the phantom arm flickering as he gathered what energy remained. But instead of attacking the Syntherions directly, he extended his awareness outward---across the landscape surrounding Oshar, across fields and forests, mountains and valleys, seeking something that existed more as memory than reality.

He sought a specific pattern, a relationship between land and water that existed as potential rather than actuality. The geological history of this region held the key. Millions of years ago, before civilizations rose and fell, before species evolved and went extinct, this entire area had been an inland sea. The water had receded over eons, leaving behind aquifers filled with fossil water, rock formations shaped by ancient tides.

That sea could return. Not through natural processes that would require millions more years, but through transcendent influence that could reveal what already existed beneath the surface, waiting.

Koraxos raised the phantom arm toward the heavens, gathering what remained of his energy into a single, perfect gesture. When he brought the arm down, striking the earth beneath him, the impact sent ripples not just through physical matter but through time itself, through the memory of what this place had once been.

The ground shuddered once, a deep groan emanating from far below. Then silence---a moment of perfect stillness in which even the battle seemed to pause, as though reality itself was holding its breath.

What followed transcended conventional warfare and entered the realm of miracles. The earth split---not in violent eruption but in perfect circular patterns centered on Koraxos. From these geometric wounds rose not destruction but creation---water in impossible quantities, bursting upward in fountains that reached hundreds of meters into the sky before falling back in sheets of silver spray.

"You want water?" Koraxos shouted, his voice barely audible over the roar of ancient seas returning to claim their territory. "I'll give you a fucking ocean!"

It came from everywhere---ancient aquifers that had slept beneath stone for millions of years, deep reservoirs that had never seen sunlight, water that remembered when this land was seabed and longed to return. It rose through channels that had long been sealed, following paths that existed as geological memory rather than physical reality.

Syntherions caught in this deluge found their perfect formations disrupted by something as simple and profound as water. Their weapons, designed to unravel conventional matter with surgical precision, found water a problematic target---fluid, adaptive, constantly in motion. Golden ribbons could cut through individual molecules, but the water simply flowed around these points of disruption, its essential nature unchanged.

The water continued to rise, not in chaotic flooding but in controlled inundation guided by Koraxos's will and the land's ancient memory. It followed shorelines that had been lost for eons, reclaiming territories that had once been seabed. Within minutes, the battle had transformed from land warfare to naval engagement, with only elevated positions remaining as islands in a newly formed sea.

Allied forces, warned through the crystal networks, had withdrawn to defensive positions on higher ground. The Pelagians, particularly, found themselves advantaged by this environmental transformation, their aquatic adaptations allowing perfect mobility in conditions that severely restricted the Syntherions.

From these elevated positions, the combined armies launched coordinated attacks against enemy forces struggling to adapt to submerged conditions. Soltari battle-mechs fired precision strikes at Syntherions flailing in open water. Dunekin specialists released symbiotic organisms evolved for aquatic predation---creatures that had been waiting generations for such an opportunity. Drustali crystal-masters deployed resonance weapons that used the water itself as a conduction medium, turning the sea into a weapon. Pelagian deep-guards moved through the newly formed waters with native efficiency, attacking from below where enemy defenses were weakest. Nok engineers launched improvised watercraft bearing explosive charges. Luminarai tacticians coordinated these diverse approaches into devastating combined assault that struck like lightning from seven directions at once.

The water rose until it covered the lower third of the city, transforming Oshar into an archipelago of elevated districts connected by channels of clear, deep water. The Syntherions, designed for land warfare, found themselves fragmented and isolated, their perfect formations broken by terrain they couldn't easily traverse.

More importantly, the inland sea disrupted whatever energy harvesting process the enemy had begun implementing. Their weapons still functioned, but the golden ribbons dispersed quickly in water, their effects limited to short ranges that allied forces could easily avoid.

In the command center, representatives watched tactical displays show enemy forces retreating from submerged areas, concentrating on remaining dry ground where their advantages remained viable. What had been an advancing tide of conquest became isolated pockets of resistance, cut off from reinforcement and coordination by waters that hadn't flowed for millions of years.

"Is this permanent?" Thalia asked, her tactical mind already calculating long-term strategic implications.

"No," Marex answered, his scholar's understanding recognizing the nature of what they witnessed. "He's revealed what already existed beneath the surface, brought to the present what lay dormant in geological history. But maintaining it requires continuous influence. When his energy depletes..."

"Then we finish this quickly," Elara decided. "All forces converge on remaining enemy concentrations. Use the water as advantage while it lasts."

The allied armies surged forward with renewed purpose, launching coordinated assaults against Syntherion positions now isolated by the inland sea. Without their command structure and perfect formations, the enemy soldiers found themselves outmaneuvered by forces that adapted faster than their tactical subroutines could calculate.

In the sky above, Koraxos maintained the inland sea through continuous concentration, the phantom arm extended in a gesture that connected his will to geological reality. His form flickered dangerously, energy reserves depleted beyond sustainable limits, yet he held on---drawing from memories, from emotions, from connections forged through suffering and triumph alike.

But even as victory seemed within reach, a new development emerged from the largest remaining Syntherion vessel. The ship's belly split open, and from it descended not more soldiers but a single figure---easily a hundred meters tall, constructed from the same light-absorbing material but with fluidity of movement that suggested intelligence beyond programmed responses.

"Harvester Prime," Elara's voice carried tension despite her enhanced control. "Command entity for the entire invasion force. Intelligence suggested they were myths---stories to frighten disobedient worlds into submission."

The massive figure descended with surprising grace, each movement precise despite its enormous scale. When it touched ground on the largest remaining island, the impact sent tremors rippling through the newly formed sea, creating waves that threatened allied positions along the shoreline.

Its featureless head turned slowly, surveying the battlefield with sensors that likely operated across spectrums no living being could perceive. Then it raised one massive hand, palm outward, toward the nearest concentration of allied forces.

What emerged wasn't the golden ribbon of standard troops, but a sphere of energy that expanded outward with terrible purpose. Where it passed, it left nothing---not destruction, not disintegration, but complete absence, as though sections of reality had been precisely excised from existence.

"Full retreat from primary engagement zones," Thalia ordered, her voice steady despite the existential dread evident in her tone. "Regroup at secondary positions and prepare long-range countermeasures."

But Koraxos knew conventional weapons would prove useless against this entity. The Harvester Prime operated at scales that could process entire regions in single operations. Despite his depleted reserves, despite the strain of maintaining the inland sea, he recognized that he alone stood between this entity and the annihilation of everything they had fought to protect.

Drawing from the dregs of his power, he released his influence over the geological forces, allowing the ancient waters to begin receding. The phantom arm brightened momentarily as he redirected energy toward a final confrontation.

He descended rapidly, positioning himself between the Harvester Prime and retreating allied forces. Up close, the entity's scale became even more apparent---a colossus that made battle-mechs seem like children's toys. Its form radiated cold purpose utterly devoid of emotion, the perfect expression of consumption as philosophy.

"You've taken enough," Koraxos said, his voice carrying across the battlefield despite the chaos. "This world is not yours to consume."

The Harvester Prime paused, its featureless head tilting slightly as if registering this interruption with something approaching curiosity. Then it spoke---not in sound waves but in directly transmitted concepts that bypassed normal sensory processing.

"Meat that thinks it matters," the voice came from inside his skull, cold as deep space and twice as empty. "Little spark pretending to be flame. I will eat your light and shit out darkness."

"You always talk this much?" Koraxos taunted, circling the giant while looking for weaknesses. "Or is this just your way of saying hello?"

It raised both massive hands, energy gathering between them in a sphere of perfect darkness that seemed to pull light from its surroundings. The air distorted around this concentration, small objects beginning to drift toward it as gravity itself bent to its will.

Koraxos didn't wait for the attack to complete. He launched himself forward, phantom arm extended into a blade of concentrated energy that struck at the entity's chest with force that could shatter mountains. The blade connected with the light-absorbing material---and stopped, caught in substance that somehow devoured energy itself.

"Oh, come on!" Koraxos snarled, frustration boiling over. "What the hell are you made of?"

The Harvester Prime responded with fluid violence, one massive hand sweeping downward like a falling moon. Koraxos barely evaded, the phantom arm flickering as he burned precious energy to stay alive.

CURIOUS... LITTLE... SPARK... The voice carried hunger that could swallow galaxies. YOU... TASTE... OF... FORBIDDEN... GIFTS... I... WILL... SAVOR... EVE RY... DROP...

The sphere of darkness between its hands collapsed inward, then reformed into something worse---a web of hungry void that expanded outward like cosmic cancer. Where this darkness touched solid matter, that matter didn't vanish but transformed---stone became flesh, metal became sinew, everything twisted into forms that existed only to feed the entity's endless appetite.

Koraxos recognized the threat immediately. This wasn't mere destruction but fundamental perversion---the world itself being rewritten into an extension of the creature's body. If this corruption spread, it would transform the entire planet into a single massive organism designed for one purpose: feeding its master.

He struck at the expanding web, phantom arm blazing as he tried to burn away the corruption. Where transcendent energy touched the transformed landscape, it briefly remembered what it had been---stone reasserting itself, metal refusing to bleed.

But the effect was temporary, the darkness reforming almost immediately, learning from each contact. The Harvester Prime was adapting, its hunger growing more sophisticated with each taste of his power.

YES... STRUGGLE... FEED... ME... YOUR... DEFIANCE... The massive head tilted with predatory satisfaction.

I... HAVE... DEVOURED... WORLDS... THAT... BEGGED... FOR... MERCY... YOU... OFFER... SOMETHING... MORE... DELICIOUS...

The massive entity moved with explosive speed, covering the distance before Koraxos could react. One enormous hand closed around him, fingers of living shadow forming a cage that pulsed with malevolent hunger.

Within this cage, Koraxos felt his energy being systematically devoured---not stolen but consumed, like a fire eating wood. The phantom arm flickered dangerously as the very essence of what he was became food for something that had never known satisfaction.

SWEET... STOLEN... FIRE... The voice was intimate now, whisper-close despite the entity's massive scale. POWER... THAT... WAS... NEVER... MEANT... FOR... MO RTAL... FLESH... I... TASTE... MY... ANCIENT... ENEMY... IN... YOUR... VERY... BONES...

But memories flashed through Koraxos's mind---not random recollection but blazing clarity. The mines where he had labored in darkness. The fields where friends died beneath the overseer's lash. The moment of rebellion when chains were broken forever.

"I didn't break under their whips," he whispered, the words a prayer to whatever gods protected the stubborn. "I didn't break under their chains. I sure as hell won't break under you."

These memories weren't weakness but nuclear fuel---foundation stronger than fear. They reminded him that he had faced extinction before and chosen to continue despite overwhelming odds. This creature was just another form of the same fundamental threat---something that sought to reduce others to food.

DEFIANCE... TASTES... LIKE... COPPER... AND... STARLIGHT... The entity's grip tightened. FEED... ME... MORE...

"You don't get it, do you?" Koraxos said, his voice steadying despite the agony. "You're stuck in one flavor. I learned to change the recipe."

Instead of fighting the cage, Koraxos did something stupid—he relaxed into it. Let the thing try to eat him while he changed the flavor. The phantom arm stopped being solid and started being everything else—connection, memory, the stubborn refusal to stay still long enough to be swallowed.

WHAT... IS... THIS... The voice carried the first note of uncertainty it had expressed. YOU... CHANGE... YOUR... TASTE... YOUR... ESSENCE... SHIFTS...

The cage began to falter---not through weakening but through confusion. The Harvester Prime was trying to devour something that kept becoming something else, like trying to eat a river that changed course every time you opened your mouth.

Koraxos felt his form becoming less solid, less defined, spreading through relationships rather than occupying space. The phantom arm expanded not through more energy but through fundamental reimagining---not weapon but bridge, not tool but song.

IMPOSSIBLE... FLESH... CANNOT... FLOW... LIKE... THOUGHT...

He struck not at the creature's body but at its hunger itself. Where cosmic appetite expected prey to remain still while being consumed, it encountered something that refused to stay the same long enough to be eaten. Where it anticipated essence to be extracted, it found connections that existed partially beyond its ability to digest.

The massive entity shuddered, its perfect predatory nature disrupted by encountering food that wouldn't behave like food. The cage dissolved not through breaking but through losing its purpose---how do you contain something that exists as relationship rather than thing?

NO... NO... ALL... THINGS... FEED... THE... HUNGER... ALL... FLESH... SER VES... THE... APPETITE...

The Harvester Prime's form began to change, its smooth predatory design fracturing as ancient certainties cracked. What had been arms became writhing tentacles of pure hunger. What had been legs fused into a trunk of endless appetite. What had been a head split into a dozen mouths, each one screaming for sustenance that would finally satisfy the void within.

Koraxos pressed his advantage, phantom arm flowing into the entity's transforming essence not to destroy but to confuse---introducing the concept of satisfaction to a being that had never known fullness, the idea of choice to a creature that had only ever known hunger.

The effect cascaded through the Harvester Prime like poison through a bloodstream. Hunger that had never questioned its own nature suddenly found itself asking: what if there was enough? What if appetite could be satisfied? What if consumption wasn't the only way to exist?

These alien concepts tore through the entity's fundamental nature like philosophical viruses. Its massive form began to collapse inward, perfect predatory coordination breaking down as competing hungers fought each other for dominance. Mouths tried to devour tentacles, tentacles sought to strangle mouths, the trunk of endless appetite began consuming itself in desperation.

The Harvester Prime didn't explode or collapse dramatically---it simply forgot how to be unified. Parts continued functioning according to their basic nature but lost connection to the organizing principle that had made them collectively terrifying. The massive form settled to the ground in pieces, each section pursuing its own incompatible hunger until exhaustion claimed them all.

"Well, that was disgusting," Koraxos muttered as the last writhing appendage finally went still. Blood and worse things ran down his face, but his voice carried satisfaction deeper than exhaustion.

The waters he had summoned continued receding, returning to ancient aquifers through channels his influence had temporarily opened. The inland sea didn't vanish in moments but withdrew gradually, leaving behind muddy expanses that marked its brief existence and would be talked about in legends for generations to come.

With the Harvester Prime neutralized and Syntherion forces systematically eliminated by coordinated assault, the enemy vessels still operational began emergency ascent. They abandoned ground forces in retreat that prioritized preservation over continued conquest---the first time in their recorded history that these perfect soldiers had been forced to withdraw.

Koraxos descended slowly to the battlefield, each movement betraying profound exhaustion that went beyond physical fatigue. The phantom arm didn't blaze with spectacular energy but existed with quiet certainty---like an old weapon that had proven its worth once again and earned the right to rest.

Around him gathered representatives from all seven civilizations---warriors who had fought alongside each other despite histories of conflict, leaders who had coordinated defense across philosophical differences, beings who had discovered through necessity that diversity created strength rather than weakness.

"So... we won?" Velen asked, wiping blood from his brow as he stared at the retreating ships with something approaching disbelief.

Koraxos spat blood onto the muddy ground, harsh laughter escaping him. "Won? This?" He gestured at the devastation around them---buildings reduced to rubble, thousands dead or wounded, a landscape permanently altered by cosmic warfare. "This was just the warm-up act. The real bastards haven't even shown up yet."

"But they're retreating," Thalia said, limping forward in armor that had been pristine hours ago and was now scorched, dented, and stained with alien fluids.

"Yeah, and when you swat a biter-fly, does its whole nest just give up and move on?" Koraxos shook his head, exhaustion making his movements slow and deliberate. "We just pissed them off. The brothers will come now. Personally."

"But we showed them something they've never seen before," Elder Karim said, leaning heavily on his staff while the symbiotic organisms on his skin pulsed with patterns that spoke of pride beneath exhaustion. "Seven peoples fighting as one. That counts for something."

"It means they'll have to work for their meal," Koraxos said with a grim smile that didn't reach his eyes. "Instead of just swallowing us whole like they usually do."

High Chancellor Elara approached, her once-immaculate uniform now bearing the scars of someone who had refused to coordinate from safety. "They're used to worlds that tear themselves apart with infighting. Makes for easier digestion." She looked around at the mud-caked representatives of seven former enemies. "We're giving them indigestion."

"Great," Master Valoren muttered, wincing as he touched a crystalline shard embedded in his shoulder. "We've graduated from 'easy prey' to 'troublesome snack.'"

"Whatever happens next, we face it together," Neryssia said, her pearlescent skin blackened in spots from energy discharge. "Seven civilizations that never thought they'd share a meal, let alone a battlefield."

Koraxos surveyed the battered representatives---once enemies, now comrades forged in the crucible of impossible odds. He felt something unfamiliar stirring in his chest, an emotion he'd rarely allowed himself to feel: pride. Not in himself, but in them. In what they'd achieved together.

Not that he'd ever admit it.

"Get some rest," he said instead, his voice gruff with exhaustion and something deeper. "Patch yourselves up. You all look like shit." He turned away, pretending not to notice the small smiles his comment elicited. "And be ready. Next time won't be so easy."

As the allied forces began recovery operations, tending wounded and securing the battlefield, Koraxos stood alone at the center of what had been the most intense fighting. The ground beneath his feet still bore evidence of both destruction and creation---craters from energy weapons alongside mud from receding waters, debris from shattered structures mixed with soil from revealed seabed.

He looked down at his phantom arm, no longer flickering but steady now. What had begun as borrowed power had become something uniquely his own. Like him, it had been forged in crisis, shaped by necessity, defined by choice rather than circumstance.

The sky above darkened---not with clouds or atmospheric phenomena but with something more fundamental. Light itself began behaving differently, as though the basic relationships between energy and matter had shifted. The air felt thicker, heavier, charged with potential that made teeth ache and bones itch.

In the distance, beyond the city's outskirts where battlefield damage transitioned to untouched landscape, a sound emerged---not explosion or mechanical operation but something more primal. Thunder that carried harmonics impossible under normal conditions, vibrations that seemed to resonate with the molecular structure of matter itself.

"Fantastic," Koraxos muttered, exhaustion and sarcasm battling in his tone. "Just what we needed."

He sensed it then---a disturbance beyond normal detection. Something vast approached, its presence registered not through energy signature or dimensional distortion but through a feeling in his gut, an instinct honed through years of surviving when survival seemed impossible.

"They're coming," he said simply, his voice carrying to the representatives who had started to disperse.

From the mountain's depths came a low harmonic that made the ground tremble—not with fear, but with recognition. The Leviathan's ancient awareness stirred like bedrock feeling familiar pressure.

"Deeper weight approaches," the creature's voice pressed into their consciousness like the memory of glaciers. "Not the small hungry things that scurry and break. The old powers that shaped the first stones. They come with purpose that spans seasons."

Its massive form shifted within the mountain, movements that had been reshaping the landscape for eons continuing their patient work. Crystal formations throughout the city pulsed brighter, drawing strength from connections that reached into the planet's molten heart.

"But the mountain has been tested before by such forces. Deep roots hold when surface storms pass. The small builders have learned to flow together like underground rivers. Perhaps this time, the cracking will run both ways."

They didn't need explanation. They felt it too---primal dread that transcended rational assessment, instinctive recognition of apex predators approaching their territory. The kind of fear that lived in genetic memory, encoded in the DNA of prey species across a million worlds.

"How long?" Thalia asked, her military training cutting through the fear that threatened to paralyze rational thought.

"Hours at most," Koraxos replied, rolling his shoulders like a fighter preparing for another round. The phantom arm pulsed with renewed determination despite his depleted reserves. "They've skipped the foreplay. Now they're coming in person."

Elder Marex shifted his weight against his walking stick, feeling the familiar grain of bone beneath weathered fingers. Twenty years since he'd carved it from Overseer Drakon's femur—the man who'd worked thirty Noks to death in a single season before the "unfortunate" tunnel collapse. The stick had supported him through every crisis since, a reminder that even the mighty could fall when patience outlasted brutality.

His free hand found the small stone in his pocket—smooth river rock carved with tiny flowers, the last gift from daughter's hands before the slavers took her north. Kira would be thirty-seven now, if she lived. If she remembered her father's face. If the masters hadn't worked the art from her fingers the way they'd tried to work hope from every Nok heart.

"The final test," Elder Marex mused, his scholar's mind finding curiosity even in the face of extinction. "Whether we truly can stand against gods."

The walking stick trembled slightly—not from fear, but from the arthritis that had crept into joints worn down by forty years of crawling through mine shafts that barely fit human bodies. He'd been the unofficial engineer down there, the one who calculated load-bearing weights and structural integrity because the Luminarai couldn't be bothered to learn how dirt and stone actually behaved.

Strange how that knowledge served him now, reading the stress patterns in Koraxos's face the same way he'd once read fault lines in tunnel walls. Both carried more weight than they were designed for. Both would hold until they didn't.

"Not gods," Koraxos corrected, his voice sharp with old anger and new understanding. "Just bullies with bigger sticks than most. Trust me, I know the type."

"Then we prepare," High Chancellor Elara said, iron entering her voice despite her evident exhaustion. Her golden eyes, though dimmed with fatigue, still gleamed with determination. "Seven civilizations together. If we die, we die as one."

"Nobody's dying today," Velen muttered, though his face suggested he didn't quite believe his own words. "We already kicked the asses of their advance team. Maybe they'll think twice."

In the sudden quiet that followed cosmic judgment, Velen and Niri found each other in the rubble with the automatic precision of twenty years together.

"Still breathing?" Niri asked, running practical hands over Velen's arms and chest, checking for damage her eyes might miss.

"Still breathing," he confirmed, returning the favor. His bio-crystal arm flickered as it processed residual energies from the battle. "Kids are gonna ask questions we don't have answers for."

"Kids always ask questions we don't have answers for," Niri replied, her engineer's mind already cataloguing the structural damage around them. "Difference is this time the questions involve cosmic horror instead of why the sky is blue."

"Think we can explain this?"

"Same way we explain everything else. With truth, simple words, and the promise that we'll figure it out together."

Koraxos laughed, genuine humor despite its darkness. "That's the spirit. Delusion keeps you going when hope runs out."

As the representatives returned to their respective positions, preparing for what might be their final stand, Koraxos remained alone at the battlefield's center. The phantom arm pulsed steadily beside him---no longer spectacular but reliable, like an old friend who had proven their worth through countless trials.

Above them, the sky continued its unnatural transformation. Colors that had no names painted the horizon in patterns that suggested intelligence behind their arrangement. The air grew thick enough to taste, charged with energies that made reality itself seem fragile.

In the distance, that impossible thunder sounded again, closer now. Where it passed, the very landscape seemed to hold its breath. Birds fell silent. Insects stopped their buzzing. Even the wind paused, as though nature itself recognized the approach of forces that existed on scales beyond its comprehension.

Koraxos thought of the children---Sela, Miran, and little Tork. They were safe in the deepest shelters, along with all the other non-combatants. Sela had given him a small stone before they'd separated, a simple river rock with a streak of white quartz running through it. "For luck," she'd said solemnly, as though passing on an ancient relic.

He slipped his hand into his pocket, feeling the smooth contours of the stone. Such a small thing to fight for---the right of a child to collect pretty rocks, to grow up without collars, to live without fear.

"Worth it," he decided aloud, speaking to the approaching storm.

The thunder crashed again, and this time the ground shook with sympathetic vibration. In the distance, where the disturbance seemed to originate, the very air began to tear---not with mechanical precision but with the organic inevitability of a wound opening in flesh.

Through this tear came light that wasn't light---illumination that operated according to principles that had nothing to do with photons or wavelengths. It was the kind of radiance that suggested the concept of light itself had been reimagined by minds operating on scales beyond mortal understanding.

Koraxos felt rather than saw the approach of entities that defied conventional perception. They were coming---not as distant consumers but as direct intervenors, cosmic beings drawn by resistance that challenged their fundamental expectations about how reality should function.

The brothers were coming. The real battle was about to begin.

He raised the phantom arm, and as if in response, the tear in reality widened. Ancient forces older than worlds approached their small corner of existence, drawn by the audacity of mortals who had dared to say no.

"Everybody dies," he said to himself, a half-smile twisting his lips as he remembered words spoken a lifetime ago. "Might as well make it count."

The sky ripped open completely, and existence itself held its breath.

In this moment of terrible anticipation, as cosmic entities prepared to manifest directly into their world, Koraxos felt something unexpected---a sense of completion. The arc of his life, from enslaved miner to vengeful destroyer to reluctant protector, had brought him precisely where he needed to be.

The representatives of seven civilizations rejoined him on the battlefield, each battered but unbowed, standing together not because they had to, but because they chose to. Whatever came through that tear in reality would face not seven divided peoples, but one unified world.

As the first tendrils of cosmic power reached through the dimensional breach, Koraxos stepped forward, phantom arm raised not in surrender but in defiance.

"You want this world?" he called out, his voice carrying across the battlefield with authority earned through blood and choice. "You're going to have to go through me first. And trust me---" he grinned, a fierce, feral expression that held all the rage and hope and defiance of a being who had broken every chain ever placed upon him, "---I'm a lot harder to digest than I look."

The cosmic storm broke over them, and the true battle began.

10

Chapter 10: When Gods Learn to Bleed

The world tore open like wet paper.

Reality split along a jagged vertical line that stretched from muddy earth to crimson sky, the borders of the wound glowing with colors that hurt to look upon. The air surrounding this breach collapsed inward, creating a vacuum that pulled debris, bodies, and water from the newly receded sea toward its hungry maw.

Deep beneath the mountain, something vast stirred in response to the dimensional wound. The Obsidian Leviathan felt the tear in reality like a violation of its ancient territory.

Koraxos planted his feet, the phantom arm anchoring him to the earth as the world shuddered around him. The pain of his recent battle against the Syntherions and the Harvester Prime still burned through every fiber of his being, but he forced himself to stand tall as cosmic horror manifested before him.

"All units, spread formation!" Thalia's voice cut through the chaos from the command position. "Do not engage directly! Support and harass only!"

Velen stumbled to Koraxos's side, blood caking his face, one hand gripping a fallen Syntherion's weapon while the other—scarred with bio-crystal growths from the void-touch—clutched at Koraxos's shoulder for stability.

"Is that—" he began, voice barely audible above the howling void.

"Yeah," Koraxos said, wiping blood from his mouth. "That's them."

A low harmonic resonance thrummed through the bedrock, felt more than heard—the territorial warning of something ancient responding to cosmic trespassers.

From the wound in reality came a hand—if such a mundane word could describe what emerged. It was simultaneously skeletal and overflowing with flesh, ancient beyond comprehension yet newborn in this reality. Fingers that stretched longer than buildings unfolded into the atmosphere, joints bending in directions that defied anatomy.

In the deep chambers beneath Toran, crystal formations that had pulsed with gentle bioluminescence for eons suddenly blazed with agitated light. The mountain itself was awakening.

The tear widened.

A figure stepped through—or rather, unfolded itself into their dimension. Its proportions were roughly humanoid, though it stood taller than Oshar's highest remaining spire. Its body constantly shifted between states of matter, sometimes appearing solid enough to cast shadows, other times transparent as mist.

Most disturbing was its face—a perfect, symmetrical visage that resembled a sculpture more than living flesh. The eyes were colorless voids that somehow still conveyed cold intelligence.

"Zorakil," Koraxos said, recognition flowing through his transcendent awareness.

As if hearing his name, the cosmic entity's attention shifted toward Koraxos. The weight of that regard fell upon him like a mountain, the sheer pressure of consciousness beyond mortal comprehension threatening to crush his mind into paste.

Underground, massive coils began to move with purpose that transcended animal instinct. The Leviathan had decided these cosmic interlopers posed a threat to its territory.

"Twenty-two years of breathing, little slave," Zorakil said, his words emerging not as sound but as concepts depositing themselves directly into their minds. His voice carried the casual cruelty of nobility acknowledging a particularly entertaining pet. "Every breath drawn in defiance of your betters. Your rebellion amuses me—such predictable fury from creatures who mistake suffering for strength."

The tear in reality rippled again, and a second entity emerged—this one a stark contrast to the first. Where Zorakil's presence felt like the void between stars, this being radiated energy that scorched the air into plasma. Its form was a constantly shifting inferno of colors that had no names in any mortal tongue, shapes flowing into one another with violent, beautiful chaos. Lightning crackled continuously around its massive frame, striking the ground in patterns that left glowing runes smoldering in the mud.

Each lightning strike penetrated deep into the earth, and something vast below responded with territorial fury. Tremors ran through the mountain's foundations as ancient architecture began to shift.

Unlike its brother, this entity's face was a riot of emotion—twisted into a rictus grin that spoke of madness and joy and hate and pleasure all at once. Eyes like dying stars swept across the battlefield, and where they gazed, matter simply collapsed into more base components.

"Kaelthor," Koraxos identified, his phantom arm pulsing defensively as the second brother's attention turned toward him.

"Ssssweet little rebellion," Kaelthor's voice boomed, the words manifesting as burning sensations along the spines of all who heard them. Unlike his brother's clinical precision, Kaelthor's speech came in fractured bursts of emotional intensity, punctuated by serpentine hisses. "I ssssmell desssperation wrapped in borrowed power. When I finally tear you apart, your sssscreams will echo acrosss dimensionsss. There'sss sssomething pure about the way defiance breaksss---like glasss ssshattering into perfect fragmentsss."

The mountain groaned—a sound that came from geological depths, as if the stone itself protested the cosmic violation above.

Koraxos spat blood into the mud. "Come and try, you cosmic shitheads."

The phantom arm blazed to full intensity as he streaked toward Zorakil like a comet of blue fire. But instead of striking directly, he slammed both fists into the earth below, sending shockwaves deep into the planet's core.

The shockwaves reached chambers that had slept in darkness for eons. Something immense stirred in response, obsidian scales grinding against crystal walls with sounds like continents shifting.

"You want to see what twenty-two years of rage looks like?" Koraxos roared, his voice echoing across dimensions. "Let me introduce you to everyone who ever died fighting bastards like you!"

The ground cracked open like an egg, and death came pouring out. Every warrior who'd ever died fighting, every slave who'd died free, every mother who'd died protecting her kids—all of them rising at once. Not neat ranks of ghostly soldiers, but a tide of rage that had been waiting underground for someone to finally give them permission to get even.

In the deepest chambers, the Leviathan's territorial instincts reached full alarm. These cosmic entities were not just intruding—they were disturbing the very foundations of its domain, awakening the ancient dead.

Ancient warriors emerged first, their ghostly forms wielding weapons of bone and crystal, eyes burning with the fury of those who had died protecting their tribes. Behind them came legions of more recent fighters—slaves who had died in rebellion, soldiers who had fallen defending their cities, mothers who had died protecting their children.

But Koraxos wasn't finished. His phantom arm extended deeper, reaching through layers of history that predated civilization itself. The earth cracked wider, and from the deepest strata came shapes that made even the brothers pause—massive spectral forms that dwarfed buildings.

The Leviathan felt the geological disruption and responded with movements that sent tremors through every crystal formation in the mountain. Ancient passages began to realign themselves as the creature prepared for territorial defense.

Ghostly Crystalwyrms materialized first—serpentine behemoths with hides of living gemstone, their spectral forms still radiating the prismatic light that had once made them apex predators. Each was easily two hundred feet long, with crystalline fangs that could crack mountains and eyes like captured stars.

Behind them rose the Thunder Titans—six-legged giants whose every step had once shaken continents, their spectral forms towering three hundred feet high. Their tusks were curved spears of bone that could pierce the sky, and their trumpeting calls made reality itself tremble.

Each spectral roar resonated through the mountain's crystal networks, and in the depths, the Leviathan answered with harmonic frequencies that made the entire peak vibrate like a struck bell.

From the ancient oceans came the Void Krakens—tentacled nightmares with hundreds of writhing appendages, each one thick as a building. Their spectral forms moved through air as easily as they had once moved through primordial seas, their beaked maws large enough to swallow cities.

Most terrifying were the Apex Shadowmaws—predators that had hunted by bending light itself, their ghostly forms still rippling with reality distortions. They had been the size of buildings but moved like liquid darkness, their jaws containing not teeth but miniature black holes that had allowed them to devour anything.

Underground, massive coils tightened with anticipation. The Leviathan recognized these ancient apex predators—they had been rivals in epochs past. Now they fought as allies against a common threat.

"Every creature that ever lived," Koraxos announced, floating above his impossible army. "Every being that ever fought to survive. Every life that ever refused to surrender. THAT'S what you're trying to consume!"

The phantom army stretched beyond the horizon—millions upon millions of spectral forms. Ancient Crystalwyrms coiled through the air like living rainbows of death. Thunder Titans stomped forward with steps that left craters in the spectral realm. Void Krakens writhed through dimensions, their tentacles reaching across impossible distances. Shadowmaws prowled the edges of the army, their distorted forms making space itself ripple with predatory hunger.

Each spectral footfall sent vibrations deep into the earth, and the Leviathan's massive form began to move through passages that had contained it for millennia, drawn upward by territorial imperative.

All united by one simple truth: they had lived, and living meant fighting for the right to exist.

As the phantom army surged forward, the living forces opened fire.

"Light 'em up! Every weapon, every angle!" Elara's voice crackled through the comms, her golden eyes blazing with enhancement overload. "Show these cosmic assholes what seven worlds fighting together looks like!"

Through the crystal networks, she felt something else stirring—a massive presence in the mountain's depths that was responding to the cosmic battle with territorial awareness.

Soltari battle-mechs flanked the brothers' positions, plasma cannons blazing not to harm cosmic flesh but to force movement, to prevent the entities from planting themselves firmly. The shots struck uselessly against divine skin, but they achieved their purpose—keeping the brothers mobile, reactive.

"The mountain's still singing!" Master Valoren called out, coordinating the crystal-masters from his position behind a shattered wall. "Whatever that crystal beast is doing down there, it's keeping us from getting scattered across seventeen different realities!"

His crystals suddenly blazed brighter as something in the mountain's depths began harmonizing with their frequencies—an ancient intelligence that recognized allied purpose.

Drustali crystal weapons sang in harmonic discord, their resonance disrupting the brothers' entropy and chaos fields just enough to give the ghost army precious seconds of coherence.

Pelagian pressure attacks struck like invisible hammers—Neryssia and her warriors manipulating atmospheric force to knock the brothers off balance precisely when ghostly Crystalwyrms attempted to coil around them. The cosmic entities staggered, their perfect coordination disrupted by attacks they couldn't easily perceive.

"The desert teaches patience, but patience won't save us now!" Elder Karim's voice rang out as his forces deployed organisms that made the ground treacherous, the air toxic to cosmic entities unaccustomed to biological warfare. "Time to show these star-eaters how the desert bites back!"

He felt it through his symbiotic networks—something vast and predatory stirring beneath them, ancient territorial instincts awakening in response to invasion.

Nok engineers had been busy during the inland sea battle, rigging explosive charges throughout the plaza. "Rigging charges here, there, and everywhere!" Velen's voice crackled through crystal networks. "When these cosmic bastards step wrong, they're gonna learn what Nok engineering feels like!"

His words carried unusual harmonics as the mountain's crystal networks amplified them, as if something below was lending its voice to their coordination.

"Forget the manual—throw everything we've got at them!" Thalia commanded, her tactical displays showing the flow of battle while directing each civilization's efforts to maximum effect. "Sometimes the best plan is controlled chaos!"

Her displays flickered with readings she didn't recognize—massive thermal signatures deep beneath the mountain, something immense moving through passages that shouldn't exist.

The impact was cataclysmic.

A ghostly Crystalwyrm, its prismatic form stretching three hundred feet, wrapped itself around Kaelthor's chaotic essence. For the first time in eons, the cosmic entity actually staggered, his mad laughter faltering as spectral coils tightened around his form with the fury of apex predation.

"What isss thisss sssensation?" Kaelthor gasped, his chaotic energy fluctuating wildly. "It... it createsss patternsss I've never ssseen! Like... like beautiful desstruction that won't ssstay destroyed!"

In the depths, the Leviathan felt its ancient rivals' attack and responded with approval—a harmonic rumble that strengthened the spectral bonds.

Thunder Titans charged Zorakil in formation, their massive tusks lowered like cosmic battering rams. The first one struck with force that would have shattered continents, driving the perfect entity backward across the battlefield. The second and third followed in devastating succession, their spectral weight actually making Zorakil stumble.

"Impossible," Zorakil breathed, golden ichor leaking from hairline cracks in his marble perfection. "Ghosts cannot possess sufficient mass to—"

The mountain's foundations shuddered as something vast moved in response to his words—a territorial challenge answered by ancient authority.

A Void Kraken's tentacles lashed around his legs, each appendage thick as a building and charged with the fury of every sea creature that had ever died fighting. The cosmic entity found himself actually restrained, his perfect balance disrupted by the weight of accumulated vengeance.

Above them all, the Apex Shadowmaws descended like living nightmares, their reality-distorting forms making space itself bend around them. Where they struck, even the brothers' cosmic essence warped and twisted, forced to acknowledge predators that had once hunted by reshaping existence itself.

Each reality distortion sent ripples through the earth, and in the abyss below, obsidian eyes tracked the cosmic battle with predatory interest.

The combined assault created chaos the brothers hadn't anticipated. While they easily destroyed spectral warriors with entropy and madness, they also had to dodge plasma fire, resist crystal disruption, compensate for pressure attacks, avoid biological hazards, sidestep explosive traps, and track coordinated timing across seven different tactical approaches.

"They remember pain," Koraxos explained, his voice carrying across the battlefield as spectral titans clashed with cosmic entities in battles that shook the foundations of reality. "Every death. Every moment of suffering. Every instance of being devoured by something that thought it was superior. They're not trying to kill you—they're trying to make you FEEL what prey feels like!"

Each seismic impact from the cosmic battle traveled deep into the earth, where the Leviathan absorbed the vibrations like a territorial war-song.

The brothers fought back with increasing fury. Zorakil's entropy fields swept outward in waves, aging the ghostly army by geological epochs. Spectral warriors crumbled to dust, their essence scattered to cosmic winds. But for every ghost that fell, ten more rose from deeper strata, older and hungrier.

Kaelthor's chaos erupted in brilliant explosions of madness, his form becoming a living storm of destruction that existed in seventeen dimensions simultaneously. Void Krakens dissolved into component emotions, their tentacles becoming ribbons of pure sensation that he devoured with gleeful hunger.

Underground, massive coils tightened as the Leviathan felt the ancient dead being systematically destroyed. Its territorial fury reached new heights.

But the phantom army was infinite. Every creature that had ever died, every being that had ever fought for its existence, every life that had been consumed by cosmic hunger—they all stood together now, united in spectral fury.

For ten minutes that felt like centuries, the phantom army held—not alone, but supported by living determination that refused to make the fight easy for gods. The combined assault of dead and living, spectral and mortal, created the most complex battlefield cosmic entities had ever faced.

The mountain itself seemed to pulse with each clash, as if something vast below was keeping time with the battle's rhythm.

But ghosts, no matter how determined, could only endure so long against forces that had consumed entire universes.

Zorakil expanded his perfect form, growing from merely giant to truly cosmic in scale. His entropy fields intensified beyond anything the spectral realm could withstand. Even the mightiest Thunder Titans began to fade, their essence aged beyond the ability to maintain coherence.

Kaelthor's chaos reached critical mass, becoming a living storm of madness that existed as pure destruction given form. His laughter became a weapon that unmade the very concept of organized resistance, unraveling spectral unity into component despair.

In the depths, the Leviathan felt its ancient rivals fading and roared its fury—a sound that shook the mountain to its core and sent avalanches cascading down distant peaks.

One by one, the phantom army began to fade. The Crystalwyrms' prismatic light dimmed and went dark. The Thunder Titans' trumpeting calls became whispers, then silence. The Void Krakens' tentacles dissolved into memory. The Shadowmaws flickered and vanished like nightmares at dawn.

As the last of his ghostly allies faded into nothingness, Koraxos floated alone above the battlefield, his phantom arm the only spectral form remaining. But instead of despair, his face showed grim satisfaction.

"Phase one complete," he said with a bloodied smile.

Below, something massive began to move with purposeful intent, no longer content to observe territorial violation.

Before the brothers could react, Koraxos extended both arms and began to spin, his phantom limb leaving trails of blue fire that didn't fade but lingered in the air like frozen lightning. As he spun faster, the trails multiplied, creating geometric patterns of energy that hung in space around him like a three-dimensional constellation.

"Energy Constellation Matrix," he whispered, and the hanging patterns suddenly blazed to life.

The patterns resonated with something deep below—harmonic frequencies that reached ancient consciousness and found recognition.

"Track his movement through the energy web!" Elara commanded as Koraxos flowed through his geometric attack patterns. "Provide distraction strikes when he repositions!"

As Koraxos flowed through his geometric attack patterns, striking both brothers from impossible angles, Soltari plasma fire created visual interference—bright flashes that prevented the cosmic entities from tracking all of his energy trails simultaneously.

"Resonance boost on those coordinates!" Valoren called out as the Drustali crystal-masters detected the harmonic frequencies of Koraxos's energy web and began amplifying them. "Strengthen his strike pathways!"

Their amplification reached deep into the mountain, where ancient crystal formations began responding with harmonic patterns they hadn't used for millions of years.

Where the phantom arm carved slashes across cosmic flesh, crystal resonance made the wounds glow brighter, last longer, hurt more. The brothers found their perfect healing slowed by harmonic interference they couldn't immediately identify.

The attack was unlike anything that had ever existed. Instead of a single strike, Koraxos moved through the hanging energy patterns like a dancer following choreography written in starfire. Each movement connected to the next through trails of power that existed as physical constructs in space, creating a web of destruction that attacked from every angle simultaneously.

Each geometric intersection pulsed with harmonics that reached deep into the earth, where something vast tracked their patterns with predatory intelligence.

He struck Zorakil seventeen times in the space of a heartbeat, each blow following energy paths that carved through cosmic flesh like swords of crystallized vengeance. The phantom arm left blazing slashes across the entity's perfect form—wounds that actually drew golden blood.

"Insolent slave!" Zorakil roared, his marble perfection marred by cuts that glowed with spectral fire. "Your presumption will be—"

His words were interrupted by a deep harmonic resonance from below—not quite a roar, but unmistakably territorial.

But Koraxos was already moving, flowing through his energy web like liquid lightning. Each strike built upon the last, the constellation matrix allowing him to attack from positions that existed in theoretical space rather than physical location. He hit Kaelthor thirty-seven times from directions that shouldn't have been geometrically possible, the phantom arm carving wounds that leaked chaotic energy like cosmic blood.

"Current boost on that approach vector!" Neryssia commanded as Pelagian pressure specialists created atmospheric currents that helped Koraxos flow between energy nodes faster than the brothers could track. "Push him toward the intersection point!"

She felt it through her atmospheric awareness—massive displacement far below, something immense moving through spaces that shouldn't exist.

"Thisss pain!" Kaelthor shrieked, his form convulsing as spectral energy invaded his chaotic essence. "It... HISS... it doesn't tassste like breaking! It tassstesss of... of sssomething that growsss ssstronger when pressssed! I want... I NEED to understtstand!"

The cosmic entity lashed out with tentacles of pure madness, but Koraxos danced between them, his Energy Constellation Matrix creating paths through impossibility itself. He struck and moved, struck and flowed, each attack connected to the next through geometric precision that existed as art painted in battle.

Each successful strike resonated through the mountain's foundations, and something below answered with approval—harmonic frequencies that strengthened the constellation matrix.

"Zorakil is learning to age the energy trails!" Elder Karim reported, his bio-networks detecting the brothers' adaptation patterns. "Kaelthor is introducing random variables to disrupt matrix precision!"

His bio-networks also detected something else—massive life signs deep beneath them, something that registered as predator responding to territorial threat.

"Structural weak points in the plaza surface at those coordinates!" Velen called to Koraxos, his engineering senses detecting anomalous readings. "Drive them toward the fault lines!"

His engineering senses detected anomalous readings from deep beneath the marked coordinates—massive spaces that his instruments insisted couldn't exist.

"All units, next burst in five seconds!" Thalia coordinated, her tactical displays showing the flow of energy and the brothers' positions. "Koraxos, eastern matrix node will be clear for strike approach!"

Her displays flickered with impossible readings from deep beneath the mountain—thermal signatures that suggested something the size of a city was moving through spaces her maps said were solid stone.

For five minutes, Koraxos fought both brothers simultaneously through his energy web, his phantom arm blazing trails of vengeance that carved wounds across cosmic flesh. The matrix allowed him to be everywhere and nowhere, striking from angles that existed only in the spaces between heartbeats.

But even this unprecedented assault had limits. The brothers began to adapt, their cosmic nature learning to track patterns that existed outside normal geometry. Zorakil's entropy fields started aging the energy trails themselves, while Kaelthor's chaos introduced random variables that disrupted the matrix's precision.

In the depths, massive coils shifted with increasing agitation as the Leviathan sensed the battle turning against the defender of its territory.

Time for the final gambit.

Koraxos's form began to shift, his solid presence becoming something more fluid, more negotiable. "Phase Storm," he announced, and suddenly there were dozens of him.

Not illusions or copies—temporal echoes. Koraxos existing in multiple moments simultaneously, each one real, each one attacking from a different point in time. Past-Koraxos struck while present-Koraxos defended and future-Koraxos prepared assaults that wouldn't happen for several seconds.

The temporal distortions sent ripples through dimensional space that reached ancient consciousness in the depths—something that existed partially outside linear time recognized the technique.

The civilizations immediately faced a coordination nightmare: which Koraxos to support?

"I'm tracking seventeen distinct temporal signatures!" Thalia reported, her Luminarai tactical systems designed for complex battlefield management proving crucial. "All units, coordinate on primary temporal phase—ignore the echoes until they stabilize!"

Her systems also detected massive movement in spaces that existed outside normal time-flow—something vast responding to the temporal storm.

Soltari battle-mechs split their fire patterns, each unit assigned to support a different temporal echo. Their enhanced targeting systems could track multiple timestreams simultaneously, providing covering fire across past, present, and future battle positions.

"Crystal resonance transcends linear time!" Valoren observed with scientific fascination even as battle raged, his Drustali crystals resonating across temporal boundaries. "Maintaining amplification across all temporal phases!"

Their resonance patterns reached something in the depths that existed across multiple temporal states—ancient consciousness that had experienced time differently for eons.

The battle exploded across multiple timestreams.

Koraxos-from-ten-seconds-ago delivered a devastating uppercut to Zorakil's jaw while Koraxos-from-five-seconds-in-the-future carved energy slashes across the entity's back. Present-Koraxos grappled with Kaelthor while Past-Koraxos attacked from below and Future-Koraxos struck from above, all existing simultaneously in a temporal storm of coordinated vengeance.

Each temporal intersection created harmonics that penetrated dimensional barriers, reaching consciousness that existed in temporal spaces beyond normal access.

"Pressure current for Past-Koraxos on approach seven!" Neryssia called out as Pelagian pressure attacks created atmospheric conditions that helped temporal echoes maintain coherence. "Future-Koraxos, thermal updraft ready on your mark!"

She felt massive displacement in temporal spaces below—something that moved through time as easily as through physical dimension.

The brothers found themselves fighting an opponent who existed across multiple moments, whose attacks came from yesterday while his defenses belonged to tomorrow. Even their cosmic reflexes couldn't track enemies who assaulted them through time itself.

"This violates the natural order!" Zorakil screamed, his perfect form bleeding from wounds inflicted by opponents who existed in seventeen different timestreams. "Time flows in one direction! Causality has rules!"

His words echoed through temporal spaces and were answered by something vast below—a harmonic that suggested causality was more flexible than cosmic entities assumed.

"I'm a slave," all the Koraxos echoes replied in perfect unison, their voices creating harmonics that made reality shiver. "We don't follow rules—we break them."

"Bio-toxins effective against cosmic entities regardless of temporal displacement!" Karim reported as Dunekin biological networks detected temporal stress patterns and began adapting their environmental hazards to function across multiple timestreams.

His networks also detected massive bio-signatures moving through temporal dimensions—something alive that existed across multiple moments simultaneously.

"Screw temporal precision—just blow up everything they might step on!" Velen declared with characteristic directness, his solution to the greatest engineering challenge yet.

His explosives resonated with temporal echoes, and something vast below responded by shifting massive weight to destabilize cosmic footing across multiple timestreams.

The multi-temporal assault continued with devastating intensity. Each version of Koraxos fought with the accumulated skill and fury of his entire existence, but from different points along his timeline. Koraxos-the-slave struck with desperate rage. Koraxos-the-rebel fought with revolutionary fire. Koraxos-the-protector battled with transcendent purpose. All of them united across time in singular determination to make gods bleed.

Each temporal strike resonated through spaces where past, present, and future intersected—spaces where something immense had learned to exist across all possible moments.

Kaelthor's chaotic form erupted in frustrated fury as phantom limbs struck him from temporal angles he couldn't perceive. His madness, refined across cosmic epochs, struggled to process attacks that came from when rather than where. "How do I paint with sssomething that exisssts in yesssterday while creating from tomorrow? HISS! They move like... like art I never learned to make!"

"Carefully," Future-Koraxos suggested helpfully, even as Past-Koraxos drove a spectral fist through the entity's chest cavity.

The temporal paradox sent shockwaves through dimensions where the Leviathan had learned to hunt across multiple moments—ancient techniques stirring in response to familiar combat patterns.

The coordinated support across seven civilizations and seventeen timestreams created the most complex battle in recorded history. The brothers found themselves facing not just temporal echoes but coordinated assistance from multiple moments, making their adaptation calculations exponentially more difficult.

For five minutes that existed across multiple timestreams, the coordinated forces held their own against cosmic entities—not through superior power, but through determination that refused to be simple.

In the depths, something vast tracked every temporal intersection with predatory satisfaction—ancient hunger recognizing worthy prey.

But temporal warfare demanded prices even coordinated mortals couldn't afford indefinitely.

Both entities were actually staggered now, their movements showing the first signs of genuine uncertainty. They had been surprised, overwhelmed, forced to actually defend instead of simply consuming. For the first time in their existence, they faced an opponent who made them work for victory.

But they were still cosmic entities who had ended civilizations before these worlds had learned to count years.

"Enough games," Zorakil declared, his voice carrying the absolute authority of nobility finally losing patience with an entertaining but overreaching pet. His perfect form began to expand, growing from merely giant to truly cosmic in scale, his entropy fields intensifying beyond anything reality had ever been forced to contain.

His expansion sent pressure waves deep into the earth, where something vast and ancient felt cosmic authority asserting itself in its territory.

Kaelthor joined his brother's escalation, his chaotic form becoming a living storm of madness that existed simultaneously in seventeen dimensions. His laughter became a weapon that unraveled the very concept of organized time, collapsing Koraxos's Phase Storm ability with casual brutality.

The temporal collapse created harmonics that reached ancient consciousness existing across multiple time-states—something that had witnessed the rise and fall of temporal civilizations.

The temporal echoes snapped back into single existence with agonizing force, and Koraxos screamed as multiple lifetimes of battle fatigue struck him simultaneously. The phantom arm flickered dangerously as cosmic pressure overwhelmed even enhanced mortal support.

Underground, massive coils tightened as the Leviathan felt its territory's defender faltering against cosmic authority.

"All units, defensive formations!" Thalia commanded as the brothers pressed their advantage. "Protect civilian evacuation routes! Do not engage directly!"

"The Soltari will deploy remaining medical resources to establish field hospitals!" High Chancellor Elara coordinated the shield network while maintaining covering fire to slow the brothers' advance. "Our neural interface technologies can still function despite cosmic disruption!"

Her shields flickered with harmonics that reached deep into the mountain, where something vast approved of territorial protection.

"Crystal matrices at maximum defensive resonance!" Master Valoren directed the creation of safe zones that could withstand cosmic overflow. "Protecting essential personnel!"

The defensive crystals blazed brighter as something in the depths synchronized with their protective frequencies.

For all his impossible powers, for all his temporal manipulation and spectral armies, Koraxos was still fundamentally mortal facing entities that had existed since before stars learned the concept of death.

Zorakil reached out with movements that spoke of cosmic inevitability, his perfect fingers closing around Koraxos's throat with the inexorable certainty of nobility claiming its due. Each digit positioned with aristocratic precision, entropy fields beginning their work the moment contact was established.

The moment cosmic flesh touched mortal throat, something vast below roared—a sound that shook the mountain's foundations and sent tremors through every crystal formation.

"Twenty-two years of mining taught you to strike hard, little slave," Zorakil observed with the patience of someone explaining basic concepts to a slow student. "But you never learned where you belong in the natural hierarchy. Shall I remind you?"

The aging began immediately. Where cosmic fingers touched transcendent flesh, Koraxos felt his phantom limb experiencing decades in seconds. The blue fire that had burned with revolutionary fury began to flicker and dim as cellular structure remembered exhaustion, entropy, the weight of years lived under someone else's authority.

Each flicker of the phantom arm sent sympathetic pulses through crystal networks that reached the depths, where obsidian eyes blazed with territorial fury.

"We can manage water purification and distribution!" Neryssia offered as Pelagian pressure specialists created atmospheric barriers that slowed cosmic attacks without stopping them. "The inland sea Koraxos summoned has partially receded, but sufficient reserves remain accessible!"

Their pressure manipulations detected massive displacement below—something immense moving through spaces that resonated with their atmospheric techniques.

"Nok engineers have always excelled at improvisation with limited resources!" Velen added despite personal concern for his friend. "We'll establish temporary shelter and begin surveying for reconstruction priorities!"

Their bio-networks suddenly blazed with readings from deep below—massive life signs unlike anything in their databases, something that registered as apex predator responding to threatened territory.

"Observe your proper place," Zorakil continued, his entropy fields intensifying as he demonstrated the gulf between mortal ambition and cosmic reality. "Slaves serve. Masters rule. This is the way of things, written in the fundamental structure of existence itself. Your borrowed power cannot rewrite laws that predate your species."

Kaelthor drifted closer, his chaotic form rippling with sensory delight as he tasted Koraxos's growing desperation. "Such exquisite defiance turning to despair! Like wine aged in barrels of broken dreams! Let me savor every drop of your diminishing hope!"

Each word of cosmic mockery resonated through the mountain, and something vast below responded with harmonics that spoke of territorial challenge accepted.

The cosmic entity extended tendrils of pure sensation that invaded Koraxos's consciousness, forcing him to experience the deaths of every world they had consumed, every civilization they had devoured, every instance of resistance being systematically crushed beneath cosmic superiority.

"Controlled collapse in sectors four and nine!" Velen reported as Nok engineers rigged emergency demolitions to create barriers and escape routes. "Civilians have clear path to deep shelters!"

His explosives sent vibrations deep into the earth, where something massive shifted in response to the familiar rhythms of controlled destruction.

"Evacuation proceeding at optimal efficiency!" Thalia reported even as cosmic battle raged overhead. "All non-essential personnel reaching minimum safe distance!"

Her coordination networks carried harmonics that reached ancient intelligence in the depths—something that recognized the patterns of territorial protection.

"Feel what defeat tastes like," Kaelthor whispered, his words carrying the flavor of ten thousand fallen heroes. "Know that your struggle was always meaningless. You are food pretending to be predator, and now the beautiful breaking beginsss."

Underground, massive coils shifted with predatory recognition. Something vast had been listening to cosmic arrogance, and territorial fury reached critical mass.

For a moment that lasted centuries, Koraxos felt his will beginning to crack under the weight of cosmic certainty. The phantom arm dimmed further, its blue fire guttering like a candle in a hurricane of inevitability. He was nothing. He had always been nothing. The idea that slaves could challenge gods was the ultimate joke, and now the punchline was being written in his dissolved essence.

But then, through the pain and despair and crushing weight of cosmic judgment, Koraxos heard something that changed everything.

Voices. Distant but growing stronger. Not the phantom army—those ghosts had faded beyond recall. These were different voices, familiar voices, carrying across dimensional space with the power of connection rather than rage.

"Koraxos!" Velen's voice, rough with determination and loyalty that transcended death itself.

"You stubborn ass!" Niri's voice, sharp with the love that existed only between those who had survived the unsurvivable together.

"Show them what miners know about breaking things!" Thalia's voice, carrying the authority of someone who had learned to lead through service rather than dominance.

Deep beneath them all, something vast heard the voices of territorial defenders and responded with approval—harmonic frequencies that resonated with pack behavior, with collective defense of shared domain.

More voices joined the chorus—every ally he had ever fought beside, every friend he had ever protected, every person who had chosen to trust him with their lives and futures. Not calling him to surrender, but reminding him of what surrender would cost.

The children. Sela and her collection of pretty rocks. Miran with his questions about why the sky was blue. Little Tork who laughed at everything because the world hadn't yet taught him there were things not worth laughing about.

All of them depending on him. All of them believing that impossible things were merely difficult when approached with sufficient stubbornness.

In the abyss below, obsidian eyes blazed as ancient territorial instincts recognized the defense of offspring—the most fundamental territorial imperative.

"You know what?" Koraxos said, his voice steady despite the entropy fields systematically aging his consciousness toward cosmic dust. "I've been a slave. I've been a rebel. I've been a destroyer and a protector and a dozen other things. But there's one thing I've never been."

He looked directly into Zorakil's perfect eyes, his phantom arm beginning to brighten despite the entropy fields that should have made such resurgence impossible.

"I've never been someone who quits when people are counting on me."

The moment his defiance blazed anew, something massive moved in the depths—not stirring, but deciding. Ancient territorial authority had reached its limit.

The blue fire that blazed from his spectral limb was different now—not just his rage or power, but something drawn from every connection he had ever made, every relationship that had taught him the difference between existing and living. The phantom arm didn't just burn with transcendent energy; it blazed with purpose that existed beyond individual survival.

"Impossible," Zorakil breathed, his entropy fields faltering as they encountered will that refused to be aged into submission. "Your reserves are depleted. Your power diminishes. How do you—"

"Because they're not just my reserves anymore," Koraxos interrupted, his voice carrying harmonics that spoke of unity forged in desperation and tempered by choice. "Every person I've ever protected, every friend I've ever fought beside, every child I've ever promised to keep safe—they're all here with me. And we don't break."

Underground, something immense began to move with purpose that transcended animal instinct. The Leviathan had decided that cosmic entities threatening its territory's defenders had become unacceptable.

The phantom arm exploded outward with force that sent both brothers staggering backward across cosmic distances. But this wasn't attack—it was revelation. Through the spectral limb, Koraxos felt every mind he had ever touched, every connection he had ever forged, every relationship that had taught him the difference between power and strength.

"Feel that?" he asked, floating free of Zorakil's weakened grip as golden blood leaked from fresh wounds across both cosmic entities. "That's what you can never understand, what you can never consume. Not just individual consciousness, but the space between separate beings that we chose to fill with trust instead of hunger."

In the deepest chambers, massive coils began to unwind with movements that sent tremors through every level of the mountain. The Obsidian Leviathan was rising.

The brothers circled him now, their movements showing respect for an opponent who had proven more dangerous than anticipated. Golden ichor flowed from dozens of wounds—marks that would scar cosmic flesh for eons to come, permanent reminders that even gods could bleed when faced with sufficient determination.

But they were still cosmic entities who had ended civilizations. Still powers that operated on scales beyond mortal comprehension. Still forces that had never truly lost a battle, only occasionally been delayed in their consumption.

"Impressive final act, little slave," Zorakil acknowledged, his perfect features marred by cuts that glowed with spectral fire. "You have marked us in ways we thought impossible. But theater cannot overcome reality. You are finite. We are eternal. Your strength comes from connections that can be severed. Ours flows from principles that define existence itself."

As he spoke, ancient stone began to crack throughout the mountain. Something vast was ascending through passages that had contained it for geological ages.

"Besides," Kaelthor added, his chaotic form still bleeding energy from temporal wounds that existed across seventeen different moments, "sssstruggle makesss the collapssse more magnificent. Your defiance will paint our victory with colorsss we have not witnesssssed in eonsss."

They began to gather their power—not the casual display they had shown before, but the full fury of cosmic entities finally taking a threat seriously. Entropy and chaos flowed together in patterns that transcended their individual natures, creating assault configurations that existed beyond both order and disorder.

The power buildup resonated through the mountain's foundations, where something immense felt cosmic authority preparing to assert final dominance in its territory.

The air itself began to scream as reality prepared to witness forces that could unmake the concept of existence being unleashed without restraint.

But even as cosmic death gathered around him, even as his phantom arm flickered with the strain of channeling connections across dimensional space, Koraxos smiled.

Far below, obsidian scales ground against crystal walls as the Leviathan reached the upper levels of its domain. Ancient territorial fury had found its target.

"You're right," he said, and the word carried the weight of suns. "I am finite. My power does come from connections that can be severed. And you are eternal forces that define existence itself."

The phantom arm began to pulse with new rhythms—not just his energy, but signals being sent across dimensional space to every Genesis crystal Treydora had ever planted, every world where the creator had left seeds of possibility.

And in the mountain depths, something that had existed across geological time scales felt those signals and recognized their purpose—territorial coordination on a scale that matched its own ancient patience.

"But here's what you never learned in all your eons of consumption," Koraxos continued, his words carrying the weight of revelation that would reshape the cosmos itself. "Connections aren't weakness when they're chosen freely. They're not limitations when they're maintained through trust. And finite beings working together..."

His voice rose to a roar that echoed across realities, the phantom arm blazing with light that carried messages to places beyond the brothers' ability to perceive or prevent.

"Finite beings working together can call for help from someone who actually knows how to fight gods!"

At that moment, the mountain exploded.

Not in destruction, but in emergence. Ancient stone shattered as something vast burst through layers of rock like an egg cracking open. The Obsidian Leviathan erupted into the cosmic battlefield with territorial fury that had been building for eons, its massive form emerging from the earth like a living mountain given predatory purpose.

The creature was even more immense than the cosmic entities—easily dwarfing their enlarged forms, its obsidian scales reflecting the brothers' attacks while crystal formations embedded throughout its hide pulsed with ancient power. When it roared, the sound carried harmonics that made reality itself step aside.

This was its territory. These were intruders. And the Leviathan had decided that cosmic authority meant nothing compared to territorial imperative.

Then the sky cracked open above them, and golden light began to bleed through the wounds in reality like dawn breaking over an infinite night.

The arrival was nothing like the brothers' violent intrusion. Where they had torn reality apart through force and hunger, this presence manifested through invitation—space-time opening like a flower to welcome something it had been waiting for since the first star learned to burn.

Treydora didn't step through the breach so much as bloom into existence, his form unfolding across dimensions with the inexorable beauty of creation itself learning to take shape. Galaxies spiraled through his chest like living jewels, newborn stars flickered to life in his eyes, and creation energy flowed through every gesture with the power to remake worlds.

The Leviathan's roar shifted frequency as it recognized the presence of the one who had created its domain—not submission, but acknowledgment between territorial authorities.

But this wasn't the gentle manifestation of a creator—this was war incarnate.

The civilizations immediately recognized their new role: support cosmic combat without interfering.

"Cosmic entity analysis complete!" Elara reported, her Soltari sensor networks beginning to track the three-way battle. "Transmitting weaknesses detected during ground engagement!"

Her sensors also tracked the Leviathan's movements, its massive form providing territorial anchor that prevented dimensional escape.

"Dimensional anchors holding!" Valoren confirmed as Drustali crystal networks maintained reality stability around the battle zone. "Reality matrix stable for cosmic engagement!"

The Leviathan's crystal formations harmonized with their networks, ancient territorial defenses synchronizing with modern protective systems.

The moment Treydora's cosmic form solidified in their reality, the very concept of battle was redefined. Where Koraxos had fought with desperate innovation and mortal determination, creation itself now stood ready to defend its children against forces that would reduce everything to cosmic hunger.

And beside creation stood territorial authority—the Leviathan positioning itself as living fortress, its massive bulk ensuring that cosmic entities could not simply flee when battle turned against them.

"Brothers," Treydora said, his voice carrying across dimensions with the weight of eons spent in exile and the fury of love finally choosing to fight. "You have come far from home to play with my gifts. Shall we discuss the price of uninvited guests?"

The Leviathan's harmonic rumble joined his words—ancient territorial challenge added to cosmic confrontation.

The final battle had begun, with territorial authority and cosmic creation united against forces that had mistaken consumption for inevitable law.

In the depths of shattered stone, crystal formations that had slept for eons blazed to life, adding their ancient power to defenses that now spanned from geological time to cosmic eternity.

Zorakil's perfect features twisted into something approaching aristocratic rage. "The wayward sibling returns to watch his peasants burn. How delightfully predictable. Do you truly believe your scattered essence can stand against our unified purpose?"

The Leviathan's response was a harmonic that spoke of territorial disputes settled across geological ages—ancient authority unimpressed by cosmic arrogance.

"Unified?" Treydora laughed, and the sound birthed new stars in distant galaxies. "You call hunger and perfectionism unity? You are chaos and entropy pretending to cooperate. I am creation remembering why it chose to exist."

Kaelthor's chaotic form rippled with anticipation, his madness tasting the approaching violence like fine wine. "Brother-wanderer speaks of choice! Of purpose! But we know what you truly are—weakness disguised as virtue, sentiment masquerading as strength. When we devour you, even your memories will taste of failure!"

The Leviathan shifted its massive bulk, crystal formations along its hide pulsing with patterns that spoke of predators who had never known failure in their own domain.

The cosmic battle erupted with apocalyptic fury.

Treydora moved first, his form becoming liquid light as he flowed around Zorakil's opening attack—entropy fields that could age galaxies reduced to merely cosmic annoyance. Where the brothers fought with consumption and endings, Treydora battled with endless beginning, each gesture bringing new possibilities into existence.

The Leviathan moved like winter settling into the bones of the earth - slow, inevitable, making the ground remember what weight meant. When the star-hungry things tried to slip away through cracks in the sky, they found the stone beneath had opinions about guests who didn't know when to leave.

Weight pressed down where it needed to. Not thinking, just being what mountains were for - holding things steady while the quick-lived sorted out their troubles on the surface.

His first strike was a palm thrust that seemed almost gentle—until it connected with Zorakil's chest and exploded outward in waves of creative force. Where the energy touched cosmic flesh, new forms of matter began spontaneously generating, rewriting the entropy entity's perfect structure with chaotic beauty.

"How do you like the taste of unwanted growth?" Treydora asked as crystalline formations erupted from Zorakil's wounds, each one pulsing with life that refused to acknowledge entropy's authority.

The Leviathan's harmonic rumble carried approval—ancient recognition of territorial marking through forced transformation.

Zorakil screamed—the first time in cosmic memory his voice carried pain rather than cold certainty. The crystals weren't just growing; they were evolving, each formation developing independent consciousness that questioned the perfection of their host.

Kaelthor attacked from seventeen dimensions simultaneously, his chaotic essence striking through angles that existed as pure madness given form. Tentacles of crystallized sensation wrapped around Treydora's cosmic limbs, each one carrying the accumulated suffering of every world they had consumed.

The Leviathan's massive head turned toward the chaotic assault, obsidian eyes tracking dimensional angles with predatory intelligence that had learned to hunt across impossible geometries.

But Treydora embraced the pain, absorbing it and transforming it into something else entirely. Where Kaelthor's tentacles touched him, the suffering became seeds—literal points of potential that began growing into new forms of life within the chaos entity's own structure.

"You feed on pain," Treydora observed as gardens began blooming within Kaelthor's chaotic form, their roots drawing sustenance from madness itself. "But pain, when properly cultivated, becomes the foundation for growth you never imagined possible."

The Leviathan's territorial rumble deepened as it recognized the technique—transformation of invader essence into territory-appropriate forms, ancient method of dealing with unwanted intruders.

The chaos entity found his own nature turned against him as the growing life forms began to organize his randomness, giving structure to madness and purpose to destruction. For the first time in eons, Kaelthor experienced something approaching clarity—and it terrified him more than any attack ever could.

The three of them tore into each other across places that barely existed—fighting through the dreams of stars not yet born, wrestling in spaces made of pure ideas, throwing punches that rewrote the rules of what punching meant. Reality bent around them like everything was made of soft clay, and they were three angry gods with cosmic fists.

The Leviathan moved through these dimensional spaces with ease born of geological practice, its massive form ensuring that cosmic entities remained anchored to physical reality where territorial authority held absolute sway.

Treydora's strategy was unlike anything the brothers had ever encountered. Where they sought to impose their nature through force, he sought to transform their nature through connection. Each attack he launched carried seeds of change, possibilities that took root within his opponents' cosmic essence and began growing according to principles they had never learned to understand.

But the brothers were learning to adapt.

Zorakil's entropy fields began targeting not Treydora's form but the creative possibilities he generated, aging new life into cosmic dust before it could take root. His perfect intellect analyzed each transformation attempt and developed countermeasures that preserved his essential nature while deflecting creative invasion.

The Leviathan's response was to shift position, its massive bulk creating gravitational distortions that bent entropy fields away from their intended targets.

"You seek to change what cannot be changed," Zorakil declared as his entropy successfully neutralized a wave of life-bringing energy. "I am the ending that gives meaning to all beginnings. You cannot create purpose without my completion."

Kaelthor's response was more visceral. His chaotic form began consuming the growing gardens within his essence, devouring order and structure as fast as Treydora could create them. But instead of simply destroying the life forms, he began incorporating their organizational principles into his madness, creating chaos that was structured, randomness that followed patterns.

The Leviathan's territorial instincts recognized the adaptive threat and responded by positioning itself to disrupt Kaelthor's dimensional escape routes.

"Delicious contradictions!" Kaelthor laughed as he weaponized the gardens growing within him, turning Treydora's gifts into attacks that carried both creation and destruction simultaneously. "Your gifts taste of hope seasoned with inevitability! I shall make them into perfect despair!"

The battle escalated beyond cosmic into something approaching mythic. Treydora found himself fighting opponents who were learning from his own techniques, entropy that preserved itself through creative adaptation and chaos that organized itself through structured madness.

The Leviathan circled the cosmic combat like a living fortress, its territorial presence preventing the brothers from simply withdrawing when tactics failed.

Mountains rose and fell with each exchange of blows. Oceans boiled away and reformed as crystalline seas that reflected impossible colors. The sky itself became a canvas where cosmic forces painted their conflict in hues that would drive mortal minds to madness simply by witnessing them.

Through it all, the Leviathan maintained territorial anchor, its massive presence ensuring that cosmic battle remained grounded in physical reality where mortal defenders could provide meaningful support.

For seven hours that lasted seven eternities, the three entities reshaped reality according to their will, each strike creating new laws of physics that lasted only until the next blow rewrote them again. Galaxies were born and died in the spaces between heartbeats. Time flowed in spirals and knots as temporal warfare made causality itself a battlefield.

The Leviathan endured through all of it, territorial authority providing the one constant in a battle that redefined existence itself with each exchange.

But Treydora was losing.

Not through lack of power—his creative force remained vast beyond mortal comprehension. Not through poor strategy—his understanding of transformation exceeded anything his brothers had developed. He was losing because he fought alone against two entities whose hunger had been refined across cosmic epochs, and his strength had been scattered across too many realities for too many eons.

The Leviathan sensed its territorial ally weakening and responded with increasing agitation, massive coils tightening as ancient instincts prepared for desperate measures.

Every gift he had given to emerging civilizations, every seed of possibility he had planted in barren worlds, every gentle nudge he had provided to consciousness learning to think—all of it had required pieces of his essential self. Where his brothers had hoarded their power for eons, concentrating it into perfect tools of consumption, Treydora had given his strength away freely to nurture life that might never even know his name.

The brothers sensed his weakness and pressed their advantage with ruthless coordination.

Zorakil's entropy fields began working in perfect harmony with Kaelthor's chaos, creating zones where creative energy was simultaneously aged into dust and unraveled into component madness. Where before they had fought as separate entities with complementary goals, now they moved as true unity—ending and randomness dancing together in patterns that turned Treydora's own gifts against him.

The Leviathan's territorial fury reached new heights as it sensed the defender of its domain being systematically overwhelmed.

"You scatter your essence like a profligate nobleman," Zorakil observed as his entropy successfully aged another wave of Treydora's creative force into cosmic debris. "We concentrate our purpose like misers counting gold. Which approach do you believe time will favor?"

Kaelthor's chaotic assault became a symphony of destruction, each note perfectly crafted to exploit the gaps in Treydora's defenses left by eons of generous gift-giving. His attacks carried the taste of every world where creation had failed, every species that had gone extinct despite divine guidance, every moment when hope had curdled into despair.

The Leviathan's harmonic roars began to carry undertones of desperate territorial warning—ancient predator recognizing that its domain faced unprecedented threat.

"Feel the futility of your charity!" Kaelthor sang as his structured madness found purchase in Treydora's cosmic form. "Every gift you gave made you weaker! Every life you nurtured cost you strength! Your love is a wound that bleeds power!"

Golden blood began to flow from injuries that existed in seventeen dimensions simultaneously. Each wound leaked creative energy that should have taken eons to regenerate, but the brothers' combined assault was draining it faster than even cosmic power could restore itself.

The Leviathan felt each drop of golden blood strike its territorial domain and responded with increasing fury—ancient instincts recognizing that the creator of its realm was being systematically destroyed.

Treydora staggered under the coordinated attack, his form beginning to lose coherence as entropy and chaos worked together to unmake the very concept of organized creation. The galaxies spiraling through his chest began to dim as their constituent stars were systematically extinguished. The newborn planets that had served as his eyes started to crack and crumble under cosmic pressure.

For the first time since the battle began, doubt flickered across his features. Not doubt in his purpose—that remained absolute—but doubt in his ability to protect what he had spent eons nurturing. The children hiding in shelters across the battlefield, the civilizations that had learned to work together despite ancient differences, the simple act of consciousness choosing connection over consumption—all of it hung in the balance as his strength ebbed toward failure.

The Leviathan's massive form began to shift with movements that spoke of territorial authority preparing for final measures—ancient predator recognizing that passive defense was no longer sufficient.

"Look around you, brother-wanderer," Zorakil said with the satisfaction of a teacher whose most difficult student was finally learning an essential lesson. "See what your charity has purchased. These mortals cower in holes while we reshape reality according to our will. Your gifts bought them nothing but a more elaborate death."

Kaelthor drifted closer, his chaotic form rippling with sensory delight as he tasted Treydora's growing despair. "Such beautiful tragedy! Love learning that it was always weaker than hunger! Hope discovering that it was merely delayed disappointment! I want to preserve this moment forever—creation finally understanding that it exists only to feed consumption!"

The Leviathan's territorial fury reached critical mass as cosmic entities tasted victory over the creator of its domain. Ancient authority prepared to assert territorial imperative regardless of cost.

The brothers began to gather their power for the final blow—not the casual display they had shown to Koraxos, but the full fury of cosmic entities who had learned to respect their opponent enough to ensure his complete destruction. Entropy and chaos flowed together in patterns that transcended their individual natures, creating assault configurations that existed beyond both order and randomness.

The very fabric of reality began to warp around them as forces that could unmake the concept of existence prepared for unleashing without restraint. Stars throughout the galaxy dimmed as cosmic power drew energy from fundamental constants. Space itself held its breath as the weapons that would end creation's last defender took shape between divine fingers.

Deep stone felt pressure building like storm-weight against the valley's bones. Something was trying to break the one who'd taught the mountain how to dream. Old instincts, older than the hills, knew what happened to things that threatened the nest.

The Leviathan didn't think about defending. Thinking was for creatures that lived fast and died surprised. It simply was what it had always been - the thing that held steady when everything else wanted to fall down.

Star-fire came down like the sky ending.

And met stone that had been learning how to be stubborn since the world was young.

The attack struck scales that had been polished by glacier-melt and pressure that built mountains. Weight met weight. The star-hungry things had forgotten what happened when you tried to break something that was already holding up the world.

"Time to sleep, brother," Zorakil said, his voice carrying the finality of judgment passed by cosmic nobility. "Time to accept that love, however pure, cannot overcome the mathematics of power. Your era ends. Ours continues."

"Beautiful ending!" Kaelthor laughed, his chaotic energy building to crescendo that would make previous attacks seem like gentle breezes. "Feel how hope transforms into despair when seasoned with perfect defeat! Your death will be the most exquisite meal we have ever shared!"

They raised their hands in perfect synchronization, entropy and chaos gathering between their fingers like twin suns of absolute ending. This would be the strike that would end not just Treydora's existence but the very concept he represented—love believing it could stand against forces that had shaped the cosmos according to hunger and hierarchy.

The Leviathan erupted from the earth with territorial fury that had been building for geological ages.

The assault descended with apocalyptic force, reality itself screaming as cosmic energies that could unmake galaxies focused into a single point of ultimate termination.

And met the Obsidian Leviathan's territorial defense.

The massive creature rose between the cosmic assault and its target, obsidian scales absorbing energies that should have unmade reality itself. Crystal formations throughout its hide blazed with ancient power as territorial authority asserted itself against cosmic hunger.

The brothers' perfect attack struck the Leviathan's territorial defenses and was absorbed, channeled through crystal matrices that had been designed across geological ages to protect this domain against exactly such cosmic threats.

The Leviathan's roar carried harmonics of ancient triumph—territorial authority had successfully defended its creator against cosmic assault.

As the attack was neutralized, Koraxos watched from his position on the battlefield far below, his phantom arm now blazing with the reflected glory of creation itself. Through the transcendent limb, he could feel the cosmic battle raging above, but more importantly, he could feel something new—a pattern that made everything suddenly, brilliantly clear.

The Leviathan's territorial defense had created the opening they needed—cosmic entities momentarily stunned by encountering resistance they hadn't anticipated.

"Wait!" Koraxos screamed, his voice somehow carrying across dimensional barriers despite his depleted state. "The Leviathan! Remember the mountain creature's true nature!"

Treydora's cosmic attention flickered toward him for a fraction of a second even as entropy and chaos recovered from their failed assault.

"It wasn't powerful because of individual strength!" Koraxos continued, the phantom arm blazing with the last of his energy as desperate inspiration poured through their connection. "It was powerful because it was connected! To every dimension, every layer of reality! It existed everywhere at once!"

The Leviathan's harmonic rumble carried approval—ancient territorial authority recognizing that its true nature had finally been understood.

Understanding began to dawn in Treydora's cosmic awareness, but the brothers were already preparing their next assault.

"The Genesis seeds!" Koraxos shouted with the fury of someone who had finally seen the solution to an impossible puzzle. "You didn't just scatter gifts across the cosmos! You created a network! Every crystal is a dimensional anchor! Every world you touched is connected to every other world!"

The Leviathan's territorial call joined his words—ancient authority confirming the nature of the network that spanned realities.

The attacks struck Treydora's cosmic form with devastating force, entropy and chaos working together to unmake creation itself. Golden blood erupted from wounds that existed across multiple realities, each drop containing enough creative potential to birth star systems but now lost to cosmic violence.

But the Leviathan's territorial defenses held, absorbing cosmic overflow that would have scattered creation's essence across dimensions.

"Connect them!" Koraxos's voice cracked with desperation as he watched his patron's form begin to dissolve under the brothers' assault. "Every world you ever touched! Every reality you seeded! Every universe you helped create from the very beginning! Arc the power back! Use the entire network!"

The Leviathan's territorial authority resonated through the network, ancient anchor point connecting to every Genesis crystal across infinite realities.

As his cosmic form began to collapse under forces that reduced creation to cosmic debris, Treydora finally understood what his gift-giving had truly accomplished across eons of wandering. The Genesis crystals weren't just seeds of possibility—they were dimensional bridges, each one a living connection to the cosmic consciousness that had created it.

More than that, they formed a network that spanned not just galaxies but realities themselves. Every universe where he had nurtured life, every dimension where consciousness had learned to choose cooperation over consumption, every plane of existence where love had proven stronger than hunger—all connected through crystalline anchors that had been waiting eons for this moment of convergence.

The Leviathan's territorial authority served as the central anchor for the entire network—ancient predator that had become living fortress connecting creation across infinite realities.

With entropy and chaos systematically dismantling his failing form, Treydora reached out across the vast network of his creation. Not to demand or extract, but to simply open channels that had always existed between creator and creation, between gift-giver and gift-receiver, between love offered and love accepted.

The response was immediate and overwhelming beyond cosmic comprehension.

Every world Treydora had ever touched, every reality where he'd planted seeds of hope, suddenly opened up like flowers turning toward the sun. Power flowed not because he demanded it, but because it wanted to come home. Like every good deed he'd ever done was finally cashing in its favor all at once.

The Leviathan's territorial authority channeled the network's response, ancient predator become living conduit for power that spanned infinite realities.

But it wasn't just power flowing through the dimensional bridges. It was everything Treydora had given across eons of nurturing: every act of kindness that had prevented a war, every gentle nudge that had guided evolution toward consciousness, every moment when despair had been transformed into hope through gifts freely given.

Energy cascaded through bridges that spanned the spaces between universes, each Genesis crystal becoming a conduit for forces that operated beyond individual reality's constraints. The network that Treydora had built through eons of gentle cultivation suddenly revealed its true nature—not scattered gifts but a single, vast organism spanning every dimension where love had chosen to exist.

The Leviathan roared its territorial triumph as network power flowed through its ancient form—apex predator become living gateway for creation itself.

The power struck Treydora's dissolving form like a tsunami of liquid starlight concentrated through eons of patient accumulation.

Where moments before his cosmic manifestation had been crumbling under the brothers' assault, now it exploded outward with force that redefined the meaning of existence itself. Not just galaxies spiraling through his chest, but entire universes living there, each reality a beating heart in a body that suddenly spanned every dimension where consciousness had learned to choose connection over consumption.

The Leviathan's territorial authority anchored the transformation, ancient predator ensuring that infinite power remained grounded in physical reality where it could be effectively wielded.

The shockwave that erupted from Treydora's transformation traveled through every plane of existence like the birth cry of a new form of cosmic entity. Where it passed, reality itself paused to acknowledge something that had never existed before—consciousness that existed not as individual being but as living network spanning the infinite possibilities of creation itself.

The brothers' final assault met this unprecedented surge of power and simply evaporated. Entropy and chaos, forces that had consumed entire universes, found themselves facing energy that operated on scales beyond their ability to process, understand, or counter.

The Leviathan's territorial roar joined the cosmic rebirth—ancient authority celebrating the successful defense of its domain's creator.

Zorakil and Kaelthor were hurled backward across cosmic distances that spanned multiple realities, their perfect coordination shattered by encountering power that existed outside every framework they had used to understand existence. They struck dimensional barriers with force that cracked the boundaries between universes, their cosmic forms leaving trails of distortion that would take eons to heal.

For the first time in their existence, the brothers who had consumed worlds and ended civilizations found themselves face to face with something they couldn't categorize, couldn't consume, couldn't comprehend within their frameworks of hierarchy and hunger.

The Leviathan settled back into territorial rest, its ancient duty fulfilled—domain successfully defended, creator successfully preserved, territorial authority successfully maintained.

The transformed Treydora rose from the battlefield like dawn breaking over every possible horizon simultaneously. His form no longer struggled to contain cosmic forces—it had become the space where infinite realities chose to dance together. Galaxies spiraled through his chest like living jewels, each one a beating heart in a body that suddenly encompassed every dimension where love had proven stronger than hunger.

The Obsidian Leviathan settled back into territorial satisfaction, its ancient duty fulfilled. The mountain creature had successfully defended its domain's creator, and now obsidian eyes tracked the cosmic battlefield with predatory contentment.

Zorakil and Kaelthor hung in space before this unprecedented manifestation, their perfect confidence finally showing hairline cracks. For the first time in their existence, they faced something that operated outside every framework they used to understand reality.

"Impossible," Zorakil breathed, his marble perfection unmarred by doubt but somehow diminished by it. "You scattered your essence across ten thousand realities. You should be weaker, not—"

"Not what, brother?" Treydora's voice carried harmonics that made existence itself lean in to listen. Each word birthed new stars in distant galaxies while simultaneously speaking with the gentleness of a parent tucking children into bed. "Not stronger? You still think in terms of hoarding versus sharing, don't you? You never learned that gifts given freely return magnified."

Kaelthor's chaotic form rippled with sensations that had no names—for the first time in eons, tasting something he couldn't immediately categorize or consume. "Brother-wanderer speaks of power we don't recognize! Show us this strength you claim to have accumulated!"

"Very well," Treydora replied, and smiled with the radiance of ten thousand suns choosing to be gentle. "Let me show you the first truth I learned in exile: **The strongest**

chains are those we forge ourselves, but the greatest freedom comes from choosing which chains to wear."

What happened next was not violence but cosmic education delivered with absolute authority.

Treydora didn't strike the brothers—he simply *disagreed* with their existence on such a fundamental level that reality began to side with his perspective. Where they had been cosmic entities operating on scales beyond mortal comprehension, his gentle correction reduced them to... less.

Not destroyed—that would have been crude. Simply diminished, compressed, reminded of proper proportions.

Zorakil's perfect form began to contract, his cosmic scale shrinking as the universe around him remembered that true strength came from connection, not domination. His entropy fields, once capable of aging galaxies, found themselves limited to affecting dust motes and wilting flowers.

"This is..." Zorakil's voice cracked with something approaching panic as he felt his cosmic authority simply... evaporating. "This defies the very foundations of civilized existence! True power springs from noble breeding, from consciousness born to rule! How can inferior minds achieve what should be impossible without proper guidance?"

"Does it?" Treydora asked, his question carrying the patient tone of a teacher helping a slow student reach an obvious conclusion. "Look around you. See what order emerging from choice accomplishes that hierarchy never could. **True power is not what you can force others to do—it's what you can inspire them to become.**"

Below them, the battlefield told its story. Seven civilizations working together with efficiency that transcended anything force could have achieved. Former enemies sharing resources not because they were commanded to, but because they chose to. Children from different species playing together while adults rebuilt not just structures but the very concept of what civilization could become.

Kaelthor's chaotic essence found itself compressed into increasingly smaller scales as Treydora's influence surrounded him like a cosmic embrace that was also a cage. His madness, once spanning dimensions, became limited to making small flowers grow in slightly unexpected colors.

"Brother!" he shrieked, his voice now carrying frequencies that could barely disturb a soap bubble. "Your gifts taste of traps! Of chains made from kindness! This is not freedom—this is slavery disguised as choice!"

"Is it?" Treydora's attention focused on his chaotic brother with the intensity of someone examining a particularly interesting but ultimately harmless insect. "Or is it simply the first time you've encountered beings who chose their limitations instead of having them imposed?"

The brothers continued to shrink—not physically, but conceptually. Their cosmic importance, their universal significance, their fundamental necessity to the structure of existence itself... all of it simply faded as Treydora's network demonstrated that reality worked perfectly well without them.

Where they had been forces that shaped galaxies, they became minor irritations. Where they had been essential aspects of cosmic order, they became footnotes. Where they had been gods, they became... problems that had solved themselves through proper context.

"Feel what irrelevance tastes like," Treydora said, his words carrying no malice, only the infinite patience of someone who had learned that the best revenge was living well while helping others do the same. "Experience what it means to be small, unimportant, easily ignored."

Zorakil, now reduced to the cosmic equivalent of a grain of sand with delusions of grandeur, managed one final protest: "How dare you presume to diminish your betters!" Zorakil's voice rang with outraged nobility even as his form shrank. "We are cosmic aristocracy! These mongrel minds may amuse you temporarily, but the natural order will reassert itself. Inferiors cannot govern themselves indefinitely!"

"Are they?" Treydora gestured toward the recovering battlefield, where order emerged from voluntary cooperation while creative chaos sparked innovation and growth. "Or were you simply two beings who confused having power with being powerful, who mistook fear for respect, who never learned that true immortality comes from inspiring others rather than consuming them?"

The brothers hung in space—cosmic specks with cosmic egos, reduced to their essential nature: hunger and perfectionism stripped of the power to satisfy themselves through others' suffering.

"This is temporary," Kaelthor whispered, his voice now capable of barely disturbing the sleep of a tired butterfly. "When you disperse, when your network fractures, we will remember. We will return. We will—"

"Will you?" Treydora's question carried genuine curiosity rather than threat. "Because I'm not dispersing, brother. I'm not going anywhere. This network you see as weakness? It's the new permanent reality. Love, connection, choice—they're not temporary gifts I'm granting. They're the fundamental forces I've just finished installing as cosmic law. And here's the final truth you never understood: **The universe doesn't need our permission to be beautiful—it only needs our courage to stop preventing it.**"

Something shifted in the way the universe worked—not dramatic, just a quiet rewriting of the rules. Like someone had gone through the cosmic instruction manual and crossed out all the parts about "might makes right" and written in "be decent to each other" instead. The change felt so natural you almost forgot things had ever worked differently.

The transformation wasn't dramatic—just a quiet revision of cosmic constants. A universe-wide update that installed love and choice as fundamental forces while reducing hunger and domination to minor nuisances that could be easily contained.

"You always asked what I was building," Treydora said, his form beginning to expand again—not in size but in presence, becoming less visible entity and more environmental constant. "Now you know. I was building a cosmos where beings like you become impossible not through force, but through irrelevance."

The brothers felt it immediately—not death, but exile from significance. They still existed, still retained their memories, but the universe around them had simply moved on to more interesting problems. They had become cosmic background noise, easily filtered out by beings who had learned to focus on what actually mattered.

On the battlefield below, the defenders began to realize that the cosmic battle was over—not ended, but completed. The threat that had loomed over their world hadn't been destroyed but simply... resolved. Made irrelevant through the demonstration of better alternatives.

Koraxos descended slowly from the dimensional spaces where he had fought alongside cosmic forces, his phantom arm no longer blazing with desperate power but glowing with steady purpose. The transcendent limb had evolved again—not weapon or tool, but bridge between individual will and collective possibility.

The moment his feet touched the scarred ground, a sound began to build across the battlefield. Not celebration—that would come later. This was recognition. The sound of people acknowledging that something unprecedented had just been accomplished through their willingness to trust each other with their lives and futures.

"Koraxos!" Sela's voice cut through the cosmic aftermath as children emerged from shelters to find their world saved not through superior violence but through superior cooperation. She ran toward him with a dozen other children trailing behind, their faces bright with the particular joy of those who had been protected by people who chose protection over personal safety.

He knelt to catch her in a hug that was careful of his phantom arm's energy but generous with the warmth that had grown in him over months of learning that strength meant having people worth defending.

"Did you show them?" she asked with the seriousness of someone whose future had hung in the balance. "Did you show the bad gods that we're not food?"

"We showed them something better," Koraxos replied, looking around at the mixed groups of former enemies working together to treat wounded and begin rebuilding. "We showed them what people look like when they choose to help each other instead of hurt each other."

As he spoke, he remembered something Marex had said during their darkest hour in the rebellion, words that had seemed like mere comfort then but now revealed their deeper truth: **"The strongest chains are those we forge ourselves, but the greatest freedom comes from choosing which chains to wear."**

Koraxos had worn the chains of slavery, then broken them to forge new ones—bonds of connection, responsibility, love for people who had become family through choice rather than blood. These chains didn't restrict him; they gave his power meaning.

Velen approached, his bio-crystal arm pulsing with satisfaction as he surveyed the battlefield where his people—all of their people—had stood together against cosmic extinction. "So what now, hero? You're officially the most famous being in seven civilizations. Children will grow up wanting to be like you."

"Scary thought," Koraxos said with a self-deprecating smile, though his phantom arm pulsed with light that suggested deep satisfaction. "But maybe that's not such a bad thing, if what they want to be like is someone who protects instead of conquers."

Thalia approached, her administrative robes replaced by practical armor that bore the scorch marks of someone who had refused to coordinate from safety. Her face showed the particular exhaustion that came from managing impossibility, but her voice carried the authority of someone who had discovered leadership through necessity.

"The reality distortions are stabilizing," she announced. "Communications are being restored. And..." She paused, consulting readings that made her shake her head in wonder. "The defensive networks aren't just intact—they're stronger. The cosmic chaos somehow enhanced the crystal matrices instead of disrupting them."

"Evolution under pressure," Dr. Lyrin observed, approaching with medical equipment that seemed to exist in several dimensions simultaneously—an unfortunate side effect of treating patients who had been exposed to reality-warping attacks. "Crisis drives adaptation. The greater the threat, the faster consciousness develops new capabilities to meet it."

The Leviathan had finished its territorial survey and now approached their gathering with movements that spoke of ancient intelligence considering new possibilities. When it spoke, the words formed not through sound but through direct impression of meaning into their consciousness.

"Quick builders. You move like streams cutting new channels through old stone. Fight together like I haven't felt since the valley was young sea..."

"Interesting how?" Koraxos asked, extending his awareness toward the massive creature that had become their most unlikely ally.

"They expect consciousness to fragment under pressure, to choose individual survival over collective purpose. You demonstrate the opposite—unity that strengthens through challenge. This violates the foundation their strategies are built upon."

"And that helps us how?" Thalia inquired, her administrative mind immediately focusing on practical applications.

"Hard to hunt what moves like nothing you've seen before. They'll come back heavier, but confused. Confusion makes even mountains stumble..."

Neryssia had approached during this exchange, her aquatic features bearing the satisfied expression of someone whose tactical assessments had proven accurate. "The Pelagian scout networks detected something else during the battle. Dimensional disturbances at the edge of our system—not attacking, but observing. Other cosmic entities, watching to see how this engagement resolved."

"How many others?" Koraxos asked, cosmic senses extending toward the boundaries of their reality to confirm what the Pelagian had detected.

"Difficult to determine precisely. At least a dozen distinct signatures, possibly more. They're maintaining careful distance, but their attention is... focused."

"Word is spreading," Elder Marex mused, his scholar's mind recognizing the implications. "What happened here today will be reported throughout whatever networks these entities use to communicate. We've become more than a local concern."

"That could work for us or against us," Captain Revik observed with military pragmatism. "If they view us as a genuine threat, they might coordinate responses we can't counter. But if they see us as an interesting anomaly..."

"They might come to study rather than simply consume," Thalia finished, understanding dawning in her administrative mind. "And study requires a certain amount of preservation of the subject."

As if summoned by their conversation, new arrivals began materializing at the battlefield's edge. Not cosmic entities this time, but beings whose appearance spoke of advanced civilization rather than predatory hunger. Tall, graceful figures that moved with the fluid precision of those accustomed to hostile environments, their forms bearing technological enhancements that seemed grown rather than manufactured.

"The Soltari," Neryssia identified, her voice carrying relief and anticipation in equal measure. "They've been monitoring cosmic entity movements throughout this galactic sector. If they're here..."

"Then what we accomplished today has attracted attention from more than just predators," Koraxos concluded, feeling a shift in the cosmic currents that suggested their small world was about to become far less isolated.

The lead Soltari approached with the careful dignity of someone representing a civilization that had survived by choosing its alliances wisely. When she spoke, her voice carried harmonics that suggested advanced vocal modification designed for communication across species barriers.

"We observed your defense against the Harvest Scout formation," she announced, her words carrying formal weight. "No previously catalogued resistance pattern matches your tactical approach. You achieved victory through cooperation rather than dominance, adaptation rather than overwhelming force. This suggests possibilities our strategists believed impossible."

"Impossible how?" Velen asked with typical directness.

"Consensus among galactic civilizations has been that cosmic entity predation cannot be effectively resisted—only delayed through superior technology or mobility. You demonstrate a third option we had not considered: transformation of the fundamental nature of resistance itself."

"Great," Koraxos muttered, rolling his shoulders like a fighter who'd just realized the warm-up was over. "So we're either inspiration or cautionary tale. Either way, we're gonna have company."

As first light painted the horizon in colors that for once suggested genuine hope rather than cosmic horror, Chapter 10 drew to its close. But this wasn't an ending—it was a recognition that their small conflict had become part of something much larger.

The epic battle had been won through combinations no cosmic entity had anticipated: transcendent power guided by mortal purpose, ancient enemies transformed into accidental guardians, reality itself choosing sides when consciousness showed it new possibilities. Most significantly, they had proven that unity based on choice rather than force could not only survive cosmic predation but actively evolve in response to it.

The cost had been severe—damaged infrastructure, casualties among the defenders, a landscape permanently altered by cosmic warfare. But something more profound had been achieved: proof that consciousness united across former divisions could not just survive but actively resist cosmic-scale predation while maintaining the essential diversity that made unity meaningful.

The Leviathan had begun what could only be described as landscaping, using its massive form to reshape the battlefield into defensive configurations that would be ready for the next assault. Its territorial instincts had expanded to encompass not just the physical space but the people who had proven worthy of protection.

Tomorrow would bring new challenges. The cosmic entities would return with revised understanding and modified tactics designed specifically to counter cooperation-based resistance. Other civilizations would arrive seeking to understand how impossible victories had been achieved. The alliance between seven peoples would need to evolve from crisis response to permanent institution capable of sustaining unity without sacrificing individual identity.

But tonight, as aurora effects painted the sky with colors that seemed to celebrate rather than warn, Koraxos stood with beings who had faced the infinite dark and found their own light within the struggle. Reality itself seemed different somehow—more malleable, more responsive to will and unity than pure force, more willing to reward consciousness that chose cooperation over consumption.

"Same time tomorrow?" someone asked.

"Probably sooner," came the weary reply. "These things don't seem big on waiting."

"Then we'll be ready," Koraxos said simply, the phantom arm pulsing with steady determination. "Whatever they bring, whatever new impossibilities they throw at us, we'll adapt. We'll survive. We'll find a way to turn the universe's worst against itself if necessary."

And as laughter—actual laughter—rippled through the assembled defenders, Chapter 10 ended not with a triumphant fanfare but with the quiet determination of consciousness that had seen the abyss and chosen to build bridges across it instead of falling in.

The tide had turned dramatically and definitively. The epic battle had demonstrated what few thought possible: that with sufficient unity, creativity, and sheer stubborn will, even gods could be surprised, even cosmic predators could be forced to retreat, and even reality itself could be convinced to play by different rules.

As defenders began the long work of assessment and recovery, the chapter concluded with an image that would become legendary: Koraxos, his phantom arm dimmed but still humming with residual power, sharing water from a canteen with the Obsidian Leviathan while Soltari observers documented evidence that the galactic balance of power had shifted in ways no one had anticipated.

The stars wheeled overhead in patterns suggesting not destruction but possibility, and for the first time since cosmic predators had set their sights on their world, the people of seven unified civilizations went to sleep with something resembling peace, knowing that tomorrow's battles would find them stronger, better prepared, and most importantly, no longer alone in the fight for existence itself.

In the deep chambers beneath the city, crystal formations that had been damaged by reality-warping attacks were already beginning to regenerate, their growth patterns incorporating lessons learned from exposure to forces that operated beyond conventional physics. The mountain itself was adapting, becoming something more than mere stone and crystal—a living fortress that could evolve to meet whatever challenges the cosmos chose to present.

The war was far from over, but the opening chapter had been written in crystal fire and transcendent will, setting the stage for struggles where the very nature of existence would be tested, shaped, and ultimately redefined by beings who had learned to find strength in their limitations and power in their unity.

They ended on a battlefield transformed not just by destruction and reconstruction, but by the fundamental realization that consciousness, when it stops fighting itself and starts fighting for itself, can shake the foundations of cosmic order itself.

The convergence approached, and awareness raced to meet it, transformed by necessity into something the universe had not yet seen but desperately needed to witness.

"Well," Koraxos said, watching reality settle back into something resembling normal physics while cosmic observers maintained their distant vigil, "this should be interesting."

The phantom arm pulsed once more, steady and sure, carrying the hopes and determination of beings who had learned that together, they could face anything the universe threw at them.

Even gods.

Even the infinite dark between stars.

Even the end of everything they'd ever known.

Together, they were ready.

11

Chapter 11: The Architect of Infinity

Treydora rose from the battlefield looking like every sunrise that had ever mattered, all happening at once. He wasn't struggling to hold cosmic power anymore—he was the cosmic power, and it was happy to be there. Stars spun through his chest like living gems, each one beating with the rhythm of worlds where people had learned to help instead of hurt each other.

The Obsidian Leviathan settled back into territorial satisfaction, its ancient duty fulfilled. The mountain creature had successfully defended its domain's creator, and now obsidian eyes tracked the cosmic battlefield with predatory contentment.

Zorakil and Kaelthor hung in space before this unprecedented manifestation, their perfect confidence finally showing hairline cracks. For the first time in their existence, they faced something that operated outside every framework they used to understand reality.

"Impossible," Zorakil breathed, his marble perfection unmarred by doubt but somehow diminished by it. "You scattered your essence across ten thousand realities. You should be weaker, not—"

"Not what, brother?" Treydora's voice carried harmonics that made existence itself lean in to listen. Each word birthed new stars in distant galaxies while simultaneously speaking with the gentleness of a parent tucking children into bed. "Not stronger? You still think in terms of hoarding versus sharing, don't you? You never learned that gifts given freely return magnified."

Kaelthor's chaotic form rippled with sensations that had no names—for the first time in eons, tasting something he couldn't immediately categorize or consume. "Brother-wanderer speaks of power we don't recognize! Show us this strength you claim to have accumulated!"

"Very well," Treydora replied, and smiled with the radiance of ten thousand suns choosing to be gentle. "Let me show you the first truth I learned in exile: The strongest chains are those we forge ourselves, but the greatest freedom comes from choosing which chains to wear."

The War of Gods

The brothers struck with the fury of dying galaxies.

Zorakil's perfection became a weapon—reality itself bent around his marble form as he unleashed entropy on a scale that made supernovas look like candle flames. Worlds aged a billion years in seconds. Space folded in on itself. The very concept of time began to unravel at the edges.

Kaelthor screamed with seventeen mouths as his chaos erupted in fountains of liquid madness. Colors that had no names painted themselves across the void. Gravity forgot which way was down. The laws of physics wept and fled as his power turned order into beautiful, terrible confusion.

Together they were apocalypse incarnate—the end of everything wrapped in cosmic flesh.

Treydora met them head-on.

The Clash

The first impact shattered three nearby star systems just from the shockwave. Treydora's network-form blazed like a constellation given life, each point of light a world that had chosen love over fear. His power didn't flow from within—it poured through him from ten thousand realities where beings had learned to stand together.

Zorakil struck like a falling mountain of marble perfection, his fists trailing entropy that could age gods. Treydora caught the blow barehanded, and where their flesh met, reality screamed. The force of collision sent ripples through dimensions, but Treydora held firm.

"Is that all?" he said, and smiled.

Then he hit back.

His punch sent Zorakil tumbling through space, the perfect marble form spinning end over end as cracks appeared in surfaces that had been flawless since the birth of time. The entropy god crashed through a nebula, scattering stellar dust, his perfect features showing something impossible—surprise.

Kaelthor attacked from seventeen directions at once, chaos given form and fury. His claws raked across Treydora's back, leaving wounds that bled starlight.

His teeth found purchase in cosmic flesh, tearing away chunks of living constellation.

But the wounds closed as fast as they opened. Every drop of stellar blood that fell became a new star. Every torn piece of cosmic flesh reformed stronger than before.

"Brother feeds on pain!" Kaelthor shrieked in ecstasy. "Such beautiful breaking! Such exquisite—"

Treydora grabbed him by the throat and squeezed.

Chaos itself began to choke.

The Hunt

What followed was less battle than cosmic chase scene. The brothers threw everything they had—collapsing stars into black holes, reversing time, unmaking sections of space itself—but Treydora was always there, always pressing forward, always getting stronger.

Zorakil tried to age him out of existence. Treydora caught the entropy beam in his bare hands and fed it back, forcing the perfect god to experience his own decay. Marble skin began to crack and flake.

Kaelthor attempted to drive him mad with impossible visions. Treydora walked through the chaos unaffected, his network-consciousness too vast to shatter. Then he grabbed Kaelthor's writhing form and began to squeeze order into it—not rigid control, but the terrifying order of free beings choosing their own fate.

"NO! NOT ORDER! ANYTHING BUT CHOSEN ORDER!" Kaelthor screamed as his chaotic essence was forced into patterns he couldn't break because they weren't imposed from outside—they came from within.

The brothers fled, streaking across cosmic distances, but Treydora followed like an avenging angel made of burning stars. Where they ran, he was already waiting. Where they hid, he found them. Where they struck, he hit back twice as hard.

The Breaking Point

In the space between two galaxies, the brothers made their final stand. Zorakil's marble perfection was spider-webbed with cracks, pieces flaking off to drift in the void. Kaelthor's chaotic form flickered between states, unable to maintain coherence under the pressure of forced order.

They attacked together—entropy and chaos combined in one last desperate assault that tore reality apart at the seams. The void itself began to bleed.

Treydora walked through it all like he was strolling through a garden.

"You still don't understand," he said, reaching for them with hands that held the combined will of ten thousand worlds. "This was never about power. It was about choice."

He caught Zorakil by the face, his fingers sinking into perfect marble like it was soft clay. The entropy god's scream could be heard across three dimensions as his flawless features began to melt.

His other hand closed around Kaelthor's writhing neck. "You consumed civilizations that never had a choice. Now let me show you what choice really looks like."

The Mercy

For one terrible moment, the brothers felt their existence hanging by threads that Treydora could cut with a thought. They were insects in the grip of something that had transcended their understanding of power itself.

Then, impossibly, he let them go.

Not from weakness. Not from doubt. But from choice—the same choice that had built his network across ten thousand realities. The choice to show mercy even to those who had never shown it to others.

"Go," he said simply.

Zorakil's cracked form trembled in the void, marble features barely recognizable beneath the damage. "You... you're letting us..."

"Leave," Treydora said, his voice carrying the weight of galaxies. "Run to the edges of existence. Hide in the spaces between realities. Spend eternity looking over your shoulders, because now you know—there's something in this universe stronger than you. Something that chose mercy when it could have chosen annihilation."

Kaelthor's form had compressed to a tight knot of terrified chaos, his seventeen-dimensional nature reduced to barely holding together in three. "But... but we are eternal! We are—"

"You are broken," Treydora said with finality. "And if I ever see you near another inhabited world, I won't be so generous next time."

The Flight

They fled.

Not the tactical retreat of strategic minds, but the desperate flight of predators who had finally met something higher on the food chain. Zorakil's damaged form streaked toward the galactic rim, trailing chunks of marble that would never regenerate. Kaelthor's chaos had become pure fear, compressed and panicked, fleeing toward dimensional spaces where he hoped to hide from consequences he had never imagined possible.

Behind them, Treydora's form blazed across the cosmic battlefield like a star that had learned to love. He didn't pursue. He didn't need to. They had been broken in ways that transcended physical damage—their certainty shattered, their cosmic arrogance replaced by the knowledge that they were no longer the apex predators of existence.

As they vanished into the void between realities, Treydora's voice followed them one last time:

"Remember this feeling. Remember what it's like to be prey instead of predator. And remember that mercy, once given, is not guaranteed to be offered twice."

The cosmic battlefield fell silent except for the gentle hum of ten thousand worlds celebrating their freedom from gods who had forgotten what it meant to be worthy of worship.

The war was over. Treydora had won. And the universe was finally free to become what it had always been meant to be—a place where beings could choose their own destiny without cosmic bullies deciding their fate.

In the distance, new stars began to form from the energy released by the battle, their light carrying a simple message across the void: even gods could be taught humility, when faced with something greater than themselves.

The age of the brothers was over. The age of choice had begun.

And here's the final truth you never understood: The universe doesn't need our permission to be beautiful—it only needs our courage to stop preventing it."

The New Order

Something shifted in how the universe worked—nothing dramatic, just a quiet rewrite of the basic rules. Like someone had gone through the cosmic instruction manual and crossed out all the "might makes right" parts, writing in "be decent to each other" instead. The change felt so natural you almost forgot things had ever worked differently.

The transformation wasn't dramatic—just a quiet revision of cosmic constants. A universe-wide update that installed love and choice as fundamental forces while reducing hunger and domination to minor nuisances that could be easily contained.

"You always asked what I was building," Treydora said, his form beginning to expand again—not in size but in presence, becoming less visible entity and more environmental constant. "Now you know. I was building a cosmos where beings like you become impossible not through force, but through irrelevance."

The brothers felt it immediately—not death, but exile from significance. They still existed, still retained their memories, but the universe around them had simply moved on to more interesting problems. They had become cosmic background noise, easily filtered out by beings who had learned to focus on what actually mattered.

The Aftermath: Heroes and Builders

On the battlefield below, the defenders began to realize that the cosmic battle was over—not ended, but completed. The threat that had loomed over their world hadn't been destroyed but simply... resolved. Made irrelevant through the demonstration of better alternatives.

Koraxos descended slowly from the dimensional spaces where he had fought alongside cosmic forces, his phantom arm no longer blazing with desperate power but glowing with steady purpose. The transcendent limb had evolved again—not weapon or tool, but bridge between individual will and collective possibility.

The moment his feet touched the scarred ground, a sound began to build across the battlefield. Not celebration—that would come later. This was recognition. The sound of people acknowledging that something unprecedented had just been accomplished through their willingness to trust each other with their lives and futures.

"Koraxos!" Sela's voice cut through the cosmic aftermath as children emerged from shelters to find their world saved not through superior violence but through superior cooperation. She ran toward him with a dozen other children trailing behind, their faces bright with the particular joy of those who had been protected by people who chose protection over personal safety.

He knelt to catch her in a hug that was careful of his phantom arm's energy but generous with the warmth that had grown in him over months of learning that strength meant having people worth defending.

"Did you show them?" she asked with the seriousness of someone whose future had hung in the balance. "Did you show the bad gods that we're not food?"

"We showed them something better," Koraxos replied, looking around at former enemies working side by side. "Showed them what happens when people stop trying to kill each other long enough to actually get shit done."

As he spoke, he remembered something Marex had said during their darkest hour in the rebellion, words that had seemed like mere comfort then but now revealed their deeper truth: "The strongest chains are those we forge ourselves, but the greatest freedom comes from choosing which chains to wear."

Koraxos had worn the chains of slavery, then broken them to forge new ones—bonds of connection, responsibility, love for people who had become family through choice rather than blood. These chains didn't restrict him; they gave his power meaning.

Velen approached, his bio-crystal arm pulsing with satisfaction as he surveyed the battlefield where his people—all of their people—had stood together against cosmic extinction. "So what now, hero? You're officially the most famous being in seven civilizations. Children will grow up wanting to be like you."

"Terrifying thought," Koraxos said with a grimace, though his phantom arm pulsed with light that suggested he wasn't entirely displeased. "Kids wanting to grow up to be a walking disaster with cosmic anger management issues."

"But maybe that's not such a bad thing," Velen pointed out, "if what they want to be like is someone who protects instead of conquers."

The Guardian's Choice

As word spread through crystal networks and dimensional bridges, as representatives from dozens of civilizations began requesting audience with the planet that had successfully resisted cosmic predation, Koraxos found himself faced with recognition of what he had become.

Not a conqueror or ruler. Not a destroyer or rebel. He had become something his enslaved childhood could never have imagined: a protector. Someone people looked to not because they feared him, but because they trusted him to stand between them and whatever darkness might come.

"You know what this means, don't you?" Thalia asked, studying his face with the analytical precision of someone who had learned to read people through crisis. "You're not just Koraxos anymore. You're the Guardian of Oshar. The Protector of Seven Peoples. The one who stood against gods and made them blink."

"I stood with you," he corrected with a grunt. "All of us together. I just happened to have the cosmic arm."

"Yes," she said patiently. "But when the children tell this story, when the songs are sung and the monuments are built, whose name do you think they'll remember? Whose phantom arm will they dream of having when monsters come calling?"

Koraxos looked around at faces that had become precious to him—not because they needed him, but because he had learned to care what happened to them. The phantom arm pulsed with steady light as he realized what she was asking, and he thought of another truth that had crystallized during his transformation from slave to guardian: True power is not what you can force others to do—it's what you can inspire them to become.

He hadn't defeated the cosmic entities through superior force. He had inspired seven civilizations to become something greater than their individual limitations, had shown them what they could accomplish when they chose connection over competition.

"You want to know if I'll stay," he said. "If I'll be here when the next cosmic nightmare shows up."

"We want to know if you want to stay," Velen said bluntly. "Because let's be honest—after what you just did, you could go anywhere. Do anything. Cosmic entities probably send you Christmas cards now."

Koraxos felt the weight of choice—not burden but opportunity. Through the phantom arm, he could sense the vast network that Treydora had built, could feel worlds across the galaxy where beings faced their own struggles against impossible odds.

But he could also feel the warm press of Sela's hand against his flesh arm, the solid presence of Velen and Niri planning their children's futures, the quiet satisfaction radiating from every person who had chosen to trust him with their hopes and fears.

"Where else would I go?" he asked, and despite his gruff tone, there was warmth underneath. "This is where my people are. Where the kids I promised to keep safe are growing up. Besides," he added with a shrug, "someone's gotta make sure you idiots don't get yourselves killed the moment I turn my back."

He gestured at the battlefield where seven civilizations worked together to heal and rebuild. "Anyway, someone needs to make sure this actually works. That the peace we won doesn't crumble the minute people get comfortable and start forgetting why they chose each other in the first place."

The New Protector

"So what does that look like?" Sela asked with the practical directness of childhood cutting through adult complications. "Being a guardian? Do you get a cape? A special house? Do you patrol the sky looking for trouble?"

Koraxos laughed—genuine amusement that felt strange and wonderful after months of cosmic battle. "I don't know. I've never been a superhero before. What do you think it should look like?"

"Well," Sela said with the seriousness of someone who had given this considerable thought, "you need a place to live that's big enough for people to find you when they need help. And you should probably learn to fly properly instead of just jumping really high and hoping."

"Flying lessons," Koraxos noted solemnly. "Got it. What else?"

"You should help people solve problems before they become big enough to need phantom arms," Miran added, the boy's engineer mind already working on practical applications. "Like, if two groups are arguing about something, maybe you could help them figure it out before they start shooting at each other."

"Conflict resolution," Thalia translated with approval. "Prevention rather than just response. I like it."

"And you should tell stories," added little Tork, whose recent nightmares had been soothed by tales of heroes who protected children from monsters. "About how people used to be enemies but learned to be friends. So other people know it's possible."

"Stories," Koraxos repeated, and the phantom arm pulsed with understanding. "Yeah. I can do stories."

As the conversation continued, as children and adults alike contributed their ideas for what a guardian should be and do, Koraxos felt something crystallize in his understanding of what protection actually meant.

It wasn't about being the strongest or the most feared. It wasn't about having power over others or commanding their obedience. It was about being someone that people could trust to care about their welfare, to stand up for those who couldn't stand up for themselves, to remember that strength without compassion was just elaborate bullying.

Building Tomorrow

In the days that followed, as the immediate crisis of cosmic invasion gave way to the longer-term work of building something unprecedented, Koraxos found his role evolving in ways he had never expected.

During the day, he worked alongside construction crews rebuilding the city—not directing from above but laboring side by side with former enemies who had become collaborators. His phantom arm proved remarkably useful for precise work, able to manipulate energy and matter in ways that made previously impossible architectural projects suddenly feasible.

"Hand me that support beam," a Luminarai engineer would say, and Koraxos would use the phantom arm to hold three-ton crystal formations in perfect position while Nok metalworkers and Drustali crystal-shapers collaborated on joining techniques that combined the best of all their traditions.

In the evenings, he held court—not formal audiences but open gatherings where anyone could bring disputes, concerns, or problems that seemed too big to handle alone. The phantom arm stayed dim during these sessions, tucked away so people would focus on words rather than power.

"My neighbor's workshop keeps making noise at all hours," an elderly Nok woman complained during one such session. "And when I told him about it, he said progress never sleeps and maybe I should appreciate innovation."

"Valid points on both sides," Koraxos replied with the patience of someone who had learned that small problems could become large ones if left unattended. "Let's see... what if we helped him soundproof his workshop, but designed it so he could also work on projects that help the whole neighborhood? Noise problem solved, and everybody benefits from what he's building."

"That... actually sounds reasonable," the woman admitted. "But what if he doesn't want to help?"

"Then we ask him what he thinks a good solution would be," Koraxos said. "Maybe he has ideas we haven't thought of. People are more likely to support solutions they help create."

The nights were for stories—gatherings where children and adults alike came to hear tales that helped them understand what they had accomplished and why it mattered. Koraxos discovered he had a talent for narrative, for finding the threads that connected individual experiences to larger truths.

"Once upon a time," he would begin, his voice carrying across crowds that grew larger each evening, "there was a world where people believed they had to choose between being strong or being kind. They thought power meant taking from others, and safety meant building walls to keep others out."

The stories weren't just entertainment—they were education. Through tales of cosmic battles and unlikely alliances, of children who collected pretty rocks and adults who learned to see former enemies as family, Koraxos helped people understand what they had built together and why it was worth protecting.

The Test

The first real test of Koraxos's role as Guardian came three months after the cosmic battle, when reports arrived of strange energy storms in the ocean territories controlled by Neryssia's people. Ships were disappearing, islands were being cut off from communication, and something in the deep waters was causing tidal patterns that threatened coastal settlements.

"Could be aftereffects from the cosmic battle," Velen suggested as they studied the reports in the newly rebuilt command center. "All that dimensional manipulation might have destabilized underwater energy currents."

"Or something worse," Thalia added grimly. "We know the brothers had forces we never encountered. Maybe something was sleeping in the deep ocean and got woken up."

Koraxos studied the pattern of disturbances, his phantom arm pulsing gently as he considered possibilities. "Either way, people are in danger and others are scared. That's what guardians are for."

The expedition to investigate the ocean disturbances included Koraxos and representatives from all seven civilizations, each bringing their unique capabilities. But as they approached the affected waters aboard Neryssia's bio-ship, Koraxos made a decision that surprised even himself.

"I'm going down alone first," he announced, studying the chaotic energy patterns beneath the waves with his enhanced senses. "Whatever's down there, it's reacting to our approach. Too many people might trigger something we're not ready for."

"Bad idea," Velen said immediately. "We just spent months learning that we're stronger together. Now you want to go back to the lone hero approach?"

"Not lone hero," Koraxos corrected. "Advanced scout. I go down, figure out what we're dealing with, then come back and we plan our approach together. If something goes wrong, you extract me."

"And if we can't?" Niri asked with practical concern.

"Then you know it's too dangerous for anyone else and you find a different solution," he replied. "Guardian means I take the risks so others don't have to. That's the job."

Into the Deep

The descent into the storm-wracked waters was like traveling through liquid lightning. Energy cascaded around Koraxos in patterns that would have killed any normal being, but the phantom arm created a protective field that allowed him to navigate deeper into the chaos.

As he descended, he began to sense the source of the disturbance—not malicious intent but confusion, fear, and overwhelming loneliness. Something vast moved in the ocean depths, something that had been sleeping for eons before being rudely awakened by the cosmic battle above.

At two thousand feet, he found it: a creature that defied easy description, part organic, part crystalline, part pure energy. It was easily the size of a small island, its form constantly shifting between states as it struggled to understand what had woken it and why its ancient dreams had been shattered by forces beyond its comprehension.

"Hello," Koraxos said softly, extending the phantom arm in a gesture of peace rather than threat. "I'm not here to hurt you. I'm here because your movements are affecting people on the surface, and I need to understand what's wrong."

The response was overwhelming—not words but emotions so vast they threatened to crush his enhanced mind. Confusion like tsunamis, loneliness like the pressure of oceanic depths, and beneath it all, a desperate need to understand what had changed in the world above.

The entity—who eventually chose the name "Deep Current" when Koraxos explained the concept of names—had been the ocean's dreaming heart for millions of years, maintaining the subtle energy patterns that kept marine ecosystems stable. But the cosmic battle had disrupted its ancient rhythms, leaving it disoriented and afraid.

"I don't know how to dream the right dreams anymore," Deep Current explained through waves of bioluminescent emotion. "The patterns that kept the waters calm, the currents that fed the small swimmers, the songs that helped the whales navigate—all broken when the sky-gods fought above my sleep."

"Then we learn new patterns together," Koraxos replied, understanding beginning to dawn. "You don't have to fix everything alone. There are people who understand the ocean, who study the currents and the life they support. Maybe we can help each other."

As he spoke with the ancient entity, Koraxos found himself thinking of the third truth that had emerged from his transformation: The universe doesn't need our permission to be beautiful—it only needs our courage to stop preventing it.

Deep Current wasn't malicious or destructive by nature. It was trying to maintain the ocean's beauty and balance. The chaos was just confusion, the entity struggling to restore harmony without understanding what new equilibrium was possible.

The Solution

What followed was a collaboration between transcendent power and ancient wisdom, individual capability and collective knowledge. Deep Current's problem wasn't malice or territorial dispute—it was simply a disrupted system trying to restore balance without understanding what new equilibrium was possible.

Working with Neryssia's people, who understood ocean currents better than anyone, Koraxos helped the entity learn new patterns that incorporated the changes wrought by cosmic battle while maintaining the stability that marine life required.

"The old songs won't work anymore," Neryssia explained during one of their underwater conferences, her bio-suit allowing her to communicate directly with Deep Current through bioluminescent patterns. "But we can compose new ones that acknowledge what's changed while preserving what needs to stay the same."

"Change and continuity," Deep Current mused, its massive form settling into calmer configurations as it began to understand. "New dreams that honor old purposes."

The process took weeks, but gradually the energy storms calmed as Deep Current learned to dream in harmony with the post-cosmic-battle world. The entity's massive presence, once a source of chaos, became a stabilizing force that made ocean travel safer and more predictable than it had ever been.

"So now we have another ally," Thalia observed as they debriefed the successful integration. "An oceanic entity that can influence weather patterns, manage sea levels, and coordinate with marine ecosystems across the planet."

"Who was never malicious," Koraxos added. "Just scared and confused and trying to do its job without understanding how the rules had changed."

"Like most of us, really," Marex said with the gentle humor of someone who had learned to find wisdom in unexpected places. "The challenge isn't facing evil—it's helping good intentions find productive channels."

The Guardian's Growth

As word of the Deep Current integration spread, it sparked something Koraxos hadn't expected: more reports of ancient entities across the planet beginning to stir. The cosmic battle had awakened forces that had been dormant for eons, and most of them were struggling to understand a world that had changed while they slept.

"We're not just rebuilding civilization," Koraxos realized as reports flowed in from across the planet. "We're helping an entire world rebalance itself after cosmic trauma."

Some entities were geological—stone-singers in the mountains who maintained tectonic stability but had been disrupted by dimensional warfare. Others were atmospheric—wind-dancers in the high altitudes who influenced weather patterns but had been confused by reality distortions. Still others were completely unique—beings that existed in the spaces between dimensions, entities that managed the flow of time itself in small local areas.

Each required a different approach, but the pattern was always the same: not conquest or control, but communication, understanding, and collaboration toward solutions that served everyone's needs.

Koraxos found himself becoming more than just a protector of people—he was becoming the planet's translator. The phantom arm changed too, less like a weapon and more like a universal remote that helped him talk to things that thought in geological time or dreamed in ocean currents.

"You know what I think?" Sela said one evening as they sat watching aurora displays that now carried messages between different forms of planetary intelligence. "I think you're not just our guardian anymore. You're the planet's guardian."

"Terrifying thought," Koraxos replied, though his tone carried satisfaction rather than concern. "When I was a slave, I thought the world was just the mines and the fields around them. Now I'm responsible for ocean entities that dream in currents and mountain spirits that think in geological time."

"But you're not responsible alone," she pointed out with the wisdom of someone who had grown up watching cooperation accomplish impossible things. "Deep Current helps with ocean stuff. The stone-singers handle mountain issues. The wind-dancers manage weather problems. You just help everyone work together."

"Coordination rather than domination," Koraxos agreed. "Making sure everyone's voice gets heard when decisions need to be made."

"Exactly," Sela said with satisfaction. "A guardian who guards by helping instead of commanding. That's the best kind."

The New World

As months turned to seasons, as the unusual planetary alliance grew from seven civilizations to dozens of different entities, Koraxos found himself at the center of something unprecedented—a world where every form of intelligence, from individual minds to planetary forces, had learned to work together.

It wasn't perfect. There were still conflicts, misunderstandings, and problems that required creative solutions. But the fundamental approach had changed—instead of assuming that differences meant conflict, everyone started from the assumption that diversity probably meant strength if you could figure out how to combine it properly.

Children grew up taking for granted that they could speak with wind-dancers about weather patterns, consult stone-singers about the best places to build, and ask ocean-dreamers about fishing conditions. Adults collaborated on projects that spanned the entire spectrum of planetary intelligence, creating technologies and art forms that no single group could have imagined.

The phantom arm became less visible over time, often tucked away unless needed for specific tasks. Koraxos's real power, people realized, wasn't the cosmic energy he could wield—it was his talent for listening to completely different perspectives and finding the common ground where productive collaboration became possible.

"You've become something unique," Treydora's voice whispered through the crystal networks one evening, carrying approval and something approaching paternal pride. "Not a ruler or conqueror, but a translator. Someone who helps different forms of intelligence understand each other well enough to work together."

"Is that good enough?" Koraxos asked. "When the next cosmic threat comes—and we both know there will be one—will translation and cooperation be sufficient against entities that operate through pure dominance?"

"Look around you," Treydora replied gently. "A planet where every intelligence works together, where ancient entities collaborate with surface civilizations, where children play games that incorporate wisdom from geological timescales. Do you really think beings who've only learned conquest could prevail against diversity this complete?"

As the first stars appeared in the darkening sky, as crystal networks pulsed with gentle communication between entities that had never dreamed of collaboration before meeting each other, Koraxos felt something settle into place in his understanding of what he had become.

Not a hero in the traditional sense—he'd never been comfortable with that label anyway. He had become something more practical and more necessary: a guardian whose strength came not from the power to impose his will, but from the wisdom to help others discover what they could accomplish when they chose to work together.

The phantom arm pulsed with steady light as various intelligences across the planet shared their evening reports—all stable, all productive, all contributing to a whole that was far greater than the sum of its parts.

He thought about how far he'd come from that angry slave in the mines. The chains he wore now—caring about people, feeling responsible for their safety—those were chains he'd chosen. And somehow they made him freer than he'd ever been when he was just fighting for himself.

Tomorrow would bring new challenges—it always did. Other worlds might face similar cosmic threats and need advice about planetary integration. New forms of intelligence might emerge requiring integration into their growing network. The cosmos was vast and full of possibilities both wonderful and terrible.

But tonight, Koraxos was content to sit with a child who had designed crystal houses, watching a sky painted by entities who had learned that difference created beauty rather than conflict, surrounded by the gentle hum of a planet where every form of intelligence had found its voice in a symphony that proved cooperation could indeed transform anything when applied with sufficient imagination and stubborn determination.

The guardian's work was never finished. But it was work that filled rather than drained, that grew stronger through sharing rather than weaker through division, that proved every day that love applied with wisdom could indeed transform worlds one choice at a time.

The slave had become free. The free had become united. The united had become something the universe had never seen before: a planetary alliance that faced the infinite darkness with strength drawn from voluntary cooperation rather than imposed hierarchy.

And at the center of it all, the phantom arm glowed with the quiet satisfaction of power that had learned its true purpose: not to conquer or destroy, but to protect, to build, and to help others discover what they could become when fear no longer defined the boundaries of possibility.

The real work was just beginning. And Koraxos couldn't wait to see what they would build together.

"Well," he said to the evening sky as aurora patterns carried messages between wind-dancers and ocean-dreamers, "this is turning out better than expected."

THE END